P9-CQP-368

Lindsey, David L.

The rules of si-
lence

DUE DATE		D384	24.95

THE
RULES OF SILENCE

THE
RULES OF
SILENCE

DAVID LINDSEY

WARNER BOOKS

An AOL Time Warner Company

Warner Books, Inc., 1271 Avenue of the Americas, New York, NY 10020

Visit our Web site at www.twbookmark.com.

 An AOL Time Warner Company

Printed in the United States of America

First Printing: April 2003
10 9 8 7 6 5 4 3 2 1

Library of Congress Cataloging-in-Publication Data
Lindsey, David L.
      The rules of silence/David Lindsey.
          p. cm.
      ISBN 0-446-53163-4
      1. Kidnapping victims—Fiction. 2. Billionaires—Fiction. 3. Extortion—Fiction. 4. Criminals—Fiction. 5. Texas—Fiction. I. Title.

PS3562.I51193 R8 2003
813'.54—dc21   2002033059

For Joyce,

my constant shelter from the

solitary storms of the imagination.

Acknowledgments

While every writer is ultimately responsible for what he has created, it requires a great deal of midwifery to turn a novelist's imaginings into tangible books, and to put those books into the hands of readers. I want to thank some of those who have nurtured me, and my writing, through the complicated process of publication.

Foremost among those to whom I am indebted is my agent, Aaron Priest. I first met Aaron in 1975 when I was in New York on business, and he was just starting his literary agency, operating out of a tiny office on East Fortieth Street. I hadn't yet begun writing, however, and it wasn't until 1982 that he sold two novels for me, beginning a partnership that now has lasted through two decades and twelve novels.

The literary agent toils at a mysterious alchemy, impossibly combining words and dollars in the ever-hopeful pursuit of forging the bright ore of a writing career that will serve to the mutual benefit of all the parties involved. It is an enigmatic profession involving a complex brew of relationships among author and agent and publisher and public.

Aaron, it was my good fortune to have stumbled into your

office twenty-seven years ago. Of all the obvious benefits that have accrued to me from that encounter, there is one that supersedes them all: You have made it possible for me to have a career in the intimate company of the English language. I still find that extraordinary. I am unabashedly grateful to you for providing me the privilege of being a novelist.

Beyond that, the years themselves have burnished the friendship, through thick and thin, from Texas to Manhattan. *Mil gracias, mi amigo.*

Over the course of twelve novels just about everyone in Aaron's office has helped me along. My thanks to Molly Friedrich for stepping in when stepping in matters so much; to Lucy Childs who fields anxieties with such good-natured aplomb; to Frances Jalet-Miller whose special touch is not forgotten; and to Lisa Erbach-Vance who is the most efficient, dauntless, and gracious person I've ever worked with.

My thanks to Larry Kirshbaum and Maureen Mahon Egen who brought me to Warner Books three novels ago. It is no small thing to put faith in a writer, and then to ride out the ups and downs of his career. The kind of commitment that requires should not be overlooked in the scheme of things, and isn't.

Thanks to Jamie Raab for sweating out the proposals and deadlines and editing, and to Harvey-Jane Kowal and Sona Vogel for attending to the sea of details that have to mesh throughout the hundreds of pages of a book.

And a special expression of appreciation goes to editor Jessica Papin who relentlessly pursued the better novel inside the first draft of this book. Thanks, Jessica, for your generous and insightful guidance.

THE
RULES OF
SILENCE

Chapter 1

Benny Chalmers stared through the opened window of his pickup. He wore a soiled and sweat-stained khaki shirt with long sleeves, dirty jeans, and beat-to-hell cowboy boots with tops that reached nearly to his knees. He was red-faced from forty-one years in the searing border country sun, and his forehead was as white as a corpse where his Stetson had protected it.

It was four-thirty in the afternoon, and Chalmers was sitting in the middle of twenty-one million acres of rugged terrain known to ecologists as the South Texas plains and to everyone else as the Brush Country. They were fifty miles from anything other than an isolated ranch house every twenty or so miles. But they were only two hundred yards from Mexico. The sun was white. As far as you could see in any direction was an endless parched landscape of head-high thickets of cat claw and black brush interspersed with prickly pear flats and mesquite.

Chalmers was watching a rancher's *vaqueros* load 126 head of mixed-breed cattle into Chalmers's cattle truck. He had been hired to take them to another ranch near Bandera two hundred miles north. The cattle were being held in a sprawling maze of pens made of rusty oil rig drill pipe. A long iron-and-wood ramp ran from the pen's chute into the back of the trailer, a massive twelve-wheeler, triple-decker Wilson.

Fifty yards to Chalmers's left, a helicopter had just landed in a tornado of dust. The 'copter had disgorged three men wearing guns, boots, and the familiar deep green uniforms of the U.S. Border Patrol agents. They were interested in watching the *vaqueros* load the cattle, and they were interested in Chalmers's big rig.

"Goddamn it," Chalmers muttered, squinting into the sun. The cattle were bawling and rocking the huge trailer as they clambered up the ramp and into the cavernous belly of their transportation. The cattle that were still in the pens milled and shuffled around in the hot dirt, kicking up dust that hung heavily above the whole operation in a rusty haze.

Chalmers had trucked cattle for border ranchers for twenty-two years. He knew more backcountry roads through the remote border ranches from El Paso to Brownsville than any man alive. And he knew about the hidden airstrips, too, and about the stepped-up Border Patrol activity because of the increase in smuggling of drugs and humans. He also knew that the odds were getting shorter against him.

He watched the three Border Patrol agents huddled at the rear of the trailer, looking in three different directions from behind their sunglasses. They were talking among themselves without looking at one another, the dust from the loading operation drifting over them and sticking to the sweat that stained their dark uniforms.

Then the agents disappeared around the side of the sixty-five-foot-long truck and trailer, and when they emerged from behind the cab of the red Mack tractor, they looked toward Chalmers and waved. He waved back, sticking his beefy arm out the pickup window.

"Adios, boys," he said under his breath. He turned back and looked out the windshield again and stared at the rusty fog and the cattle and the *vaqueros*. But he didn't relax until he heard the chopper's engine start, its low whine cranking up slowly, revving to lift.

He wiped his forehead on the sleeve of his shirt.

Chalmers smuggled people, but his operation was more than just a little special. To frustrate the noses of the Border Patrol dogs, he built two cubicles in the curved top of his trailer right in the middle of a big bunch of stinking, shitting cattle. The cubicles were twenty-four inches high (a little more than the thickness of a man lying flat on his back), sixty-two inches long, and twenty-four inches wide. He piped air-conditioning from the cab into the cubicles and put long, narrow water tanks in there with hoses to drink from. A man could live three days in there easy and hardly feel it.

Two people only. Delivery guaranteed. But the fee was high. And Chalmers knew damn well what that meant. Whoever came to him willing to pay his price had to have something more waiting for him in the States than working on a framing crew or wiping tables in a fast-food joint. This was elite human smuggling he was offering here.

And it worked. He'd made nearly $750,000 in six months. Cash.

At dusk Benny Chalmers finished up the paperwork with the rancher, using the hood of the rancher's pickup as a desk. They shook hands, and he said that he was going to get a bite to eat right there in his truck and then head out. Leaning on the front of the truck, he watched the rancher and his *vaqueros* drive away from the holding pens in their pickups, pulling horse trailers.

Half an hour later Chalmers stood at the edge of the brush, having a serious conversation in Spanish with four Mexican coyotes. His truck idled in the dying light behind him, its tiny amber lights glowing like long strands of embers. Real coyotes yipped and keened out in the endless night of desert brush.

The coyotes Chalmers was dealing with were heartless men who had lots of money, more than the U.S. government doled out to its law enforcement agencies. They bought the best electronic countermeasures that technology could produce, and here they were to prove it, bunch of sorry-ass Mexican smugglers wired up with headphones and mouth mikes like some damned singing kids on MTV.

Chalmers was sweating, nervous, wishing to hell he hadn't agreed to this particular load. He should have quit one load back. The last one should've been his last.

The kid who was apparently in charge of this spoke softly into the mike curved in front of his mouth, and they all turned and looked south toward the river and Mexico. Silence. A minute. Two. Three. Five. They all saw the chopper's distinctive blue light before they heard it, its baffled engine making no more noise than a quiet cough in the distance.

Suddenly Chalmers developed some respect. He'd seen this machine only once before, but he'd heard plenty of stories about it. He could've charged twice what he'd asked. Jesus.

The black chopper landed on a sandbar in the river, stayed no longer than a minute, then lifted up again and wheezed away into the darkness. They waited.

Soon a small group of men emerged from the grease brush, seeping out of it like shadows pulling loose from shadows.

There were three men with two black-hooded figures. The hooded men were dressed better than the others and communicated only by sign. He could tell that they could see through the strange sheen of the fabric. The more muscular of the two hooded men carried a cheap plastic net bag with a couple of mangoes and oranges in it.

One of the three escorts spoke with the young MTV smart-asses, and then the little shit in charge turned to Chalmers and spoke to him in perfect, unaccented English.

"Okay, bubba," he wisecracked, "this does it for us. We don't have anything to do with the other end."

Chalmers nodded, and the kid handed him a thick envelope. Chalmers calmly took a small Maglite out of his pocket and started counting. He didn't care how many people were standing around waiting for him. This right here was what it was all about. He was looking after his end.

It was all there. He looked up. "Okay."

"Let's get these guys loaded up," the kid said.

The two hooded men climbed up the side of the trailer and crawled feet first into the tiny compartment in the top of the cattle trailer. They never said a word. Once they were inside, Chalmers, standing on the rails on the outside of the trailer, started explaining to them in Spanish how to operate the air vents and the water hoses.

It was two-thirty in the morning when Chalmers delivered his cattle at another set of isolated holding pens on the Braden Ranch southwest of Bandera. This was the Texas Hill Country, rolling hills studded with oaks and mountain juniper. The Medina River was so close that you could smell it.

In the early morning darkness, Chalmers told the rancher he'd have to tidy up a few things on his trailer before he drove away, said adios to him, and watched the headlights of the last pickup ascend the caliche road that climbed out of the shallow valley.

Then Chalmers turned and heaved his heavy body up on the rails of his trailer and climbed to the top. With a small ratchet he unscrewed two bolts and lifted out the panel that concealed the two cubicles.

5

"*Está bien,*" he said, and climbed down the rails again.

From the ground he watched as the first man wriggled from his cubicle in the near dark. He was no longer hooded, which immediately set Chalmers's antennae to quivering. As the first man helped the second one—also without his hood now—negotiate the difficult exit onto the sides of the cattle trailer, Chalmers noticed that the first man was clearly younger and more muscular. Bodyguard.

They were stiff and moved slowly, but eventually they made their way to the ground. Even though it was dark, Chalmers deliberately kept his head down as the bodyguard produced a cell phone and placed a call. The older man walked a little ways from the truck, unzipped his pants, and pissed into the darkness, his back to them.

Chalmers made a big deal of being busy putting something in order on the tail end of the truck, but he kept a wary eye on the younger man's hands. This was where Chalmers became a liability instead of a necessity. When the man finished his conversation, he came over to Chalmers.

"Which way's the road?" he asked in English.

"Right behind you," Chalmers said, his eyes averted, tilting his head toward the caliche track into the brush. His own rig pointed straight at it.

"Okay," the man said, his voice saying a kind of thanks and a kind of good-bye. "Wait half hour," he added, then turned and walked away toward the other man, who was pacing back and forth.

They exchanged a few words and then, without turning around, walked away into the cobalt darkness, headed for the only road out of the valley.

Slowly Chalmers eased over to a toolbox under the steps of his rig and took out a pair of binoculars. He moved away from the truck and sat on the ground, his legs pulled up, and rested his elbows on his knees. He put the binoculars to his eyes and focused it on the two men. The nightvision lenses illuminated them in a slightly fuzzy, green world. They were still together. They didn't look back.

He sensed it a millisecond before he felt it, the cold, thick tube eased firmly against his right ear. He knew. He went weightless, and his heavy, weary body levitated slowly and then stopped a few inches above the ground, the cold tube pressed against his ear keeping him from tilting. He was still watching the two men walking away in a green world when his head exploded.

Chapter 2

The Lincoln Navigator climbed over the caliche track to a larger caliche road, this one wider, flatter, and graded. The Navigator turned right and quickly picked up speed to a fast clip. Behind the SUV the dust churned up into the cloudless darkness, where the glow of the three-quarter moon caught it and turned it into a plume of powdered silver that hung momentarily in the night and then slowly sank and settled away into the dark landscape.

When the Navigator hit the highway, it turned left and headed west. The man in the front passenger seat handed back two paper sacks with hamburgers to the men behind him, who hadn't had anything to eat except a few mangoes and oranges during the past twelve hours.

As the Navigator sailed over the rolling, winding highway through the Hill Country, the two men in the backseat ate, staring out through the windshield at the headlights threading the darkness. They all listened to the terse transmissions in Spanish coming over the complex of equipment stuffed under the dashboard and in the console between the two front seats. The space was so cramped that it resembled a cockpit.

Wearing headphones and a mike, the front-seat passenger occasionally spoke a word or two in flat, dispassionate Spanish, often changing frequencies. A computer screen in the center console displayed a map with remarkably sharp resolution and a stationary bright red spot in the upper right corner. The Navigator's progress was represented in the lower left center of the screen by a green pulsing dot, jerking its way on an irregular trajectory toward the upper right corner.

They turned north.

"What about those guys?" the older man said in English, referring to something he'd heard on the radio. He wanted to speak in English now. Get his head into it. His neck was stiff, and he could smell cow shit in his clothes. Riding in the top of a cattle truck was not his usual mode of travel.

"They're in place, both of them."

"You've checked with them, about the techniques?"

"Many times."

The older man sighed in disgust and dropped the rest of his hamburger into the sack. Fucking hamburger. He wiped his mouth with the paper napkin. It would sit like a stone in his stomach. He tossed the sack onto the floor. Fucking stupid American hamburgers.

"And the other two?" he asked.

"The same."

"The same what?" he snapped.

"They're ready. Their techniques are well planned. They are waiting to hear from you."

Outside, the countryside was lighted by the waxing moon that raced along beside them. Hills rose up the size of pyramids, mounded and disguised by time, mile after mile of them. Occasionally they would fall away and a valley would open up, and sometimes fields, and sometimes meadows, rolled out

10

under the moonlight. Now and then, in the distance, the windows of a solitary ranch house burned like isolated embers.

"Planning something like this, on this side," he said to no one in particular, looking out the window, "we can't be too careful. This time there's no such thing as too much planning."

The men listened. They were already nervous, all of them. The stakes this time were higher than they had ever been, and everyone knew that the older man behind them had a short and deadly fuse when the stakes were high. They had been planning this a long time, and now with the arrival of the cattle truck, there was no turning back.

The Navigator turned west again.

The older man liked the sounds of the radio transmissions. It meant his men were tending to business. There was always something to double-check. There was always a tiny, bothersome oversight to eliminate. He settled into the corner of his seat.

"This guy's going to think the devil's got him by the *huevos*," he said. "He's going to wish his mother had choked him to death the minute he was born, right there between her legs."

TUESDAY
The First Day

Chapter 3

Titus Cain and Charlie Thrush were at the far half of the one-mile course when they decided to stop jogging and walk the rest of the way back. They'd done three and a half miles, and the temperature was a hundred and two. It was six-fifteen in the afternoon.

They loped to a walk, sweat streaming from them, their athletic gray T-shirts and shorts stained dark with it. They strode through the misters flanking either side of the cinder track at fifty-yard intervals, head-high sprayers that formed a wet cloud of ten or twelve feet in diameter that Titus had installed for a distance of several hundred yards on the back half of the track.

Charlie, a tall, lanky man in his early sixties, turned and went back to the mister and stood in the cloud of spray.

"Damn, this's saving my life," he gasped, bending over and putting his hands on his knees as he caught his breath, the fine spray beading on his silver hair.

Titus, breathing heavily, too, paced back and forth through the cloud.

"We should've gone to the pool. This's brutal."

There were nearly two hundred employees at CaiText now, and Titus had deliberately fostered a health-conscious environment by making it convenient for them to jog or swim or play handball without having to leave CaiText's twenty-six-acre campus. The roughly oval cinder track, situated at the back of the company's complex west of downtown, wound through an airy stretch of Hill Country woods dominated by oaks and elms and mountain laurels. It was a choice site, sitting on the crest of a hill and commanding an expansive view of the valleys that fell away to more hills to the west.

"We're gettin' old," Charlie said, straightening up and grinning.

"We?"

Titus had known Charlie since his early years at Stanford, when CaiText was just a dream in Titus's mind. At the time, Charlie was an electrical engineer and software designer doing research in microengineering. He was in the process of pioneering some of the early uses of computer-guided laser surgery, which he later patented. In the years since, the patents had made him enormously wealthy.

Over the years their friendship remained strong, and Charlie and his wife, Louise, regularly visited Titus and his wife, Rita, in Austin. Though nearly twenty years separated the two women, Louise's impulsive and exuberantly curious nature had kept her young and was a complement to Rita's commonsense practicality. They had become good friends from the moment they met.

During their visits to Austin, Charlie and Louise had fallen in love with the Texas Hill Country and eventually bought a four-hundred-acre ranch south of Fredericksburg about an hour's drive away. They built a retirement home there, and the two couples saw each other frequently. In fact, Rita and Louise were now on a three-week trip together in Italy.

Titus heard a lone jogger behind him and turned to see a chunky guy with thick black hair and a beet red face just shutting down from a jog to a fast walk. He was trying vainly to dry his glasses on the tail of his sweatshirt.

"Hey, Robert," Titus said as the guy approached. "You gonna make it?"

The guy shook his head. "Heat index's gotta be a hundred and twenty, hundred and thirty."

"It's the humidity," Titus said. "Don't push it too hard." He slapped the guy on the back as he passed by. When he was through the mist he put on his glasses again, but he didn't pick up the jog. He just kept walking. Titus watched him.

"You ever meet Brister?" he asked Charlie, nodding at the young man.

"Yeah, sure. In the R and D labs."

Often when Charlie was in town, he would hang out at CaiText for a few hours, spending time in Research and Development exercising his curiosity. He was something of a celebrity with the researchers there, and they got a kick out of talking to him. His "no boundaries" thinking was just as radical now as it had been when he was a young man, and everyone in the division had great affection for this eccentric and brilliant man.

The two men moved out of the spray and started back to the clubhouse, keeping to the shady side of the track.

"Poor guy's life's a horror story right now," Titus said. "His wife has brain cancer. The slow kind that takes your life away by moments and millimeters, leaving you breathing, but haunted."

Titus paused. "I'll tell you, Charlie, it makes you count your blessings. I just can't imagine what I'd do. . . ."

"Yeah, I know," Charlie said, running a hand over his sweaty face. "I've thought about it, too. Not exactly like that, maybe, but just from the point of view of us having done okay doing the kind of work we like to do. Not everybody's got that."

"Not everybody's got someone like Louise, Charlie. Or someone like Rita. We're lucky about those two women, that's what I'm talking about."

Charlie suddenly laughed, shaking his head.

"I got an e-mail from Louise yesterday," he said. "She said she was shipping something home, and if it got here before she got back, I wasn't supposed to uncrate it under any circumstances. Uncrate it!? What the hell's she done?"

They were both laughing as they walked through the long arcade of arbors into the palmy courtyard outside the club. CaiText employees were sitting around small tables in their swimsuits and jogging clothes in the shade of the oaks that covered much of the campus. The setting had a westward view of the hills.

Afternoon, Mr. Cain. Hot enough for you, Mr. Cain? The women smiled. Titus stopped and chatted with them a few moments before he and Charlie moved on, going through the club, past the swimming pool with its echoing voices, and on to the men's dressing rooms.

Titus Cain was an egalitarian. He shared everything with his employees. There were no special facilities for him or any of the CaiText executives. His locker was just one of the hundreds of lockers in the same locker rooms with everyone else. He swam with everyone else, jogged with everyone else, and worked as hard as everyone else.

But, like being the most beautiful girl in school, just being who he was naturally set him apart. After you get so far up on the food chain, egalitarianism is largely a symbolic sort of thing anyway. You're really never going to be buds with the men and women at the bottom. And in Titus's case that really didn't matter to them. But it did matter to them that he cared enough about them not to set himself apart in the day-to-day scale of things where they had to live out their lives.

Titus Cain might have a lot more money than they did—multimillions more—and most would probably admit that he was smarter than they were—in a certain wide-angle sense that the world seemed to reward—but the important thing was, he never acted as if he believed he was a better human being because of those things. And they liked him and respected him for that.

The two men went to their lockers, took off their sweaty clothes, showered, and dressed. A few minutes later, they were in CaiText's underground parking garage at their SUVs.

"You sure you don't want to stay over tonight and drive back tomorrow afternoon?" Titus asked.

"Naw, I'd better get back," Charlie said, opening the back of his Pathfinder and throwing in his dirty jogging clothes. "I've got to do some stuff around the house tonight, and tomorrow I've got to cut down an old dead tree by the office. I've been putting it off." He slammed the back door. "But thanks for the invitation. Maybe I'll take you up on it near the end of the week. I've got to come back in and do some legal stuff downtown."

"Give me a call," Titus said. "Careful driving back."

He opened his Range Rover and climbed in. He started the engine to get the air conditioner going and flipped open his cell phone.

As he pulled out of the garage and circled up to the front gates of the complex, he waited for the only sound in the world that he really wanted to hear.

Chapter 4

"Hello, Titus," she said. "Tell me about your day."

"You first. You've got to be having more fun than I am."

He heard her yawn. It was two o'clock in the morning in Venice, but he didn't care, and she never complained. Rita didn't sweat the small stuff.

"Well, in the morning we went to Burano, where Louise way overspent on Venetian lace, and then we went to Murano, where I spent a very sensible amount for some gorgeous glass. Snoozed in the afternoon. Dinner—a wildly delicious dinner— at La Caravella."

"Sounds hectic," he said. He steered the Rover past the security booths and then pulled into the overlook just outside the gates. In the near distance below, he could see Austin between the shoulders of the hills. It sparkled promisingly at the end of the groove of the valley. When he looked the other way, the Hill Country was turning purple beneath the last tangerine light of sunset.

"And your day?" she asked.

"Business. Uneventful. Charlie was in town. We had lunch,

jogged this afternoon, and then he headed back. I'm on the way home right now."

"I saw on the Internet that the temperatures have skyrocketed in the past week."

"Blistering. Hundred one, hundred two, every day. No rain in sight. Things beginning to burn."

"Summer."

"Yes, ma'am."

"Well, we're both having a great time. Louise is a dear and fun to be with, as always. Yesterday she spent all day photographing the colors of the walls. I had a good time just watching her. She's just endlessly curious, finds something beautiful to appreciate every time she turns around, and sometimes, literally, right under her feet."

"You just tagged along."

"I never just tag along. I carried her camera stuff for her, kept track of the rolls of film, dating and numbering them."

"You kept track of the time and already had the place picked out where you'd eat your next meal."

"Yep, you bet I did."

Titus laughed.

"Well, you know Louise," Rita said. "She just follows her nose around all day, and when it occurs to her that she ought to eat she just wanders into any old place close by. Listen, ever since we both got sick that time in Barcelona I quit doing that with her. I've always got something checked out."

"The way Louise pokes around in the back streets, I can't imagine you finding guidebook recommendations everywhere you go."

"Nope, but I give the place a good look-over with my old nursing eye. If it doesn't pass muster, I make a good excuse and steer her to someplace that seems a little less threatening gastro-wise."

"She doesn't mind."

"No. She knows what I'm doing. We rather enjoy each other's eccentricities. As it happens, I like where she wanders, and she likes where I eat."

They visited for a while, and as much as he wanted to keep her on the line, he really did feel guilty about waking her at this hour. After a few more minutes, he hung up. But he didn't drive away immediately. For a while he looked at the city.

A dozen years earlier, Titus Cain had been a far-from-home Texan, part of a team working for CERN, the Geneva-based physics laboratory, when researcher Tim Berners-Lee developed hypertext markup language, which had led to the conception of the World Wide Web.

Though he'd been just on the periphery of that new development, Titus saw the profound implications of what was happening as quickly as anyone else. He came back home and founded a tiny company that created software for specialized computers in biomedical engineering research. He marketed his company over the newly developing Internet, and while the World Wide Web was still in the early stages of its academic origins, Titus Cain was communicating with research laboratories on every continent, literally years ahead of other software developers. CaiText became the standard software provider for laser applications medical researchers all over the globe.

Growing his company held more attraction for Titus than creating the software itself, and he quickly moved out of the science of it and into the business. Soon he was living the familiar cliché of the successful young entrepreneur: His work became his social life, his play, and his family all rolled into one. Then one day he woke up and discovered that because of his work, he actually had none of the others.

He forced himself to take a two-month vacation, and then

three months later he set off on another two-month trip. The time away from the grind was a revelation. He followed his curiosities all over the world, but he was uneasy and restless and didn't even know it.

All of that changed one sweltering September afternoon when his rafting party rounded a bend in a deep gorge of the Boquillas canyon of the Rio Grande and came upon another rafting group. There had been a serious accident. The guide was unconscious with a broken collarbone, and two members of the party were lying on a sandbar with injuries that hadn't yet been dealt with. Most of the members of the tour group seemed bewildered and at a loss, but the few who could still pull their rattled nerves together were taking orders from one person, a tall, calm, mud-spattered blonde who was ignoring the hand-wringing and tending to the injured.

It was his first glimpse of Margarita Street, a registered nurse from Houston who turned out to be the archetypal independent Texas girl.

That moment changed his life. Thank God.

It took him only fifteen minutes to get home, ten acres of woods and hillside on the eastern slope of the hills west of the river. The wrought-iron gates swung open for him, and he wound his way up to the house, twelve thousand square feet of native limestone and Italian tile. His home was big and comfortable, with sprawling porches and courtyards and half a dozen varieties of tall Texas oaks to shade it. Titus had spent more than he would ever admit to anyone to make sure that the house didn't appear ostentatious and to guarantee that the place would never be described as grand. It looked like a sturdy Texas ranch house, and that was that.

He parked the Rover under the pecan trees at the back of the house and was greeted by his two laid-back redbone hounds, who were pleased to see him but not frantic about it.

He petted them both, gave them good, solid slaps on their shoulders, and then walked through the broad breezeways to the back lawn.

Looking forward to the smell of peaches, he headed down through a long allée of mountain laurels to the small orchard below the house, the two hounds sauntering along behind him, swinging their tails. It was the end of the peach season, and he picked a fat Harvester freestone. He started eating it as he continued on the path to a work site just over the shoulder of the hill, where stonemasons were building a reservoir to retain rainwater runoff from the buildings for irrigation.

It was nearly dark when he got back to the house. While he was feeding the two redbones, the security lights came on around the grounds and lighted his way back to the veranda.

He went into the kitchen, got a beer out of the refrigerator, and glanced out the kitchen window to the lights in the allée through which he had just walked. He saw a glimpse of something at the edge of the lights, almost something. Coyotes, probably. Shit. The damn things were getting braver and braver all the time, every year closer into town. But why weren't the hounds bawling?

He stepped outside to the deep veranda that stretched across the back of the house and turned the lights down to a mere glow. He sat at one of the wrought-iron tables and looked out to the courtyard that began at the edge of the veranda, and beyond that to the star jasmine hedges that dropped down toward the orchard.

He had taken another couple of sips when he noticed something missing. The fountain in the courtyard was silent. He could've sworn it was splashing when he'd walked past it earlier on his way down to the orchard with the dogs.

And where were the dogs? They ought to be here now, scratching, sniffing at his shoes, wanting to check out the beer he was holding. Had they taken off after the coyotes after all? If so, why didn't he hear them bellowing?

He was holding a mouthful of beer when he became aware of dimensions in the darkness of the courtyard, the shadows taking on the shape and bulk of substance as three figures emerged slowly from separate corners. He couldn't swallow. His heart rolled hugely and lost its rhythm.

The men moved a little closer without appearing to move their legs, magically, their positions staggered so that they were not aligned. He saw their weapons now, and just before he thought he was going to pass out, his heart kicked in again, and he swallowed the beer.

Chapter 5

At that moment a fourth man came through the laurel allée as if he'd been there all along and approached the courtyard from the side. He stepped into the pale light spilling off the veranda.

"Don't be alarmed, Mr. Titus Cain," he said with Spanish-accented English, "you are safe. Perfectly safe. Please, everything is fine."

He stopped at the edge of the veranda as if awaiting permission to go farther. Of average height and weight, he was perhaps sixty-four, sixty-five, with wavy, gray-streaked hair. A narrow nose, long upper lip. Nice looking. He was wearing a dove gray suit and a white shirt with broad navy stripes, very English, no tie, the collar open, the suit coat buttoned.

"I've come to visit with you, Mr. Cain, to have a conversation about concerns of mutual interest."

Titus clung to fragments of logic. His alarm system was the best. So these people had to be very good. The fountain was on the same circuit. He hoped they hadn't killed the dogs.

"I would like to sit down with you," the man said, holding his hand out to one of the wrought-iron chairs as if asking permission.

Titus couldn't bring himself to speak or even nod.

The man stepped onto the veranda and approached politely. Watching Titus carefully, as if he were trying to discern his disposition, he pulled one of the chairs away from the table and sat down. His suit was silk. Very silk. French cuffs, the glint of a discreet gold bracelet on his right wrist. Gold ring with a cabochon garnet.

Slowly, as if he were demonstrating there were no tricks up his sleeve, he reached into his coat pocket and took out a pack of cigarettes. He offered one to Titus, who just stared at him. The man took one for himself and lighted it, laying the pack on the table with the lighter.

"My name is Alvaro," he said. He smoked. "What I am about to tell you will take some lengthy explanation," he said, "but from this moment, Mr. Cain, I am afraid that you must consider yourself *secuestrado.*"

Titus gaped at him.

"Yes, kidnapped," Alvaro said.

The shadow men stayed in the shadow courtyard. Titus heard the coyotes now, yippingyippingyipping on the far side of the valley, below the amber lights of houses clustered near the crests of the next ridge of hills.

Alvaro smoked, clenching his teeth as though there were something tart but savory in the taste of the cigarette before opening his lips to exhale.

"First of all," he said, "I must give you a few moments to control yourself, to comprehend the reality of your situation. For the next half hour or so, I am going to explain to you how your life has changed. *¿Bueno?*"

Titus's ears were ringing. His face was hot, and he felt a little giddy.

"As you must already know," Alvaro went on, "this kind of enterprise is much practiced in Latin America. In the past it has been a very crude business, and it still is most of the time. Unnecessarily complicated for everyone. Idiots in the mountains holding hostages in filthy conditions. The idiot K and R people based in London or Paris or Washington negotiating with the idiots in the mountains on behalf of the sweaty corporate lackey worrying about how much his employer's insurance is going to go up. Wild demands negotiated down to stupidly small sums. Imbecilic police."

Titus was dumbstruck. This guy just wasn't for real. It was like going to the theater with Rita, one of those productions in the round where the actors come out into the audience to include them in the drama. He was always uneasy with that.

Alvaro rested his right elbow on the arm of his chair, his forearm vertical, cigarette tucked deep into the crotch of his first and second fingers. His eyes grew lazy.

"Forget all of that," he said, flicking his hand dismissively. "As you will see, this is something quite different altogether. First, this is occurring right here in the U.S.—Texas, no less—not in Latin America.

"Second, we are not going to take you away. No. You are free to go on living your life normally, as you please.

"Third, no negotiations. No haggling.

"Fourth, no police, no federal authorities, no intermediaries, no K and R guys. In fact, no one will ever know that this has even happened."

Titus's adrenaline high had greatly heightened his perceptions. The sticky smack of phlegm in Alvaro's throat when he spoke certain words was amplified to the point of distraction. And though the light on the veranda was only a glow, Alvaro sat before him in sharp three-dimensional clarity, outlined very precisely from the darkness behind him, his face glimmering like a hologram.

"I have gone to a great deal of trouble to learn about you,"

Alvaro went on. He looked around and lifted his chin. "This house, for example, is as familiar to me as my own home. I could find the light switches in every room in the darkness. I know your company and its history inside out. I know your biography better than my own father's."

He spoke with a grounded sureness, without animation, his voice almost devoid of inflection.

Titus hadn't taken another swallow of his beer. He was entranced. Immobile, he waited for the emerging revelation. It was like seeing the moment of his own death coming down a long road, a small speck, slowly, slowly growing larger as it made its shambling approach. It was a horrible thing to see, and fascinating. He couldn't pull himself away from the spectacle of it, even to flee.

Alvaro continued. "CaiText is worth two hundred and fifty-six million dollars, Mr. Cain. I want the equivalent of a quarter of that."

In the warm breeze of the summer night, Titus went slowly, serenely cold.

Alvaro waited, seemingly understanding what Titus was going through.

"Are you all right, Mr. Cain? We have a long way to go yet."

Titus couldn't answer.

"The most important thing in this entire negotiation," Alvaro said, "is secrecy. I want to acquire the money in clean, legal silence. Indirectly, of course. Through business arrangements."

Titus's mind latched on to the words *business arrangements*. Reality. Something he could wrestle with. Something he understood. The hallucination shuddered.

The embodied shadows drifted now and again in the darkness, and like the hour hand of a clock, they moved without moving. They were here, and then they were elsewhere. But they were always there.

"What kind of business arrangements?" Titus finally managed to ask. A negotiation. A deal, something that required him to rein in his wildly scattered thoughts.

"I have a number of enterprises that I want you to invest in," Alvaro answered. "Foreign enterprises. You will be given opportunities to invest in international charities. Good causes. All of them are front companies through which the money will wash away to places unknown."

He smoked the cigarette again, clenched his teeth, parted his lips, and let the stench seep out into the air. Titus thought he saw an ocherous tint to the smoke, to the edges of it, maybe. The stench seemed not to have its source in the cigarette so much as in Alvaro's own rancid nostrils or, more precisely, from somewhere within him.

"Why me?"

"Oh, there are many reasons, Mr. Cain, but there are a few obvious ones. Neither you nor your company is flamboyant. You keep a very low profile. You are relatively small, but the company has been a solid and profitable enterprise for more than a decade. And you have refused to take it public. You are a wholly owned, private company. You are CaiText. You answer to no one, normally an enviable position."

Titus could hardly make himself formulate the next question in his mind, but it wouldn't go away. It kept trying to take shape, a venomous idea lingering in the place of hazy fears at the back of his mind.

"And why," Titus heard himself say, his stomach tightening, "would I do this?"

Alvaro closed his eyes lazily and nodded as he drew on his foul cigarette. "Yes, of course," he said. He stared at Titus as if making judgments about him, about how much to tell him or about how to tell him. "There will be critical junctures in our negotiations, moments when I will expect you to perform precisely as I've directed. There will be certain criteria that you will be expected to meet. Maintaining secrecy. Meeting deadlines. Following precise instructions. There will be no, as they say, no wiggle room in your response to these instructions."

He paused for emphasis.

"I am not a patient man," Alvaro added. "I will never say to you, 'The next time you don't follow instructions . . .' No. You will receive instructions only once. And to answer your question, why would you do this . . . It's very simple. People are going to start dying, and they will die at a rate of my own choosing based upon how well I think you are cooperating. And they will continue to die until I have sixty-four million dollars."

Chapter 6

Titus should have seen it coming, but he hadn't. The hallucinatory feel of his situation returned instantaneously. The flagstones on the veranda swung around and floated above him, and the fountain in the courtyard hovered upside down over the dark night sky that spread out in front of him like a black valley rich with sparkling flowers.

Jesus Christ. Jesus. Christ.

"We have to move on, Mr. Cain," Alvaro said.

Titus looked at him. "Move on?"

"Yes. Do you understand your situation?"

He understood what this guy had said, yes. But he was still waiting for it to seem real.

"Mr. Cain, do you understand?"

Titus would try. He would address the business of this . . . hallucination, and he would follow the lines of logic.

"Yeah," Titus said, "I understand." It just didn't seem real. "When . . . am I going to learn more about the 'business arrangements'?"

"Soon."

"You don't want it all at once?"

"Oh, I'll take it all at once, but I happen to know that you can't get it that quickly. However, I'll want the first payment immediately."

"How much will that be?"

"I'll let you know."

Titus quickly ran over his personal assets in his mind. How much was this maniac going to ask for? Titus was beginning to come around, as if he were regaining consciousness. "My financial people will be flabbergasted if I start dumping millions. It won't make any sense to them."

"You'll have to be creative to avoid curiosity," Alvaro said. "I don't want anyone suspicious about what you're going to be doing. That would be unacceptable."

"What kind of enterprises are you talking about?"

"Oh, a wide variety. I'll get to that later. The main thing is, when all is said and done it must appear that you've simply made a series of business decisions that have resulted in these unfortunate losses. Everything you do has to lead to that appearance. The way you set up these acquisitions, all of it."

"I'll look like a fool for making decisions like that," Titus said.

"I have people who will work with you," Alvaro said, "to give it the best face possible." He paused. "But, really, I don't give a damn about how it will make you look, one way or the other. You need to understand that. So long as it isn't suspicious. That's the important thing. I really can't emphasize that enough."

Moment by moment, reality was filtering back into Titus's thinking. The disabling numbness of shock lessened, and he came to himself as if he were awakening from a drugged stupor. Fear was still there, potent and sweaty, and there was a stirring of resistance, too. Though he was still reeling, there was a germinating seed of anger.

"As for your law enforcement agencies," Alvaro said, "don't do it. It's a gamble. If you call them, and you are able to keep it hidden from me temporarily, you may indeed save your money. But I will find out about it sooner or later, and then it will cost you your peace of mind for the rest of your life. If I can't get to you, I'll get to people you know. Friends. Family. You will be responsible for what happens to all of them, for everyone you've ever known."

He paused and lolled his head as if weary of trying to be convincing.

"Mr. Cain, believe me, I've done it all before. I know the tricks men want to play. I know that after I leave here tonight you will begin scheming of ways to escape your situation with your money and your life intact. I know you will do this because you are an intelligent man—after all"—he spread his arms out and looked around him—"look at the fortune you have created by your own ingenuity, your own cleverness. No? So, who am I to come in here and give you instructions, do this, do that, as if you were stupid and couldn't figure out a way to outsmart me? Right?

"But . . . listen to me, Mr. Cain." Alvaro lifted his chin and pronounced his next words with exaggerated care. "You-can-not-do-it. And if you try, you will create a fucking monster. As of tonight your life has changed, as surely as if you had discovered a terrible disease inside you, and there is nothing you can do about it. The only thing in your power regarding this situation is to do as you are told. It will save lives."

He cocked his head at Titus. "And that's no small thing, is it?"

Again, Titus was speechless. How could he possibly respond to such . . . insanity? He couldn't even formulate a question that didn't seem surreal.

A tiny red light out in the courtyard caught Titus's eye, just a couple of winks and it was gone, and one of the dark smudges drifted away from the others and stood alone. Titus could hear the man talking. His head was throbbing. He reached out and put his now tepid bottle of beer on the wrought-iron table.

"Suicide," Titus said abruptly.

"That's always an option," Alvaro said, unfazed. "But you're really not the issue. I want the money. I don't care if I get it from you or from your wife. It's irrelevant to me. The important thing is that I get it."

"I could put it all into a trust. I wouldn't have any control over it."

"Mr. Cain, please understand: People die if I don't get the money. It's not a matter of how clever you can be, or how clever your lawyers can be. Anything you do that prevents the transfer of sixty-four million to me will cause people to die. You go to the FBI, they die. You find a financial escape hatch, even more people die. It's very simple."

"How many people?" Titus asked stupidly. But he thought of only one person. Rita. Jesus Christ. Rita's face lodged in his mind—an unthinkable association that crowded out the faceless plurality of all the others that might have been there.

"How many people do you know?" Alvaro asked. It was a ghoulish response that left no doubt that he would take it further than Titus could bear. Titus didn't answer.

"Well," Alvaro said, turning in his chair with a little gesture to the shadows, "that covers the big picture."

Titus heard the dogs and then saw them coming, lumbering along through the allée of laurels with their noses down, scanning the earthy scents. They were happy to be out of wherever they were being kept and came onto the veranda and straight to Titus.

He bent to the dogs and petted them firmly, as they liked.

It was so good to see them. This was reality; these slobbering, affectionate old friends were reality.

But when the dogs turned to Alvaro, expecting the same treatment, he stopped them with a scolding grunt. They flinched away, casting puzzled, wary glances at him, and then stood looking at him, their tails hanging still.

In that moment Alvaro made another gesture, and Titus saw a flash from the shadows and heard a muffled *pumft! pumft! pumft! pumft!* The first dog's head flew back, and he dropped on his folded legs, his brains thrown twenty feet back against doors into the house. The second dog, caught in mid-turn, stumbled as if tripping, the bullets catching his brain at such an angle as to buy him another millisecond. He emitted a muffled yowl, and his hindquarters collapsed, and for an instant his front legs remained rigid, refusing death, his head extended awkwardly as if to maintain his balance. And then he went down.

Titus was on his feet instinctively, which brought the shadows instantly into the light at the edge of the veranda. Three men, Hispanics in dark street clothes, small, high-tech automatic weapons, headphones.

Alvaro was as cool as boredom. He put his hand up and signed for Titus to step back away from him. Titus did, his heart rattling around in his chest, driven by fear and fury and simple astonishment. Alvaro stood and moved closer to his men, closer to the dark. He lifted his chin at the dogs.

"It's that easy, Mr. Cain." He shrugged. "Friends. Relatives. Strangers. I hand them into your safekeeping. Don't hand them back to me. They're all dogs to me."

He turned and stepped into the darkness.

Chapter 7

Titus stood on the veranda as if he had just walked out of the house and had forgotten what he'd come to do. He stared at the silent fountain in the courtyard and listened to the cars starting in the drive at the front of the house. He heard car doors slamming and heard the cars driving away, their engines fading as they wound their way down the hill and into the night.

He turned and looked at the dogs. Jesus. He had to think. He had to be clearheaded. He had to think things through all the way to their logical conclusions.

After walking over to the first dog, he knelt and worked his hands underneath. He was warm and limp and bloodsoaked. Titus avoided looking at his head. When he picked him up he felt that odd density of death, a strange thing he had known before with animals, how they seemed so much heavier after they had died.

He carried the dog through the courtyard, into the allée of mountain laurels and out into the darkness, where a broad, sloping path led down to the orchard. At the back of the orchard, where the only light was the reflected glow of the city lights haloed over the ridge of hills, he put the dog down on a flat plot of thick Bermuda grass. Then he returned for the second dog.

With a pickax and shovel he got from the reservoir work site a hundred yards away, he began digging in the loam. It took him the better part of an hour to get the hole deep enough to discourage the coyotes and feral cats from digging them up, and then he laid the two dogs one on top of the other and filled in the hole.

When he was finished he was soaked in sweat, his clothes ruined, smeared with dirt and dog's blood that combined into a sad crust. He returned the pickax and shovel to the reservoir site and then walked back up to the house, where he got a hose and washed the pools of blackening blood from the veranda.

He crossed the courtyard and went through to the walled enclosure surrounding the pool. Behind the poolhouse there were showers and dressing rooms and a large storage room where they kept the tables and chairs and other accessories they needed for entertaining.

Outside the dressing rooms, he removed his clothes and mud-caked loafers and threw them into the trash cans. Naked, he went to the ice machine in the cabana beside the pool and filled a plastic bucket there with ice and threw the ice into the pool. He did this repeatedly until the ice machine was empty. And then he dove in. He swam four laps slowly, back and forth through the cold pockets of floating ice, trying to clear his head.

Once out of the pool, he made his way to a deck chair and sat down. He started trying to work it out. For a moment his thoughts just wouldn't gel. He couldn't come up with anything at all. He just wanted to call Rita, hear her voice. But that was out of the question. He didn't trust himself to hide his emotions, and to make her suspicious—maybe even frighten her—

without having some kind of plan in place was simply irresponsible.

If he was going to believe this guy's threats, then there was nowhere to go. No options. But Titus found that inconceivable. There were always options, weren't there?

How would this guy know if he contacted someone? Obviously he had some kind of tactical team. How thorough were they? There were bound to be bugs in the house. The phones were probably tapped. And it didn't take geniuses to pick up cell phone transmissions. Would he be followed, too?

Still, doing nothing was out of the question. Alvaro had said: Even if you do contact law enforcement people and are able to hide it from me temporarily . . . So maybe his surveillance wasn't as infallible as he would like Titus to think. Sure, he'd want Titus to believe that he, Alvaro, was all over him, that Titus couldn't even have a change in his pulse rate without Alvaro knowing about it; but what if that wasn't true? Was Titus just going to roll over and believe that? It's a gamble, Alvaro had said.

Titus sat up in his chair at the memory of that remark. A gamble. Well, where there's a gamble, there's also a chance, isn't there?

He stood up, his mind racing. No police. No FBI. No law enforcement agencies. But Titus remembered a guy. Four years ago, one of Titus's female employees was abducted from the CaiText parking garage. It developed into a hostage standoff situation (it turned out to be a bad marriage turned worse) that lasted a couple of days. Among the various law enforcement–type consultants brought in during the ordeal was a guy named Gil Norlin. It was never clear to Titus who brought him into the situation or whom he answered to, but he was always sort of hanging around on the edges of it. Never fully engaged, never having any authority for anything. Yet Titus noticed that

41

people did consult him, even the FBI agents, but always quietly, to the side.

Titus heard later that he was a former CIA officer, retired now. A consultant. He had left Titus his card, avoiding his eyes, Titus remembered. Titus headed for the house.

Wearing his robe, he rummaged around in his office for twenty minutes before he found the old card in an outdated Rolodex at the back of a drawer.

He looked at his watch. At this hour the winding roads of the wooded hills were sparsely traveled, and even Titus would be able to see someone following. On the other hand, it really didn't matter. Even with all the advanced technology available today, a call from a spontaneously chosen pay phone was still a safe call. Even if Alvaro's people had a surveillance tag on the Rover and knew he was making the call, they wouldn't know whom he was calling or what the call was about.

Alvaro had specified no law enforcement. But he knew that Titus would have to make arrangements with a variety of people in order to raise the money Alvaro was demanding. For all he knew, Titus could be calling his banker, his broker, his accountant, his lawyer. Surely those conversations could be private and not considered a violation of Alvaro's bans on communication? Was Titus to have understood from Alvaro's instructions that he could never have another private conversation? That just didn't seem realistic. It was worth the risk of pushing the envelope a little to find out just how tight a grip this guy had on him.

He grabbed the card from his Rolodex, threw on some clothes, locked the house—feeling stupid, considering what had just happened—and went out and got into the Range Rover.

It took him only ten minutes to get down the winding narrow roads below his house to the lone all-night convenience store at an isolated intersection in the woods. He hadn't seen anyone following him so far, although he knew that his countersurveillance skills had to be less than great.

There were no other cars there. He placed the call from the pay phone outside. That number had been changed. He dialed the new number. He got a recording that gave him yet another number, where he received a cell phone number, where he got a recording to leave a pay phone number and state if he had an emergency. He did both.

Agitated, he sat in the Range Rover with his window down so he could hear the phone ring and stared at the bright interior of the store. Nobody was in there except the night clerk. No other cars were parked outside except his. The two of them, the middle-aged woman suspended in fluorescent isolation as she stared into space from her stool behind the cash register and Titus staring at her from his solitary, lightless cubicle, were polar opposites, bound together by their dissimilarities. Black-and-white metaphors for the bewildered.

When the phone rang he was out of the Rover in an instant and picked up the receiver on the third ring.

"Yes?"

"Yeah, this is Titus Cain. I met you about four years ago. There was this abduction—"

"Yeah, I remember."

"I need to talk to you."

"What's the situation?"

"Extortion. Death threats if I call law enforcement. This phone call's a big risk."

"How were the threats made? Letter?"

"Three armed gunmen showed up at my house about an hour ago. Shot my dogs right there in front of me and gave me ultimatums."

"Give me the address where you are right now."

"I imagine I'm being followed. My car's probably—"
"As long as you're not tagged personally, we'll be okay."
Titus gave him the address.

He left the Rover at the convenience store and rode with Gilbert Norlin through the winding, wooded roads of the hills while Norlin made the necessary maneuvers to make sure they weren't being tailed. Titus surprised himself by not being able to speak. Norlin didn't press him, and they rode in silence for a while. Titus's tongue-tied confusion embarrassed him, but there literally wasn't anything he could do about it. Finally he could control his voice, and he began to tell Norlin everything, chronologically, in as much detail as he could remember.

By the time he had finished, they had arrived at the deserted building site of one of the many new homes under construction in the hills. They got out of Norlin's car and walked to the house slab where the framing was just beginning. They sat on the slab, surrounded by the smells of lumber and concrete and freshly moved earth.

Now it was Norlin who remained silent. Titus waited, his heart loping along as if it were trying to outrun what he was sure would be Norlin's grim appraisal of his dilemma.

Finally Norlin asked, "How difficult is it going to be to do what he wants, to move the money?"

"Depends on how much he asks for first. I've got, I don't know, a good chunk in markets I can dump immediately. I'll take a loss, but I can do it. Beyond that I'll have to sell pieces of the company. It's just going to look bizarre to . . . hell, to everybody. I've built CaiText on cautious, conservative business practices, for God's sake. I've got a reputation for that.

"Just six months ago, after years of planning, I let all the division heads buy into the company. That's worked great all these years with one other guy who's been with me from the beginning. But on top of that, six months ago, we borrowed heavily for our expansion program—a program all the division heads planned and proposed to me. Everyone's excited about it, and we think it's going to have a huge payoff.

"Now, can you imagine how this is going to look if I start shifting assets so I can start laying out millions of dollars on foreign investments? This isn't going to work."

"But you don't have any specific instructions yet," Norlin said. "You don't know the immediate requirements."

"No."

Norlin wasn't saying much, and that was making Titus nervous, filling him with the worst kind of dread.

In the reflected glow of the city lights across the river, Titus could see enough of Norlin to remember him from four years ago. Of middle height, he had thinning hair, a face with no jawline. His shoulders were rounded, tending to a slight hunch.

Norlin shook his head. "I don't blame you for not going to the FBI. I wouldn't have, either. But that's not what they'd want me to say to you. The conventional wisdom is that the sooner they're involved, the better."

Norlin sat with his arms locked straight, his hands palms down on the edge of the slab, looking at Titus.

"But this doesn't look too damned conventional to me," he said. "You know what the percentages are for catching kidnappers in the U.S.? Ninety-five percent. That's mostly because things like this don't usually happen here in the States. The people who get into it here are loners, emotional basket cases to start with. Crazies who think they're going to magically solve the sad problems of their empty lives by stealing another living human being."

He paused.

"But if something like this, if this was what kidnapping

45

was like in the States, that ninety-five percent would be shattered. Why? Because this is business, and these people aren't crazies. Not in the sense I'm talking about, anyway. That thing with the dogs, that was a promise, not a threat. You can expect these people to do exactly what they say they're going to do."

"This is it, then?" Titus was incredulous. "This is it? I just get ready to cough up sixty-four million?"

"No, I didn't say that."

"Then what in the hell do I do?"

Norlin didn't say anything. He was thinking, and the fact that he wasn't just firing off action points, wasn't rolling out a game plan, wasn't giving Titus go-to names, scared the shit out of him. Norlin was Titus's cop show equivalent of his one phone call, and he wasn't coming through.

Titus wiped the sweat off the side of his face. This wasn't what he'd wanted. He'd wanted Norlin to be reassuring, to have answers. He felt his chest tightening; he felt time running out; he felt desperate.

"I'm no good to you," Norlin said.

Jesus.

"I'm not. Wherever this guy's coming from—Colombia, Mexico, Brazil—he's from another world. Believe me, these guys do not breathe the same air we do. Listen, last year in Colombia alone, nearly a billion dollars were paid out in kidnapping ransoms. Big business. And it just doesn't get any more serious than this."

Norlin shook his head, thinking.

"What I'm seeing here, this is some kind of hybrid operation. I don't know. I've never heard of this kind of thing happening in the States. I've never heard of this much money being demanded. I've never heard of them wanting to keep the money transfer 'legal.'"

His voice was flat. He wasn't getting excited about it, he was just laying out the facts.

"Killing friends, family, for negotiating leverage, that's routine in Latin America, India, Philippines, Russia, those places, yeah. But here in the States? Shit. I don't know what they're thinking. It's just way, way out of whack. It's hard to believe."

Titus thought he heard a glimmer of hope.

"You think this could just be a huge poker hand, then? He's calling my bluff? If I cough up some money, he hits it lucky? If I don't, he'll just disappear? He took a shot at it, and it didn't really cost him anything to try."

"No." Norlin was quick to come back. "That's not what I'm saying. You've got to believe this guy." He shook his head. "Everything's accelerated in the last two years. There's a harder edge to everything, terrorism, international crime. Law enforcement's pressing harder, intelligence community has gotten back into the trenches. Everything's more extreme. Looking down the road, we knew we were going to be seeing things we'd never dreamed of seeing before. This is the kind of thing we were afraid of. And the worst part of it is, we're just not geared up yet to deal with something so damned brutal."

Chapter 8

Titus turned and sat on the slab again, a few feet away from Norlin. He felt a little light-headed, his thoughts alternating in velocity between a stunned, sluggish incredulity and the frenetic, revved-up hyperjitter of panic. He wanted to stand up again. He wanted to pace. He wanted to be able to think methodically. He wanted more air. He wanted to wake up.

"I'm going to give you some advice," Norlin said. "Your situation, there are going to be pressures put on you, deliberately, to make fast decisions. And you're going to have to do it. You won't have any choice. But it's going to be tough because sometimes—and it's just the odds, you can't fight it—sometimes you're going to make the wrong decisions. The consequences are going to be painful."

"What's that mean, exactly?" Titus wanted it spelled out, bad news in black and white.

"It means that after it's done, it's done. If you're going to second-guess yourself, you'll go crazy before this is over."

"Odds are, people are going to die, you mean."

"Think of it like this: This man is bringing you a sick situation. He created it. You didn't. He's going to force you to make choices where nobody wins. When that happens, re-member who started it. You're just playing the hand that this guy's dealt you."

Titus let this sober insight sink in. Norlin didn't rush him. Titus could smell the freshly cut brush around them, the stuff that had been carved out of the hillside for the construction site. He could smell the earth, an odor, a fragrance, really, that made him think of his dogs and of the weight of them as he'd put them into the hole he'd dug at the back of the orchard.

"Okay," Titus said, "I understand." And he did, but he didn't want to believe it. He wanted to believe that he could avoid the grim scenario that Norlin was predicting. He wanted to believe that in most cases that might be true, but he'd be able to avoid it. He'd figure out a way not to have to live through that kind of dark dilemma.

"I'm going to put you in touch with someone," Norlin said, standing. In the dim ambient light from the city in the dis-tance, Titus watched him step off the concrete slab and go over to his car. He reached in and took out an oversize cell phone—encrypted, Titus assumed—and came back over to the slab.

"I've got to repeat this," Norlin said. "This is not the way the FBI would want it done. They'd say it was irresponsible. And normally I'd agree with them. But . . . " He hesitated only slightly. "The truth is, if I were standing where you're standing right now, I'd want this guy to hear my story. And I'd want to know what he thinks about it. He may say, Go to the FBI. Then you should go, and you won't have to worry about whether you're doing the right thing or not. You can believe what he says."

"But he may say something else," Titus said. "And if he does, I go with that. I believe him on that, too."

"That's right."

"Where is he?"

"I don't know. I'm getting ready to find out."

"You have a lot of faith in him?" It was a question, and an observation, and a concern.

"I worked with him at the CIA. He's been contract for a long time now. He's solid, like I told you. Does his best work out of the box."

"Out of the box. I need a little more on that."

"He's several points removed from any official equation. If he screws up, there's no blowback. He's one of a very few who know going into a situation that he's on his own. Guy like that, nobody owns his ass. And nobody helps him out of a bind, either. He's alone. He's given the edgiest operations, and when he succeeds, the intelligence community wins big. And silently, which is really the only way to win. But when guys like him go down, they go down alone. They just disappear. Forever."

"Why do they do it?"

"Big, big money. And because they can't help themselves. They're addicted to the adrenaline. Or they have private demons that can only be satisfied by putting everything on the line every time." He shrugged. "Or for reasons that maybe only God understands."

"But that's CIA work. Intelligence stuff. Why would he be interested in this?"

Norlin shrugged. "Big, big money. Or maybe he'll have other reasons."

Titus considered this. "And you think this is the way to go, then, with this guy who's . . . good at working outside the box?"

"Look, Mr. Cain, I may not have the goods to advise you on what's happening here, but I can promise you this: This Alvaro doesn't even know there is a fucking box. Believe me, if I can find him, you're going to need this guy."

Without saying any more, Norlin turned and walked away,

past his car, onto the dirt track that led away from the construction site to the road below. Titus could hear him murmuring out in the dark.

Titus stood and twisted his shoulders to relieve the tension. He stared out over the valley. No city view here, but he could see a coil of Lake Austin, the surface of the water glazed in reflected light. He felt desolate. Isolated. Completely at a loss. The woods around the construction site were dense, and when he looked up toward the lighted sky, he could see the black circle of the trees surrounding him out of his peripheral vision. He stood that way a long time, long enough to lose track of time. Long enough to be startled by Norlin's voice.

"You're in luck," Norlin said, coming up out of the darkness.

Titus was surprised to see Norlin step up and stretch out his arm, handing the cell phone to him.

"He just happens to be close by," Norlin explained. "He's in San Miguel de Allende, Mexico. His name's García Burden."

Titus took the heavy phone and put it to his ear in time to hear one ring and then:

"Titus Cain?"

"Yes, that's right."

"García Burden. Gil's told me the basic story. If this is what it seems to be, it's extraordinary."

His voice was soft, a surprise, though Titus hadn't had any preconceptions. He had a bit of an accent, but Titus had no idea what it was. García. No, it wasn't Hispanic, the accent, not like Alvaro's, anyway. It was something altogether different.

" 'If'?" Titus asked. "Why wouldn't it be?"

"Who knows?" Burden said cryptically. "But your visitor's not who he says he is. His scheme is complex and would require a lot of experience in this sort of thing. So I'm fairly sure he's using a bogus name, which means he's on all the international border watch lists. He must've entered the States illegally. That's significant and supports the ransom story."

"How does it do that?"

"He's too cautious to have come in under a fake passport. Too much risk with the new technology now. This kind of man wouldn't enter the States under the sorts of conditions illegal entry would require for anything routine. This has probably been in the works for a long time. He's come in for the kill . . . so to speak."

Burden seemed to be all over this.

"How long before he gets back to you?"

"He didn't say."

"It'll be very soon. But he gave you no instructions?"

"No."

"So there are no 'rules' for you to offend yet."

"I'm not supposed to contact any law enforcement agency."

"Well, he would consider me in that category, so if he knew about this, you would've already offended him. This conversation would justify the first hit."

The word *hit* struck Titus like a board to the side of the head. Jesus. It was stunning to hear that word in the context of reality, of his reality. But then, did he really believe Alvaro was going to start killing people if Titus didn't—what—follow instructions?

Burden responded to Titus's shocked silence.

"No, don't make that mistake, Mr. Cain," he said. "This man doesn't threaten. He probably even told you that himself. He's eagerly awaiting his first opportunity to show you how quickly he'll react to your failure to follow instructions."

"Then you do know him."

"I don't know. But I do know the kind of man he is. In that sense, yes, I know him." Burden abruptly shifted gears. "I want to work with you on this, Mr. Cain. Are you interested?"

Titus glanced at Norlin, but he couldn't see anything beyond a dark figure.

"Of course I'm interested, but I've got to think this over. I'm not going to decide to do this right now."

"I'm only asking if you're interested in talking."

"Yeah, of course I am."

"There's not a lot of time. You should come tomorrow."

"Down there? San Miguel?"

"Yes. We need to be here when we talk. I have things to show you, to explain. My archives are here. They're not portable."

"But what if he tries to get in touch with me while I'm gone?"

"I'll explain how to handle that."

"I don't know if I can make it tomorrow. My security system's been wrecked, and I've got to get someone to start debugging this place."

"Did he tell you not to call in security people?"

"No." Titus cringed. Was that another offense? Was he expected to live with Alvaro listening to every word spoken in his own home? He couldn't do it. He wouldn't do it. "He didn't say specifically not to do it."

"Then you've got a choice to make. Get used to it, or be ready to live with the consequences, if there are any."

"I can't live like that."

"Fine. Do you know people who can do that for you?"

"I own a software company. We work with electronic security constantly."

"You're going to need some highly specialized people, Mr.

Cain. You've got a very specific kind of problem there. It's not the same. Surely you can see that."

Shit. Titus felt stupidly naive. He was going to have to start thinking differently.

"Mr. Cain, this is my profession. This is what I do. Let me send someone to you. They know about the latest technology. They know this game. Okay?"

"Yeah," Titus said. "Okay."

"They'll be there tomorrow," Burden said. "Now, you're coming down here tomorrow so we can talk?"

"Yeah—"

"Do you speak Spanish?"

"No."

"Doesn't matter."

"What do you want me to do, just fly down there?"

"No. I'll get instructions to you. And Mr. Cain, you need to understand right now that nothing is 'just' anything anymore. From now on you are an extraordinary exception to the general rules of just about everything."

WEDNESDAY
The Second Day

Chapter 9

Any significant sleep had been impossible during the night. Titus had lain in bed watching the black hills against the cobalt dark sky and was still watching as the sun rounded the curve of the earth, scattering the night before it.

At nine-fifteen the next morning, a van and a pickup with no markings pulled into Titus's driveway. They stopped within a large enclosure of high hedges that screened the parking area from the city.

Mark Herrin was a quiet young man with a ponytail and a gentle smile. He was a full head taller than Cline, his partner, who had a fraternity-neat haircut and a tendril of a black tattoo creeping out of the white collar of his shirt along his left jugular vein.

They introduced themselves, and Herrin said, "García said to assume everything in the house is hot."

"I'm not positive about it," Titus said. "I do know the security system's been bypassed."

"We'll give it all a good cleaning," Herrin said with a kind of lazy indifference. "Actually debugging a place like this takes a lot of equipment. We're going to have to haul some things inside. Big stuff." He looked around at the hedge enclosure. "This is a big break, having this protection. I don't like working under the opposition's constant supervision, you know," he said, throwing a look across the valley toward the river.

"Then you think the house is being watched?" Titus asked.

"If you're a target, you're a target," Herrin said simply. "If this guy's serious, there's no such thing as half-assed in this business."

They stood there between the driveway and the veranda while Herrin had Titus corroborate the information Burden had passed on to him, and then he asked him a lot of additional questions.

"Okay," Herrin said after a while. "We need to go inside and look around. Now, when we start locating these bugs and jerking them out of there, they're going to know about it. So after we pop the first one, the cat's out of the bag. But there's no need to give them a heads-up, either. So when we get in there let's don't talk about what we're going to be doing, okay?"

Titus led them inside and showed them through the house. Once they had a feel for the layout of the place, Titus left them alone to wander through the house and survey the size of their job.

Remembering what Herrin had said about the house being watched, Titus walked down the allée to the site where the stone workers were facing the reservoir. They came in every morning just after sunrise to get an early start on the heat, using the code to the front gates on the property. Titus had been using these men for years to do work around the property, but now he wasn't comfortable with someone having access to that kind of freedom to the grounds.

Standing in the shade of an oak, he talked with Benito, the foreman, and told him that he was going to have some other men on the property working on some electrical problems, and he didn't want that many crews and trucks there at the same time. He said he'd give Benito's crew two weeks' paid vacation—beginning right now. When they came back, they could pick up where they'd left off.

Benito was surprised, but two weeks' paid vacation smoothed over a lot of puzzlement, and Titus shook his hand and headed back to the house. He could hear the crew loading their tools into the truck behind him.

Titus returned to the kitchen and looked at his watch. He had about forty minutes before he had to leave. He picked up his cell phone and walked outside to call Carla Elster, his assistant at CaiText.

"Carla, listen, I don't really have any must-do meetings during the next few days, do I?"

"Nothing on your calendar but the weekly touch-base reviews with the department heads," Carla said. "But, uh, Matt Rohan did call late yesterday and wanted to see you for about half an hour when you had time today. He didn't say what about. As usual. And Donice McCafferty called for an appointment. I'm guessing she wants to ask if CaiText will sponsor their charity drive again this fall. And I was supposed to remind you that there's a retirement party on Friday for Alison Daly in accounting."

There was no wasted motion and no wasted moments in Carla's life. She was disciplined, focused, organized, and faithful to her routines. She had to be, because without it her life and Titus's life would fall apart. At least she was convinced they would.

Carla had been his assistant since the day he'd signed the corporation documents to start CaiText. Until he'd met Rita, Carla had been the one person he'd depended on to give him a grounded second opinion and an honest, compass-correcting perspective on whatever was preoccupying him at the time. She was like a sister to him.

"Okay, well, if you could just put all of that on hold for right now, I'd appreciate it."

"On hold? For how long?"

"A few days, maybe. I'm going to be out of pocket a couple of days."

Pause. "Okay." Pause. "Everything okay?"

"Yeah, sure." He stopped. Jesus. He was tempted, enormously tempted, to say something to her, to relieve some of the pressure he felt, but he kept remembering Alvaro's words: *I don't want anyone suspicious. . . . That's the important thing. I really can't emphasize that enough.*

"Titus," she said, "what's going on?"

At forty-six, Carla was a single mother of twin daughters who were soon to enter their freshman year at Vanderbilt University. Her husband had left her six years earlier when the girls were in the sixth grade, and Carla had immediately galvanized her mind and turned her life into a regimen. She was determined to do it all without him, and she did. She'd be damned if she would let her life fall apart in his absence. A man who would leave his wife and young daughters to fend for themselves couldn't have been all that valuable in the first place, she decided. She wouldn't let him be.

Titus had helped her throughout the whole ordeal. Whenever she needed to take off from work for the girls' school events, she never even had to ask. He boosted her salary to compensate for the loss of half her income, and he made sure the girls had summer jobs at CaiText so Carla didn't have to worry about them during the day.

Her husband had maddeningly given her the house in West Lake Hills without a whimper. The fact that he didn't think it worth fighting for infuriated her. And he didn't even fuss that much about the level of alimony she had demanded. He was in such a hurry to set up housekeeping with his new girlfriend that he practically ran from everything they had built together over fourteen years of marriage.

And then there was Darlene, his new woman. Darlene was half Carla's age. She was a blonde; Carla was a brunet. She was tall; Carla was not so tall. She was health-nut thin and tight; Carla was practical medium and not so tight. Darlene didn't work; Carla had worked for CaiText their entire marriage and was as loyal to Titus and the company he was building as if she owned half of it. The striking differences in the two women were an additional humiliation. Darlene was everything that Carla wasn't.

But that had been six years ago. She had created a new life and a new self. She had made a stable home for her daughters while she had nurtured them through the storms and stresses of adolescence. They were good girls, and she was proud of them.

Now, though, with the girls away from home for the first time at summer jobs in Denver that Titus had gotten for them, and soon to be off to their first year at the university, Carla found herself with a spare moment once in a while, for the first time in eighteen years. She was dating a man, Nathan Jordan, who was considerate and sensible and comfortable with the girls, who liked him very much. She was entering a new season in life, and it looked as if it were going to be a good one.

"Everything okay with Rita?" she asked.

"Yeah, everything's fine. I talked with her last night."

Pause. He could feel her listening to his voice, reading between the lines of the way he sounded. She was all over this.

"Come on Titus. What's going on?"

"I'm under a little pressure here," he said. "It's nothing to do with Rita. It's . . . financial. And it's personal, company's not involved. But Rita doesn't know about it yet. It doesn't seem right to go into it with you before I've had a chance to tell her."

"Well . . . is it . . . disastrous? I mean, hell, Titus, give me something to put this in perspective."

"Several months back I made some . . . risky investments. I've just learned that they've gone bad. I've lost a hell of a lot of money. I'm working out how to deal with it. I can tell you more in a few days. But right now, Carla, you're the only person who knows about this. Understand?"

"Yeah, Titus, I understand," she said, and he could hear the sympathy and the actual hurt in her voice. "Listen, I'm sorry to hear this. If I can do anything . . . I'll do anything I can."

"I've got to go," he said.

Chapter 10

Herrin's assistant with the jugular tattoo drove out of Titus's place in his pickup, his windows rolled down in the late morning heat, obviously alone, as anyone could see. In a hidden compartment under the bed of the pickup, Titus lay in the dark, guessing the truck's route by following the right and left turns as they made their way down the winding roads to Westlake Drive and headed toward town.

The ride downtown hardly registered on Titus. He carried no additional clothes, only his laptop, as Burden had instructed. He felt webby headed, his reflexes sluggish from the lack of sleep, his mind only slightly distracted by the rattling of equipment in the pickup's toolboxes and by the smell of plastics and electrical wiring.

Cline let him out in the first level of the Four Seasons underground parking garage, and Titus took the elevator down to the second level, where he met two men waiting beside a rental car. No introductions.

While one of the guys went over Titus with a debugging instrument, the other one opened his laptop and put it through a series of checks as well. Satisfied, they told him to lie down in the backseat of the car, and they drove out of the garage. A few minutes later they told him he could sit up, and he stared out the window into the bright summer light while they headed east out of downtown to Austin-Bergstrom International.

They bypassed the main terminal entrance and circled around behind to the charter flight hangars. The car drove straight onto the tarmac to a waiting King Air 350, and in twelve minutes Titus was in the air.

Alone in the cabin, he watched as the earth fell away outside the window, and when they began passing through the white, cumulous clouds, he reclined his seat as far as it would go. Still trying to understand how this could be happening to him, he fell asleep.

Awakened by the quickly sinking Beechcraft, he sat up just as they were touching down. Zipping past the window was a narrow valley, the grass lush with the summer rains and scattered with up-reaching fingers of *garambullo* cactus and huisache trees with gracefully outspread canopies. As the pilot turned the aircraft and cut back on the engines, Titus saw a black Suburban waiting at the edge of the isolated airstrip.

The driver was a hefty Mexican behind sunglasses and a mustache, polite but taciturn, and soon they were sailing along the valley's dirt road. Beyond the nearer rolling hills, the Sierra de Morenos stretched out in the blue distance as far as Titus could see. Finally they reached a two-lane paved road and turned south.

San Miguel de Allende was a small hillside town in central Mexico, a couple of hours north of Mexico City. Rich in colonial history, it was crowded with handsome churches and elegant homes clustered along narrow, and sometimes steep, cobblestone streets. It was famously beautiful and long had been a favorite retreat for wandering American writers and artists and eccentric expatriates with dubious pasts. For several decades now it had become a popular second-home destination for well-to-do Americans and a cosmopolitan international crowd.

After rambling into the heart of town, past the Jardín, and then up into the higher neighborhoods, the driver eventually squeezed the Suburban into a cobbled lane of simple, sun-washed walls. He stopped the groaning vehicle on a steep incline and said something in Spanish, gesturing at a massive, dark wooden door set in a fading cornflower blue wall. A jacaranda, lavish with blossoms like broken pieces of the sky, sheltered the doorway. To one side, a brilliant bougainvillea splashed over the top of a rock wall as if the stones were holding back a sea of magenta.

Titus got out with his laptop and waited for his driver to pull away up the hill before he crossed the lane. He stepped down from the steeply rising sidewalk to the level threshold of the cathedral-size door, banged the brass door knocker in the shape of a woman's hand, and waited as the sound echoed and died between the high walls of the lane.

Very quickly a normal-size door inset into the larger one was opened by a grandmotherly Indian, who smiled at him with bright teeth generously framed in gold. Her abundant black-and-gray-striated hair was parted in the middle and worn in two braids that reached down past her thick waist.

Greeting him in Spanish, she stepped back to invite him inside, a brown hand pressed gracefully to the front of her white blouse, which was embroidered with broad, alternating bands of russet and gold. Her skirt, a dazzling thing of cobalt and black stripes, stopped just an inch above her bare, stubby toes.

Talking to him all the while, she ushered him through a short corridor into the diffused brightness of a colonnade that enclosed a garden courtyard. The quadrangle of arches drew his eyes upward, where the dappled light fell past the second-floor colonnade through the canopies of trees.

Continuing her lilting but unintelligible monologue, the woman gestured politely for Titus to wait on a long wooden bench against the ocher walls of the deep ambulatory. And then she disappeared. Wooden birdcages with varicolored finches and canaries hung along the colonnades, and a fountain in the center of the courtyard added its splash to the high-pitched chatter of the birds.

Just as Titus took a deep breath, he was startled by an outburst of shouting. A woman's voice shrilled from one of the doorways on the second floor, a staccato, singsong flood of an Asian language delivered in spirited anger.

Then silence.

Slowly the birds, stopped by the verbal eruption, resumed.

Before Titus could even begin to imagine what that might have been about, a voice above him said, "Welcome to my home, Mr. Cain."

Titus recognized the voice and looked up to the left side of the courtyard balcony.

García Burden was leaning his forearms on the stone balustrade, looking down at him. He was tallish and lean, and his dark hair hadn't seen a barber in a good while. His unbuttoned black shirt hung open, the sleeves rolled to his elbows. A gold medallion on a chain around his neck dangled over the balustrade.

"We're just about ready for you up here," Burden said. "There are stairs over there." He gestured toward a stone staircase. "Just come around the balcony," he said, swinging his arm past the open doorways.

Burden was buttoning the front of his shirt as Titus approached him, and as they shook hands Titus noted that they were very nearly the same height. But Burden's age was difficult to determine. He might've been near Titus's age as well, but the crow's-feet at the corners of his brown eyes were deeply cut and had the effect of seeming to distort his age. And there was something in the eyes themselves that made Titus take a second look, something that made him think they had seen more than their share of remarkable things, many of them unnerving.

"Based on what you and Gil have told me," Burden said, his soft voice even softer now that they were near, "I've got it narrowed to three men. I've got photographs."

He turned and led Titus through the open doorway in front of which he'd been standing.

The house was old, with the three-foot-thick walls typical of colonial architecture. The room they entered was huge and probably had been several rooms at one time. Though they were only passing through, heading for another opened doorway on the other side, Titus quickly caught glimpses of antique desks and bookcases, a sitting area with sofa and armchairs, a round library table stacked with books, some still open, a fountain pen cradled in the gutter of one. The only light in the room came in through the deep casements of the doors and windows.

As they went out the other door and onto another balcony, Titus realized that the simple blue wall that faced the street concealed a sizable compound. Here they looked down on a second garden courtyard twice as large as the first one and surrounded by several two-story casitas also connected by two levels of colonnades. Towering *flamboyan* trees cast a lacy veil of shade over everything.

Titus followed Burden into the first casita and through a time warp into the twenty-first century: a long narrow room chilly with air-conditioning, numerous computers and servers, a movie screen, a huge television screen, and videophones.

Three women moved about the room, working at various tasks, ignoring Burden's arrival.

"Let's show him what we have," he said to no one in particular, and one of the women nearby turned around and sat at the computer. Titus was surprised to see that she was a Mayan Indian, her flattened features distinctive and unmistakable.

While she typed, Titus glanced at the other two women: an attractive Asian woman who appeared to be in her late forties, her hair worn in a precisely cut bob, dressed in a very smart, straight black skirt and dove gray blouse; and a busty woman of middle height and middle age, plain with Scotch-Irish coloring, roan hair, and a sweet, blue-eyed smile.

Burden stood with his arms crossed, staring over at the TV screen. When the first photo flashed up, he looked at Titus. Titus shook his head. Second photo. Burden looked at Titus. Again Titus shook his head.

"Oh?" Burden seemed both surprised and eager. "Really? Well then, here's your man."

Third photo. It was Alvaro in a grainy photograph blown up from a small surveillance negative, crossing a street—Titus thought it looked like Buenos Aires, maybe—a newspaper tucked under his arm as he glanced back in the direction of the photographer, though not at him.

"Yeah," Titus said, "that's him."

"Cayetano Luquín Becerra. Mexican," Burden said.

Titus was both relieved and anxious, the way a man might feel when his doctor tells him that they've finally identified the mysterious disease that's been crippling him. He didn't know if this was good or bad.

"Let me see your laptop," Burden said, and when Titus gave it to him, he handed it on to the Asian woman. "We're going to tune it up a little," he explained. "When she's through, all communication from this man to you will automatically be forwarded to us. It's perfectly safe. He won't know. And we'll build very thorough firewalls for you so our own communications will be secure as well."

He looked at Titus and jerked his head at the huge photograph on the screen.

"Good news and bad news," he said. "Come on, we'll talk about it."

Chapter 11

As they walked into the study again, Titus expected Burden to turn on some lights, but instead he walked over to an area where there was a sofa and armchairs and gestured for Titus to take a seat anywhere. Both men sat down.

"No one—no one in my business—has set eyes on Tano Luquín in three and a half years," Burden said. "The guy who took that picture you just saw, he was the last man. He's dead now, the photographer. It's been more than fifteen years since Luquín was seen in the U.S. This is significant."

"In what way?"

"Well, I'm not sure. Is he here purely because of the size of the ransom? *¿Quién sabe?* Could be. Maybe not."

Titus was sitting on the sofa, facing the wall at one end of the room, the one opposite Burden's desk, which was behind him. As his eyes adjusted to the low light, he realized that a large portion of the wall was taken up with a black-and-white photograph about four feet high and easily twelve feet long, recessed in its own niche in a simple black frame and surrounded by bookcases. The image was of a reclining nude woman.

"Look, I don't feel like I've got a lot of time," Titus said, nervous at Burden's peaceful demeanor. "How do we get started here?"

"You'll get a complete dossier on Luquín," Burden said, "you'll know who you're dealing with. But, briefly, here are the high spots. Tano grew up in a well-to-do family in Mexico City, university education. He was never really interested in any legitimate business pursuits, and by the late seventies he was already gravitating to the drug trade. By the turn of the decade he was down in Colombia doing petty errands for people who were contracting their services to Pablo Escobar, who had already become a notorious legend. Tano had a feel for abduction, and was soon kidnapping for hire, again for people who were working for Escobar.

"His expertise in *secuestro* grew during the eighties as Escobar's need to discipline and persuade his competitors increased. But Tano, demonstrating a rare wisdom in that line of work, never worked directly for Pablo. He always made sure he was a couple of connections removed, letting others take the credit . . . and the heat if something went wrong."

Titus only needed to move his eyes a flicker to shift them from Burden to the photograph, which was becoming a distraction as it continued to emerge from the surrounding shadows.

"So, when Escobar's empire began to rattle apart in the late eighties," Burden went on, "Tano could see the end coming and got out of Colombia. He spent the early nineties in Brazil and had been living in Rio de Janeiro for several years when Escobar was finally killed in Medellín in December of 1993.

"But Tano had been busy in Rio, honing his skills. According to the Ministério da Justiça, Tano's MO was all over four of the largest high-end kidnappings that occurred in Rio between 1991 and 1997. All of the targets were foreign executives, and these four incidents brought Tano a very nice income of nearly fifty-three million dollars in ransoms."

"What were the size of the ransoms?"

Burden nodded. "Interesting. They increased steadily over the four events. Tano was beginning to study his targets with more deliberation, and what he learned about them shaped the way he handled their abductions and ransom demands. It determined the way he designed their ordeals."

All of this was stated in a gentle way, as if Burden were a mild-mannered psychiatrist explaining the rationale for a therapy regimen. Occasionally he gestured gracefully with his hands, which Titus now noticed were unexpectedly elegant. Sometimes he would run his fingers through his hair to get a wavy lock of it away from his eyes.

"Tano's technique improved, too," Burden continued with a hint of pleasure in his eyes, as if he were relishing what he was about to reveal. "I'll run through the four cases for you. It's important that you understand what's about to happen to you.

"Number one. The target was a French executive with a multinational corporation. Corporation brings in their insurance company's recommended K and R team. Negotiations take three months. Kidnappers come down to one-half of their original demand. K and R people bungle the negotiations. Victim dies in the process, but Tano gets 5.3 million dollars.

"Number two. German CEO. Kidnappers contact the family this time, not the corporation. Kidnappers let the family apply the pressure to the corporation, while the kidnappers save themselves a lot of sweat. But the family consults with Rio's Policía Civil kidnap squad. Things slow down, victim's hand arrives special delivery. Family has a meltdown. Puts pressure on corporation, which eventually agrees to pay seventy percent of the original demand: 8.5 million dollars.

"Number three. Spanish executive. But this time the kidnappers know that the executive and his family are the major stockholders in the corporation. No K and R people allowed to participate. Victim will be killed if Policía Civil are brought in. Family agrees, but then they drive a hard bargain. So a brother-in-law, representing the company in Buenos Aires, is kidnapped also. Not for additional ransom, but to put pressure on the original negotiation. Pay up or he dies. The family continues to belabor the amount of the demand. Brother-in-law, hands and feet bound with wire, is set on fire in the long private drive that leads up to the family's estate. Family pays ninety percent of the original demand: 16.8 million dollars.

"Number four. British CEO. Also wealthy major stockholder. Kidnappers are clear: No K and R, no Policía Civil. Huge ransom demand. Several of the corporation board members have pull in British government. Supersecret Special Event Team flown in under the radar of Brazilian government. But they're out of their league, lose a couple of guys, muck up the negotiations. They're pulled out just as secretly as they came in, tails between their legs. But they've caused a hell of a lot of trouble for the kidnappers. Immediately two other corporation employees die—in an automobile accident. Kidnappers notify family that other employees will die (accidentally) if ransom isn't paid. They pay up. The kidnappers got one hundred percent of the ransom they had asked for: 22 million dollars."

When Burden stopped, Titus thought he saw a pleased expression that indicated that the case synopses he'd just been through drew some telling conclusions. But with the recounting of each incident, Titus only grew more depressed. In fact, Burden's serene demeanor was beginning to get on his nerves. Titus's entire life had been uprooted not more than fifteen hours earlier, and it was far from clear whether it could be salvaged. In light of that, he found Burden's composure and apparent lack of a sense of urgency offensive.

"I don't see any damn reason for optimism here," Titus said. His stomach was knotting. "I want to know where the hell you think you're going with all this."

Burden's calm expression gave way to something more sober, and he reached over to a side table and picked up a remote control. The light rose on the long photograph on the wall, illuminating it slowly, subtly. The picture was stunning.

The nude woman reclined on her right side against a charcoal background and looked directly at the camera with a sad, penetrating gaze. Her hair, darker than the background, fell over her left shoulder and stopped just above her left breast. Her left arm lay languidly along the fluid line of her waist, hip, and thigh, while she supported herself on the elbow of her right arm. In her upturned right hand, which rested in a position equidistant between her breasts and the dark delta between her thighs, she held a tiny, huddling, jet black monkey so incredibly small that it was completely contained within her palm. This queer, startled little creature gaped at the camera with outsized eyes, as if he were seeing the most astonishing thing that a monkey could ever behold. Its silky, ebony tail was coiled desperately around the woman's pale wrist, his wee hands pressed together in an attitude of prayerful concern.

"She," Burden said, "is the sister of the Spanish executive in Tano's case number three, the widow of the man who was set afire in the driveway of the family home."

"Jesus!" Titus stared at the woman. "When was this taken?"

"Two weeks after her husband's funeral."

"What?"

"Her idea. Every detail."

"Why?"

Burden looked at the picture, studying it as if it were an image of infinite fascination for him, as if he could turn his attention to it at any time and find it provocative and of enduring curiosity.

"Often," he said, "with women, the why of how they express their grief over the violent death of someone they love is inexplicable. I mean, the 'logic' of how they express it. It's an intensely inward thing. Deeply embedded. The fact that she seems, here, to be acting in a way that's the absolute opposite of private or personal"—he shrugged—"well, it only seems so. We misunderstand her."

Titus looked at Burden studying the photograph and wondered what was going through his mind. He glanced around the room. There were framed black-and-white photographs in a variety of sizes hanging on the walls, propped against bookshelves, resting against the sides of his desk, sometimes two or three stacked one in front of the other. All of them, all that Titus could see, were of women, mostly portraits.

"It's my guess, however," Burden went on, "that if this woman's husband could know today what she has done in her grief, he would be shocked. The incident in extremis that prompted her behavior was his death, so as long as he was alive he would never have seen this . . . unusual aspect of her psyche."

Church bells began ringing, first one and then another farther off, then another in a different direction, and still another. The air was singing with them.

Burden broke his gaze at the photograph and stood.

"I want you to remember this photograph and this story, Mr. Cain. As we decide how to address your dilemma, at some point along the way—this inevitably happens—you're going to be tempted to believe that you know best about how to extricate yourself from this ordeal that you are about to suffer.

You're going to think that you don't need to listen to me, that you have better instincts for what ought to be done at some particular point or another."

He paused a beat and almost smiled, his face taking on an expression that Titus didn't really understand and which made him uneasy.

"If you don't want me to see how your own wife might react to your death," he said, glancing at the photograph, "you need to listen to me. You need to do what I tell you to do . . . the way I tell you to do it."

Surprised at Burden's abrupt conclusion, Titus stood, too.

"Lália will be here in a moment to show you where you can freshen up," Burden said. "I'll join you downstairs for lunch in twenty minutes."

Without any further explanation, Burden left Titus standing where he was and walked out of his study.

Chapter 12

Standing alone in the room, Titus looked again at the picture. Burden's rather creative warning was vivid and had blindsided him with its almost cruel undertone. It was unnerving, as he imagined Burden had intended it to be.

He picked up one of the books lying on a library table and read the title: *The History, Culture, and Religion of the Hellenistic Age*. He flipped through it and saw that the pages were heavily annotated in brown ink. He picked up another: *Spanish Red: An Ethnogeographical Study of Cochineal and the Opuntia Cactus*. Again heavily annotated. He bent down and looked at the book lying open, the fountain pen in its gutter: *The Liar's Tale: A History of Falsehood*. More marginalia in brown ink. The book next to this one had a dozen page markers sticking out of it: *The Natural History of the Soul in Ancient Mexico*.

Titus was surprised. He had expected to find books on intelligence systems, cryptography, international crime, terrorism, drug trade . . . kidnapping. None of that here. But clearly Burden had his resources. The room where the three women were working must have held a vast amount of information, and he remembered that in their telephone conversation Burden had mentioned his archives.

A shadow in the doorway caused him to look up. Lália was standing there, smiling at him in her radiant colors. He followed her light, barefooted step around the balcony to the other side. She left him alone in a spacious bedroom where the linens smelled of lilac and the fireplace scents hinted vaguely of November fires.

While she waited outside the door on the loggia, he washed and splashed cool water on his face and combed his hair. He was tempted to call Rita—it was the dinner hour in Venice—but, again, he didn't have anything to tell her except that he was in trouble. That wouldn't do.

His neck ached, and he recognized the stiff beginnings of a tension headache. Tucking in his shirttail, he thought of the photograph of the Argentine widow and her monkey, and of how Burden had chosen to give it a position in his study that practically defined the place. Titus was sure that there was more to the picture than met the eye or that was hinted at in Burden's explication. And he was sure, too, that there was more to García Burden than a lifetime of knowing him would ever allow anyone to understand.

He followed the colorful Lália downstairs to a dining room, one entire wall of which was open to the courtyard. Sitting alone, he was served by two young Indian girls who urged him to go ahead and eat.

For a little while he enjoyed the food and beer. The echoing birdsong spilling out of the colonnades and dying into the undertones of the fountain were almost soporific, even comforting. Then, unexpectedly, this momentary peace caught in his throat like a sob, and he found himself on the verge of tears. Jesus, what was happening to him? He put down his beer and fought to control himself, baffled by the sudden burst of intense feelings. Embarrassed, he swallowed. And then swallowed again.

While he was struggling to calm himself, he saw Burden come in through the entrance corridor and enter the loggia across the courtyard. By the time he got to the dining room, Titus had reined in his wobbly emotions.

Burden sat down with him, and one of the girls brought him a plate of fruit and slices of various melons. He took one of the lime slices on the side of his plate and drizzled the juice over the melons. He ate a few bites, then picked up with their conversation as if he'd never left.

"I'll tell you an anecdote about Tano Luquín," Burden said quietly, chewing a bite of cantaloupe. "Just a few months before he left Colombia to avoid being caught up in Escobar's disintegration, I saw an interesting example of how he works. It was one of Escobar's contracts, Tano twice removed, of course. I was in Medellín on another matter, but I had seen enough of Tano's work by then to be able to distinguish it from all the others.

"Culturally, you know, Colombians have ardent family allegiances. They're loving and loyal to their children, aunts, and uncles, devoted to the idea of family. This is true across all levels of society. An admirable societal characteristic that any culture would be proud of. But Colombia is a culture of extremes, and this worthy quality has a perverse downside in Colombia's criminal world. When a criminal enterprise requires violence, everyone understands that to hurt a man's family is to hurt the man in the deepest way possible. So this is done with disgusting regularity and predictability."

Burden ate some more melon, staring out to the courtyard in thought, leaning on his forearms. He went on.

"An enemy's wife is killed. His sisters, brothers, children, are ideal targets. Often there is horrible mutilation, and sometimes the man is forced to watch it all as it happens. That's always a favorite touch. It's a spiritually vicious thing, intended to destroy the man within the man, his heart of hearts. It's never enough just to kill his body. No, they want to lacerate his soul as well. And if they could figure out a way to punish him beyond death, they would send someone straight into hellfire to get the job done.

"It's fascinating to me, these Janus faces of familial devotion. One gives strength to the other, becomes, in a weird way, its raison d'être. You just wonder why one never mitigates the other. Why do they never see the faces of their own wives or children or siblings in the faces of the people they mutilate? Why doesn't that arrest a brutish hand or . . ."

He shrugged and drank from his bottle of beer. "But then, that's really a human irony, isn't it. Maybe there's a peculiar Colombian twist in these instances, but they certainly aren't alone in their lack of a moral imagination. Tano isn't Colombian, but his tactics were learned there and are the same."

One of the Indian girls floated in to check their bottles of beer to see if they wanted fresh ones. No sooner did she leave with the empty ones than the other girl arrived with the new ones, the bottles cold, a fresh lime slice sticking out of them. Burden went on.

"Well, it was in this environment that Tano Luquín came to maturity in the art of kidnapping, and then surpassed his training and became the maestro of his own kind of abduction."

He squeezed the lime into his beer, almost reluctant to get to the anecdote about Luquín that he'd promised.

"This man—his name was Artemio Ospina—who had to be punished had three children," he resumed, glancing after the girl who had left the room, "all under the age of twelve. The oldest was his only daughter, and Artemio adored her for tender reasons." He shook his head. "Anyway, Artemio was abducted off the street and taken to his home. There he and his daughter were placed side by side and forced to watch while his wife and the remaining children were . . . dismembered . . . their body parts were . . . intermixed, reassembled into savage and surreal re-creations like horrible Hans Bellmer dolls."

He paused. "I was there afterward. I saw it"—he pointed two fingers at his eyes—"with my own eyes. Unbelievable."

Another pause. "You never see it all. The human mind's capacity for bestiality is boundless. You never see it all. There's always something even more unimaginable, out there, waiting for you. Just waiting.

"That night Artemio was given his freedom, allowed to go on living, as best he could, with those insane images. But Tano wasn't through with him."

They had finished eating and were sitting there, sipping their beers. Burden glanced toward the kitchen.

"Come on," he said, picking up his beer. Titus accompanied him up the stone stairs to the balcony and around to his study. They returned to the places where they had sat before, and Burden resumed his story.

"That same night, Artemio's daughter was taken away. But Tano made sure he continued to see her. Every few months after that, Artemio was hunted down wherever he was and forced to look at photographs of his little daughter in various acts of unspeakable humiliation. She was now working in the child sex trade.

"There were torments in these photographs too brutal to speak. The imagination recoils. Her soul rotted away in little pieces right before her father's eyes.

"This would have gone on forever, but after nearly a year the man destroyed himself. I don't know how he lasted that long."

Titus sat in silence, appalled. He heard the canaries in the courtyard below, their tiny voices crisp and light on the air that floated up to them.

"What in God's name had he done?" Titus asked. The punishment, as Burden called it, had to have been provoked by something terrible.

"He was one of my agents," Burden said. "A common man, an intelligence officer. An extraordinary man. And that's not a contradiction. Ordinary men are capable of unbelievable heroics. There's something transcendent about it."

Burden stopped. He almost went on, and then he stopped himself again. Then he said:

"And Luquín never even knew for sure that Artemio worked for me. He only suspected it. Artemio never admitted it."

"Not even to save his family?"

"To save his family? That was never a possibility. That's not the way Luquín works. To fall under his suspicion is to have been judged guilty. Artemio knew that. Confession. No confession. It made no difference. The truth was the only thing Artemio had that Luquín couldn't get, and even in the midst of the horror of his misery and grief, Artemio clung to that one scrap of dignity. Luquín would not have it."

Titus was speechless. The enormity of Luquín's bestiality came more alive with every image provoked by Burden's story.

"The point of telling you this," Burden said, picking up one of the many women's portraits lying around, "is to help you understand what is happening to you."

He looked a moment at the woman's picture and then put it down and leveled his eyes at Titus.

"Your ordeal has begun. This is no time to be indecisive. This is no time to deceive yourself into believing you can avoid what is about to happen to you by negotiating with this man."

Titus's stomach tightened. It was the second time Burden had used the word *ordeal*.

"Look," Titus said, feeling his fear and his frustration commingling into a confusing impatience, "I don't want anyone to die, but . . . You say, don't make the mistake of thinking I can negotiate with this man. Okay, well, that doesn't leave me many other choices."

Burden had been lounging in his armchair, but as Titus spoke he gradually straightened up and sat forward, and Titus saw something happen in his face, something subtle but unmistakable that expelled the equanimity that had seemed to define him.

"There's the question," Burden said, "of whether or not you should go to the FBI and risk the consequences of Luquín finding out that you'd done it." He paused. "I'm telling you, he will find out. It's impossible that he won't. You have to ask yourself: How many people am I willing to let him kill before I accept this?"

He looked at Titus with an expression drained of politesse. "You need to know, Titus—"

His use of Titus's first name had an effect on Titus that was sudden and totally surprising. It immediately brought them together in alliance, as if they were banded together by heart and blood and ideal.

"—one or two are already dead. I don't mean literally, but I mean that they're as good as dead. He'll have to do it, so that he'll know that you know. He understands that you won't be able to comprehend him in the correct way until you know the shock of that."

"That's inconceivable," said Titus, who was also leaning forward on the sofa now. "That doesn't make any sense."

Burden looked at him as if he were trying to see something in Titus that hadn't yet been made apparent to him. It was almost as if he were trying to determine whether Titus himself could be trusted.

"It would be a mistake, Titus, for you to believe that this is only about you and Luquín. Right now the lens is focused on you, but only because Luquín has focused on you. There's more to this picture than you can see from your vantage point. You are only one detail among many, but for now you've become a very important detail."

Burden stopped and sat back in his armchair. But he didn't resume his formerly languid posture.

"In the next hour or two we'll have to decide many things," he said. "I believe you're a good and honest man, Titus. I believe you'll be honest with me."

Burden waited, sobriety returning to his eyes, deepening the lines that gathered there.

"I should tell you," he said, "the end of the story of the little girl." He paused, his gaze distracted toward some invisible place across the room. "I finally tracked her down, a few years later. Her grave, that is. It was . . . only . . . three weeks old. Just three weeks. I had"—he turned his eyes on Titus again—"I had her exhumed. I wanted to see her . . . with my own eyes. I had to know . . . beyond any doubt, that her hell was over for her."

He swallowed. He was still looking at Titus, but he wasn't seeing him. He swallowed again.

"But she had suffered so . . . and that changes a person physically. Still, I'm almost . . . certain . . . that it was her."

Chapter 13

Charlie Thrush's land was a dozen miles southwest of Fredericksburg. His home, made of native stone, sat near the center of a small valley laced with spring-fed streams and was heavily wooded with chinquapin and live oak. A thread of sycamores crowded the banks of the largest creek that ran the length of the valley.

Even though Charlie was not a rancher, he'd always liked the idea of it, and after he and Louise had lived in their new home for several years, he'd quickly settled into the life of a gentleman rancher.

This afternoon Charlie had a fairly simple problem to deal with. For the last four years an old dead sycamore had stood solitary and forlorn near the back corner of Charlie's office, a three-room building nestled in a sycamore stand seventy-five yards from the main house. Charlie had been meaning to cut it down every year after it died, and now its skeletal presence had become symbolic, a kind of nagging reminder of his procrastination. Finally he put it on his "to do" list for this month, and today was the day he had set aside in his mind to finally get the job done.

He had meant to get started early while the day was still cool, but he had gotten sidetracked in the peach orchard, and by the time he thought of the tree again it was late morning and he realized he wouldn't get to it until after lunch.

It was a hot postnoontime, with the sun standing still in the meridian, when Charlie headed for the tool shed with a couple of Mexican laborers who had come through a few days earlier looking for work. They'd heard that Charlie was clearing the underbrush around an oak mot spring several hundred yards from the house. Charlie had put the men to work and was letting them live in a shack not far from the spring. But the truth was, they'd turned out not to be very good workers, and he'd decided he was going to let them go. But yesterday he'd told them he wanted them to help him cut down the old sycamore. He'd let them go tomorrow.

With the men carrying the sixteen-foot ladder and Charlie lugging his twenty-inch Stihl chain saw, they headed for the tree. The Mexicans raised the ladder as high as it would go and leaned it against the sycamore in the fork of one of its largest bare branches. They steadied it while Charlie serviced the chain saw and then clipped the saw to the harness he'd made for carrying the saw up into trees when he worked alone.

Working a chain saw from a ladder could be exhausting, so he had rigged the harness so that he could turn off the saw and let it hang from the strap, freeing his hands to reposition himself and steady his footing when he started on another part of the tree. For a man his age, it was slow work.

He climbed up the ladder, steadied himself, and started the saw. He revved the throttle trigger a few times until the saw idled easily, and then he started cutting, reaching up to cut the higher limbs while his energy and muscles were still fresh.

As the limbs tumbled down, the Mexicans gathered them on the ground and dragged them over to one side. It went fast since the limbs were bare of foliage, and he was soon ready to shift the ladder to another position. But then something went wrong.

Just as he was about to cut off the saw, the throttle trigger snapped and the saw revved up to a whining full-throttle scream. Bracing himself against his thighs on the ladder, he reached over with his other hand to the kill switch. But it didn't work. It slipped back and forth freely without cutting off the engine.

With the engine screaming, he moved the chain brake forward with his forearm, but the chain kept churning; the brake bolts were too loose to engage it.

Then Charlie felt his ladder move.

He looked down and saw that the two Mexicans had attached a rope to one of the legs of the ladder and were standing back out of the way. One of them was slowly pulling the ladder out from under him. It was like seeing a bird fly backward or a coyote climbing the sky. It didn't relate to anything logical at all. It just looked ridiculous.

He yelled at them: What the hell are you doing?! What the hell?? Hey!!

In an instant, with the heavy chain saw screaming in his hand, the horror of possibilities flew at him:

If he dropped the saw to hang on to the tree limb with both arms, the saw would swing from the harness and the torque of the whining engine would pull the chain into him, spinning crazily, cutting his legs off. . . .

If he hung on to the limb with one arm and the chain saw with the other, eventually his strength would give out and he'd fall, and from this height he'd surely tumble onto the churning chain. . . .

If he could step up another step and rest the saw on the

limb before the ladder was pulled out from under him, he could unclip the saw from the harness and let it fall free. . . .

He stepped up one step even as he felt the ladder going sideways out from under him, and for an instant the screaming saw teetered on the limb and then slipped over on the other side as the ladder was jerked away.

It all happened in one smooth, fluid stream of action, not in discrete moments, but in one continuous flow of time. It is said that at the moment of death the sense of hearing is the last to go. He couldn't really say. The sensation of the shrilly whining chain ripping wildly into him was startlingly painless. It eviscerated him, thrashing about inside him, the torque of the engine whipping it about like a frenzied, live thing, reaming him out as if he were a gutted deer hanging in a tree.

He smelled the hot engine spewing oil and gasoline.

Numbness came quickly, and he wasn't sure how or when he let go of the limb with his arms. He was aware of his body whirling around and around, entangled with the pitching saw. He was aware of being whipped about. He actually heard the liquidy sound of himself being flung and splashed.

He thought an arm went with a swipe of the chain.

He saw sunlight and earth and the Mexicans looking up and watching, their expressions curious but not surprised. He saw the trees and the woods and sunlight and even dark spatters flying through the air.

Somewhere in his midsection something separated and pulled loose and fell away.

The whining was vicious and deafening. His lungs flew out of his mouth. His sight failed. It wasn't so bad; and the screaming faded away, too, and though he felt nothing, he was aware of the sensation of swinging.

Chapter 14

The roan-haired woman from Burden's archives room brought over two thick ring binders containing Cayetano Luquín's dossier. Burden cleared a space on the round library table and left Titus with the two volumes while he returned with the woman.

The dossier was a straightforward biography with photographs interspersed throughout. There was a detailed index with cross-references to other volumes in Burden's archives and to various U.S. and foreign law enforcement and intelligence agency archives. Titus was surprised at the amount of personal minutiae in the file (clothing sizes, dining habits, video rental preferences, medical records) and that considerable space was given to Luquín's psychological profile.

At one point, while following up a footnote, Titus came across a reference to a paper by García Prieto Burden, lecturer at the Centre for the Study of Terrorism and Political Violence at the University of St. Andrews, St. Andrews, Scotland.

The reports of the four Rio de Janeiro abductions were given in more detail than Burden had related to Titus, but there were also cross-references to even longer accounts. Any word that was cross-referenced and had expanded data in another file was printed in a distinctive typeface. Even though the dossier seemed thorough and packed with information, there were also ample signs of copious deletions, information Titus was not allowed to see.

As if he were prescient, Burden walked into his study just as Titus was finishing the last pages. He stopped a little way from the library table where Titus sat. The deep casement of the doorway leading out to the second courtyard behind him framed him in its light, the shadow of the room too dark for Titus to make out the language of his features.

"What do you think?" Burden asked him.

Titus was nearly dizzy with information that was so outrageous that he sometimes felt as if he had been reading a work of fiction. The dossier, together with Burden's own accounts of Luquín's rampages, filled Titus with fear. The man was like a virulent disease that, by some strange biological perversity, had become a specific threat at this time to Titus's friends and family.

But Titus had tried to read between the lines, and it seemed to him that the curious deletions in Luquín's files were pointing to Luquín being a threat on a scale that far exceeded high-dollar extortion and kidnappings, even if the ransom was in the tens of millions of dollars. Titus was getting the impression that Luquín's lethal reach embraced continents. Burden had already alluded to this, but the deletions in Luquín's files clearly indicated that allusions were all that Titus could expect to get from Burden.

"This is scary as hell," Titus said. "That's what I think." He swallowed, looking at Burden's silhouette against the light. "But . . . help me understand this . . . if Luquín started killing people . . . I mean, he's threatening me with a kind of slaughter here. He might get by with that in Colombia, but not in the States. How could he?"

Burden looked at him, saying nothing. He just stood there in silence, waiting, waiting until Titus remembered. Of course it could happen in Austin. God, if we'd learned nothing else from the recent past, we'd learned that anything could happen anywhere. Death, even outrageous death, gave no special dispensation to accidents of geography or nationality.

Chastened by Burden's silence and by the sound of his own naiveté echoing in his ears, Titus ducked his head and then looked up again.

"Okay, that was stupid," he conceded, "but still, help me understand how he's going to carry out his threats and maintain the silence he's promising, and demanding, at the same time. I mean, what are the logistics of what he's talking about? Mayhem and silence just aren't compatible."

Burden's silhouette, his hands in his pockets, one shoulder angled a little lower than the other, moved out of the doorway and drifted into the shadows gathered at the edges of the bookcases. The ambient light was too little, and Titus couldn't see him well. Outside, the day was turning soft, descending toward late afternoon.

"Look at what's going on here," Burden said from a corner. "He's not going to do in Austin what he does in Colombia or Brazil. This is not a stupid man.

"Go back to the Rio cases. With each case Tano learned something to do, and not to do, in each subsequent abduction. First case: He learned the K and R people only made matters less lucrative and less efficient for him.

"Second case: He eliminates them by contacting the family instead of the corporation. But he still has to put pressure on the family to put pressure on the corporation to pay up. Working with two separate entities is still inefficient.

"Third case: This time he makes sure that the victim and his family are major stockholders in the company. They'll have more leverage in making the company pay than a mere employee would. Still, the demands are on the family, not the corporation. When there's a glitch, he has to kidnap a relative of the original victim before the family presses for payment and Luquín gets his money.

"Fourth case: This time he made sure he chose a victim who was a major stockholder in the company. But it was publicly held, and some of the board members insisted on this supersecret SWAT team's intervention. Caused Tano a lot of trouble. Still he had to threaten to kill additional employees to force their hand."

Burden moved along the wall of books until he stopped at the feet of the reclining nude woman with the monkey.

"Fifth case: You. What's he learned? To whittle down his irritants. No K and R people. No police. No corporate interests versus family interests. No publicly held company with a board to answer to. And even more ingenious, no crime. You'll be buying foreign companies. No noise. Everything done silently—and with seeming legitimacy."

Burden stopped. He took a few steps toward Titus.

"No noise," he said. "What does that say to us, Titus? Do you think he's going to commit a series of brash, Colombian-style assassinations in Austin? Remember: He said that when this is all over no one will even know that any crime has been committed. Use your imagination."

He came across the room and stood on the other side of the table from Titus. Thinking, he put his fingers on the fountain pen that lay in the gutter of the opened book.

"Imagine this, Titus. Let's say you decide that working with me isn't the way to go. You go to the FBI. Luquín discovers this immediately and disappears. You tell the FBI everything, but the fact is, you don't really have any proof that what you're telling them actually happened. Except the dead dogs. We've already cleaned up the bugs. Their files on Luquín are sparse, and he's been off the radar screen for a decade. They find your story interesting, curious, but frankly, a little suspicious, too. But it's all over, and you've averted a huge loss of money. You've saved lives. Close call.

"Six months from now a friend dies unexpectedly. A car wreck. Or a hunting accident. Or a heart attack. Afterwards you get an e-mail: 'Hello, Titus. I told you not to go to the FBI. You should have listened to me.' You go to the FBI again and tell them what's happened. They listen. You're a respectable man, so they take you seriously. But, really, there's just nothing they can do about proving that an accident like that was actually a murder caused by a bad guy from Brazil.

"Time passes. A friend's wife in San Francisco drowns while swimming laps in her pool. You get an e-mail: 'Hello, Titus. It's me again. You should have listened to me.'

"Five months later, the teenage daughter of another friend in Boca Raton, all the way across the continent, overdoses on drugs. Shocking, because the child had absolutely no exposure to such things. You get an e-mail: 'Hello, Titus . . .'"

Burden slid the fountain pen along the gutter of the page an inch or two.

"Do you see how this could happen?" he asked. "Every time you go to the FBI. But you understand, Luquín won't always go after your closest friends. He'll scatter the deaths across the country and across relationships. Maybe even extended family members of your employees. Six months apart. A year apart. Can you imagine how many people would die before the FBI could ever establish a connection in a scenario like that? If they ever did?

"Can you imagine how it's going to make you look to keep

going back and saying: Please! You've got to believe me. That tractor accident in Iowa was really a murder. It's this guy in Brazil who wanted to extort sixty-four million dollars. . . . And Luquín's going to make sure you can't capture his e-mails. There'll be no proof. It could go on and on.

"Tano Luquín is no ideologue," Burden went on. "He knows nothing about ideals or dreams or political causes, and he cares nothing for them. He's a common criminal. Venal. Violent. Egotistic. He's the kind of man who can be found in every generation and in every culture. A predator. You have something he wants, and he's going to take it.

"But the difference is that today clever men like Luquín have so many more powerful resources in the technology at their disposal. To anticipate them, you have to be willing to imagine beyond your assumptions, to be willing to make that leap into the realm of the unbelievable. I can assure you, they have. Luquín is wealthy. His methods and resources are sophisticated. His imagination and appetites are unrestrained."

Burden's point was well made, and chilling.

"Okay," Titus said, "just tell me this: Can you stop him? Can you save lives?"

Burden didn't answer immediately, and with every second he hesitated, Titus's hopes diminished with a grim effect on his spirit.

"I think I can stop him," Burden said. "I can save lives. But I can't save all of them. I've told you that. That's what I think.

"You have to remember," he continued, "Tano's ego is tied directly to his stature in his own mind. He's warned you. You go against that warning, and you've insulted him by not respecting his power to dictate to you. He's going to make you pay for it. And he's going to make sure you know you're paying for it."

Titus was feeling trapped.

"I could just cough up the money. Get it over with."

"Yeah, you could do that," Burden agreed. "And maybe that would end it for you. But it would also guarantee that Luquín would go on doing what he does, and with even more resources. You'd guarantee that someone else would be put through the same hell that you're going through. And your money would be financing it. I don't know about you, but I wouldn't want that on my conscience."

Titus found it a little difficult to get his breath.

He looked toward the windows and the opened doorway. He felt alienated, estranged from his life before last night. Adrift. Outside, the light and the sounds were foreign. The language was foreign. The smells belonged to other people, and the rhythm of life belonged to another culture. It all contributed to a sense of uncertainty.

Uncertainty, however, was only part of it. His anger was still there, too, slowly evolving into a determination to fight back. Somehow. But not at the cost of someone else's life. Not even one. Burden was probably right that Luquín would find out if he went to the FBI. Sooner or later. And then there was Burden's other prediction, that someone was going to die anyway, regardless, just so Luquín could establish his authority.

He looked at Burden, who was studying him just an arm's reach across the round table, his face a narrative of the effects of sustained secret struggles. Whatever his life had been like, it wasn't entirely hidden from anyone who cared enough to try to understand what they were looking at. It was sculpted into his face and had shaped the sorrowful angle of his eyes. Whatever it was this man knew, he'd paid dearly for it. Titus couldn't ignore that.

And then there was Gil Norlin's advice: If you follow this guy's recommendations, you won't have to worry about whether or not you're doing the right thing. You can believe what he says.

Titus took a deep breath, one that reached down into the place that made him what he was, to the place that defined him.

"Okay," he said to Burden, "let's do whatever it is we have to do. And let's do it as fast as we can."

Chapter 15

"Guys like Tano have brilliantly taken advantage of the effects that terrorism has had on U.S. domestic security," said Mattie Selway. She was the roan-haired woman Titus had seen in Burden's war room earlier in the day. She had joined Titus and Burden in the study, bringing with her a black ring binder that she kept in her lap, occasionally flipping the pages back and forth, making notes.

"They foresaw that for the immediate future, at least, the preponderance of the U.S.'s law enforcement, intelligence services, and domestic security would be poured into reacting to this new threat. Addressing a crisis like this creates a kind of tunnel vision in the national psyche. People want the damn thing solved, they want it to go away. The government wants to accommodate them. Luquín knew that in the States it was going to be all eyes—and money and commitment—on international terrorism for the foreseeable future. We've seen this in the FBI's reassignments, pulling huge numbers of agents from narcotics operations, others from violent crime units, others from white-collar crime, to work in counterterrorism."

The sun had fallen behind the towering *fresno* and *eu-*

calipto trees outside and was sinking toward the Sierra de Morenos in the west. They sat in an eerie twilight that Titus was beginning to associate with Burden himself.

"Several things stand out as interesting to us," she continued. "One: the size of the ransom, of course. That's probably a reflection of his confidence in his plan. Two: the way he wants it paid. Smart. It'll work. After you've made your investments, the money will evaporate like a morning mist. It just won't exist anymore, lost in the vast electronic void. And third: the fact that Luquín himself has crossed the border for this."

"I think this last one's the one that'll give us our opening," Burden said from a dark pocket of the room. He was continuing to roam the parameters of the gloomy space. "Mattie thinks the unusual financial arrangements are our best bet. In any event, there are some basic preparations. Your computer's ready to go. I talked to Herrin about an hour ago, and he says they're finding phone taps and bugs all over your house." He stopped and looked across at Titus through the dim light. "And you need to get your wife back here," he said.

Before Titus could open his mouth to respond, the Mayan woman appeared in the opened doorway where the balconies led to the buildings next door.

"García," she said, "we've got Luquín coming in on Mr. Cain's laptop."

Within moments they were all standing around one of the desks, staring at the screen of Titus's computer, reading the incredible message.

Following is a list of enterprises in which you will want to invest and/or contribute. I suggest you begin immediately with 15% of the $64 million you wanted to utilize.

Please complete that transaction within 48 hours of this message.

Follow that with an additional 32% investment of the total within 72 hours.

Marcello Cavatino Inversiónes, S.A., in Buenos Aires will be happy to provide you with the professional services necessary to execute these transactions.

The list of businesses and charities followed. One in Mexico, two in Brazil, one in Lebanon, one in St. Kitts, two in Monaco. Titus stared over the Mayan girl's shoulder and gaped at the computer screen.

"Bonnie, see if you can find them," Burden said to the Asian woman, who was now wearing jeans and a Oaxacan embroidered *huipil*. She went to work on another computer.

Titus stared at the screen and sat in one of the chairs without saying a word. He was shaken. How many times could he be surprised like this? He didn't know what he'd thought Luquín's first message would be, but he hadn't expected this.

"What's the matter?" Burden asked. "Liquidity?"

Titus was oblivious. The money. Jesus. He should have written it down on a piece of paper and looked at it. The whole thing had been so unreal that he hadn't yet focused on what it would mean to divest himself of $64 million—a quarter of Cai-Text's net worth. Seeing the beginnings of the process on the computer screen was unnerving.

"That's nearly ten million dollars in two days," Burden said, "and then nearly twenty-one million three days after that."

"Yes, I can get the ten. I'll have to work on the twenty-one."

"Okay. Well, we have to move fast now," Burden said, glancing at his watch. "It's three-thirty, for all practical purposes."

Mattie turned to Titus.

"Luquín's job here is a lot easier than laundering money," she said. "With laundering you're trying to cover up where the money came from. In this case that's not a problem. Luquín wants to hide where it's going. So when Cavatino disperses your investments among these seven enterprises, that'll probably be the last time we'll really know anything for sure about it. From those places it'll be buried under an avalanche of trade."

"García," Bonnie said from her computer, "the companies are coming up. All of them. No, wait, one of the charities, the one in Monaco, isn't showing yet. All the companies are less than a year old. Marcello Cavatino Inversiónes, S.A., has been around three years."

"Good. Do some work on them."

But Burden was waiting, still staring at the computer screen with Mattie and the Mayan girl, as if they were all expecting another message. The room was silent except for Bonnie's fingers snapping on the keys across the room.

The ping of another message was like a gunshot.

"Here we go," the Mayan girl said, and the screen flashed a short, terse message.

Charlie Thrush has paid for your stupidity. You should have lived with the surveillance.

Titus was standing again, again staring over the girl's shoulder. It took him some time—he had no sense of duration—to make the two words fit into the context of the moment. Charlie Thrush?

Then Burden asked, "Where did Thrush live?"

The past tense of the question hit Titus like a blow to the stomach. Suddenly he had no moisture at all in his mouth. "On a ranch west of Austin."

"Where? Exactly."

"Fredericksburg. Near there." He thought he was going to be sick.

"Rosha," Burden said, and the Mayan girl swiveled to another computer and began typing furiously.

Titus saw Charlie talking, his lanky frame sprawled in a chair in front of one of his computer screens, his long fingers flapping on the keys as if he were playing the piano, his head half turned as he talked, explaining the theory behind the calculus and the quantum mechanics on the screen. He saw him with his head buried in a book in a small pool of light in a dark room. He saw him handing Rita a wicker basket of his own peaches with a crooked grin, telling her that Titus still didn't have the knack to grow anything as sweet as these.

"Here it is," Rosha said, reading a paraphrasing. "A little over three hours ago the Gillespie County Sheriff's Office got a call to the Thrush ranch on Schumann Creek. It just says that they responded."

Titus experienced a sensation of being somewhere else. He felt a hand on his shoulder, and then the seat of a chair touched the back of his knees. He sat down. He heard the computer keys snapping snapping snapping. He was weak. Shaky. He listened to them talk as if he were not in the room. He wasn't aware of looking at anything or even of seeing anything. He wasn't aware of himself at all, in any kind of context.

"Here it is," Rosha said again. "Speer Funeral Home. Accepted the body of Charles Thrush from the Gillespie County EMS half an hour ago. Cause of death: ranching accident."

There was an awkward quiet in the room. They didn't

know the man. They didn't even know Titus. What did he expect from them? Weeping? Charlie's death was as removed from them as a weather report from the Azores.

Burden was the one who broke the silence, his voice soft and edgy at the same time.

"You see how this is going to work," he said.

Titus could feel his face burning. His emotions were indescribable, a swarm of embarrassed fear and anger and panic. There was nothing here he could identify with. The indictment of his responsibility in Charlie's death was unavoidable. Burden had even asked him if Luquín had forbidden the security sweep. Titus remembered his feeling of claustrophobia at imagining he would have to live with Luquín listening to every word he spoke. He remembered saying, I can't live like that. Well, apparently he could have. And should have. But now, how in God's name was he going to live with this?

He worked his mouth for moisture.

"Rita's with Louise Thrush in Venice," he said. "I've got to get them back here." Then, before he had the last word out of his mouth, he looked at Burden in panic. "Jesus Christ. Luquín knows that, doesn't he."

He listened to the connections going through, then the phone ringing. It was two-thirty A.M. in Venice. After their conversation she wouldn't go back to bed.

Burden's women had made themselves busy, turned away to terminals or absorbing paperwork, a gesture of privacy that he appreciated even though it was only symbolic. Burden himself waited in a chair at the next desk. He had not turned away; he wanted to hear the conversation.

"It can only be you, Titus," Rita answered from the edge of sleep.

"I'm sorry," he said.

"I know you know what time it is here," she said huskily, and he imagined her looking at her watch on the bedside table. "You know, hon, if you'd waited just a few more hours, I would've been awake anyway."

He didn't really know how to try to make himself sound. It didn't much matter. In a few more words she'd pick up on it anyway, hear it in his voice.

"I've got some bad news, Rita," he said.

Pause. He imagined her going suddenly still in the dark, factoring in his words, his tone of voice.

"What's the matter? Are you okay, Titus?" Her voice was calm, her "I won't panic no matter what he says" tone of voice. Firm, prepared. She would be sitting up in bed now, frowning in the dark, straining to pull the words out of him.

"Yeah, I'm fine," he said. "It's Charlie."

"Oh, no . . ." She was holding her breath.

"He was in an accident today, out at the ranch. He's dead, Rita."

"Oh, *no!*" She repeated it. And then she repeated it again. And then again.

He hated this more than anything, doing this to her at so great a distance, handing to her the responsibility of telling Louise, of getting them both packed and on a plane, comforting her for thousands of miles on the way back home.

They talked for half an hour, and he told her the truth: He didn't know much. He'd try to get more information. He didn't tell her he was in Mexico, of course. He'd work all that out later. He lied to her, comforted her, planned with her. Rita was best if she was planning. It calmed her; it helped her deal with the unknown, with the unavoidable but frightening unravelings of life.

He told her he was going to charter a private plane to bring them home. She thought this was unusual but didn't protest too much, and he said he would make the arrangements and get back to her with the details.

It was a strange and wrenching conversation, made all the worse for Titus because he was among strangers. And worse than that, because he knew the truth.

Chapter 16

The subdued tempo that followed the confirmation of Charlie Thrush's death didn't last long. It was nearly dusk as Mattie, Titus, and Burden followed the loggia around to Burden's study. The doors and windows of the large room were still open as before, and it was lighted only by a few scattered table lamps and the low, eerie illumination of the long photograph of the nude widow.

As soon as they were inside, Titus turned to Burden.

"I'm flying back tonight," he said. "That pilot had better not think he's going to be spending the night here."

"No," Burden said. "He's ready."

"Okay," Titus said, "then let's get down to it. As far as I'm concerned, you can go after Luquín any way you want to. Just tell me what you need, what I'm supposed to do."

Burden turned to Mattie. "Will you get the telephones for me? And bring back Titus's laptop."

As she walked out the door, he turned back to Titus.

"Look," he said, "the first thing I want you to understand is that Luquín and I have this much in common: Silence is our mantra. We have to keep him in the dark about this meeting.

He can't know that you've contacted someone for help and that you're being advised. He needs to believe that your responses to his demands are yours alone, and that you're totally focused on getting the money he wants. He needs to believe that you're paralyzed, holding your breath waiting for the next word from him.

"He must not know that we know he's in Austin. Any hint of that, and he'll vanish. Keep in mind: The people he works with are very good. They've probably been in Austin several weeks getting ready for this. We're at a great disadvantage, so we have to be smarter. Unflinching. And absolutely silent. Without that we don't have any hope of success here.

"Second thing: You can't undo this once it gets started, Titus. You understand that, don't you?"

"I hadn't thought about it," Titus said. He paused. "But now I have. Do what you have to do."

Burden nodded. "Let's talk about where you think this is going. Ultimately."

"What do you mean?"

"I mean, what do you think is the end of this, Titus? Where is this headed?"

"I want this guy out of my life," Titus said without thinking. "I want this ordeal to end. I just told you."

Burden had been standing near the bookshelves by the doorway, and now he moved slowly around the room, again roaming through the pools of light, disappearing into the dusky corners, easing along the unlighted spans of the book-lined walls, slipping through another pool of light. Finally he stopped and came over to Titus, who had continued to stand near the library table.

"Keep in mind," Burden said, "that Luquín has set the rules, and they're non-negotiable. Go to the police: People die. Don't pay the ransom: People die. Keep the whole thing secret, or people die. He's defined the rules of the game. We don't have much room to operate."

The two men were looking at each other.

"Okay," Titus agreed.

"Let's say you pay the full ransom Luquín's demanding," Burden continued. "Will that be the end of it? Or will he want something more? And if he's willing to just walk away with what he's got, are you okay with that? Even though he's killed people in the process?"

"Then you believe him when he says—even though he has his money—he'll come back and kill people if I disclose what's happened? If I go to the FBI after the fact?"

Burden leveled his eyes at Titus. "He wants you to understand, Titus, that he's in total control here. That's what Thrush's death was all about. It was a demonstration of your new reality. He's gone to elaborate lengths to cover all the bases. You turn this over to the FBI after it's over, and you're signing death warrants for a hell of a lot more people. He's told you. I'm telling you."

Burden ran his hand through his hair. "Keep repeating that to yourself, Titus. You either accept his conditions or more people die. Then ask yourself this question: If I agree to keep it all quiet, to save a lot of lives, am I okay with this guy just disappearing when it's all over . . . with the money . . . and having killed one, two, three? four? . . . of my friends?"

"Just get to the damn point," Titus said. By now he had a raging headache, and he was agitated and furious and afraid. But he knew what the point was. He really hadn't thought this through to the hard questions yet. He just wanted to be rid of it all, assuming, in the back of his mind, that in the end, even though he might lose millions of dollars, justice would ultimately be done. As in a movie, the good guys would come in and take care of it.

"The end could get rough," Burden said. "I'll take the responsibility for that. But if I do this thing for you, I don't want you coming to me with pangs of conscience when it's looking scarier than you'd imagined it would be. Once I start, I won't stop."

Titus's heart began racing. It was dark outside. He hadn't had much sleep in the last twenty hours, and the stress he'd been under made the little sleep he'd had feel like none at all.

He moved toward Burden until they were an arm's reach apart.

"Is there some chance I could end up in prison for what's going to happen once you start this?"

Burden stared into Titus's eyes. "None whatsoever."

"Then the pangs of conscience you're talking about, that has to do with what might happen to Luquín?"

"That's right."

This time it was Titus who hesitated a moment before he spoke, but when he did, there was no hesitation in his voice.

"Then you don't have anything to worry about. I'm not going to have any pangs of conscience over that."

They were looking at each other in silence when Mattie entered the study from the balcony, carrying the phones and Titus's laptop.

"It's all ready," she said, walking past them and placing everything on the library table.

The two men moved to the table, and Burden picked up one of the cell phones and handed it to Titus.

"Don't ever let this out of your sight," he said. "It's encrypted. Mattie will give you the dial codes. It connects you to me, and to Mattie and the others. It's your lifeline.

"The laptop's ready. Mattie will give you encryption codes for this, too. We'll use both the phones and the laptop to communicate.

"For the most part, you just do whatever you have to do to comply with Luquín's demands. Keep in mind, there's going to be some surveillance. There's nothing you can do about it without more retaliation from Luquín, but be aware that it'll be there."

"How much? What kind?"

"Not a lot. Luquín's people don't want to attract any attention. So they're not going to be swarming. Most of it will be mobile. A van cruising, trying to pick up snippets of cell phone traffic. Maybe some photography. But it'll be very discreet. He's not going to be all over you, but he's going to be watching.

"As of right now, I'm committed to moving as quickly as possible to try to save lives. And that'll save money, too. Remember this: Just because you're not hearing from me doesn't mean I'm not there. There's a hell of a lot to arrange. I won't be getting much sleep. Communicate as often as you want. You won't always get me, but you can always get Mattie. I'll get back with you as soon as it's possible for me to do so.

"Okay, Mattie's going to finish briefing you on communication procedures. I'm going right now to arrange for the pilot. Someone will be here to pick you up within the hour to take you to the airstrip."

Titus nodded. His mind was already moving so far and so fast ahead that he was almost carrying on two conversations in his head simultaneously. All he could think about was the logistics of getting Rita out of Europe and on her way home.

Chapter 17

AUSTIN

Luquín paced slowly back and forth along the deck that was perched on the edge of the cliff, one hand in his pocket, smoking his cigarette, the smoke a blue breath drifting away from him into the darkness. Now and then he paused and looked out into the night.

There was nothing much to see in the direction he was looking. Far below the sapphire surface of the wide river twisted through the cobalt darkness, and on the other side the long slope of the rising land ascended to black hills with sparsely scattered lights glinting through the dense woods. Occasionally a light would flicker and stretch out and die, the headlights of a car negotiating the narrow, unlighted lanes that rambled through the thickly wooded hills. The house that held his attention was straight in front of him, a mile and a half away as the crow flies.

"We'll hear from him tomorrow," Luquín said. "How many bugs have they taken out?"

"Half a dozen, so far."

"I told you," Luquín sneered, "he is going to be so predictable, arrogant bastard. So fucking confident. Nobody's going to bug his place and get away with it. I wish I could have seen his face when he realized what he had done." He shook his head in amusement. "I would have had to find another excuse to kill Thrush if Cain had left the damn bugs in place." He snorted. "It's going to be a pleasure working this asshole."

He smoked. "But I can't figure out why we haven't picked him up on any of the bugs that are still in there. We haven't even heard him coughing or pissing or anything."

"We're picking up the technicians."

"I know that, Jorge. But we're not picking up Cain. What's he doing?"

"You've scared the shit out of him, Tano," Macias said. "He's probably not even breathing in there."

Jorge Macias was Luquín's Mexican chief of operations. In his mid-thirties, Macias was barrel-chested and handsome in the Latin lover sense of the term. He was self-assured and self-centered and easy with violence.

When Luquín had business in Mexico or Texas, it was Macias who saw that it ran the way it was supposed to. His teams laid the groundwork. His teams ran the intelligence. His teams provided the brutality when brutality was required. (It was Macias's people who had smuggled Luquín across the border in the top of Benny Chalmers's truck.) And from years of experience, he had become deft at passing down the bad news to the lower ranks. If they made blunders, he gave them one chance to rectify their mistakes. Another failure, and they disappeared. Others took their place with the full knowledge of what had happened to the men before them. Predecessors' mistakes were never repeated. There were no exceptions.

"What about the guys sweeping the house?" Luquín asked.

"Just technicians. Our guy on the ground hasn't picked up

any guns. Cain has a very high quality security system at Cai-Text, and he probably knew these guys through those connections. He runs a very tight operation. It looks like routine sweeping, just what we anticipated. Nothing more than that."

"And you think these are the guys he called from the pay phone."

"Probably. He couldn't stand it. Wanted to do something about it as fast as he could."

Luquín planted his feet firmly apart, drew slowly on his cigarette, and stared across the night river. A boat moved steadily over the water, going away from the city. Its lights reflected off the sapphire, and the sound of its engine grumbled off the sides of the cliffs.

"I'm trying to imagine," he said, as much to himself as to Macias, "what he must be thinking. The man is careful. He doesn't make big mistakes. He weighs the pros and cons, follows the rules, and makes safe, reasonable decisions. He is predictable, as we have seen. Now, how does he react to the realization that he is responsible for his friend's death?

"He's going to go over and over in his head how this happened," Luquín went on, answering his own question. "He's going to reconfirm in his mind that I didn't specifically say: Don't sweep the house. So then he's going to think, My God, I've got to try to feel my way through this. That son of a bitch Luquín is unpredictable. I've got to read his mind. How in the hell am I going to do that!"

Luquín smoked, resting his elbows on the deck railing as he peered into the night, as if the tiny lights of the houses in the distance were a fortune-teller's cards and he could see there the answers to all of his concerns.

"And then," Luquín said, "he is going to begin to get crazy. A careful man finds it very stressful to deal with unpredictability. He sees no fucking way to figure it out. And that begins to wear on him. It begins to eat at him. And that's good."

Jorge Macias listened to Luquín talk. The man had no equal at what he did, and working for him was always an education in perversity. Over the years, Luquín had evolved from being just another assassin in the drug wars, a culture that bred assassins like maggots and treated them with just about as much respect, to being a kind of philosopher of the business of death. The amount of time Luquín put into knowing the psychological biography of the person he focused his attention on was extraordinary in this business. That was why he was so greatly feared by those who knew enough to fear him. And that was why he was so effective.

Macias would become a wealthy man from this one job alone. But there was a price for it. When you worked with Luquín there was always a price. The man didn't feel he was getting his money's worth out of you if you didn't pay a price, and that usually meant some kind of suffering. Before this was over, Luquín was going to require him to do something that would be anguishing, either physically or emotionally, and that was why Macias had already sworn to himself that this would be the last time he would work with this madman.

Macias's cell phone rang, and he pulled it out of his pocket and turned away from the deck railing. With his head down, listening, he began walking idly around the lighted pool. Luquín turned and watched him. He liked telephone calls during an operation like this. It meant action. Things were happening near and far to his advantage. The wheels turned; the plan moved forward.

He flicked the butt of his cigarette, and it made a high, expert arc and landed in the near edge of the pool, floating on the aqua light. He watched Macias, who was on the other side of the pool now, the half of his body facing Luquín shimmering with turquoise light reflected from the surface of the water. By the time he got around to Luquín again, he was ending his conversation. He snapped the phone closed and joined Luquín at the railing again.

"That was Mateos in Venice. His informant in Mrs. Cain's hotel just reported that she received a telephone call a couple of hours ago. Unfortunately that's all he knows. The informant wasn't in a position to monitor the call." Macias looked at his watch. "That would have been about two-thirty in Venice. An unusual hour to receive a call."

Luquín dug another cigarette out of the pocket of his guayabera and lighted it. "So that means that Mrs. Thrush and Mrs. Cain will be on their way home sometime tomorrow morning." Luquín smiled slowly, and then it grew into a soft, delighted laugh. "Goddamn, I love this guy Cain. Doing that woman long-distance would have been so inconvenient."

Luquín turned again to the dark valley and to his own thoughts, bending slightly, his elbows resting on the railing. Macias stepped away and took out his cell again. He glanced upstairs, where his two men were at their posts watching the street at the front of the house. He glanced at the shadows next to the house, where he could barely make out the black-on-black image of Roque, Luquín's personal bodyguard, sitting spookily in the shadows. It was Roque who had climbed up into the top of the dark cattle truck with his boss. He was never far away, like a sick memory you couldn't get away from.

Macias looked back at Luquín. His back was palely lighted as he stared into the night. A puff of smoke from his cigarette left his head and wandered away in a long blue stream. It looked as though his hair were on fire.

*   *   *

The night flight from San Miguel seemed interminable. But while the King Air was eating up air miles over the Sierra Madre Oriental and the north Mexican desert, Titus was busy arranging the flight back to Austin for Rita and Louise. He called an international charter service in Houston that had planes on the ground in Milan's Malpensa Airport. He and Rita had agreed that once she talked to Louise, it was highly unlikely there would be any more sleep for them, so he arranged for the charter service to pick them up at Marco Polo International outside Venice as soon as the service could get a crew together.

With that done, he called Lack Paley at his home in Austin. Paley was Titus's chief legal counsel, and Titus told him that he wanted him to initiate the process to do three things:

1. Get with Terry Odell, Titus's stockbroker, and borrow $10 million against his personal investments portfolio and immediately invest the entire amount in a certain way in the entities he would name. Use Marcello Cavatino Inversiónes, S.A., in Buenos Aires to facilitate the transactions. These transactions had to be completed by three o'clock the next day.

2. Get with Lee Silber and borrow $21 million, using interest in CaiText as the collateral.

3. Prepare documents to sell off even more of CaiText in the way Titus would describe.

Then he outlined the timetable.

After Paley got over the shock of his instructions, they spent the next forty minutes working out the general idea of how all this would work. Titus told him to keep the plans strictly guarded, though he didn't explain why.

After landing in Austin, Titus took a shuttle to the airport Hilton. Burden was assuming that Luquín would have Titus's home surveilled, as he had done during his other operations in Rio de Janeiro, and he didn't want Luquín to know that Titus had left his house. Cline would pick him up in the morning, and Titus would go home the same way he'd left, in the hidden compartment in the bed of Cline's pickup.

Titus flipped on the television the moment he walked into the hotel room. The flight home had been filled with obsessive preoccupations as he had replayed again and again the what ifs, the shouldn't haves, the whys. Then he'd reviewed his conversations with Burden and tried to put into perspective what he had agreed that Burden should do. He could only hope that in the morning the things he had agreed to wouldn't look dramatically darker.

He didn't want to think anymore. He took off his clothes and fell into bed, staring over his feet at CNN. He hoped to God it would keep him from thinking.

THURSDAY
The Third Day

Chapter 18

Herrin was waiting for him in the driveway behind the hedges when he swung his legs off the retractable hidden platform under the bed of the pickup. They walked toward the veranda, Titus carrying his now modified laptop in its case. Herrin was drinking coffee from a chrome high-tech mug that looked like the thermal equivalent of a cryonic canister. They stopped and stood in the shade of the morning glories.

"I've talked with García," Herrin said, "and he's brought me up to speed."

Titus nodded. Jesus.

"Can we talk in my office yet?" he asked, clearing his throat.

"Yeah, we can. As a matter of fact, I swept that first."

They walked through the courtyard past the fountain to a back door near the rock wall gate that led to the swimming pool. They went into a broad hallway, its atrium flooding the corridor with morning light, and turned into the first double doorway to the right.

Titus's office was spacious, and he walked across the room and put his laptop on his desk, a brandy-colored rolltop from an old bank in El Paso. He plugged in the laptop and turned it on. In the center of the room a long antique walnut table scattered with his latest projects, some brought from CaiText, some for his own private interests, was washed in diffused light from an octagonal cupola that hovered over the center of the room and burnished the two-hundred-year-old walnut. Titus walked past it to the windows and looked out to the courtyard and to the orchard beyond. To his left he could see into the walled patios that surrounded the pool. He turned around.

"Okay," he said. "Now you bring me up to speed."

"We're making good progress," Herrin said. "This stuff's pretty slick. I like it. But it's a slow go. I'm keeping a floor plan of the house on the island in the kitchen. I'm marking the rooms that've been swept so you'll know where you can talk and where you can't." He swigged from the chrome mug. "García told me he wanted to leave a couple of places hot."

"Fine. Why?"

"Yeah. He said there might be some things we're going to want these guys to overhear, so we're going to overlook some bugs. We want it to look like we're good at this, but not quite good enough. They're expecting to lose most of them anyway. But the places we keep hot have got to be in rooms where it's logical that you'd think you're safe."

"You mean the bathroom. The bedroom."

"Yeah. In fact, I've already found the ones in your bedroom. They're more sophisticated than the others, much harder for us to find. They wanted these girls to stay put. So I left them in place. I suspected García would want to leave some."

Through the windows at the end of the room, Titus saw a scarlet tanager on the courtyard wall, an incredible brilliance for an instant, then it vanished.

"Okay," Titus said. "I understand that. Then go ahead and leave them."

"You'll have to be on your toes in there," Herrin reminded him.

Titus nodded. Yeah, there was going to be a lot of that.

Suddenly Titus's encrypted cell phone rang. He took it out of his pocket and opened it.

"This is García. You have a minute?"

"Go ahead."

"I've been up all night arranging a couple of mobile teams to work with us in Austin," Burden said. "About three people in each team. One team's already there, one will be there in a couple of hours. Herrin's going to be coordinating some things with them, too, and he's going to need to set up some additional equipment. Is he going to have room in that guest house for several more monitors?"

"Yeah, there's plenty of room."

"Great. I'm about an hour out of Austin. We need to get together pretty soon and go over some things. Right now, though, I need you to get back to Luquín. Have you heard any more from him?"

"Nothing."

"Okay. Use the laptop and follow Luquín's communication instructions. All of this is about the money, so let's talk money with him. Here's how I think you should handle it."

Burden's instructions were precise, and he laid them out with a simple, straightforward explanation of his reasoning. Titus was surprised at the boldness of what Burden wanted him to do, in light of what had happened with Charlie.

Though he was still in near shock at the fatal consequences of his own decisions made the day before, he knew that Burden's aggressive approach was necessary. He knew, too, that this couldn't be done without his own full commitment. This was no time to lose his nerve, though he had to admit that he had never before had so much riding on nerves that had been so badly frayed. But, by God, he wasn't about to fold now. For all that had been lost, there was so much more to save. Despite how grieved he was over Charlie's death, he knew in his gut that it was Luquín who had killed him. Deep down it made him furious that Luquín was trying to pin the responsibility for that great sadness on him.

"Yeah, good. I'll do it," he said when Burden finished.

"Okay. Then we're set. I'm going to call Herrin again and go through some things. I'll let you know when I get into town."

"One thing," Titus said. "In two hours Rita and Louise Thrush will be landing here in Austin. I want to get Rita out of here. I want her somewhere safe. Somewhere away from this business."

There was a silence at the other end.

"What's the matter?" he asked. "What's the problem?"

"I don't know if that's a good idea," Burden said.

"Jesus, why wouldn't it be?"

"Keep reminding yourself: Luquín wants the money. The money. His methods are crude in some ways, but the bottom line is that he's trying to play you psychologically. He's hoping that the killings will gain your cooperation, that those deaths will guarantee you'll cough up the money. But he's smart enough to know that going after Rita could have just the opposite effect. It could send you over the edge. He's not going to risk that. She's safe. Just as safe as you are. He wants the money. This is about the money."

"You're telling me she's not at risk?"

"That's right. Right now I don't think she's at risk. What's more, if you do that, you could trigger another death. He doesn't want you thinking for yourself like that. He doesn't want you independent. He wants to dictate what you do and don't do." Pause. "I think it would be a huge mistake, Titus."

Titus was livid. Was he supposed to believe that he couldn't even protect Rita? That he was supposed to just leave her sitting here, vulnerable, until Luquín decided he wanted to kill her? He held his tongue. He was boiling inside, but he held his tongue.

"We'll talk about it again later," he said tersely. "I'm going to have to think about this."

Chapter 19

Half an hour before Titus sat down at his computer to contact Luquín for the first time, a King Air 350 similar to the one Titus had flown in to San Miguel and back took off from the airstrip in the resort of Lago Vista on Lake Travis and headed for Austin, twenty-five air miles to the southeast.

Aboard the ten-passenger Beechcraft were six real estate developers who wanted a closer look at greater Austin. It was a common occurrence in a city that had attracted a lot of development in the past decade. And despite the fact that the economy had slowed all over the country, the roving eyes of developers were never still. Always hoping that the next upturn in the market was just around the corner, they were ever vigilant, thinking that if they timed it right, they could fall right into the money pot again with a well-placed housing development or a shopping mall or an office complex.

With the aircraft approaching Austin-Bergstrom International's tracking range, the pilot radioed the control tower, explained what his passengers wanted to do, and requested permission to circle the city at a specific altitude of twenty-two thousand feet. After a few exchanges of information, the

Beechcraft received its permission from the Austin-Bergstrom tower and fell into a series of patterned loops over the city, most of their turns concentrating on Austin's southwest quadrant, where much of the development had been in recent years. It covered both sides of Lake Austin from Emmet Shelton Bridge to the Austin Country Club, a swath of real estate that included some of the city's most desirable neighborhoods.

As the aircraft began its first series of turns, the passengers swiveled their chairs to the cabin walls and opened concealed computer consoles that folded down out of the mainframe. Antennae telescoped out from the belly of the plane, and the technicians put on headphones and powered up their computers.

Each technician wore two earpieces so he could monitor two different radio-frequency transmissions simultaneously. Each was responsible for monitoring a selected range of frequencies in the cell phone bandwidth. Whenever they picked up an encrypted transmission, their computers immediately nailed the radio frequency and time, recorded the plane's position and the angle of reception of the signal. When the coordinates were locked in, they began recording the transmissions and then moved on to the next channel and continued scanning.

The object of this first collection flight was to scoop up as many encrypted transmissions as possible in their two hours aloft. The recordings were transmitted to the team that Burden had told Titus was already in place, a large panel van carrying encryption crunchers who quickly went to work on the content coming down from the Beechcraft. The first order of business was to determine which transmissions were in Spanish. Once the Spanish transmissions were identified, they were sent to Herrin and Cline, who started mapping and analyzing the sources of the transmissions.

*   *   *

Mark Herrin sat at his computer in Titus's guest house and watched the data scroll down the screen.

"Jesus. Good stuff!" he said into his headset mike. "What kind of technology do they have in that thing?"

"Expensive," Burden said from some undisclosed location. When the scrolling slammed to a stop, Herrin saved the information to a new directory.

"Whoa! One hundred and twelve separate encrypted conversations in the southwest quadrant in two hours?!"

"Not a surprise," Burden said. "Encryption's gotten to be something of a status symbol these days."

"But, damn, this many?"

"Well, a lot of people think they have a lot of status," Burden said dryly. "We'll get another look when they go back up in a little while. If we're lucky, we'll find something for them to take a second look at. Now we'll wait for the guys in the other van to tell us which of these things are in Spanish."

Chapter 20

Through the screen door and the opened windows of the old motel room, he looked out at the dappled shade of the afternoon on the circular gravel drive around which the dozen paint-flecked cottages sat in mute dishevelment. Trashy hackberry and chinaberry trees shielded the entire compound in a murky gloom that contrasted sharply with the bright sun-washed street a short distance away at the motel's entrance. In the center of the circular drive was a weedy miniature playground, a weather-splintered seesaw, a swing set with two broken swings, a rusted merry-go-round. No child had touched them in decades, and they were haunted by silence and by the absence of little bottoms and little hands.

From the sagging bed where he sat, he could see the bungalow directly across from him. An older couple was sitting in front of it in clunky rusted lawn chairs, smoking. They wore outsized shorts over their inflated stomachs and pale, spindly legs. From behind their sunglasses they stared straight ahead without animation, like the listening blind.

The Bungalows Motel was built in 1942, and it had not changed except for the necessary piecemeal repairs that the decades regularly forced upon it. It used to be out on the edge of town, but the years and the city had swallowed it. Now it occupied a section of South Congress Avenue that was invisible, except to people who were also invisible and who no longer had anything to do with the world in which they lived.

Shirtless and perspiring, he wiped his damp hands on his trousers. He was conscious of the odors of dank and aging surroundings, of puggy linens and mildewed upholstery and wood furnishing soured by decades of cursory cleaning with cheap, sweet cleansers. All this forced a weight of melancholy on him that was unexpected and uncomfortable.

He didn't like this motel, and even though he had been here only a few hours, there was something about the place that gnawed at him in a way he couldn't explain. It was the dank odor of mildew. He had figured it out, finally, but that didn't make it stop. There was no mildew where he'd come from. The odors of cheap hotels and apartments were quite different there. They didn't give him this oppressive feeling that chewed at his thoughts.

He didn't usually give a damn where he was. He was summoned. He went. He did his work. He waited. If no one called, he just stayed where he was, living however life was lived there. The world was interesting. Or it wasn't. It was different everywhere. Or it was the same everywhere. Sometimes it was both in the same day. It depended on what it was. There was an infinite variety of things to be different or to be the same. In the end, though, it didn't matter to him one way or the other. He just observed that it was . . . or that it wasn't.

He had never smelled anything like this before in his life, and it was driving him crazy. It didn't make any sense at all. Why would this smell get on his nerves so much? The humidity. The slimy feel of the sweat under his arms. He imagined the hair under his arms mildewing and turning rancid. Rotting.

Tufts of it falling out and sticking to the sweat against his body. Itching.

Sometimes he went to cities he'd been to before. It happened often. But it seldom seemed as though he'd been there before. It was just new all over again. As alien as the inside of a casket.

The old couple across the way were beginning to get on his nerves, too. They sat there like two corpses, their bodies distended by the heat. He imagined he could smell them, as well. He imagined that when their bodies began to crack open and ooze, they would begin to tilt over a little. As they tilted, their sunglasses would kick up on one side, maybe slip a bit down their noses. The ooze would begin to cake on them, and their limbs would swell and discolor and stiffen with gases, making them tilt even more.

No need to think like that. He'd change the subject. He'd already forgotten the name he was supposed to be. It didn't matter. He had his ID. He'd check it if he needed to know.

Sometimes it was a good thing not to remember who you were.

Chapter 21

When the charter jet pulled up at the hangar in the blazing afternoon sun, Titus was waiting on the tarmac with Derek and Nel, the Thrushes' son and daughter, who had flown in from Denver. He had already had a lengthy conversation with them and had heard the shocking details of Charlie's death from the son. Derek had talked about his father's death too readily and in startlingly clinical detail. It was the kind of obsession you sometimes saw in people who were still trying to deal with something horrible, still trying to absorb it and make it real in their own minds. Titus could hardly bear it.

The meeting with Louise was anguishing. They stood in the sun and everyone cried. Louise was already assuming the role of sturdy survivor. After all, she'd had a long flight to think about it, and it was clear that she and Rita had talked it through at great length.

After they moved into the shade of the hangar and visited a little while longer, Titus and Rita said good-bye to them, and Louise headed back to Fredericksburg with her children.

Titus and Rita went to the Range Rover and started back across town. Rita sat with her head against the window, tired and emotionally drained. She was wearing black Capri pants, sandals, and a white blouse, her blond hair kept out of her face by her sunglasses pushed back on her head. She looked exhausted.

During the drive back, Titus said nothing. In fact, much of the half-hour trip was made in silence. So much had already been said, and Titus was trying to figure out how in the hell he was going to say the rest of it. At the same time, he kept checking his rearview mirror for surveillance. He wasn't sure what he was looking for, and as Burden had said, there was nothing he could do about it, but he couldn't help scanning the traffic and wondering which of these ordinary-looking people were actually working for Luquín.

As they pulled in through the gates and headed up the curved drive to the house, he said, "I've got some people working here," he said.

"Doing what?" she asked without concern.

"For one thing, working on the security system," he said. "It's on the blink."

He pulled up beside Herrin's trucks and got out. He got her bags from the back, and they went into the shade of the veranda and through to the kitchen, where they encountered Mark Herrin carrying an armful of digital meters.

Titus introduced them, and Herrin had the good sense to make himself immediately scarce. As he walked out of the room, Rita was standing by the island counter and her eye caught the list of rooms that had been swept. She read it at a glance, dropped her carry-on bag on the floor, and turned to Titus.

"What's going on here?" she asked.

"We've got some trouble," he said, "but we can't talk about it here. Let's take a walk."

They walked through the allée of laurels together, each

with an arm around the other, and sat on the low rock wall that ran behind the orchard. Thirty feet away, the freshly dug grave where he had buried the dogs remained a bare reminder of their changed lives. Mourning doves burbled in the peach trees. He began at the beginning and told her nearly everything.

Rita was stunned, of course, and while Titus was telling her what had happened during the last two days, his own words sounded bizarre even to him. She interrupted him only a few times to ask questions, but most of the time she sat quietly, her lack of a reaction more telling of the profound effect this was having on her than if she had wept and railed.

After he finished, neither of them spoke for a little while. Midday was well gone, and the heat was building in the orchard. Cicadas droned in the woods.

"God, Titus," she said. "Good God."

She stood, unable to sit still, and he watched her move away a few paces to the edge of the shade of the burr oak that was sheltering them from the sun. She turned around and crossed her arms.

"Are you absolutely sure of this? That this man's responsible for Charlie's death?"

"Yes."

Dumbfounded, she stared at him. Then her eyes reddened and the tears came so suddenly and profusely that it was odd to see, even disarming. She didn't hide her face, and her mouth didn't contort, but her chin quivered. Her crossed arms shifted until she was hugging herself in the summer shade with the bright light behind her. The tears just came and came until her cheeks were lacquered with them, and they dripped off her chin in a copious mixture of fear and anger and grief.

"Oh, horrible," she finally managed to say with a kind of sob. As she looked at him, he knew that she already understood intuitively, without having to reason it out, that all of their yesterdays had been absurdly innocent. Their future had been abruptly truncated and, perhaps, reached no farther than the distance between them. All around them lay the debris of their assumed well-being. The past, the normal life, had been as naive as a child's daydream.

Then Rita began wiping her cheeks with her palms and fingers, sniffling. She produced a tissue from her pants pocket and wiped her nose. She cleared her throat. She bent her head and pulled her hair behind her head as if she were going to put a band around it, but she didn't.

"God," she said, and looked up and dropped her hands. She took a deep breath and put her hands on her hips, wrists turned in, then exhaled and fixed her red eyes on him. "Louise's life has been devastated because of us!"

She couldn't think of what to say because what the hell did you say to this? She couldn't stop staring at him, and he could tell that she was having a hard time trying to absorb the enormity of what he was talking about.

"Rita, I want you to go away, to get out of here. I'm going to talk to Burden about putting you up at a safe house. Someplace where . . . you won't have to worry—"

"What! What in God's—what are you thinking, Titus?" She was looking at him as if he'd suddenly begun speaking in an unintelligible language. "That's . . . unthinkable. No! I will not! I'm staying right here. Whatever's going to happen, happens to both of us, Titus. I can't even believe you'd think I'd do such a thing," she said, her voice holding off a quaver.

"It's crazy for you to stay—"

"You're crazy," she snapped. Tears weren't in her eyes, but they were in her voice. Everything was happening in a slightly surreal way, anger and fear and love melting together in disregard, their characteristics blurring and smearing across categorical boundaries.

"You tell me what's going on here, Titus," she said. "you've told me what happened, now you tell me what's going on."

Still sitting on the rock wall, he looked out over the land that fell toward the creek.

"Burden's going after this guy, Rita, and he's moving fast, but there are no guarantees."

He wanted to be honest with her, but he didn't want to tell her everything. He didn't want to tell her his fears, or the grim probabilities, or that he was trying to ignore where it was all going. If he was lucky, they could get through this without her learning things that would be hard for her to live with when it was over.

"Oh, for God's sake, Titus. What have you gotten into here?"

"What have I gotten into?" He was furious at her remark. "This came to me! Rita, listen to me: This son of a bitch is going to kill someone else. Think of that! He's going to kill someone else. And then someone else, and then . . . Friends, all of them our friends! I don't give a damn how Burden stops him, and I'm going to do everything and anything in my power to help him do it."

Again she could only stare at him. A scrum of bluejays moved through the orchard, fighting and screaming, flinging themselves about like crazed hotheads, blue flashes tumbling through the orderly rows of peach trees. They battled their way to the other side and out, carrying their internecine hostilities into the cedar brakes toward the creek. In their wake, silence, then the doves began again, the voices of solace.

Rita had that look on her face, the odd angle to her mouth that she had when she was suddenly frightened and hadn't yet had time to order her mind and overcome the adrenaline-driven confusion. He had seen it when she had heard about her father's hunting accident and when she had heard about her mother's illness. And he still ached when he remembered seeing it the day the doctor had told them that the fetus was horribly deformed.

"This is impossible to believe," she said, "all of this. I just don't know how to . . ." She took a short, jerky breath. "I can't believe you've done this without the police. The FBI . . ." She was shaking her head. "Somebody with a legal responsibility."

"I just went over that with you, the reasoning behind it."

"Well, I think you've lost your mind, Titus."

"I'm trying to save lives," he said.

"And you think this is the way to do that? With this . . . vigilante?"

He started to come back at her, then stopped himself. "I trust Gil Norlin's advice," he said.

"Great! A guy you met briefly four years ago, and even then he was a little slimy."

"I never said that."

"You told me he was shady."

"He just wasn't working up front like the rest of them," he said. "That's all I meant by that."

Again they glared at each other. This was killing him. He watched her eyes reddening again.

"Titus," she said, and her voice had a break in it that surprised even her, he saw it in her face, "are we going to regret this?" She was actually trembling. Titus had never seen Rita tremble—ever.

"I'm making the decisions I have to make," he said, "and I'm making them the best way I know how. You've got to understand, there are no guidelines for this, Rita. This is like waking up from a nightmare and discovering that being awake didn't stop the dream. I'm just having to work through it the best way I can."

He hesitated. "I need your help, Rita. I can't do this without you."

Her expression shifted. She wasn't sure she wanted the conversation to go in the direction his tone of voice was suggesting. At this point her emotions weren't attuned to conciliation.

"I need you to cooperate with me here," he said. "I'm going to have Burden find you a place to stay where I know you'll be safe—"

"Titus!" Rita stopped him, her eyes holding him, her face rigid with anger and frustration.

He knew what she was thinking: He doesn't understand . . . doesn't even have a clue what he's asking. But he did. The fact was, she was the one who didn't have a clue. Her loyalty scared the hell out of him because it put her at risk, and he could hardly live with the idea of the possibilities that presented themselves.

They stared at each other.

"I've got to unpack," she snapped, and spun around and headed up to the house along the allée.

He didn't try to stop her. He knew better. She was tired. She was emotionally worn out. She was scared. This was the way Rita reacted to those stresses. When she was afraid she got angry, because she could feel the edges of control slipping away from her and that was the most frightening thing of all. She needed time. God help them, they all needed some time, but he didn't think they were likely to get what they needed. Luquín was going to steal as much time as he could along with the money. He was going to keep the pressure on.

As he watched Rita's back flickering through the shadows

of the laurels in the allée, the droning of the cicadas grew louder, as if someone had turned up the volume. The heat seemed to have gone up a notch, too, extruding the fragrances of summer, of superheated vegetation, the undercurrents of peaches, the good odors of earth. It all seemed so much more appealing to him now, so much more desirable, than it had a few days before when he had taken it for granted. He relished it, understanding now as he'd never understood before that it was finite, that it wouldn't last forever because it couldn't. It had always been only a temporary thing, but he'd just never thought of it that way before.

Chapter 22

The coordinates from the Spanish-language transmissions dribbled in slowly, sent immediately from the first mobile team as soon as the coordinates had been identified. When the first few pinged on Herrin's screen, and Burden's, too, as he waited in the second mobile unit, Burden was immediately speaking into Herrin's earpiece.

"What are the stats on your new program?" he asked.

"It'll pull us into a target area of about a one-hundred-meter radius," Herrin said, focused on the screen.

"Good. Let's just see if we can eliminate anything outright. Maybe a retail site, a law firm, law enforcement. Something that might have a legitimate need for encryption. We're going to be interested in residential. Leased property, most likely."

Herrin stayed at the computer for nearly two hours before all the transmissions had been scanned by Burden's mobile unit. When the Spanish-language transmissions had been pulled out of the list of 112 encrypted calls, the list had shrunk to only 14. He had called Burden back.

"Okay," Burden said. "The Beechcraft will be in position again in fifteen minutes. So what have we got?"

Herrin brought up the summary on both screens.

"Of the fourteen encrypted Spanish-language transmissions," Herrin said, "two originated in a country club, one in a real estate office, three in lawyers' offices, and two were APD Chicano squad transmissions."

He rubbed his face and then leaned on his elbows and stared at the screen. He was sitting in the path of one of the air-conditioning vents in the guest house, and the chilled air was welcome.

"That leaves only six transmissions to look at," Herrin continued. "Three originated on this side of the lake, three on the other side. The ones on the other side are known addresses. The ones on this side were mobile. But we still don't have any content."

"They said the encryption's tricky," Burden said. "It didn't take much to find out if they were English or Spanish, but the actual translations themselves are another thing."

"Any guesses?"

"No. But I'm hoping the mobile ones go back to one of the houses on the other side," Burden said. "If they do, then I'm hoping we'd have their base and their surveillance unit."

Herrin stared at the screen and unwrapped the clear cellophane from a cube of taffy candy and popped it into his mouth.

"We've got just this one more shot," Burden said. "That plane's scheduled for a job in Maracaibo beginning tomorrow." Herrin was sucking nervously on the taffy, sucking on the taffy, thinking, thinking, and then he bit into it and chewed it up in a couple of bites.

"I'm going to call the plane," Burden said. "I'm going to tell them to stay with those six channels, and go ahead and scan as many of the new ones as they can during the two-hour flight."

Herrin waited, eyes fixed on his screen, one leg bouncing on the ball of his foot as if he were a manic adolescent. Running live operations made him forget to be laid-back.

"Damn," Burden said into Herrin's earpiece, "this isn't much. If they just happen not to be transmitting during these four hours . . ." Pause. Silence. Then he said, "But I have a hunch that their timing's good. On the first flight the Beechcraft was in position and operating within only a couple of minutes of Cain's e-mail to Luquín. If Luquín was going to react quickly, and he always does, he should've been making encrypted calls within the time frame of that first flight. He just has to be in one of those three houses."

Chapter 23

Jorge Macias stood at the deck railing that overlooked the lake, a cell phone pressed to his ear as he watched a girl in a banana yellow bikini lying on the bow of a rumbling ski boat resting in the water a hundred meters below. He wore black linen trousers and a dove gray silk shirt unbuttoned to mid-chest, the dark hair of which peeked through the plackets of his shirtfront. He was talking to his mobile surveillance crew, who had picked up and reported the arrival of Rita Cain.

As he listened he watched another girl, wearing a black thong and holding a drink in her hand, as she leaned over the side of the boat and talked to a man in the water getting his skis ready. A second man stood at the steering wheel telling him what to do.

"Ah, very good," Macias said, "exactly, exactly. I needed some good news. Still no sign of bodyguards, anything like that? . . . *Bueno, bueno.* Great."

The girls preened in the sun. Girls like that, *qué chichis.* And then the girl on the bow stood and got into the boat. The driver, looking back, gunned the engine. The prop dug into the water and the boat took off. Suddenly the guy in the water was skipping along the surface of the lake on his skis, heading into the glittering ripples of the water.

Macias watched them head into the sun. Shit.

He glanced back at Luquín, who was sitting on the other side of the pool at a table in the shade of the trees. He was smoking and was focused intently on the screen of his computer, as if he were gazing at the center of the universe, sending and receiving encrypted messages through Rio, Mexico City, Buenos Aires, Beirut, Monaco. He had hardly stopped to eat. He had slept little. He was irritable. He was as volatile as nitroglycerin and even more difficult to handle.

But everyone involved in this one was on edge. It was dangerous running something like this in the States. There was a lot of pressure because everyone was getting paid double his usual fee, and because of that, Luquín expected superhuman performances from all of them.

As Macias watched, Luquín suddenly straightened up in his chair, his eyes locked on the small screen. Macias stopped hearing anything that was being said to him over the cell phone. Luquín leaned closer to the screen as his expression hardened.

"I'll get back to you," Macias said. He closed the cell phone and had started around the pool when Luquín suddenly bellowed a curse and jumped to his feet. He snatched up the laptop from the table and flung it into the air. It whiffled into a high arc, still open, the screen lighted with its last message, and then plummeted into the exact center of the pool, where it hit the water with a soft slurp and fluttered slowly to the bottom.

Macias stopped. Luquín glared across the water at him, his legs apart in a combative posture.

"Goddamn it," Luquín barked, "get me a computer."

Macias broke into a sweat as he went into the house and snatched a laptop from the dining room table. As he headed outside with it, his mind ran through all the places they'd anticipated glitches, trying to guess what might have caused Luquín's outburst.

"I don't believe this guy," Luquín said. His voice had returned to a conversational volume. His fury had gone underground. Now you needed to be afraid of him.

Macias set the laptop on the table, opened it, and hit the power button. Then he went around to the other side of the table so that he could watch Luquín's face. Luquín finessed the keys, his fingers barely making a sound as they whispered over the little gray plastic squares.

They waited for the secure site to materialize, and then Luquín pulled up the message that had caused his outburst. He turned the laptop around and shoved it at Macias.

"That *pinche cabrón*," he said, smiling, his voice languid in disdain.

Macias looked at the screen.

I have the $10 million ready for Cavatino, but I'm not putting it through until I talk to you again, face-to-face. We have to understand something. I've done nothing to disobey your instructions. If you're going to kill people even when I follow your directions, then I'll keep my money and you can go to hell.

Macias couldn't believe his eyes. Cain had just kissed off another life or two. Macias could feel Luquín looking at him over the top of the computer screen, waiting for a response.

"Well, at least you know he hasn't got anyone advising him," Macias said. "Nobody in the business would have let him do that."

Luquín said nothing. His eyes drifted away from Macias and held in the middle distance, seeing nothing.

"So what is he doing?" Luquín asked.

"Maybe he can't handle the killing. Maybe he's going to freak out."

"He doesn't do that. Maybe he hasn't seen enough killing, that's what I think."

This was Luquín's big gamble, *jugar el todo por el todo,* all or nothing, and he had pored over psychological profiles of Cain as if he were a professional psychiatrist. From these documents Luquín had created his own understanding of Cain's psychology that allowed him to anticipate Cain's reaction to every pressure that Luquín applied even before he applied it. This, however, was a kink in the plans.

But Luquín's impatience with this surprise was only that, impatience. In Luquín's mind, his superiority was firmly established. Cain might make a sudden move that required a sudden reaction, but it was only a momentary diversion.

"This is an interesting development," Luquín said. "Defiance? After knowing he was responsible for his friend's death?"

"But he thinks the killing was unjustified," Macias said. "Maybe he doesn't think he's responsible at all. He thinks you're out of line."

Luquín slowly pulled a cigarette out of the pack on the table in front of him, as if a quick move would make him lose his train of thought. He lighted it and stared out into the heat.

"Maybe," Luquín said, thinking. "This guy is a complicated mixture, a pussy with brass balls." He laughed. "Yeah, that's a good description. I'm just surprised the balls came into play at this point. After a little more pressure, maybe. But I thought the first killing would knock him off his feet, that it would take him some time to recover. Then, maybe, I'd have a tough time with him." He smoked, nodding to himself. "Yeah, this is interesting."

Macias watched Luquín. This was interesting for him, too.

Normally, having a target show this kind of defiance would already have resulted in an order for a swift, brutal death, but for some reason, this time, Luquín was not so predictable. This time he was willing to exercise a little patience, even if it was capriciously granted. Still, for him to show any at all was extraordinary. Maybe Luquín wanted the money even more than he wanted to make a machismo point with Cain. Luquín's greed was legendary. He wanted those millions.

But there was more to it than that. Though Macias was not directly involved, and Luquín never spoke to him about it, Macias knew that something bigger was at stake. Luquín was once again doing business with some of his old friends in the Middle East. Business in Mexico.

Macias wasn't officially in the loop, but he knew more about this than Luquín believed. Not much went on in Mexico that Macias didn't know about. And the strange activities of his old *compadre* Luquín were no exception.

Even by Luquín's standards, this Middle Eastern business was insanely dangerous. No wonder Luquín was volatile sometimes and uncharacteristically pliant at others. He was playing a game of snakes and ladders, *jugar a la vida.*

"Can that be done?" Luquín asked, shifting his eyes to Macias. "A safe meeting with this *cabrón?*"

"It can be done, Tano. But are you sure you want to do it?"

Luquín cut his eyes at Macias. "Fear. And flexibility. Huh? This requires a brutal hand . . . with a delicate touch now and then to give him hope. We have to be flexible, Jorge. We've never done it in just this way before. We have to be . . . sensitive to the possibilities. The blade here. A blessing there. We do what we have to do . . . for sixty-four million dollars, huh? You can do this? No problem?"

"Sure, we can do it. But we have to control the logistics. And we need to make him think that we need time for you to fly in for the meeting. We don't want him to know you're close by."

Luquín thought a moment. Then he reached out and turned the laptop around and started typing.

> Okay. One meeting. Wait for instructions. You would do well to meet your deadline for payment tomorrow.

Luquín turned the laptop around again and showed his message to Macias.

"I'll contact my people and start setting it up."

"Send it," Luquín said.

Macias tapped the key, and Luquín shoved back his chair and stood. He wanted to see the laptop in the water. He walked over to the pool and stopped, the toes of his loafers almost over the edge. He looked in and there it was, sitting at the bottom like a single eye in a man's forehead. He smoked, and the smoke was whipped away in the breeze that blew along the cliffs above the lake.

His eyes picked up the movement of an oak leaf that had fallen into the water. It was floating about crazily, the variable breezes slinging it this way and that, first in manic pursuit, then in unstrung flight across the aqua sea.

That's the way he wanted Titus Cain, he thought, just on the edge of hysteria, his heart racing, his mind not quite able to stop long enough to gain the traction of reason, but having enough control of his faculties to know that the faster he unloaded the money, the sooner the deaths would stop. That was the kind of pressure that Luquín had to reestablish in his meeting with Cain. Cain had to be buffeted constantly, given no time to drift. He had to be driven.

Chapter 24

On the way back from the orchard, Titus stopped off at the guest cottage while Rita continued on to the house. The living room of the cottage was now crammed with computers and a variety of electronic equipment that he hadn't even bothered to try to understand.

Herrin gave Titus a quick overview of how it would all work and was bringing him up-to-date on the results from the Beechcraft when Titus's cell phone rang. It was Burden.

"Have you seen Luquín's response?"

"No."

"He's going to do it. He's going to meet with you."

Titus was stunned. He didn't know what he'd expected, but he was definitely taken aback at the prospect of meeting face-to-face with Luquín again.

"What'd he say?"

"He'll send you his instructions, so stay close."

"Did he say why he was agreeing to meet with me?"

"No, but he's not as sure of himself as he wants you to believe. I think he wants to look at you, reassure himself. This is good. We'll see his instructions, so just do what he says. We'll take care of our end of it."

"Which is?"

"I want to go over that with you in detail," Burden said. "I'm going to get to your place early tonight, and I'll put it all together for you, tell you where we stand. What do you have to do to make the first payment go through?"

"A phone call."

"Good. I want you to do that right there in front of him. And what about the next payment?"

"I'm working on it."

Burden paused, and Titus heard something in the background, people talking, radio transmissions.

"Look," Burden said, "I want you to be prepared . . . Thrush isn't going to be the only one. I just don't want you to start thinking . . . that anything's magically changed here."

Titus was aware of the acrid odor of electronics, of warm plastics and rubber-coated wiring. Familiar smells. But what he was feeling at the back of his brain, the hum that oscillated deep behind his chest muscles as if his heart were about to fibrillate, was not only unfamiliar, but also frightening. Waiting for another death was harrowing. He wondered if this was what a man felt when he lost control of his reason, if these sensations were the beginnings of what would later be called blind rage.

"No," Titus said, "I understand that hasn't changed."

After ending the call, Titus stepped outside and stood in the shade at the front of the guest cottage. The shadow would grow as the sun fell farther behind the orchard, heading toward the hillside where the men had been working on the reservoir. He looked down through the splintered light of the allée of laurels and slipped into one of those moments when all that was familiar and commonplace swiftly bled away from his awareness, until he found himself estranged from his own experience, caught in a queer and alien moment.

Then, just as quickly, he snapped out of it and took the cell phone out of his pocket and called Carla at the office. He asked her if she could bring her laptop and come to the house for a few hours' work. It wasn't an uncommon request. Titus liked working from the house whenever he could, even in the early years.

He walked across the courtyard, past the fountain, and into the broad atrium hallway. He found Rita in their bedroom, unpacking. She heard him, but she didn't turn around from the bed where she had opened her suitcases. She was snatching things out of the bags, still agitated.

"Listen," he said, "let's don't leave it like this."

When she spun around to say something that he knew had been building up inside her, he gestured with a vertical forefinger and then pointed to his ear, reminding her of the bug.

Caught off guard, she just stared at him, holding her breath. Then she snapped, "Not now, Titus, for God's sake." And she turned around again and went on with her unpacking.

"Carla's coming over," he said to her back. "I've got to get some things done."

"Then do it," she said without stopping, covering the bed with slips and skirts and underwear and shoes.

Titus turned and walked out of the room.

When Carla stepped into his office nearly an hour later, he was at the long worktable reading Luquín's message on his laptop screen for the tenth time. When he looked up and saw her face, he knew that she knew that something was going on. She put her laptop on the table across from him and flipped it on before she'd even slipped off her shoulder bag.

"I just saw Rita in the kitchen," she said, giving him a significant look as she shrugged off the bag. "What happened to the trip? She was upset."

"Sit down," Titus said, and as she did he started telling her about Charlie Thrush's accident. Astounded, she asked questions—she always asked questions—and then commiserated. It didn't take her long to realize, either, that this terrible news was falling on top of the stress Titus was already under from the huge financial loss he'd told her about yesterday.

They talked a little while about notifying certain people at CaiText, and Carla made a list of those whom Titus thought should be told immediately. They, in turn, could tell others.

"God, this is just one thing on top of another," she said. She hesitated and then went right into it. "What about . . . the financial thing you mentioned? Is that what you want to deal with now?"

"Mostly."

"And does Rita . . . ?"

"She knows everything."

"How's she . . . ?"

"We're working on it."

Carla nodded. After an awkward silence Titus said, "I'm going to have to sell off a piece of the company, a small piece, about eight percent."

Carla's mouth dropped open.

Titus instantly flushed. This was humiliating.

"I've got Lack Paley working on it, and it ought to be done in a couple of days."

"A couple of days?!" She was floored.

Angry and embarrassed, Titus swallowed, and then he knew she had seen it. He'd never felt exactly like this in his life. All the good common sense, the sound judgment, the caution and steady stewardship he'd used to build CaiText, and which was a trademark of the way he conducted business, were being destroyed by the actions Luquín was forcing him to make. It would have been bad enough if this disparagement had been justified, but to have to deliberately bring such wrong assumptions upon himself was nearly more than he could stand.

"You needed to know this," he went on, his face burning, "in case something about it leaked out and you started to get inquiries."

If he felt this way telling Carla, who knew him so well, with whom he had shared so much of his life, and who knew more about him than anybody besides Rita, how was he going to feel when this perceived irresponsibility became public? What would people think when the business press seized on this? What would happen to his reputation when his colleagues and managers and employees believed he had behaved so recklessly? How was he going to deal with that?

"If . . . if I do get questions, what . . . what do you want me to say?" she asked.

"Just tell them you don't know anything about it. Tell them it's legal stuff. It's out of your bailiwick."

She nodded, still looking at him, but the expression on her face had moved from shock to suspicion, as if she were beginning to see that there was far more to this than Titus was telling her.

"That's a big hit," she said, pretending to believe him and knowing that he could tell she was pretending, "that bad investment."

He nodded. Carla was a faithful jogger, and the same inner discipline that drove her regimen of physical training shaped her sense of integrity. It wasn't his withholding that was eating at her here. Titus didn't tell her everything about the business, of course, and she never expected him to. But she knew that something else was going on here, something was wrong.

They sat in silence.

"Look," she said, leaning toward him, her short, brindled hair framing her face and raised eyebrows in a kind of tousled discipline, "when I came into the house a minute ago, I saw some kind of technician coming out of the guest house wearing headphones. I walked into the kitchen and there was Rita standing at the sink, staring out the window. When I hugged her she didn't even react to my surprise at seeing her home early."

She kept her eyes on him.

"And just now, when I walked through the house to come in here, I saw another technician wearing headphones." She paused for emphasis. "It looked to me like he was listening to a little bookcase."

She shrugged. Who was she to find that odd? Her forearms were resting on the table, and when she paused her hands opened and her fingers spread out as if she were trying to convey a feeling of sincerity. Her fingernails were carefully manicured to an oval-edged practicality. She never wore polish.

"I'll go along with the bad investment story," she went on. "That's fine." She nodded. "Okay? But listen, Titus, something's terribly not right here, I think. Are you sure . . . you know, that you don't want to go into it just a little bit?"

He stared at her. He was tempted. The room had been swept. Who could possibly know if he said anything to her? He didn't have any doubt about her being able to keep a secret, but he felt that telling her would be like splashing her with a radioactive chemical. It could only be dangerous for her to know.

"Give me a week," he said, swallowing again. "We'll talk about it then."

"You and Rita," Carla said, "everything's okay there?"

"A lot of tension," he said honestly. "But we're okay."

162

She nodded solemnly. "Good," she said. "Then you can handle anything else, can't you."

"Yeah. I can handle anything else."

His right hand was resting by his laptop, and she reached over and touched the back of it with the back of her hand.

"Okay," she said. "Then I guess we'd better get some work done."

Titus worked several hours with Carla, and by the time she left it was late in the afternoon. He checked for messages and found that Luquín's instructions for the meeting had arrived. They were terse: At exactly twelve-thirty A.M. he was supposed to drive through the gates of his property and make his way by a specific route to an isolated intersection in the hills, where he would receive further instructions. He sat down and stared at the screen. Burden would have this by now, too. Surely Titus would hear from him soon.

He found Rita in the kitchen, making pasta for dinner. She was still agitated, and he didn't really have anything to add to what he'd said before. Her temper was on a hair-trigger setting, and he knew that there would be little to gain from an argument with her.

He opened a bottle of wine, poured a glass for each of them, and then helped her make the salad. They ate dinner under the most strained silence that he could ever remember between them. He doubted if either of them would be able to digest what they were eating.

Chapter 25

The room was dark and he was lying on his side in his under-wear, looking out through the parted curtains of the opened window. The glow from a street lamp floated over the weedy compound, where the swing set and the merry-go-round and the slide stood out against the glow-haze like the ruins of child-hood. It could've been anywhere, that playground. Aban-doned. Things abandoned looked the same everywhere, and childhood, in some places, was grotesquely abbreviated.

The idea of childhood nauseated him, and he got up and went into the bathroom and vomited. He washed his face and walked back into the other room and fell onto the bed. He sighed and rolled over on his back. The sheets were limp, al-most sticky. He pulled the wadded screws of toilet tissue from his nostrils. He didn't know which was worse, the discomfort of the tissue or the odor. Immediately he tasted the stink of mildew and dank walls.

He got out of bed and went to the opened door. Maybe it was too hot to sleep, though he didn't know. There were so many other reasons not to sleep. He looked at the cottage across the gravel drive where the old couple slept. He could hear their window unit humming. He'd tried his, but the air that came out of it was repulsive with rot and the stale breath of strangers.

Through the screen door he could smell the dust that fogged up gently from the gravel drive when cars crept into the motel compound, and he could smell, faintly, the hot asphalt of the sun-heated streets. He could smell weedy vegetation. And he could also smell the first untainted light of tomorrow, even though it was still many hours away. And just beyond that . . . once, he thought he could smell the quintessence of eternity. But it dissipated instantly, and he wasn't sure.

He reached up, and as carefully as he would touch a spider's web he placed the tips of his fingers on the filthy screen of the door. It was caked with particulate matter of cigarette smoke laden with strangers' breath. He moved his fingers lightly across the screen, and he could feel the soiled wire with the grain of his fingerprints.

Then through the screen he saw the face. He went cold, and sweat covered him in an instant. Squinting, he peered through the filthy screen into the gloomy shadows. There, where the lower limb of the tree draped past the edge of the old couple's cottage, that line was the arc of the right eyebrow. The darkened trees behind were the shadow of the cheek, and the curve in the drive was the curve of the left side of the jaw.

He swallowed, blinked, and tried to refocus to make the illusion go away. But it wasn't an illusion, and it had been watching him all along.

He couldn't remember when he'd first seen the face, too many cities ago, too many streets ago, too many deaths ago. Sometimes it was hidden in things, like just now, sometimes it was on people on the sidewalk or in a crowd. He could never tell if it was a man or a woman, if it was angry, or wistful, or menacing. And now, as he tried to distinguish a furrowed brow, a sad decline of the eyebrow, tension at the corner of the mouth, the face began slowly to recede so that the tree was no longer the arc of an eye, the cottage was only a cottage, the drive was only a dusty caliche smear.

He accepted that. The bizarre had long since ceased to be bizarre. The outrageous and the mundane settled together on the same indistinguishable plane of experience where visions became reality and reality dematerialized. Sometimes, physiologically, as now, he reacted. Sweat. Heart palpitations. The instant urge to urinate. But emotionally, he was calm. Stable. Unshakable.

Something moved through the screen, a breath, a soft expiration.

He slipped off his underwear and stepped out of it. He raised his arms and put them on either side of the door frame and spread his legs and stood in the doorway facing out. The waft moved in through the screen and covered his body. It moved around him like a loosened spirit, searching for a roost within. It touched every pore, encircled his dangling genitals, set his pubic hair vibrating.

He was standing like that when the figure materialized at the edge of the darkness and stopped. The two regarded each other across the murky distance. Then the figure moved toward him, approaching right up to the door, and stood close to him, their faces separated by inches. They looked at each other through the filter of the screen; neither moved. He saw a glint of moisture in the other's eyes.

"¿Mé recuerdas?" the other man asked softly.

With his body forming a corporeal X across the open space of the door, he remained silent, motionless.

And then:

"Ahhhh," he purred in his chest as recognition coalesced out of muddled memory. "Sí, García. Yo recuerdo."

*   *   *

Still naked, he sat in one of the two chairs in the motel room and Burden sat in the other, the rumpled bed between them like a huge coffee table. The frail light from outside was enough for the two men to see ghostly highlights of each other. It was hot in the room.

"I didn't know it was you who had sent for me," he said to Burden, sitting back in the chair.

Of course he didn't. His latest address was handed around in certain dark streets like a very dangerous illicit drug. People were eager to turn loose of the paper it was written on. He never knew who would hire him next until the people showed up, and most of the time he dealt only with go-betweens. Sometimes he never knew for sure who'd paid him for the things he did.

"Tell me about yourself," he said.

The words were amiable enough, but simply dealing with him was inherently menacing. Yet Burden wasn't afraid of him, though he recognized his instability. No one at Burden's level would come to him themselves. Burden knew that this fact was not lost on the other man and that it set Burden apart in his eyes.

"I left the Agency. Freelancing now," Burden said.

"I heard that. I've heard some stories. You tend to leave stories behind, like droppings. Where do you live?"

It was a question no one in his right mind would've answered truthfully.

"San Miguel de Allende part of the time. Paris part of the time. San Francisco. London—"

"Okay, okay." The man rocked his head from side to side. "Did you ever marry that woman?"

"No."

"But you're still with her."

"Of course."

"Of course." The man's body was pale, washed in the pale light coming through the window beside him. "Lucía the Gypsy. Beautiful woman."

Burden was uncomfortable hearing him talk about her. But he waited, careful not to show his discomfort.

"Why did you leave the Agency?"

"Descontento."

"Yes, but why?"

"I don't want to tell you."

"Okay, fine."

The dank little room reeked . . . of something . . . of many things . . . sweat, mildew, a lingering uric scent . . . of fear . . . of nightmares. These were the odors of broken men. Burden had smelled it in women's rooms, too, but those rooms wafted also of perfume, and no matter how cheap it was, no matter how sweet, it lessened the loneliness. But it also left behind a melancholy that was unbearable.

"I never thanked you," the man said.

"It wasn't necessary."

"Very few things are really necessary. I'm ashamed that I never thanked you. *Lo siento.*"

Burden understood, but he didn't respond. The man lived a life that had no tomorrows. Inasmuch as one man could, he lived in the present, moment to moment. It was a clean life, the life of an animal that knows nothing of the idea of future. It was a horrible life.

"I didn't know where you'd gone," Burden said.

"Did you look for me?"

"After a fashion."

He heard the man aspirate, and he thought he saw his breath shoot out in a long plume of cynicism into the pale light surrounding his dark silhouette.

"After a fashion," the man said, to hear the sound of it again. "That's a very García kind of response."

"I thought you wanted to disappear."

"I did." He coughed a little. "You did the right thing."

Now that he was actually sitting here in front of him, Burden wanted to ask him something he had always wondered about. His curiosity overcame the fear that would have prevented any other man from asking.

"How did you manage to get away from him?"

There was no immediate response. Maybe there would be no response at all. But then the man said, "It was easy. Like suicide. There's nothing easier in the world once you finally decide to do it."

Burden waited for more.

"One sleepless night . . . I lay in the dark. I saw no end to it. I reached and got a handful of the darkness and pulled on it. It came, like a black curtain coming down. And I pulled on it and pulled on it. This went on for hours. By daylight I was gone. And that was all there was to it."

Burden nodded. He had heard that the man talked this way, that for him there was no verge between normal and fantastic.

"There's a merry-go-round out there," the man said, and turned his face toward the window. "And swings. And weeds."

The curtains hung dead behind his face, a pale silhouette against a paler light.

"I have a name for you," Burden said, "but I don't want to give it to you yet." He was afraid the man would grow agitated, that knowing who it was would upset him to the point of making him unpredictable. "You remember that I often handle things differently."

"We used to say unorthodox."

"Carefully," Burden corrected him.

"Unorthodox. But it has no meaning to me anymore. It has no context. It's nothing."

"But you understand?"

"Well, you see, it just doesn't have any meaning."

Jesus. Burden saw the edges of difficulty. But for all the man's psychosis, his reputation was impeccable. It occurred to him that it was he, Burden, who was now having trouble with unorthodoxy. Here he was, insisting on a frame of reference from a madman. Well, here was a lesson, wasn't it. He shouldn't be surprised.

"Is it tonight?" the man asked.

"No."

"Then I don't want to talk about it. Do you still go to pray?"

"Yes."

"Churches? Mosques? Synagogues?"

"Yes."

"Why?"

"For all the same reasons."

"You don't see things differently now?"

"Things? Yes, things are always changing, so I see things differently. But I don't see myself differently. So I still go."

"If the stories I've heard are true," the man said, "I don't know why you still go."

Burden didn't say anything.

Silence.

"But then," the man said, "what does it matter, really? I don't think it matters at all."

They looked at each other across the dusk of the small room, silhouette to silhouette.

Burden stood slowly, suddenly feeling as if night covered the globe, as if, while he had been in this puggy little motel room, all of the time zones had melted away into darkness everywhere and morning was erased from the vocabulary of man.

"When I come back," he said, "I'll be coming to get you to do it."

Chapter 26

When Burden finally got there, Titus was waiting for him on the veranda. Burden was hot and sweaty, having been let out by his van crew on Cielo Canyon Road and then having climbed through the woods to the back of the orchard. He was dressed much as he'd been in Mexico twenty-four hours earlier when Titus had left him, faded jeans and a baggy, chocolate brown linen shirt.

They went across the courtyard past the fountain and the atrium hallway and into Titus's office, where Rita was waiting.

Their introduction was awkward. Rita was wary and standoffish and making no effort to disguise it, and Burden was sweaty and clearly pressed for time. Rita was civil enough to offer him a glass of water, which he accepted. When she returned with it he thanked her, took a long drink of it, and dove right into his explanation.

"The first order of business for us," he said, standing at the end of the table, the windows overlooking the dark orchard behind him, "is to find out how many people Luquín actually has working with him on this operation. In setting up this meeting, they'll have to put their communications and security people into play. We'll watch and count. That's all."

He took another drink of water and a deep breath. He looked at his watch and went on.

"We're at a huge disadvantage here," he said. "We can't lose sight of that. And we only have one shot at getting this count—"

"Explain the disadvantage," Rita interrupted.

Burden looked at her. Titus thought he could see him swallowing his irritation. Then he nodded.

"This is a kind of operation that Luquín has refined over years of experience," he said. "His people have probably been here several weeks doing advance work, which is how your house got its electronic surveillance. His operational point man is probably Jorge Macias, a former intelligence officer in the Mexican Federal Directorate of National Security. For years Macias secretly informed on intelligence matters to Luquín. And Macias has connections in the U.S. He's probably got four or five teams on this operation, all compartmentalized, all perfectly used to Macias's style of doing business. His people are rested, well rehearsed, and wired.

"Now, here's the way our side looks: I've been brought in at the last minute and have no intelligence on the ground. I'm having to build two crews, literally overnight, by flying people in here from half a dozen different cities, and I'm working against the clock. My people are excellent, but there are only a few of them. They're stretched as thin as it's possible to stretch. They've had to lose sleep to get here, and they won't be able to slow down or stop until this is finished. They're working under intense pressure that Luquín's people don't have to contend with because Luquín's the one who's creating the pressure. He's dictated the rules—as we've discussed," he said again to Titus, "and he's set a schedule. If you, and therefore we, don't keep to his schedule, there'll be consequences. We've already seen a tragic example of that."

All of this was laid out in a smooth, clipped monologue, and although he was polite, Titus could see Burden's impatience at being asked to spell it out.

Titus glanced at Rita, who was sitting halfway down the table. A glass of Scotch sat on a magazine in front of her. She was tense and concentrating on Burden as if she were reading his mind and if she let up even a little bit, she'd lose the link.

Burden looked at her. He was waiting to see if his response had satisfied her, but Titus thought he saw more than that, too. He remembered the portraits of women in Burden's study. The man appreciated women, and that sensibility didn't go away, apparently, because of a little stress and danger. Titus glanced at Rita. She understood what was happening. Handsome women learned to understand that look from early girlhood.

"Let's talk about what's going to happen in the next few hours," Burden said. "When you leave here, Titus, you'll be pretty much on your own. Obviously we can't afford to wire you. No use to bug the Rover, they're going to separate you from that. And even though our chase cars will be with you every moment, they're going to be giving you a wide berth. They won't risk detection, even if they lose sight of you."

"What?" Rita gasped. "You can't send him to this meeting like that."

"We have to," Burden said calmly, and then looked at Titus for help in dealing with her.

Rita was looking at Titus, too, her eyes flashing with anger and a kind of fear that she wasn't even admitting to herself.

"Think about it, Rita," Titus said. "Luquín wants the money. I control the money. Believe me, I'm in no danger from Luquín. In fact, I may be the only person not in danger. My safety's not an issue here."

"Then what the hell is the issue?"

"Avoiding detection," Burden said. "We can*not* be discovered. The only—I repeat—the only slight advantage we have in this operation is that they don't know we're here. They have no idea that anyone's on to them."

Rita stared at him. "I understand the rationale," she said evenly, "but this isn't a tactical exercise to me. This is my husband meeting alone with a killer."

Burden bent his head and wiped his sweaty forehead on the shoulder of his shirtsleeve.

"Mrs. Cain"—he locked his eyes on her for emphasis—"to be brutally honest, sooner or later you're more likely to be in danger than your husband."

"We've talked about her going away, a safe house somewhere," Titus interjected, "and—"

"And it's a stupid suggestion," Rita interrupted, cutting her eyes at Burden. "And I wouldn't do it in a thousand years. Or sooner or later. Forget it."

"Look," Burden said, "I know that this seems . . . outrageously risky to you, Mrs. Cain, I know that. But think of this: Everything you see during the next few days is going to be startling to you. This is a world you've never even imagined before, but it's the world I live in. I'm intimate with it. I see it differently from you. I read the developing events from an entirely different perspective." He paused. "To be frank, Mrs. Cain, you have to trust me. You really don't have any other choice."

"I don't know if I believe that," she said quickly.

"Rita, García and I have already been through this," Titus said. "In detail. This is the way we're going. It's too late, and far, far too risky—in terms of other people's lives—for us to change courses now."

"In detail," she said. "That's great." She turned to Burden.

"And what happens if your people are spotted? What kind of a position does that put Titus in then? What preparations have you made to deal with something like that? You've just spent the last twenty minutes explaining to us how you're at a huge disadvantage in . . . in this . . . operation, and now you're wanting me to believe that Titus is going to go off somewhere and talk with this . . . insane killer, and you want me to believe that he . . . that he's not in danger? Do you think I'm an idiot?"

Titus studied Rita closely. He could tell that she had reached a point where it was difficult for her to distinguish between her anger and her fear. It seemed that the two emotions were now so closely intertwined within her that they had become an entirely new and hybrid passion. Even as strong-minded and self-confident as she was, she had always trusted his judgment in most high-stakes situations. But it seemed that she was finding this one hard to go along with.

Fighting tears, she took another drink, but Titus could tell that she was swallowing a lot more than Scotch.

In the silence that followed, Burden ran his fingers through his hair, gave the moment an opportunity to settle. To give him credit, he seemed genuinely empathetic to her predicament.

"I can't undo your misfortune, Mrs. Cain," he said. "I can't make the danger go away or disarm the evil you're encountering. It would be cruel for me to pretend otherwise."

Rita looked away, and Burden glanced at Titus for direction. Titus nodded for him to go on.

"You need to understand," Burden said, addressing Titus, "that even if we lose visual contact with you, we're going to know where you are at every moment. It's not like you're dropping off the edge of the earth."

Standing, he pulled a small plastic packet of breath fresheners out of his pocket and came down the other side of the table from Rita. He sat next to Titus, putting the plastic packet on the table in front of him.

"Just before I came in here," he said, looking at both of them, "we pretty much confirmed where Luquín is staying."

"Pretty much?" Titus asked.

"We haven't actually seen him on the property. By intercepting encrypted cell phone transmissions in Spanish, we've narrowed it down to three houses. Now two of those have been eliminated. The one we're looking at is owned by a divorcée who divides her time between Austin and Santa Fe. When she's not here, she lets friends use it. This month she gave it to a woman from Laredo, who passed it on through a succession of her own friends. We lost the thread, but we think this is it.

"Also, one of my two mobile units is picking up cell phone action from another mobile unit—with very strong encryption—to Mexico City. But we're not having a lot of luck unraveling the encryption, and we're having trouble nailing the exact vehicle. We think it's Macias's people, and we think we can confirm that during your meeting tonight."

"And then what?" Titus asked.

"In order to coordinate a move on Luquín, we have to know where all of his people are at all times. With the first tactical move that we make against his people, there's a risk they'll be able to set off an instant signaling mechanism. Then it's all over. A special team that travels with Luquín—probably those guys you saw the other night—will quickly spirit him away. Unless our people are in place to deal with it, Luquín will be gone."

Without further explanation, Burden opened the packet of breath fresheners and dumped out the little white pellets onto the table. Then he removed the top of the box, and from the inside of the plastic container he carefully slipped out a thin sheet of plastic that looked like waxed paper.

Nestled inside the paper was a variety of irregularly shaped blotches roughly half a centimeter in diameter, some cinnamon brown, some slightly darker than flesh, some ginger. Burden pulled a pair of tweezers out of his pocket and carefully lifted one of the objects. It was translucent, thin as cellophane.

"Moles and liver spots," he said. "They're adhesive on one side and won't loosen with sweat or water, but they're easy to peel off. So thin you have to know they're there to feel them. Designed by a dermatologist"—he laid the fake mole down on one side of the unfolded plastic sheet—"and a microfluids engineer. They're actually a by-product of something else, but this not-quite-there stage of the development turned out to be perfect for this kind of thing.

"They're little transmitters—for a special kind of receiver—and they'll transmit up to ten days and about twenty miles. We want you to put these on the backs of your hands and forearms. When you've found the right place, peel one off and leave it."

Titus was bent over the table, looking closely at the moles. "And what are the right places?" he asked.

"If you can get them on another person, that's best. Otherwise, leave them in a vehicle if it looks like it's one of theirs— say, one that's got electronic equipment or in some other way gives you the idea it's something they'll use again. If they take you someplace that looks like it's a permanent staging area, not a motel room, for example, then leave a spot. In short, leave them anywhere you think will be critical for us to know about . . . when the time comes.

"Notice," Burden added, pointing at the spots with the tweezers, "that there are light and dark moles. They send different signals. Leave one kind on vehicles, the other kind on people. That way we'll know what we're looking at. Since you won't be able to see the difference in the dark, you can put one kind on each hand so you can keep them straight."

"How many of them are there?" Titus asked.

"Only eight, unfortunately."

"They've got to be expensive."

"You're looking at fifty-three thousand dollars' worth of blotches. And they're worth every dime of it."

"Then that's all you want him to do?" Rita interjected. "Just leave these things . . . around."

"That and, of course, get what he can out of the conversation." He looked at Rita. "This is essential," he said. "The information is invaluable."

"So is he," she said evenly, and she looked as if for an extra dime she would have given Burden a piece of her mind, too, but she held her tongue. Barely.

Burden didn't react or respond. "One of them will send a slightly different signal," he said to Titus, and probed through the blotches, selecting one of the lighter ones with a black dot in the center of it. "It's yours. We'll put it on your upper arm and get it out of your way. That'll leave you seven to leave behind."

"Okay, then we'd better get started," Titus said, putting both arms on the table. "I want to see how the things work, and there's not that much time left."

Chapter 27

Following Luquín's instructions, Titus steered his Range Rover through the gates of his property at exactly twelve-thirty and started down the winding half mile of private drive to Cielo Canyon Road. He had been told to make his way to Westlake Drive and then go south to the Toro Canyon intersection, where he would receive further instructions.

It didn't happen that way.

After he rounded the second steep bend of the descending drive, a man stepped out of the dark margin of the woods into the path of Titus's headlights and waved him down. When Titus stopped, the man came up quickly and opened his door.

"Please get out, Mr. Cain," he said in heavily accented English. Titus put the Rover in park and did as he was told, leaving the engine idling. The man got into the Rover and drove away without another word, leaving Titus standing in the middle of the paved road in the dark.

As the engine of his Rover receded and the buzzing sounds of lacewings filled the darkness, Titus heard the snap of a branch and turned around to see the black smear of another figure stepping out of the woods.

"Mr. Cain," the man said, approaching him. There was no flashlight. "Please put these on," the man said, and handed Titus a pair of goggles, which he slipped on. They had night-vision lenses, and the world became apple green with high-lights of leached turquoise. He could now see that the man was wearing the same device. He was dressed in street clothes, his tight-fitting knit polo shirt revealing a trim stomach and mus-cular arms. The handgun at his waist was large.

They stepped off the road and into the woods, the man in front of him. They moved downhill through the cedar and un-derbrush, not hurrying but carefully picking their way through the dense cedar thickets, their dress loafers a distinct disad-vantage on the rough terrain.

In just a few minutes they came to Cielo Canyon Road and stopped short in the edge of the woods. A car passed them as they stood only a few feet into the brush. Then another. The third car slowed, a Lincoln Navigator. It stopped, and Titus was hustled out of the woods and into the car, which started driving away before the doors were even closed.

He was in the seat behind the driver, with the man sitting next to him.

"The glasses," said the man sitting beside him, and Titus removed the goggles and handed them over.

Titus looked at the driver. The back of the head meant nothing to him. When he glanced at the man beside him, the guy was looking at him. Mexican.

A scanner attached to the dash in the front beeped and crackled, and a satellite map, crisp and clear, was mounted be-side that. As if sensing Titus's interest, the driver leaned for-ward and turned off the monitor. Sighing heavily, Titus worked off a mole from the back of his left hand and stuck it to the front of the seat between his legs.

In just a few turns they pulled into a housing development

and drove through the streets until they came to the back side of the development, where two houses were under construction.

"Get out," said the guy sitting next to him. They both got out, and the guy came around holding something in his arms. "Take off your clothes," he said.

Titus undressed, and when he was down to his shoes and underwear the guy said, "All of it." Titus kicked off his shoes, peeled off his socks, and shed his underwear. Part of his instructions from Luquín had been to leave all identification behind. Apparently they were going to drive off and leave his clothes and shoes right where they were.

"You work out?" the guy asked, handing Titus the clothes he had been holding. The driver in the Navigator snorted.

"Yeah," Titus said.

"Weights?"

"Yeah," Titus said. He put on the pants and buttoned them and then the shirt. From what he could see in the light from the opened door, it was some kind of service repairman's uniform, putty gray. After he buttoned up the shirt, the guy dropped a pair of shoes on the ground.

"Elevens?"

"Right." Titus bent down to put on the first shoe and lost his balance. Staggering, he reached out reflexively to the guy, who reacted the same, catching him with a beefy shoulder to keep him from falling. Quickly Titus righted himself and then finished putting on his shoes. He had managed to leave a mole from his right hand on the back side of the man's upper right arm.

When they got back into the SUV, the guy handed Titus a black hood.

"Put it on," the man said.

Titus slipped it over his head and immediately had to fight

claustrophobia. It wasn't just the feel of the close-fitting cloth. It was all of it, the whole menacing unfamiliarity of it.

He tried to keep track of the turns, but it was impossible; besides, he suspected the driver was doubling back and retracing his course much of the time. After Titus had shed his clothes, the two men began talking in Spanish. They must've known that Titus couldn't understand them because they didn't seem to be cautious or stinting in their conversation. Then the car hit what must have been a stretch of highway, because the Navigator sped up to a sustained speed. The conversation stopped.

Titus lost track of time on the highway, and the monotony of the constant speed and the lack of conversation conspired to create a strange timelessness. Then suddenly the car began to decelerate quickly, and without pulling off to the side of the highway, it stopped.

The doors flew open and Titus was hustled out and shoved into another vehicle—another SUV, from the feel of it. Again he found himself in the backseat. Quickly, because he didn't know how long he would be in the car, he left another mole on the seat between his legs. The car turned off the highway and accelerated quickly, roaring over a paved but undulating road, maybe a county road.

Another turn. A gravel road that climbed. Switchbacks. Slowing. A stop.

The SUV's doors opened: the driver and only one other. Different men, he guessed. Somebody took him out and, holding his arm above the elbow, guided him over gravel, then grass or weeds, and finally a couple of steps to a porch. Wooden porch. Into a front door.

By pretending to be more uncertain of his movement than he really was, he was able to reach out often with searching, fumbling hands and to touch his escort more often than he would have done otherwise. Between the car and the porch, he managed to leave a mole on this man also.

Inside, he was told to stand still and wait for instructions, then he heard the man leave and the door close behind him. He could tell someone was in the room with him, and he could smell a cold fireplace. The wooden floor underneath his feet creaked. Old. Deteriorating.

"Take off the hood, Mr. Cain."

Titus recognized Luquín's voice.

Chapter 28

He took off the hood and found himself in a one-room shack. It was lighted by a kerosene lantern that sat on an overturned bucket in front of a caved-in fireplace. The light was harsh around the lantern, giving way quickly to shadows that waited anxiously around the edges of the room. The odor of kerosene mixed with the stench of rat urine and rotting wood.

"Sit down," Luquín said. He was sitting to one side of the lantern in a canvas deck chair. His shadow, thrown against a near wall, was broken by the angles of a corner. The seat he offered Titus was another overturned bucket. He was dressed in very nice street clothes (Titus could see the silk in the trousers), which made him look entirely out of place in his surroundings, as if he'd stepped off the back lot into a movie set. They were alone in the room.

"You wanted to talk," Luquín said. He was relaxed, his arms resting on the arms of the chair, his hands dangling loosely over the ends.

Titus stepped over and sat on the bucket, five feet from Luquín. He looked hyperreal. Knowing what he had done to Charlie had altered Titus's perception of him.

"You had Charlie Thrush killed."

"Yes."

The monosyllable, so readily given, so free of guilt, was disarming.

"Do you know how he was killed?"

"No." Said with the same weightlessness of conscience.

"You don't know."

"No." Luquín twisted his head in irritation. "What do you want, Mr. Cain?"

"You shouldn't have killed him," Titus said.

Luquín raised a finger and wagged it slowly at Titus. "Be careful. You are up to your ass in shit here, and sinking."

"Why?"

"I told you," Luquín said, "that I would decide who died and when. And so I did. That surprises you? What in the world did you think I meant when I said that?"

A beetle flew in, heavily, like a miniature aircraft, and smacked into the globe of the lantern. It fell at Luquín's feet, spinning around in circles on the dusty floor with a broken wing. Luquín didn't even notice.

"What did that accomplish, killing him?"

"Did it change the way you thought of your situation?"

A rhetorical question. Titus didn't answer.

Luquín's expression soured, and he nodded. "That's what I accomplished."

Luquín's manner dripped arrogance, and Titus hated it that Luquín thought that this was the way to play him.

"Have one of your people come in with a telephone," Titus said, "and I'll put through the first ten million right now. And I'll make the next payment of twenty-one million within twenty-four hours, rather than the forty-eight you've instructed."

Luquín's eyes brightened, but even as he nodded affably in

gratified surprise, his brow puckered in skepticism. Titus could see him formulating a question and then instantly correcting himself and moving his chess piece to another square.

Without taking his eyes off Titus, he lifted his foot and crushed the beetle with a sharp pop of its crusty shell.

"Roque," he said in a voice no louder than the one he was using to speak to Titus. There were stirrings outside in the darkness, the door to the shack opened, and a man came in and stood behind Titus.

"*Tú celular,*" Luquín said, lifting his chin at Titus. The man unsnapped a cell phone from a holder at his waist and handed it to Titus.

Titus dialed Lack Paley's number and listened to it ring. Luquín was watching him like a lizard, motionless, processing. Paley answered.

Titus told him to move the money to Cavatino first thing in the morning, the moment the bank opened. He told him to get the second investment ready. Lack knew the drill, and though he didn't know what was behind it all, he knew something extraordinary was going on. That was that.

After Paley had hung up, Titus pretended to be listening. Before Roque had handed him the phone, Titus had managed to work off one of the lighter moles and was holding it between the forefinger and thumb of his right hand. He held the phone in his left. As soon as he had the mole the way he wanted it, he concluded his feigned exchange with Paley, punched the disconnect button, and with his right hand handed the phone to the waiting man. The mole stuck like a leech. The man returned it to the clip at his waist.

"That's it," Titus said to Luquín.

"We'll see." Luquín was studying Titus. He had lighted a cigarette, and as he smoked he seemed to be trying to come to some kind of conclusion.

"But," Titus added, "if anyone else dies, you won't get another dime."

Luquín's face changed as if Titus had reached out and slapped him. His surprise was genuine, and so was the gall that replaced his enigmatic expression.

"You don't have any fucking idea what you're saying," he said. "I really don't think you are capable of understanding what that would mean."

"If I let you . . . if I bargain with you over lives, I won't be able to live with myself," Titus said. "And I know that you don't understand that. But that's the way it is. It's called normal. It's not extraordinary. It's what decent people do."

"Decent people," Luquín mused, nodding. "Yes. Well, Mr. Cain, it has been my experience that there is just a hair—a very thin hair—between decent people and animals. I have learned that what works with animals, works with decent people, too."

"Fear."

"Yes, of course. Fear."

Titus listened to the faint hiss of the lantern in the following silence. Even though the windows of the shack were open, the heat was oppressive, and the acrid smoke of Luquín's cigarette mingled with the decaying odors of the old shack. Titus was sweating under his uniform, and he saw that Luquín was sweating now, too, almost suddenly.

"You are a stupid man, Mr. Cain," Luquín said.

"Within forty-eight hours you can have thirty-one million dollars in your accounts, via Cavatino," Titus said. "But if another person dies, I'll go straight to the FBI with everything. I'll have them hunt your ass all the way to Patagonia. And if they don't find you . . . I will."

Luquín flinched, and his right arm shot up as he thrust his upper body forward in his deck chair and pointed the first and second fingers at Titus, the cigarette smoldering between them. The swaggering affability was gone, and Titus saw rage. He saw Luquín's beast, a thing that had hungers that could be satisfied only if someone grieved.

Like a silent image in a wax museum, Luquín remained frozen in midgesture, his arm outstretched, his eyes fixed in midheat. His words, whatever they might have been, remained in his throat. Only the cigarette, trembling slightly, smoke waffling up from its ember, betrayed his reality.

"Do not," he managed to say in a voice made hoarse by his extraordinary effort at self-restraint, "presume anything with me, Mr. Cain." His breath was squeezed to a whisper. "You do not threaten me."

Luquín's eyes flicked to the side, and in an instant Titus remembered that Roque was still standing just a step back. The butt of Roque's gun caught him at the edge of his eye in the right temple. He heard the sound of flesh splitting between metal and bone and felt his head fling back before he went out.

Unfortunately he was out only seconds, stunned, really. He could've gotten up sooner, but the lantern kept trying to go out, and for reasons he didn't understand he seemed to have gained several hundred pounds and had to get his legs in just the right position to be able to lift himself.

He heard Luquín barking angrily in Spanish, and then Roque was on him again, and Titus covered up his head to ward off another blow. Suddenly he was horrified that he would be beaten to death. But there was no second blow.

"*La capucha*," Roque said, standing over him, and Titus felt the black hood hit him in the head.

Chapter 29

There was a driver and a camera operator with a thermal infrared videocamera in each of the four surveillance cars, all local talent. The local talent was a necessity. So much of chase surveillance was about anticipating moves, and anticipation required an intimate knowledge of the geography and the traffic ways. Burden was in the fifth vehicle, a van, where he sat in the back with two technicians monitoring three types of mapping computer screens and four live television screens picking up the cameras from each of the cars.

Burden never even met the chase people he was working with, but the driver and the two technicians in his own van were regulars that he used on these kinds of operations, flying them in from different locations.

From the moment Titus was picked up outside the gates of his property, Burden watched LorGuide monitors that registered the feedback from the moles Titus was carrying for distribution. Green dot signals registered the moles put on people, the yellow dots registered moles left on vehicles.

Using a complicated tag relay technique, the chase team was able to keep visual contact with the vehicle carrying Titus, even when he was taken into the thousand-acre greenbelt of City Park, nestled into a large U-shaped bend of Lake Austin. It was on the isolated City Park Road that Burden watched his monitors as Titus was switched to another vehicle, which then left the park's only paved road and headed out into the dense cedar brakes.

But it was also on City Park Road that the chase cars had the good luck to spot Macias's own surveillance van. They dropped off a marksman in the woods when the van entered a loop that would bring it out the same way it went in. From his blind, the marksman shot the van's right rear wheel with a paint ball filled with a black dye that popped up on the LorGuides as a bright raspberry dot.

For the two hours that Titus was in the hands of Macias's people, Burden's teams never stopped moving, dropping off cars and picking up others to avoid any vehicle being seen more than once by the Macias surveillance. It was a complex operation, and by the time Titus was dropped off at an apartment complex overlooking Loop 360, Burden's people had a good idea of the size of Macias's tactical team. Many of the vehicles and people had been tagged by Titus, and their positions could be monitored constantly.

It was two-forty in the morning as Titus guided the Rover up his private drive, past the place where the Rover had been taken away from him, and went on to the wrought-iron gate. He punched the remote under his dash, the gates swung open, and he drove through.

Suddenly a man stepped out in front of his headlights, at the far edge of their reach, and stood in the middle of the drive. Titus's heart slammed so hard, he lost his breath. No, he didn't want any more of this. And then: Had something happened?

Had they gotten in somehow? The figure grew brighter and brighter until he realized it was García Burden.

Titus stopped, and Burden came around and opened the passenger door and climbed in.

"Shit!" he said when he saw Titus's face in the dash lights. "What happened?"

"I pissed off Luquín and his man banged me with the butt of his gun. I've been bleeding like a pig, but I'm okay except for a hell of a headache."

Burden was already past it. "After you clean up I need to talk with you. I need to hear the details."

Rita conquered her every instinct to explode and instead helped him clean up the cut. Though she quickly realized that it wasn't a really serious wound, she stubbornly insisted that he needed stitches. But when Titus flatly refused to go to the emergency room, she cobbled together a butterfly stitch of her own manufacture that she said would do the job but would leave a scar as big as a third eyebrow. After he put on clean clothes, they called Burden, who had gone to the guest house to talk to Herrin and his mobile crews over the radios and secure phones.

They sat at the island in the kitchen, Titus, Rita, and Burden, with papers and radios and telephones scattered out in front of them on the black granite counter. Rita had made a pot of strong French roast coffee to help them stay alert.

Rita, Titus discovered, had actually listened to the whole thing in the guest house with Herrin, an experience that she said she had found fascinating and horrifying, but ultimately reassuring. The subdued control with which Burden and his teams had handled the hectic two hours was a lesson in a new kind of reality for her. Somehow—irrationally, she admitted—

it had made her feel as though there might be some way to get through this after all.

Burden was focused on the debriefing and repeatedly took Titus through his trip from the moment he was taken from the Rover to the moment he was returned to it. He asked Titus about the things he heard, of movements he heard, of what he sensed. What about accents? What about personalities? He asked how many people Titus could count, and then he took him over what they had seen on their monitors. He asked Titus for his guesses about this and that, and then he told Titus his own perspective of the same guesses.

They went over Titus's conversation with Luquín, and Burden asked about Luquín's manner, the way he sounded when he said certain things, the expression on his face, the set of his eyes. How did he choose his words?

Finally there was a pause in the debriefing. Burden checked his messages on his phone, looking at the readout without saying anything. Titus glanced at Rita, trying and failing to mask his anxiety. Rita caught his expression and frowned.

Burden cleared his screen, looked up, and paused.

"Okay," he said, "let's talk about it. Whatever it is. There's no time for being subtle. I don't have time to decipher signals. Bring it out in the open."

Titus shifted in his chair.

"The whole thing tonight," he said, rubbing his face with his hands, flinching when he touched the cut that he'd forgotten about. "He's running a pretty damned tight operation, isn't he."

"He always does. You can't afford many mistakes with this guy."

"I'll be honest," Titus said. "It doesn't look to me like you've got what it's going to take to do this."

Burden kept his eyes on Titus, but his expression was unreadable.

"It looks to me like the disadvantages that you outlined for us earlier add up to a damned big handicap. Too big for you to overcome."

"I've already told you our odds aren't good," Burden said. "So that shouldn't be a surprise. And if you're judging the battle by what you see on the battlefield, you're making a mistake."

"What I see," Titus said, "is a guy who's got a well-oiled machine operated by disciplined and brutal men. What I see is that he came prepared to win, and he brought men who'll do anything to make sure that he does."

"That's what you've seen," Burden said.

"Yeah."

"Well, in this business what you see isn't a good gauge of the reality. The whole plan of engagement—on both sides—is designed to be unseen. It's what you don't see that you need to worry about."

"That sounds good, García, but I can't make my decisions based on what I don't see."

"Keep this in mind," Burden said. "Those people who handled you tonight have been here a month or more, and during that time you saw nothing, knew nothing. They came into your house, many times, planting bugs, familiarizing themselves with your security system, sniffing you out, and you didn't have the slightest idea about it. Until Luquín himself told you what he'd done.

"And don't forget this: What you saw of Luquín's operation tonight you saw only because of what we did, my people and you. We drew him out, and he didn't even know what was happening. As powerful as he is, we were able to do that. Right now we're processing that information in our computers, and after I add in what I learned from you during the last hour or so, we'll have a pretty good picture of the number of people we're up against."

Burden took a sip of his coffee and glanced at Rita before he spoke again.

"You haven't done the wrong thing, Titus. Don't start second-guessing yourself now. We sure as hell don't need Ruby Ridge or Waco tactics here. We've come a long way in a short time in understanding how to deal with the Luquíns of the future. What you're seeing are the rough edges. The slicker stuff you won't see at all. We don't want spectacle. We want invisibility . . . and silence."

He paused. "One other thing: Remember our conversation in San Miguel? Once we've committed to this thing, there's no turning back. I'm holding you to that. We're sleeping with the serpent now, Titus. The only way we're going to live through the night is to be very still and very quiet until it's dead. If we wake it, it'll kill us."

FRIDAY

The Fourth Day

Chapter 30

An hour after Titus collapsed into bed and instantly fell asleep, despite the adrenaline high of his ordeal, his assistant, Carla Elster, rolled over in her bed several valleys north and looked out the window at the pale dawn. The radio alarm had just come on, and she listened to Bob Edwards on NPR intone something about a congressional hearing. She let herself stay in bed until the end of the story, which couldn't have been more than three minutes long, and then threw back the covers.

She reached for her cotton robe on the chair beside the bed, slipped it on, and tied the sash in a slipknot. She padded into the bathroom, where she washed her face, brushed her hair, and then brushed her teeth with her left hand on her hip as she examined her face in the mirror and assessed the impact of the years.

Telling herself to hell with that, she turned and went out into the hallway and down the stairs to the kitchen, where the coffee would just be finishing. She poured herself a cup, added half-and-half from the refrigerator, and carried the mug with her out the front door to get the paper.

Back inside, she sat at the kitchen table and read the headlines of *The New York Times*. She couldn't concentrate on the articles because her mind kept going back to Titus, as it had throughout the night. She couldn't stop worrying about him. Something was seriously wrong. She didn't believe the bad investment story, of course. But the most remarkable thing about it was that whatever was happening, Titus thought it was necessary to ruin his own reputation to cover it up. That must have killed him, and it pained her deeply that he felt he had to do that.

And those guys with the headphones, were they checking for electronic bugs? That's what it looked like, and Titus had completely ignored her pointed questions about it. Even more curious was his immediate insistence that his financial worries were personal. That made her suspect they weren't.

She changed into jogging clothes, still thinking of Titus and Rita. Although Rita's disturbed behavior was understandable, given the death of Charlie Thrush and the news about Titus's financial troubles, she seemed more agitated and abrupt than distraught.

At the bottom of the stairs she stopped by the secretary's desk in the front hallway to pick up her epinephrine injector, which she kept in a small sack and wore on a string around her neck when she jogged. She checked her watch as she headed down the front sidewalk and then hit the street, taking off at a slow lope.

There were sections of West Lake Hills, an incorporated town on Austin's southwest side, that felt almost rural, their narrow, winding lanes climbing the heavily wooded hills and then twisting down into the valleys. The homes themselves were often hidden from the lanes, and it wasn't unusual to jog for many blocks without seeing any of the homes at all.

Carla's route was a secluded course, and she looked forward to her peaceful early morning regimen. She liked the time alone, because once she got to CaiText it was nonstop until she returned home exhausted in the evening.

Twenty minutes into her run, as she rounded a corner at an intersection, a man was warming up at the entrance to his drive that led deeper into the woods. He fell in behind her for half a block back as she turned into a smaller street. Another half block ahead of her a woman emerged from a hedge flanking the front sidewalk of one of the homes and began jogging in front of her, though at a slower pace.

Just as Carla was about to overtake her, she heard the man coming up fast behind her. She slowed just as she was approaching the woman so that the three of them wouldn't be three abreast on the small lane as the man passed.

But he didn't pass. The woman whirled around and embraced Carla and spun her around. The man was on her instantly, stuffing a ball of foam into her mouth, and then the two of them literally carried her into the dense woods that crowded up against the lane.

Stunned, Carla didn't even know how much she struggled, but she was aware of fighting, though she was soon pinned down. The woman pulled down the neck of Carla's sports bra, and the man produced a net bag that emitted a sound that horrified her: a constant, quavering buzz.

Carefully the man placed the opening of the bag next to her left upper breast, and she went berserk. But she just wasn't strong enough. The hornets stung her repeatedly before the man moved the net down to her bare stomach, where he held it firmly against her as they stung her again.

That was all.

Then the man and woman simply held her. The man looked at his watch, and they all waited. The welts on her breast and stomach burned fiercely, as though hot coals had been spilled on her, and because she was already sweaty, they itched wildly.

They lay there, the three of them, in the tall grass a few yards into the woods, in a weird, mad embrace, waiting. What was happening? Why were they doing this? She could smell the man's aftershave, and she could feel the woman's soft breasts against her bare shoulder. The mind-numbing why of it was as stupefying as was the terror of waiting for the allergic reaction to kick in.

This was incomprehensible.

She tried to see their faces, but she couldn't. Why wouldn't they let her see their faces? If they were trying to kill her, what would it matter? Kill her?! Was that . . . could that really be their intent? That's what they were doing, but was that what they meant to do?

That made no more sense than if one of them were a butterfly.

Her allergy was acute, so the symptoms struck quickly. She began to feel her throat close up, and then her lungs seemed to collapse, as if they couldn't retain enough oxygen. She felt the quiverings of panic and coughed through the foam ball. Her stomach began to cramp, long, hard contractions of her muscles. She felt light-headed, and her heart revved up to an incredible speed.

She felt one of them remove the epinephrine injector from around her neck. Were they going to save her after all?

Suddenly she felt as if time had accelerated at an incredible velocity. She knew she had twenty minutes at most. The couple embraced her like oddly impassioned friends. The idea of how the three of them might look to someone passing by flashed through her mind. Beyond strange. She felt their warm flesh against her own. So intimate. She could hear them breathing. Or was that her?

As she began to fade in and out, it seemed that they loosened their grip on her. Was that just because she was losing consciousness, or were they actually doing that? Inexplicably she thought of her ex-husband with an angerless regret. She thought of the girls. They would be all right. She had gotten through the tough years with them, and they were leveling out. The rest of it was going to be okay. Nathan. Bless his heart. He would be dumbfounded.

There was a moment of brilliant, mind-blinding panic, and she fought her abductors. And she fought her departure. Of all the silly things to happen to her . . . Who would've thought it would be something like this, something so profoundly, utterly mystifying?

Well, she was glad she'd taken the dark sable brown suit to the cleaners. That's the one the girls would choose. But Nathan would have to think of it being at the cleaners when they couldn't find it in her closet.

Suddenly her head was bursting, and she felt nauseated. And she was so hot!

Chapter 31

Titus was shaving, a towel wrapped around his waist. His neck was stiff despite the long shower he'd taken to try to loosen it up. A cup of coffee sat on the countertop by his shaving mug, along with a half-eaten piece of toast. The outside of his eyebrow was swollen, and the flesh around it was purple. He looked out the glass wall to the pool, feeling thickheaded. The four hours of sleep had felt exactly like four hours of sleep: not enough.

Nevertheless, he had to admit the conversation with García Burden in the small hours of the morning had been fascinating. Burden had made good points about Titus's concerns that he had done the wrong thing, but he hadn't really offered anything concrete. Titus still had that uneasy feeling that his decision to work with Burden was going to result in yet more tragedy. But, as with Burden, he couldn't come up with any specific, factual data to justify his anxiety.

He washed the lather off his face and walked into his closet to get his clothes. After dressing, he felt a little less fuzzy headed as he made his way along the atrium to the kitchen. Rita was again sitting at the island, nursing a glass of orange juice.

"You want anything besides that piece of toast?" she asked. She, too, looked exhausted.

"No, I'm fine," he said, dumping his cold coffee down the sink. He turned around and leaned against the counter.

"How's your head feeling?" Rita asked.

"Lousy."

"Let me see." She got up from the bar stool and went over to him. He waited while she examined him. She was close, and he could see the blond fuzz along her temples, smell her shampoo.

"The swelling's going to be with you for a while," she said, returning to the island.

The front gate intercom buzzed behind him on the counter panel, and he reached over and pushed the button.

"Yes?"

"This is Deputy Seams with the Travis County Sheriff's Office. This Mr. Cain?"

"Yeah. Yes, it is."

"Wonder if you could open the gate for me, Mr. Cain?"

"Uh, sure," Titus said, frowning and looking over at Rita as he hit the gate button.

Rita was motionless, her questioning eyes locked on him.

"I don't have any idea," he said, and headed for the door to the veranda. Rita followed him, and they both stood in the morning shade and watched the sheriff's car come slowly over the rise on the paved drive, seeming to take too long to curve around and approach the turn that brought him behind the high hedges. He pulled up behind Herrin's trucks and turned off the engine.

Oddly, the deputy took off his regulation summer western hat and laid it on the seat of the patrol car before he opened the door. As he got out, the scratch of radio transmissions came with him and then went silent as he closed the door. He looked around as he walked over to the veranda where Titus and Rita were waiting at the edge of the flagstones, under the morning glory vines. Mourning doves soughed in the rows of peach trees in the orchard, their cooing carrying surprisingly far in the morning stillness.

He bobbed his head at Rita and said, "Ma'am," and then reached out his hand to Titus. "Ward Seams," he said, dropping the "Deputy."

"I'm Titus Cain. This's my wife, Rita."

Now the deputy bobbed his head at her again and shook hands with her, too. He looked at Titus.

"I'm sorry," he said, "but I've got some bad news for you, Mr. Cain. I understand Ms. Carla Elster is your personal assistant?"

Titus could only nod. The only thing that remained for him to know was how it had happened.

"Ms. Elster is dead, Mr. Cain."

Rita gasped, then gasped again, two expurgations of air that sounded as if she'd been hit in the stomach. Titus couldn't respond at all.

Seams talked slowly, carefully, as if he were trying to coax a frightened animal.

"She was found just about an hour ago near her home," he said. "She was lying by the roadside. Been jogging. EMS people tell us it looks like she died of allergic reaction to insect stings."

Incredibly, Rita gasped again. Seams threw a look at her again and then went on.

"She was wearing identification," he explained. "EMS took her to Seton downtown. I went by the house and neighbors told me her two daughters were out of town for the summer. They told me she worked for CaiText, and the people there told me she worked for you. That you were old friends."

He reached out and put his hand on Titus's shoulder, an unexpected gesture.

"I'm really sorry, Mr. Cain." And he seemed to be. He looked at Rita again, then back at Titus. "This is hard, I know, but I need to ask you some questions about the girls. We need to talk about how to handle it. Somebody has to tell them. We've got to decide how to go about doing that."

Rita had sat down in one of the wrought-iron chairs in the veranda and was crying as Titus stood and watched the deputy's car go down the drive to the front gate. He watched it until it was out of sight.

What he was feeling was indescribable. It was an emotion like no other, and it grew stranger as he stood under the morning glories and listened to Rita crying softly, even politely, but without consolation. There was a world of bewilderment in her weeping as well as fear and anger and stupefaction and emotions that no one had ever named.

For Titus, though, the overriding feeling was one of nausea driven by an appalling sense of guilt. If he had . . . if he had . . . if he had . . . In an instantaneous swarm of remembrances, he blamed Luquín . . . and Gil Norlin . . . and García Burden . . . and himself for not seeing at every turn where all this was going, for not having enough insight, for not having enough intelligence, for not having enough savvy . . . for not having enough guts . . .

"Goddamn it all!" he swore, and wheeled around, his face flushing, his body thrilling with the adrenaline that was exploding through him, driven by the hyperagitation of his own mind. "Goddamn it!" he repeated, and barged across the veranda and onto the courtyard, headed for the guest house, where Burden had spent what was left of the night instead of going back down the hill.

"Titus!" Rita lifted her head out of her hands. "Titus!" She stood, but she was frozen to the spot.

Titus flung open the door of the guest house with such force that it slammed against the inside wall like a gunshot. His entrance was so volcanic that Herrin and Cline, who were working at computer monitors, actually jumped to their feet in shocked surprise.

"Where the hell's Burden," he demanded, his throat thick with emotion, just as Burden stood up from the sofa where he'd been sitting, his telephone still to his ear.

"Get off the goddamned phone," Titus barked at him.

Burden said something into the phone and snapped it shut. The two men faced each other.

"You know what just happened?"

"Yeah," Burden said. "I just found out."

Titus's chest was heaving, his heart pitching, almost squeezing off his ability to speak.

"No more," he said. "That's it. No more. Not one more. Don't give me any of this shit about inevitability. Fuck that. The killings stop here. Right now."

"How do—"

"I'm going to tell you," Titus said. "You take every bit of information you have on Luquín and his people—which is considerable at this point—and you go to the FBI. Now. Right this minute. You take them everything you have, and you get their tac squads over there and arrest Luquín or kill him, and I don't give a shit which. But this insanity stops now!"

"Think about this, Titus—"

"*You* do this *now*, García"—Titus was almost screaming,

his voice hoarse with heat—"or I will. I don't give a shit
about your silence or your secrecy or your hidden agendas.
No more of my friends are going to die because of this son of
a bitch. You don't have any choice. You don't have any say.
This is the end of it."

Chapter 32

The guest house was full of electricity, more of it coursing through the people than through the tangle of cables and wires supporting the computers and communications hardware scattered around on makeshift folding tables.

Rita had burst through the door immediately after Titus, and the two of them were standing facing Burden, who, unintimidated, was nodding at them, letting them catch their breath. Mark Herrin and Cline were working feverishly at their computer screens with an improbably fierce concentration. In the midst of this momentary silence, the only sound was the white noise of humming electronics.

"I should never have let this go this far," Titus said. "My choices led to these deaths. But I'm not going to let it happen anymore."

"So your solution is to pull the plug on all this," Burden said.

From where he stood, he faced the south side of the large main room, with its high glass wall that reached to a vaulted ceiling and looked out at the last part of the laurel allée and the peach orchard.

"Look," he said, running the fingers of one hand through his hair and looking at Titus, "think about this: Knowing what you know now about Luquín, knowing that he had promised you he'd kill people if you went to the FBI"—he paused—"do you think that if you'd gone to the FBI that first night, you would've prevented either of these deaths?"

Burden paused, but he didn't want his answer quite yet. He went on.

"How quickly do you think the FBI would've found Luquín? Literally, how would that have played out? Would they have him yet"—he looked at his watch and then back at Titus—"sixty hours later? Would either of these deaths have been prevented?"

Titus stared at him. His mind was plunging into the problem, but still Burden didn't wait.

"Even if they had arrested him—an impossibility, but let's go ahead with that fantasy for the hell of it—would that have prevented these tragic . . . accidents?"

Silence.

"Or let's say Luquín would've managed to get out of the country before they found him. Do you think that would've prevented these two deaths?"

Burden glanced at Rita, who was staring at him in brittle silence.

"You need to remember, Titus, that you aren't the only one who's ever had to go through something like this because of this man. Have you forgotten that? And, believe me, I didn't tell you nearly all that I could've. The fact is, as tragedies go, things could've been a hell of a lot worse for you, couldn't they."

Titus stared at him, feeling the heat of temper still in his face. He was strung out, pummeled by his own emotions.

Leaving his questions hanging in the air, Burden moved

over to the window and looked out. He stayed that way, giv-ing no indication of what he planned to do next.

"I can't do anything about what Luquín's done anywhere else," Titus said to Burden's back. "I'm sorry about it, I am, but I can't do anything about it."

Burden turned around. "But you can do something about it here? Is that it?"

"I should've gone to the FBI to begin with."

"And Luquín would be gone now," Burden said, "and Thrush and Elster would've died anyway."

"But we'd have the FBI," Titus countered, "and the CIA, and the damned U.S. military, if we needed them, chasing his ass. There's a lot of weight there, García. What have you got chasing him?"

"And others would've died, too," Burden went on, "just like Luquín promised, because he would've been furious at you for having gone to the FBI and having cost him his damn ran-som money. On top of that, he would've gone underground, and it would take us another ten years to get our hands on him again, and all the while he would've gone on devastating God knows how many more lives." He paused. "That's what you would've accomplished, Titus."

The two men looked at each other.

"You do recognize that, Titus? You do understand that, don't you?"

"Let me tell you what I understand, García. I understand that it was because of decisions that I made that Charlie and Carla died. I understand that I can't live with any more of those kinds of deaths. I can't do anything about things that I don't understand. I'm through working off the books. I want this information to go to the FBI. Now. I want Luquín stopped. Now."

Burden came back over in front of Titus and Rita, addressing them both.

"Get this straight," he said, sounding nearly callous now, "Charlie Thrush and Carla Elster were dead from the moment Cayetano Luquín stepped onto your veranda over there two days ago. They were dead, regardless of what you did, and that's just the brutal reality of it. I think I said as much to you, didn't I? In San Miguel. I said, One or two are already as good as dead. I said Luquín would have to do this because he thinks that's the only way you'll really be able to grasp the reality of what's happening to you."

He paused but didn't move, didn't even blink.

"Luquín travels with violence and misery. He's decided to travel here. Now, you can blame me for that if you want to, but it doesn't make you right. And you can feel guilty about that if you want to, but since you didn't have anything to do with it, it seems a little irrational for you to feel responsible for it. It's just wrong to feel that way, and it doesn't accomplish anything. And, frankly, it smacks of self-indulgence."

This last remark made Titus furious, but in the same instant he could see it. He hadn't forgotten what he'd learned about Luquín, but neither had he stopped to put his own experience into perspective in light of those other horrible stories.

Burden moved away from Titus again. Though he seemed self-possessed, his few movements were actually his version of nervous pacing. Titus remembered him walking through the pools of light in his study as he tried to put his thoughts together. Now Burden stopped near one of the stone pillars that supported the high ceiling.

"You've got to stop this ambivalence, Titus. There's no time for it. You've got to understand how thin the margin for success is here even if we work closely together. We can't fight each other and win this thing."

He had hardly finished his last word when Rita spoke up.

"I want to know where we are," she said. "If you're so sure that Luquín would've gotten away if we'd gone to the FBI because they're too slow and clumsy, now that you've got all this information that your computer people are processing, why don't you take it to the FBI like Titus says, and make sure that they nail this maniac? And when you say 'winning this thing,' what do you mean, exactly?"

Burden's eyes moved between Titus and Rita. His expression was stoic, but he was clearly trying to make a decision. He shifted his weight on his feet, still leaning on the pillar. He looked over at Herrin and Cline, who were doing their best to appear oblivious to what was going on, as if they were deaf.

"Mark," Burden said, "could we have some time alone here?"

"Oh, yeah, sure," Herrin said, and he and Cline got up and walked out of the guest house without another word.

As soon as they had shut the door behind them, Burden came back over. He sat on the sofa, on the front edge of it, his forearms on his knees, his fingers loosely laced.

"The FBI doesn't want this damn information," he said. "They want me to have it. And they don't want to know what I do with it."

Chapter 33

Titus and Rita gaped at Burden, half-afraid of what they were going to hear.

"The only reason I'm going to tell you what you're about to hear is because I've got to have your cooperation, and I don't think you're going to give it to me unless you know. But, hear me on this: There's a price for knowing what I'm getting ready to tell you. You've got to go to your graves with this. If you don't, it won't matter who you are or how righteous you think your claims are, it's not going to go well for you."

"You ought to be able to give a threat more teeth than that," Titus said.

"I can, but that's not a threat. It's a matter of counsel, a cautionary word."

"I'm not promising a damn thing," Titus said.

"I didn't think you would. You're in a hell of a situation, and at this point in the game you deserve as much of an explanation as I can give you. I'm just telling you, the knowledge doesn't come free. There's a price for it. You'll have to make some tough choices about how you use it."

Burden's soft voice seemed to grow even softer as he spoke. He paused, considering what he was about to say next, and when he began again, Titus found himself leaning forward in his armchair, trying to hear him more clearly.

"There's a list," Burden said, "and Luquín's name is on it. It's a short list, and was drawn up by a select committee of ranking members from each of the branches of the U.S. intelligence community. This list is not shared with the intelligence agencies of any other nations, not even our closest allies. The individuals on this list are considered to be serious threats to the U.S.—specifically to the U.S., without regard to any other nation. The executive branch has issued a secret finding ordering a consent to silence, targeting these people for assassination."

Titus felt Rita stiffen as she sat beside him on the arm of his chair.

"There's another list. A shorter one. These individuals have been sanctioned to carry out the consent to silence. My name is on that list.

"Listen to me carefully: You've been sucked into something here that you can't fathom. It's more complex than you're able to imagine."

Titus was stunned. "How . . . how could these men be so much of a threat . . . you're talking . . . assassination?"

"Before bin Laden we didn't think it was possible, either," Burden said. "These men are known to us. So was bin Laden. These men have connections that cross political, ideological, criminal, and national boundaries. So did bin Laden. It's their ability to synthesize these connections, and to focus them on a target on a scale never seen before, that has earned these individuals a place on the list. If such a thing had been imaginable before bin Laden, his name would've been on the list, too. As it's turned out, he's the one who's made us see the necessity for even having such a list. And for seeking such a resolution."

"Jesus Christ," Titus said. Suddenly everything tilted. His perspective shifted, trying to accommodate another dimension. "These men . . . on the list, they're . . . all over the world?"

"That's right. Every speck of intelligence about these men is funneled into the operations office of a . . . certain task force. And eventually it comes to me, or one of my colleagues. That's the end of it as far as anyone in intelligence is concerned. I'm not, strictly speaking, an intelligence officer. In fact, I'm not anything. Or, more accurately, I'm whatever I need to be to get the job done."

"Why"—Rita was shaking her head in disbelief—"can't they just deal with these people in a straightforward way, through the legal system? Or the military? Or . . ."

"Consider this," Burden said. "Think of the scale of commitment that's been brought to bear on the pursuit of bin Laden and al-Qaeda, the manpower, military power, intelligence dedication, financial expenditure, legal wrangling, media attention, national preoccupation, time. Multiply that by ten . . . or more."

"But these men haven't done what bin Laden did," Rita argued.

"Neither had bin Laden before he did it. But we did know that he was some kind of threat, on some level, possibly huge. Our problem was that we had a failure of imagination. And it cost us thousands of lives and billions of dollars, and we're not through yet. Believe me, these men have every bit as much potential to assault this country as bin Laden did. Some of them have even more. They wouldn't do it the way he did it. They know we're watching for that. But they'll come up with something different.

"You need to understand, there's no failure of imagination in their minds. Look at what Luquín has come up with. And what he's doing to you isn't even his objective. It's just something he's doing to get his hands around a huge sum of money on his way to something bigger. He's financing something, and we don't know what the hell it is. But we're worried about it."

Burden looked down at the floor, his hands still clasped, forearms on his knees. His face, though impassive, nevertheless conveyed the strain he must have felt as time pressed in upon him.

"This is . . . hard to believe," Rita said.

Burden looked up. "Is it as hard to believe as Charlie Thrush's death? Or what that deputy told you just an hour ago?"

Titus said, "How do we know we can believe this?"

Then he saw something in Burden's face, an inkling, really, a slight intimation, of a hard passion stripped of the civility and of the world that had been ripped away from Titus three nights before. In the flick of an instant he glimpsed that unmentionable thing that a cultivated society allows to live at its core as long as it doesn't step into the full light, as long as it is silent and protects us from those unspeakable things that live even deeper in the darkness than it does.

"You want all of your questions answered?" Burden asked. "Listen to me, I've spent eighteen years in this business, and I've had to make a hell of a lot of morally confusing decisions. But they've never given me all the answers. Ever. Only God gets all the answers."

Burden simply looked at them, and Titus could feel him trying to understand how they were taking this. Then Burden said:

"I'm not going to say we're engaged in a war here. It's

not that easy to define, and it oversimplifies what we're facing. But we do have enemies who threaten us, who have to be engaged in a defensive struggle. And that struggle shares in some of war's demons: People die, people make sacrifices, make hard decisions, do hard things. And if we survive, we have to live with what we saw and what we did, and what we allowed others to do on our behalf. It's the price we pay . . . even if we didn't have any choice in the matter at all."

Titus glanced at Rita, and he could clearly see the strain in her face. This had blindsided her, caught her off guard even more than it had Titus.

"We can't send this struggle away to be dealt with elsewhere by other people," Burden went on. "When something like this comes to your doorstep, you have to deal with it on your doorstep. And you have to deal with the moral decisions that killing always involves. Life doesn't give us clarity of foresight. We work with what we've got. It's a human dilemma."

Before Titus could speak, Rita stood from where she had been sitting beside him on the arm of his chair. He watched her as if he were seeing her anew, loving her profile, loving the way her thick, buttery hair was gathered hastily behind her neck, always so practical. She put both hands on her hips, wrists up, and looked at both men.

"All of this is just so ridiculously horrific, isn't it," she said. "I can't stop thinking of Louise, and of Carla's poor girls. Going to sleep at night will never be the same again for any of them."

Titus didn't know what she was going to say, but he knew in his gut where she was going with it.

"Can you possibly imagine what those two . . . deaths must've been like," she said, looking at Titus now. "I have to say I've thought of it. In spite of my repulsion at the idea of it, I've been drawn to thinking of it. Can we possibly imagine the . . . odd . . . horror of their last moments?" Pause. "What are we to think of that?"

She put her hands together and pressed her forefingers to her lips as she thought a moment. Then she wiped back a few floating tendrils from her temples.

"We're not bad people, Titus. If we do this, then we do it, and we don't look back. I know that I've been dragging my feet, and that's made it hard for both of you. But if what he's telling us is the truth . . . we don't have any choice in this. This really is bigger than us, larger than our own self-interests, larger than our fears."

She turned and focused on Burden. "We don't know what . . . we're doing here. We're caught in a terrible place. If Titus is willing to trust you on this, then I will, too." She paused. "But so help me God, if you turn out not to be who you say you are, as wild as this sounds, I'll see to it that you regret what you're doing to us."

Rita and Burden stared at each other in silence. It was a moment that at once cleared the air and then suddenly filled it again with new tensions.

Titus stood up. "Let's just get the hell on with it," he said.

Burden looked up at him. "Titus, none of this ever happened. This is your own consent to silence."

"Understood," Titus said. Rita swallowed and nodded.

Burden hesitated, then decided not to belabor it.

"Okay, then," he said, "that's settled. Now, first thing: It's time you two had a conversation in your bedroom for the benefit of the listening devices we left active in there. Titus, we need for Luquín to believe that he's achieved the effect he was wanting to achieve with you by keeping the pressure on you. This is especially true since you pissed him off last night.

"You need to tell Rita that after learning of Carla's death, you want to get this ordeal over with as quickly as possible. To prevent any more deaths, you're going to give Luquín all of the money he's asking for. Forget the delayed releases, you say. You're going to start putting through big chunks of his ransom demand to Cavatino as quickly as your attorney can arrange it with your banker and your broker. Tomorrow. Or the next day. As soon as possible."

"But what if I can't deliver on that?"

"All you're saying is that you're going to speed up the original schedule he'd given you." Burden checked his watch. "That conversation needs to happen within the hour. One last thing," he said, looking at Titus. "In your meeting with Luquín last night, you gave him a pretty hard time. That took guts. But in any other circumstances, that would've gotten you killed. And that confrontational stance has a pretty stiff downside to it.

"It's my fault," he added quickly. "I should've covered this with you, but it got past me. The fact is, pissing him off wasn't what we wanted to do. The upshot of the meeting should've been that you were intimidated by your confrontation with him. He needed to have walked away from there thinking that he had you completely under his control. But in light of the effect you had on him, I think we ought to bring in some bodyguards to stay here with Rita. You may have to leave again. She may need company."

Neither Titus nor Rita said anything for a moment. They were both having the same thought, but Rita came out with it first.

"But . . . isn't that . . . wouldn't that be the same thing as Titus removing the surveillance? When they see bodyguards

DAVID LINDSEY

coming in here . . . won't that give Luquín another excuse to kill someone else?"

She was looking at Burden, but it was Titus who spoke up.

"Do it," he said to Burden. "And do it fast."

Chapter 34

He unzipped his pants, moved over a few steps, and pissed at an angle against the rock retaining wall so that it didn't make any sound. A bright green anole lizard scuttled away up the set-back rows of stones to get away from the urine.

As he relieved himself, he took stock of his situation. Bluejays complained incessantly somewhere in the peach trees. Cicadas hymned loudly in every direction, praising the rising heat. Nothing unusual. He glanced back over his left shoulder toward the guest house. The two guys who had come out half an hour earlier were still sitting on the veranda. The Cains were still inside the guest house. Whatever the hell that was all about.

He shook himself off and zipped his trousers again. Turning back to the camera, he leaned his full body against the stones of the retaining wall. They were set back row upon row from his feet to his chin, so that all he had to do was lean forward against them in an upright reclining position, as if it had been designed for him to spy from. He lowered his head to the camera, scanning the telephoto lens back and forth. No. Just the two guys.

That morning he had watched as the woman came outside, early, in her gown. She had gone out to the fountain and looked in, then she had walked over to the wall that separated the courtyard from the pool and looked at some flowers there. It was there, as she'd turned to go back to the veranda, that the sun had fallen on her across the top of the stone wall, and in an instant the gown went clear, as if it had turned to a thin sheet of transparent water. Oh, shit.

It was good for six or eight strides of her long legs, and then the thing went opaque again as the poolhouse blocked the sun. But he had gotten off two snaps, and when nothing was happening he went back to them on the camera's screen. He was going to save those.

Having thought of it, he double-checked the laptop, which was balanced on the retaining wall's top row of stones. The thing was powered up, ready to send his next series of pictures.

Suddenly the guest house door opened, and the two guys on the veranda stood, looking toward it. The problem with his position—and there was nothing he could do about it, no matter how much he moved up and down the retaining wall—was that he couldn't get a clear shot of the door itself. The allée of trees obscured it so that all he could see was the bottom half of the people who came and went, until they got to the veranda.

But now he saw three sets of legs. The woman, her husband, and another. He needed a shot of the third person. He didn't know there had been another person in there. The guy had to have arrived after dark.

Sweat trickled out through the hair at his temples and slid down the side of his face. His hands were sticky with it, and the case of the camera grew slick. Straining through the viewfinder, he concentrated on the legs of the people as they moved to the front of the allée, toward the veranda. He blinked away the sweat gathering in his eyebrows. Damn it.

Just before the three of them emerged onto the veranda, the unidentified man stopped. They talked some more, and then the guy left the Cains and headed down the allée alone.

He had to make a quick decision since the allée descended in his direction and came to within twelve meters of where he was standing. He shoved the computer into the grass—no time to put it away—grabbed the camera, and fell back into the orchard, disappearing into a stand of wild grass. Turning immediately, he faced the allée with a view through a row of peach trees.

The guy walked the length of the allée, and he could hear him talking, using his cell phone. Still he couldn't get a clear shot with the camera. At the end of the allée the guy turned and went down behind the orchard toward the woods. Where the hell was he going?

Risking discovery, he left the grass and ran, bent over in a crouch along the end of the rows of peach trees, past a toolshed. Breathing heavily and thankful that the guy was on the phone, which would distract his hearing, he came to the end of the last row of trees and dropped to his knees behind a cedarpost woodpile. He turned to the end of the allée where he expected the guy to have emerged and raised his camera. But he was nowhere in sight. Loza frantically scanned the edge of the dense woods that led down the hillside to Cielo Canyon Road below the property.

At the last possible moment he saw the guy entering the woods. He squeezed off a few shots, not sure what he was getting.

Shit. This was suspicious. Not good. Macias wasn't going to like this.

Chapter 35

After Burden left them in front of the guest house, Titus and Rita headed straight to their bedroom, where they dutifully had the conversation Burden had wanted, and then went on to Titus's study. For the next hour they sat at the long table under the sunny cupola, contacting Carla's friends and enlisting help in calling scattered relatives. Titus made sure the news of Carla's death was handled properly at CaiText and that Carla's responsibilities were temporarily covered.

But no matter how many phone calls Titus made, no matter how many shocked people he talked to or how many urgent items he found crowding in upon him demanding to be dealt with immediately, his mind was divided. He had been staring out the window, lost in thought, when he realized that Rita was finishing a conversation and hanging up the phone. She had been talking to Louise.

"How'd she sound?" he asked.

"Okay. I think she's in that just-get-through-the-funeral mode. Nel and Derek are lifesavers. And a lot of friends from Fredericksburg are coming out."

"She'll have a lot of support," Titus said. "She'll need it."

"She wants you to speak at the service," Rita said.

"When?"

"Day after tomorrow."

"Jesus. What'd you tell her?"

"Of course you would."

Before he had time to process how impossible that seemed to him, his encrypted phone rang.

"This is García. Listen, Gil Norlin's bringing in the body-guards—"

"Norlin?" Titus was surprised, though as soon as he was he didn't know why he should've been.

"He pulled together the local chase car drivers I needed last night, Titus. I use him when I need him, just like everybody else."

For some reason that last sentence stuck in Titus's mind like a neon sign.

The bodyguards were two men and a woman. They arrived in a Blazer following Gil Norlin's Volvo without any special effort to conceal the fact that they were coming in. Titus guessed they had talked that over with Burden.

First names only. Janet was tall and athletic, with makeup that looked as if it had been applied by numbers. She had an easygoing manner. At first the sound-suppressed MP5 (she told them what it was) slung across her shoulder looked incongruous, until you watched her move around with it. She wore it as comfortably as her pleated trousers.

Ryan was the shorter of the two men at six two, Titus guessed. Lifted weights. Military haircut. All-American. Looked exactly like what he was.

The tall one, Kal, was maybe six five. Not a small man, but not bulked up like Ryan. He seemed a little preoccupied, as if the team were his responsibility.

As soon as they finished introductions and a few words,

Rita and Titus took them on a tour of the house. Decisions were immediately made to lock all but the most frequently used doors and to put breach limpets on all the doors and windows. It got very serious very quickly.

After the bodyguards had been briefed and took off in separate directions, Norlin paused in the kitchen with Titus and Rita.

"Do what they say," he said. "There's no hocus-pocus here. Just a lot of experience-based common sense."

"These are your people?" Titus asked.

"I've worked with them before," he said. He was standing with his fist on his hip, his jacket pushed back a little. Titus saw Rita glance at the gun at his waist.

"And you've worked with García Burden before, too?" Rita asked. "Is that right?"

"Yeah. A few years back."

She looked at him. "Why don't you just give me some idea of what this man's like?"

Norlin flicked an uneasy glance at Titus and then looked down, collecting his thoughts.

"That's kind of touchy," he said.

"What do you mean?" she asked. Her voice had a barb to it, as if his reluctance were somehow unworthy.

"Well, you're working with him—"

"Look," she interrupted, and then she hesitated nervously—or was it angrily? "People are dying here," she said, "and any scruples you might feel of a professional nature just don't seem significant to me right now."

Norlin was looking at her. He didn't seem particularly taken aback, nor was he intimidated, but Rita had definitely cut through a lot of crap that he was used to falling back on when he was put on the spot.

"Well, he's had a full life," Norlin said with intended irony. "What did you have in mind?"

"Just give me some sense of what he's like," she said. "Something that . . . orients him in my head, gives me some perspective. Look, we're working with this man because you recommended him. Now you think about it: We don't really know you, either. You think it's just . . . the way it ought to be that just because we're scared to death here, we should start trusting people who—let's face it—are leading pretty damn murky lives? I don't know what you do. Titus has told me how he first met you, but then . . . what's that? You seem to be who you say you are, but then, how the hell are we to know, really? We haven't seen any credentials. Right? No one that we know we can trust has called us and vouched for you, have they? You know, Mr. Norlin"—she put a little extra on the "Mr. Norlin"—"we don't just intuit your integrity, or your legitimacy, for that matter. The fact that we're even working with him, Burden, or you . . . or any of these other people"—she gestured broadly toward the bodyguards, toward Herrin in the guest house—"strikes me as . . . just . . . insane when I think about it."

By the time she had stopped, her voice was quavering with a complex brew of emotions. But the torrent of words had had its effect on Norlin. He seemed to soften a little as he looked at her.

"You have a good point, Mrs. Cain," he said carefully. "But let me say, it's only insane if you think of it from the point of view of your life before Cayetano Luquín. After Luquín, insane takes on another meaning altogether. But," he added quickly, "you're right. You've been asked to take a lot on faith. Those of us in this line of work, we don't appreciate that enough."

He gave some thought to what he was about to say.

He leaned against the kitchen counter and folded his arms across his chest. His old suit, already sagging at all of its stress points, bunched up across his shoulders as if it had done this a thousand times before and knew the routine.

"On a personal level," he said, looking at Rita, "and I've told Titus this, I trust this man implicitly. But the thing is, the thing that would be hard for you to sort of get a grip on, is that my trust lies within a context of extremes. The things I trust him to do, for instance, are things that would probably shock you."

Another pause. "I could talk about him for days. Don't waste your time trying to figure him out. The only person I know who comes even close to having done that is the woman he lives with. Her name's Lucía. I don't know how many years he's been with her. She's a Roma, a Gypsy from Sicily. Photographer." He looked at Titus. "Took all—or most—of those pictures you saw in his place. She's as inexplicable as he is, and they're devoted to each other . . . way past anything I've ever seen between two people. But that's personal stuff, not exactly where we want to go.

"Look," he said, "I'll tell you what. I don't really know how to do this, so I'll just tell you a story. I could tell you scores of them, but I think this one will do for right now. I'll make it short, but I think it'll give you some idea what García Burden's life is like."

Chapter 36

"Several years ago," Norlin began, "an Algerian Islamic extremist, guy named Mourad Berkat, showed up in surveillance photos in Mexico City. He was in the company of members of a drug-trafficking cartel that had established Middle Eastern connections.

"Berkat had been a GIA terrorist in Algiers during the eighties and early nineties, but he had ambitions and had become a freelance assassin working mostly for the capos in the drug underworld in Spain, Sicily, and France. He liked poisons and chemicals, unusual for a hit man. His appearance in Mexico set off alarms.

"García was called in . . . for various special reasons. Turned out that Berkat was trying to obtain the bacterium *Clostridium botulinum*. Uh, it's an organism that produces an exotoxin, a damned lethal exotoxin, one hundred thousand times more powerful than the sarin nerve agent. But this stuff also has medical uses, as a therapeutic agent in the treatment of certain neurological disorders, for example. So it was a dual-use substance that could legitimately be found in some pharmaceutical and medical environments.

"García sent out a string of alerts to his foreign assets, but a month went by before one of them called him about a woman doctor in Paris who turned up dead in her apartment. She worked for a research clinic that specialized in neurological diseases. Berkat's photo was found in her possessions. A torn-up metro ticket led them to an apartment near Charles de Gaulle Airport, where surveillance photographs picked up a Hamas agent leaving the apartment.

"Berkat wasn't really on the Mossad's radar screen, but they sure as hell knew the Hamas guy. They quickly located Berkat in Gaza City, and then grabbed photographs of him at a café talking to Hassan al-Abed. Al-Abed had a doctorate in biological sciences from Cairo University. Back in Paris, the French DST confirmed the missing *Clostridium botulinum* from the research clinic. Now García was sure that Hamas/Berkat were working on a dispersal method for the exotoxin."

Norlin shifted on his feet. Gave it some more thought before he went on.

"Berkat disappeared from Gaza, and his trail went cold. Then three months later one of García's agents picked it up again in Strasbourg. Berkat had spent the night with a woman there who said that he'd used her computer nonstop for a whole day before moving on. García's people sucked the marrow out of the hard drive and found that he'd booked a two-week vacation cruise from Brest to St. Kitts under a French name, traveling with his wife and two kids. That was Berkat's shtick, using the family man thing as a cover. He seemed to find no end of gullible women to help him without realizing what they were doing.

"They tracked him to Belize, where he abandoned his 'family.' Now, under a different French name, he caught a flight to

Tampico, where he rented an SUV under the name of a Mexican national and headed north.

"By now everyone had to assume that his target was somewhere in the States. Even beyond the issue of national security, the people who hired García didn't want it known that a terrorist with a biological weapon had made it within even a hundred miles of our borders. At that time, we were still whistling through the graveyard and hoping the public didn't notice just how damned vulnerable we really were.

"God knows what kind of political repercussions there might be if people ever rolled their asses off their sofas and woke up to what was really going on. And the politicians didn't want the public to get the idea that Mexico was swarming with terrorists—bad for NAFTA—even though it was, and still is, a very real issue of concern. Another one of those things they hope the public doesn't wake up to.

"Anyway, Berkat just needed to disappear, and it was best if that happened in Mexico. Without the Mexican government's knowledge, of course.

"There would be no loss of intelligence if Berkat just evaporated without anyone even talking to him. We already knew Hamas was financing his run. The delivery system that he was carrying was known by its designer/creator, the good Dr. al-Abed back in Gaza. The Mossad would deal with debriefing him. Berkat was just a snake that had to be killed. His poison would die with him.

"García's choice of weapon was a particularly incendiary bomb design, just to make sure the exotoxin didn't survive or was somehow inadvertently distributed by the explosion. The bomb was loaded on a helicopter and flown ahead in the general direction of Berkat's anticipated route, the choices being narrowed down as he advanced north. Finally it was clear that he was headed for one of the border's smallest crossings, the toll bridge at Los Ebanos, Texas."

Norlin paused again. He glanced out the kitchen window and cast his thoughts to far-off places. He slowly shook his head and brought his eyes back to Rita.

"You've got to understand," he said, "that every operation is a moving target. You start out with an objective and a plan, but you know damn well that most of the plan is bound to change because you'll inevitably be blindsided by some damned surprise. It's one of the hardest things about the job. And it's one of the things that García excels at. He's cool with blindsides.

"Incidentally, his other most desirable talent is his ingenuity in making things happen without raising any eyebrows. He achieves his objective in silence. Or if that can't happen, the event is disguised to make it appear to be something other than what it actually is.

"Anyway, at a dusty village called Cerralvo, Berkat left the main highway and headed north through the backcountry desert. That was even better for García's plans. The helicopter moved ahead, landed at an isolated spot of the highway, dealt with installing the explosives, and took off again. Five miles from the bomb, Berkat pulled off the side of the road at a little food stand. And, whoa, big surprise. The surveillance team was stunned to see a woman, two little boys, and a little girl bail out of the SUV with him to get snacks. Berkat had himself another family.

"Surveillance team frantically radioed García. The helicopter had dropped him off on the other side of the bomb, and he was headed toward it from the opposite direction, watching Berkat's dot on his tracking monitor as they both converged on the site."

Norlin looked out the window over the kitchen sink again.

Titus followed his eyes and saw one of the bodyguards prowling around the poolhouse. Norlin, his forearm on the cabinet, rubbed his forehead with his other hand. He seemed reluctant to continue.

"One night a little more than a year after this happened, I sat with García in his study in San Miguel. We'd been drinking. Too much. But I remember how the crickets were raising hell in the darkness outside the opened windows as he told me in a flat, dead voice what happened next.

"García and his driver raced toward the bomb's location. About a quarter of a mile from the bomb they turned off on a dirt track and drove out into the brush and turned around to watch.

"García got out of the car and vomited in the grease brush. And then, suddenly, he lost control of his bowels. After cleaning himself up, he scrambled onto the top of the car and watched the highway through his binoculars. He could see Berkat's SUV with the woman and children heading for the border and the bomb. There would be no mistake about the bomb, a computer would make sure the timing was accurate. Everybody involved in the operation who had a radio or phone or computer was using it to message García about the woman and kids. His driver was inside the car, confirming, confirming, confirming.

"García stood alone on top of the car in the grease brush and watched through binoculars as the SUV sped along the highway.

"Then, instantly, it went up in a geyserlike explosion. It threw up a mushroom plume high into the desert's purple evening sky. García remembered the color of the sky and the color of the plume with its internal fireball. He saw it, then heard it, then felt it.

"The bomb had been designed to destroy as much evidence

as possible, and the Mexican federal police couldn't even tell how many people had been in the vehicle. They and the newspapers assumed the blast had been the work of drug traffickers' assassins, and those who suspected otherwise kept their suspicions to themselves. Whatever it was, it had been a serious thing. Mexicans learned long ago to make peace with inexplicable events."

Norlin shook his head and stared at nothing for a moment.

"Later, as Berkat's operation was dissected, and the leads gathered in those last frantic days were played out, it was learned that he had been headed for the Texas Medical Center in Houston. The effectiveness of the dispersal method designed by al-Abed for the exotoxin was a controversial question. It was an aerosol device intended for the air-conditioning system in one of the center's largest hospitals. Some argued that only twenty or thirty people would have died, but others strongly disagreed. They used words like 'catastrophic' and 'unimaginable.'

"But the speculation about body count didn't have any effect on García. There were always only four in his nightmares. He said it bothered him a lot that he never saw body parts in his dreams, only bits of charred clothing drifting down through the darkly glittering mushroom, a bright red little tennis shoe, a toddler's green-and-blue-striped T-shirt, a woman's white bra, a small dress with sashes fluttering. The colors and the kinds of clothing changed from dream to dream, but the dream never changed, and the count never changed, either. Four completely innocent people went up in a plume of fire and desert sand, over and over and over.

"Because García Burden had decided that they should."

Chapter 37

Luquín and Jorge Macias sat beneath the oak that shaded one end of the pool. They were nursing *cafecítas,* as Luquín liked to call the demitasse cups of strong coffee that he was addicted to. It wasn't espresso, just damned strong coffee. Luquín had slept late, and he'd slept like a tired old cat, deeply and serenely. That was his way. The abominations of the waking man never disturbed the peaceful hours of the sleeping man. And why should they? Waking was not sleeping. They were two entirely different things, he said.

But his confrontation with Cain had put him in a foul temper. Nobody talked to him the way Cain had talked to him, and what made it worse was that others had heard what had been said because the room had been wired for security reasons. Macias had heard it, and the sharpshooter who had waited outside in the dark, his rifle aimed through the window at Cain in case anything should happen, had heard it through his ear mike.

"No, absolutely nothing," Macias was saying. "We never saw the same car twice, all the license plates checked out. We saw nothing suspicious, and the surveillance people didn't, either. We photographed every car and put them into the computers. If any of them show up again, we'll know it."

Luquín was wearing dark trousers and a white *guayabera* that hung unbuttoned and open, exposing his thick chest. He wore sunglasses. He smoked. And sipped his *cafecíta*.

This was a dangerous enterprise under any circumstances, but doing this sort of thing inside the United States was next to insanity. Yet it was precisely there, next to insanity, that a great deal of money was to be made. High stakes inevitably required great risks.

"And the house?"

"They finally got them all. Except one." Macias was dressed, as always, in cool, limp linen. "It's in the bedroom. We put our best stuff in there. It's got boosters, little things the size of a button on either side of the room. Good reception. Filters so the sweepers can't pick them up."

Luquín looked away, across the river and the valley toward the roof of Titus's house. He was chasing thoughts, and at the moment he was replaying one of Titus's remarks that had particularly stung with insolence.

"Hunt my ass all the way to Patagonia!" Luquín snorted, mocking Titus's voice. "Patagonia, shit. What does he think? How does he feel this morning, huh? He's going to think he woke up in fucking Colombia!"

He stopped suddenly and looked at Macias. "And those two, they're gone? You got them out of here?"

"As soon as they were sure the woman was dead, they called us, and my boys picked them up and drove them to the airstrip. They'll cross the border in another hour, near Lajitas. The two guys who did Thrush are already in Oaxaca."

Luquín nodded his approval. A killing well done. He looked at his watch. "In another half hour I should hear from Cavatino."

"We saw a county sheriff's car going into Cain's place, so he probably knows about the woman by now."

"Welcome to Colombia."

Macias would be glad when it was over. When Luquín had come to him with this job and had spent two days explaining it to him, Macias had agreed to do it provided a reconnoitering trip to Austin satisfied him that his people could handle the logistics of such an operation.

After ten days in Austin, he had called Luquín and agreed to do it. But he'd wanted the complete authority to pull the plug on the operation if he thought it was about to be compromised. Luquín had balked at Macias having the last word, but he couldn't do it without Macias's U.S. and Mexican connections. Ultimately he had agreed. The deal was on.

Macias had leased the house on Las Ramitas. He had a team of three cars and six men, as well as a surveillance van with three technicians. The surveillance team was from Juarez, men out of the drug trade. The four teams were strictly compartmentalized. They never associated and never communicated except by secure radio and cell phones.

Macias knew that there were two things that had given him the edge in this enterprise. First, the fact that there was no precedent for it. What has not been done before is difficult to anticipate. That was one of the great lessons of the World Trade Center event. Innovation was difficult for the American intelligence community. The old ways of doing things were hard to change in the sprawling bureaucracy of a powerful government.

The second thing that had given him an edge was getting everyone in place in absolute secrecy. He believed he had done that successfully.

But he was nervous. There was an adverse correlative to what the crime world had learned from the September disaster in New York: The U.S. law enforcement and intelligence agencies had undergone, and were still undergoing, severe internal analysis. They were beginning to make changes. It was only reasonable for someone in Macias's position to assume that many of those changes would remain unknown, until they proved deadly to people like Luquín and Macias.

Nevertheless, this particular operation had an added incentive. If the extortion scheme worked, Macias also got a percentage of the take, not just a fee. For this kind of money he would sweat a little more than he would normally, maybe even a little more than seemed to make good sense. The size of the payoff actually encouraged risk taking.

While Macias was running all of this over in his mind, Luquín had been brooding, too. He was still furious about the way Titus had talked to him; it was the sort of effrontery that would corrode his concentration until he did something to correct the indignity.

Luquín flipped his cigarette away and then leaned forward and had a last sip from his *cafecita,* his thick fingers holding the little handle of the white demitasse cup between his forefinger and thumb, his other fingers fanned outward delicately. He smacked his lips at the rich brew as he put down the cup and sat back in his chair. He stared at Macias from behind his sunglasses.

"I've been thinking," he said, and at that moment Macias's phone rang. Luquín lifted his head in permission, and Macias answered it. He listened, then snapped the phone closed.

"This should be interesting," he said, and he reached over to the computer and tapped in an address string.

The two men listened as Titus Cain told his wife in a flat, lifeless voice that he was going to go ahead and have the rest of the ransom money processed and sent to Cavatino. If that's what it took to get this nightmare over with, he said, then that's what he was going to do. He'd had enough. There was a brief conversation between the two of them, and then it was over.

Luquín sat at the table as if hypnotized, bending forward, listening to a recording coming in over one of the laptops. When it was finished, he said, "Play it again," and Macias snapped his fingers over the keys, and they listened to it again.

"Son of a bitch," Luquín said quietly as the recording ended the second time. He stood. "This is getting damned close, Jorge," he said. "Damned close."

"Another twenty-four hours," Macias said, punching a key to get out of the file.

"Maybe."

"Maybe sooner," Macias said, punching another few keys to check his messages. And it couldn't be soon enough.

Macias checked several more files, getting routine hourly postings from each of his teams. Nothing happening. When he looked up at Luquín again, he was surprised to see him stewing, staring at Macias.

"I want to go ahead with Cain's wife," Luquín said. "She will be my going-away gift to him. When the last of the money clears Cavatino, I want you to do her. Then we'll see if he feels like following my ass to Patagonia."

Inwardly, Macias cringed. None of these operations was worth a single dollar to him if he didn't get out of them alive and well. But two bodies were never enough for Luquín. He wanted two bodies before he could even take a shit. This wouldn't be the first time Luquín had put undue pressure on an operation simply because he wanted someone else to die. And things were going so well. Machismo. It was going to get the son of a bitch killed one of these days.

Macias was about to say that he would begin putting it together when his computer pinged, and he turned to see an incoming message from Elías Loza. He glanced at Luquín and decided to wait until later to open the file.

Chapter 38

By the time Burden got down the hill to Cielo Canyon Road, he was soaking in sweat. His shoes were full of rocks and twigs, and cedar needles had gotten into his shirt and had worked their way into his skin in a dozen itchy places. He beeped his van crew and waited a couple of minutes in the woods that crowded up to the edge of the road. When they pulled up, he was inside in seconds.

Gil Norlin had gotten a rental house not half a mile from where Titus lived, a small frame bungalow built in the fifties and tucked into the woods. There weren't many of these kinds of houses left in this high-dollar part of the city, where seclusion was a large part of the real estate appeal. Probably the absentee owners of the property were asking an exorbitant price for what they had and were willing to sit on it until somebody coughed it up. Which they would, sooner or later. But the place was a dump. The small rooms were bare, empty, smelling of insecticide, and crawling with roaches.

The three-member van crew had already eaten lunch and left him a few slices of pizza in the kitchen. He took one of the delivery boxes with the last of two cold wedges of pizza littered with jelled cheese, leathery pepperoni, and flaccid olives and opened an RC. Tired, he sat on the floor in the kitchen, his back against the wall. He'd eaten only a few bites of the cold pizza and washed it down with the RC when he heard the front door open.

He heard Calò's curt bark, "García?" as he addressed the room of technicians, then heard one of them respond, "Kitchen."

Calò, an Italian whom Burden had first met in Buenos Aires, headed up a team that comprised only three people besides himself. Sometimes one or two of them were women, but mostly they were men, and there were never more than four altogether. Calò himself wasn't a big man, middle weight, dark complexion with dark hair, not muscular, not distinctive in any particular way. His face was unremarkable, and he didn't look physically imposing enough to do the things that he was in such demand to do. Close work was often misunderstood. In general his team was always a variation of himself, common in appearance, quiet, observant.

Calò walked into the kitchen and went straight to Burden as if he knew where he would be sitting. Burden was already getting up, and the two men embraced, Calò's usual *abrazo* that for him served as the sealing bond for any given operation. He turned to his three team members, all of them dressed in street clothes.

"Baas," he said, indicating a man with wide-set eyes and a soft smile, his dark hair as tightly coiled as an African's.

"Tito . . ." He pointed to a very thin young man with a little series of symbols tattooed on one cheek and a pretty mouth.

"Cope . . ." The only blond in the bunch, the oldest of them in appearance, maybe in his mid thirties. He didn't look directly at anyone.

"Good," Burden said. He'd seen Tito before, but the other two he didn't know. "The stuff's out here," he said, walking out of the kitchen and into a long screened porch that looked out onto the dense cedar woods. The porch was scattered with knapsacks and various other bags that belonged to the van crew that had spent the night there. Burden grabbed a cardboard box next to the wall, swung it into the middle of the room, and sat on the floor. The others followed suit, forming a loose semicircle in front of him.

Burden began handing out photos of the clifftop house on Las Ramitas along with several maps: the street plan, the house plan, an area plan. The four men passed the photos and maps around in silence while Burden went over the little intelligence that they had so far, acknowledging its weaknesses, knowing that every unanswered question created a risk for them.

For the next hour he went over the details of the operation, outlining the logistics of dealing with the various teams Macias had put together, emphasizing again and again the importance of absolute silence and of leaving no trace of their presence.

"No evidence at all. If you touch it, it walks away with you. No abandoned cars, no discarded weapons or casings, no bodies, no blood. *Nada.*"

"Can't be done," Calò said. "Not with this many targets." He was looking at the list of vehicles and bodyguards that Burden's surveillance crew had compiled from the previous night's operation. "Not enough intelligence. Too little time to plan. Too many targets."

"I understand that," Burden said. "But I'm not looking for a total take here. I'm just saying what you do take has got to be clean. We've got something going for us on this. You saw in the file that Jorge Macias put this operation together. In the past he's followed pretty conventional tactical discipline and procedure. Everything mobile. Everything compartmental-ized. Most important: At the first sign of operational breach, everybody disappears. No discussion. Gone." He looked around at each of them. "I want you to take out as many as you can. But if the risk of discovery is too high, if you can't do it silently, cut them loose."

"And Luquín?"

"Isolating him in that house is your main objective. I'll be responsible for him after that."

There was a pause of surprise. Calò pretended to be look-ing at the maps on the floor in front of him. But no one was going to ask Burden to elaborate.

After a few moments, Calò rose and went to the kitchen sink. He put his cigarette under the faucet, then tossed the soggy butt into one of the empty pizza boxes on the cabinet. He came back to the porch and leaned against the door frame. Everyone was sweating. The dense cedar brakes cut off any chance of a breeze reaching them through the screened porch. It was still, oppressive. Cicadas keened in the midday heat.

"Isolating him," Calò said. "That's a problem."

"Yeah," Burden said. "I know."

Calò bent and picked up his copy of the notes that had been prepared for them. He looked at them.

"Macias is staying in the same house," he said. "With his bodyguard and driver. And then there's Luquín's bodyguard and driver. That's six people. How isolated do you want him?"

"Alone, if possible."

"And if it's not possible?"

"We've got to get Macias out of there, at least. And his two people."

"Any head-on confrontation is going to cause a stink," Calò confirmed.

Burden nodded. "Can't do that."

Calò looked at his intelligence report. "We don't know their routines, their schedules, nothing."

"We just barely had time to find out how many there were," Burden said.

It was quiet on the porch for a moment, each person taking counsel of his own thoughts. Burden knew the routine and waited, letting them do what they had to do. All of the men had read the file on Luquín, so they knew the kind of man they were stalking.

Calò's teams all operated under the same rule of egalitarianism. He pulled together the best people he could find and then trusted them. Because his teams were small, any individual could pull the plug on any operation. Everybody had to be in 100 percent or it wouldn't work. A small team was like a fine mechanical watch—all the parts were essential, none expendable.

Calò's teams were assembled according to a kind of Zen-like intuitiveness. It mattered, somehow, who the target was, and the individuals he chose for each particular assignment seemed to have attitudes about the kinds of people they were going after. It made a difference, Calò said, in the synergy of violence that was a potential in each mission. He was vague about it, but Burden knew that it was important to Calò and to the team's success. It didn't matter that it didn't seem logical. He had learned a long time ago that logic was only a part of this business, sometimes a surprisingly small part of it.

Burden interrupted the silence. He had to say this before anyone spoke up.

"Look, I know this thing is full of holes," he said, "and we'll never get them all plugged. The thing is riddled with risks. Bad odds. But I just wanted you to know that I know that I'm bringing you into a mess. Calò, you can vouch that this isn't the way I work. But I couldn't walk away from a chance at Cayetano Luquín. And, unfortunately, this thing had to happen fast, or not at all."

There was no response from any of them. These were not men who felt any emotional need to pat Burden on the shoulder and say, That's okay, we understand.

"These guys are ex-Mexican intelligence, you think?" Caló asked Burden.

"That's my guess. It's only a guess."

Everybody was quiet again, looking at the maps, thinking, playing it out in their minds, trying to see the worst of it.

"Okay," Caló said finally, looking up, "let's decide. You have reservations, we discuss them right here, right now. It's go, or no go, right now."

He turned to his left and looked at Baas, who nodded without any hesitation. Caló's eyes moved to the right, to Tito. Tito was thinking, preoccupied, absently moving a delicate finger over the tattoos on his cheek. Then he nodded. Finally he looked at Cope, who was resting against the wall next to Burden.

"I don't like the skimpy intelligence." He had a strong Aussie accent. "I don't like the last minute feel to this thing. And isolating Luquín . . . shit, that sounds like a snake pit." He looked at Burden. "But I've read this asshole's files, and I'd like to help you with this one. And you've got a reputation that washes over a whole lot of shit." He nodded at Caló. "I'm okay with this."

Caló snapped his head at Burden.

"We're in," he said. "We'd like to look at your LorGuides now. First, we start with who's where so we can start setting priorities, and at the top of the list is isolating Luquín. That's the bitch. Everything comes down to that."

Chapter 39

Burden was sweating. He was fascinated. The man was sitting where he had sat the night before, but now he was dressed. Nearly. He wore the trousers of a suit. No shoes. No shirt. His skin glistened in places with perspiration. His hair was slicked back with water.

Burden had watched him walk into the dank bathroom. Standing next to a plastic shower curtain with turquoise fishes to and froing amid rising blue bubbles, he had stuck his head under the faucet and run cold water on it. Then he'd stood up and let the water drip over his neck and bare shoulders as he'd combed back his thinning hair in sleek convenience.

Then he'd come back into the room and sat in the chair by the window. He'd rested the ankle of one leg on the knee of the other. His trousers were limp in the heat, and Burden imagined the sweat underneath them.

Burden liked talking to him.

"Where do you stand now with your list?" he asked.

"Four of five."

Burden nodded. Should he say, That's good? He said nothing.

In the afternoon heat, the room smelled horribly of dank. The old motel was only just on the edge of reality. Its reality was all past, and there was no future at all, or so little of it as to make it incapable of being quantified. The curtains by the man's head were creamy with age, their white as distant and irretrievable as the children who had played on the merry-go-round.

"Can you name them?" Burden asked.

"Only you, García, would ask that." He paused. "Sotomayor. Zabre. Vega. Mojarro."

He spoke their names as if he were reciting the rosary, a relished exercise. Breathed words. Each syllable was pronounced with precision, pungent with remembrance. To Burden, the recitation was scintillating. And despairing. It was a recitation that almost pulled from Burden the antiphonal response after each name: Yes. Yes. Yes. Yes.

Cicadas and grasshoppers hummed in the high dead grass that grew up around the seesaw and broken swings.

"And that leaves . . . ?" Burden said.

The man turned his eyes on him. He was by the window, beyond which the July sun sizzled through the cysted leaves of the hackberries. The light behind the rancid curtains created a gauzy, luminous veil behind him. In this backlighting his features sometimes deepened out of sight, nearly making him a silhouette. But the whites of his eyes remained distinct, shards of bright in dirty shadow.

"Only one more," the man said without speaking the name.

"Do you worry about not finishing?" Burden asked.

"No."

"Why?"

"There's no rush."

"You don't want to get it over with?"

"Why?"

"I don't know. To finish it."

"And then what?"

"I don't know."

"Exactly."

"Just to have it done."

"Closure?"

That word sounded strange coming from a man like him. Burden wouldn't have believed he even knew the word.

"I guess."

"No. There is no closure."

That was why there was no future. It wasn't going anywhere. And the man wasn't going anywhere. Like Zeno's arrow, he was only where he was, in the instant. His existence was within a continuum that was neither past nor future, neither leaving nor arriving. It was all of a piece. And yet, like the arrow, he miraculously advanced all the same, between instants, where there was neither time nor memory, neither hope nor disappointment.

The man wasn't ordinary. Maybe he had been before it happened, but not anymore. Some men rise above the ordinary because of who their fathers were, or because of the amount of money they have made, or because of something they have done, or because of the women they have bedded or lived with or married. But this man rose above the ordinary because of what had happened to him, of what he had seen and lived with . . . and because of what he had become as a result.

A fly appeared and lighted on the man's bare right shoulder. In the sunlight it threw a shadow twice its length across the collarbone. The man looked at it to see what he'd felt, then ignored it. The fly was thinking, and so was its host. Moving in advancing jerks, the fly went down into the concave shallow near the man's neck, the relief of trapezius, it was called. The fly stayed there, out of sight.

That, Burden thought, was an odd thing.

Burden watched the relief of trapezius, waiting for the fly to emerge. The shallow wasn't that large. The fly must be sitting in just the perfect square centimeter deep enough to conceal it. What were the odds of a fly positioning itself like that, to become lost in a man's anatomy?

The man raised his right arm from where it rested on the arm of the chair and wiped at the sweat trickling out from under his other arm. Burden watched for the fly to shoot off into the room somewhere. It didn't. Now both the man's arms were resting on the arms of the chair again. He coughed softly, a kind of grunt. Burden cut his eyes to the relief of trapezius. Nothing. It was as if the fly had crawled into a tiny hidden orifice and entered the man's body. Gone.

"It's going to be tonight," Burden said.

The man didn't react. Burden felt sorry for him. It wasn't much of a life, at least the way Burden measured it. Only a few things kept this man alive. And after all five of them were done, he would find solace in suicide. It was as predictable as night. Burden could hear it in his voice.

But Burden knew that was unfair. One man measuring another man's life was always unfair, or unbalanced, or a misunderstanding. In reality you never knew what another man's life was like, and even if you thought you knew, you wouldn't get it right. You never knew, because the only thing you had to measure by was your own life, and that was such a limited thing. You had to live a long time in your imagination to approach another man's life with any sympathy or genuine understanding at all.

Burden thought of Lucía; he didn't know why. He thought of her looking through the viewfinder of her Hasselblad, the world upside down, but even so she understood it and recorded it through a lens of kindness that in itself was misunderstood. He was curious that the man had asked about her. He was curious about it, and he wasn't. Men who lived on the cusp of hell sometimes tended to be sensitive to kindness. It was a little-known fact about great sinners. It was often misunderstood, mostly by people who mistakenly believed they had little in common with those who were lost.

"It's Tano Luquín," Burden said. "I've found him."

The man quit breathing. The movement in his sternum just stopped. Slowly he turned to wax, and his eyes became glass. Though he had been perspiring before, now he began to glisten profusely, as if overwhelming emotion had sucked away his breath and condensed it within him into an oleaginous concentrate that now oozed from every pore.

Then something caught Burden's eye. On the man's shoulder the fly had crept to the cusp of the relief of trapezius. It had stopped, its black head only just emerging from the verge of the shallow. And there it waited.

Chapter 40

"I don't know what to think," Rita said. Norlin had left soon after finishing his story of Mourad Berkat, and she had gone straight to the sink to run a glass of water while Titus had walked out to Norlin's car with him. Now he was gone, and Titus had just come in through the kitchen door. Rita was standing with the back of her hips against the sink, the glass of water in one hand, her hand on her hip.

Titus looked at her and shook his head, then went straight to the refrigerator and took out a bottle of beer. He popped the top off with a bottle opener and took a long drink. Feeling weary, he sat on one of the stools at the island, put the bottle down, and rubbed his face and eyes with both hands.

"I'll tell you something," he said. "That was a pretty damned surprising story. But you know, it shouldn't have been. García told us himself—in so many words—what he does. Face it, Rita, we're pretty naive about these things. We're just . . . naive."

"I don't think Mr. Norlin picked that anecdote randomly, as he claimed," Rita said. "It's tied to what's happening now. Something else is going on with Luquín."

"Yeah, I'm sure there is. We'd be not only naive, but stupid to think there wasn't. Hell, García told us that. We're just a piece of this story. As grim as it is for us, it gets worse the more you know."

He stared out at the veranda. For the first time in a couple of days, he thought about the dogs. Shit. How many years ago had that been?

"That woman," Rita said, "and those children . . ."

He knew what was coming.

"That make you think of us?" she asked.

"Yeah," he said honestly, "it did."

"What if he wants Luquín as desperately as he wanted that Algerian man?"

"You want me to be honest with you," he said, pulling his eyes away from the veranda to her, "he probably does."

She stared at him. Rita could deal with shock. She would pull herself together and deal with it.

"I think that's part of what Norlin was telling us," Titus said, "leaving it up to us to read between the lines. Maybe he didn't know what or how much García had told us, but I think he was trying to get us to understand the scope of our situation. That it's not just about us.

"But that's not all there is to it," he went on. "This isn't the same kind of situation. Just imagine . . . the names on that list. Those men . . . every circumstance is different. They're scattered all over the world, live in all kinds of situations, in caves, in mansions. Some educated and intellectual, some ignorant. It's got to be unbelievably complex. I think we'd be making a terrible mistake to think that every one of these situations is the same, that we can predict the way one plays out based upon the way that another one played out.

"I'll tell you something," he said, turning toward her. "It probably would've been easier on us in some ways if we'd known this much truth—I won't say the whole truth, but this much, at least—going into this. But he couldn't tell us. And if we hadn't been on the verge of blowing this thing apart, he wouldn't have told us when he did. Jesus, think of what's going on here."

He took another long drink of the beer. It was cold. It was good. And it reminded him of before all this, when evil was something in books or movies, when life was simple, and he didn't even know it.

He went on. "But I've got to say, as scared as I am, knowing what we know now has put a different twist on this thing. If this is what García and Norlin say it is . . . we've got to hang in here. We've even got . . . I don't know . . . an obligation, to work with these guys."

"An obligation to help them assassinate someone?" Rita was incredulous.

Titus focused on her.

"Think about it, Rita. If they're telling us the truth, do you feel good about working against them?"

"Well, I don't feel good about helping them."

"Exactly."

"And you keep saying 'if' they're telling us the truth."

"Look, Rita. There's nothing . . . nothing . . . we can do about being in a hell of a situation here. We've just got to do the best we can. I know that sounds lame, but what in the hell other answers do you have?"

Through the kitchen window he saw Kal making his way through the wrought-iron gate in the stone wall that led to the pool and come across the courtyard to the veranda.

It was midafternoon. It seemed an eternity until dark, yet at the same time, it all seemed to be hurtling along so fast that everything could easily fly out of control.

The door from the veranda opened and Kal stepped in.

"Excuse me," he said. "Ryan and I are going to take a look around. Janet's on her way in here from the other side of the house."

"Okay, thanks," Titus said. He walked to the door and watched the two men through the window, striding quickly down the allée of laurels, their MP5s strapped over their shoulders in plain sight.

"Routine stuff," Janet said, walking into the kitchen as Titus was looking out. "It always takes a while before you feel entirely comfortable in a new situation," she added by way of a casual explanation. All three of the bodyguards belonged to the "never show concern because it scares the client" school.

Titus watched them until they disappeared around the knoll.

"It's a big place," he said. "There's a lot to get comfortable with."

"They're used to it," Janet said. "And they like it, which is even more important." She turned her head, tilting it slightly toward her earpiece, and then looked at Titus.

"Kal wants you to come down to the orchard."

Titus looked out and saw him coming back around the knoll at the far end of the allée. He went outside and headed down to meet him.

"You been taking pictures down here lately?" Kal asked, putting his foot up on a boulder at the edge of the trees as he retied his shoelaces.

"Pictures?"

"Yeah, down here." He lifted the other foot and retied that shoelace as well. Titus saw his earpiece and the tiny mike hugging his cheek and curving around toward his mouth.

"No."

Kal reached into his pocket and showed Titus a black plastic disk, the cap of a film canister.

"Thing's new," he said. "I think you've had a visitor."

He looked up and squinted into the bright western light slanting in at the far end of the allée. "Come on," he said to Titus, and they started up the allée.

They got to the entrance of the orchard just as Ryan was heading into the rows of peach trees from the back side. Kal stopped where the front corner of the orchard met the allée. A retaining wall faced with stone blocks stood shoulder high where the orchard began, following a slow, outward-swinging arch as it circled around behind the house and the pool and then sloped to natural grade on the far side of the orchard.

Kal stood with his back to the orchard and looked at the house, trying to see what the man could have seen if he was looking at the house from this vantage point. It made Titus queasy to realize again just how vulnerable to Luquín's surveillance he and Rita had been during these past few days. Luquín literally could have put his hands on them any time he wanted.

Without saying a word, Kal went through the two stone pillars where an old gate used to be, and he and Titus started walking, following the low retaining wall's outward arc. They could hear Ryan coming up through the orchard, and soon they saw him approaching, walking slowly through the trees, scanning back and forth in a very deliberate manner.

Suddenly Kal stopped. He stared at the ground. The wild grass that grew there was flattened out and the ground had been churned about, the crescent shapes of a heel print partially visible here and there in the powdery surface dirt.

He didn't have to explain anything to Titus. Both of them started looking around as Ryan walked up.

"He was here," Kal said, and the two guards started walking back and forth along the base of the wall.

Titus didn't know exactly what they were looking for, but

their subdued urgency reminded him of his dogs when they'd picked up a fresh scent with the constant sweeping of their noses to the ground. They were methodical, but more than a little juiced.

Suddenly Kal stopped and dropped to his knees, his legs straddling the churned-up ground. He stared at the retaining wall right in his face. The stones were a standard quarrying size of sixteen inches wide by eight inches high by twelve inches deep. Solid limestone blocks.

He stared at them closely, his eyes sweeping along the rows as they traveled upward. Gradually he got up off his knees to a crouch, then eventually he was standing upright again. At waist high he reached out and grabbed one of the stones. It was heavy and Titus helped him, as the two of them slipped a loose stone out and let it drop to the ground.

There was a cavity behind the stone, and Kal reached in up to his elbows and grabbed something. When his hands came out he was holding a dark charcoal laptop and a wadded clear plastic bag that looked as though it had been used to protect the laptop.

"Looks like he left in a hurry," he said.

Chapter 41

"I'm working on it now," Herrin said, "but the encryption's pretty damned good. I can't make any promises about how long it'll take."

They were in the guest house, and Burden was coming in on the speakerphone. They didn't know where he was, and he didn't say. But in the momentary hesitations of conversation, there was the distant sound of boat traffic.

"Listen, Titus," Burden said, "this's my screwup entirely. I got sloppy. The worry here is that this guy got a shot of me. We won't know whether he did or not until Mark breaks the encryption. If he did, Luquín'll evaporate, abort this thing. He may already be gone. We may be spinning our wheels here and don't even know it. But if he did ID me . . . if Luquín knows I'm here, it'll get rough. There'll be a steep price to pay for this, Titus."

The afternoon heat had driven them inside. The sun was now at forty-five degrees in a clear sky, nothing to block the heat until the horizon swallowed the light. Macias had yet to open the e-mail from Elías Loza. With an attachment. Something made him cautious, made him not tell Luquín what he had. He glanced at Luquín, who was pacing back and forth in front of the windows looking out onto the deck.

Macias opened the file. No message, which was odd. He opened the first attached picture file. The familiar allée of trees, the legs of people under the canopy of the trees standing in front of the guest cottage. Two men and a woman. He guessed the Cains and one of the technicians. The second picture file: a longer shot showing the two technicians on the veranda and the three people still at the front door of the cottage. There was another person in play now in addition to the technicians they already knew about. Third picture file: Loza's camera concentrating on the unidentified man, who had left the Cains and started down the allée alone. Fourth and fifth picture files: taken from another position, not the retaining wall. The unidentified man at the edge of the woods, his left arm holding a cell phone. But the angle was bad, mostly from the back. The last shot showed the man glancing back as he entered the woods, just his eyes showing over the top of his hand, which was holding the cell phone.

Macias had been sitting with his elbow resting on the dining room table as he stroked his mustache with his index finger, thumb under his chin. His finger stopped. Everything that had been swirling around in his mind, so many of the details to be balanced in his scheme that he had been preparing for a full month, came to a sudden halt. All sensory perception evaporated except his sight, and his sight registered nothing but the eyes . . . and something vaguely familiar about them. Where had he seen these eyes before?

Chinga——! What in the fuck was this? He looked up, glancing at Luquín, who was absently picking at a scab on the back of his hand and gazing out across the pool to the valley below and the hills beyond toward Cain's house. He shot a glance at Roque, who was sitting to one side of the room, reading—well, looking at the pictures in—a copy of *People* magazine.

Macias went back to the photograph, just to confirm his sensation of something familiar. Shit, yes. But he didn't know who this was. He didn't know.

But it wasn't necessary that he know who this was. The fact that he was there, the fact that he was leaving Cain's property in secrecy, was a clear indication that something was going on behind the scenes. Something was cooking. They were not, after all, seeing everything that Cain had going on.

Unable to control it, Macias could feel the slow arrival of a dark, hairy fear. How had his people missed this? What was Luquín going to do when he heard about this? If they could believe what their bug had picked up, in twenty-four hours Tano would have his money. How was he going to react to this late-arriving revelation that threw everything into question?

Could they believe the bug? Something was going on here. And how long had this unidentified man been working for Cain? Who was he talking to on the cell phone? What had he been doing in the guest cottage? Macias knew they had set up an electronic control room in there to deal with communications countermeasures, if nothing else. But what if there was something else? What if Macias was only hours away from an implosion here?

His mind was racing, hurtling ahead in an effort to anticipate what his situation might be, what his options might be. Was he too late? Just in time? Ahead of Cain's game? What was Cain's game? How good was his game?

Just then Macias's incoming e-mail pinged again, startling him. From Loza. Another picture file. Only one. Macias opened it. It was a photograph of two men crossing the courtyard behind Cain's veranda. Both men were carrying automatic weapons slung over their shoulders.

Macias sat very still, not wanting to attract attention to himself until he figured out what he was going to do. Why hadn't Loza sent a message with the picture files? Had he been in a hurry? Had he been caught before he could send a message! Did Cain know that Loza had sent these? And to whom?

Did Cain really intend to pay up the money the next day in order to save lives? Or was this just a ploy to keep Luquín hanging around until they could move against him? Was Cain setting a trap?

Did Macias have time to turn things around, to salvage the situation?

The questions flew at him so fast, he felt he was experiencing the emotional equivalent of data overload. But in this case it was fear overload, and the threatening result was not a system crash, but uncontrollable panic.

He could save Luquín's life by evacuating him right now. Just walk over to him and tell him, put him in the Navigator, and take him to the airstrip. He would be safe in Mexico in time to watch the evening news.

But did this unidentified man's presence mean that it was all over? If Macias followed his own rules, yes. Any sign of a countering effort meant quitting the scheme. This was the fucking U.S., after all.

On the other hand, they were only hours away from collecting a damned fortune.

Macias immediately closed the Loza e-mails and erased them. He tried to clear his thoughts. Think. That guy could've been anybody. Just because he was there didn't mean he was competent or accomplished at whatever it was he was doing. Didn't mean he was a professional. Maybe Cain was trying to play Spy Man.

But what if this was a serious move? What if this was the endgame and Macias's greed was clouding his reasoning? Both Macias and Luquín had agreed that the reward was worth the risk, but if it failed, well, then they had differing points of view. Luquín took every failure as a personal insult. As irrational as that was, it didn't change the fact that he believed it.

And now, the arrival of bodyguards meant that Luquín's order to kill Rita Cain was impossible in the short term.

The pressure for Macias was sudden and excruciating. Cayetano Luquín would have him killed for this one. If not immediately, then later, when Macias was least expecting it. Tano would see the failure of this operation—the loss of so much money—as an unforgivable betrayal.

Suddenly, getting Luquín out safely seemed less of a priority. In fact, it actually seemed like a stupid move.

This wasn't a time for half measures. Everything had to be put on the table for consideration.

Chapter 42

The two fishermen had been maneuvering the bass boat along the northern bank of Lake Austin for half an hour, every so often putting in next to the cliffside woods, tying up temporarily to an overhanging tree and then casting their lures into the shade along the bank. The boat was covered with a canvas canopy to keep the searing afternoon sun off them as they dabbled along, heading in the direction of the looming steel arches of the Loop 360 bridge.

They were having lousy luck. The ski boats were active on this particular afternoon, roaring up and down the center of the long lake, throwing an endless series of swelling wakes toward the wooded shores. The fishermen stubbornly worked their way in the direction of the bridge, stoically tolerating the rolling action of their boat, casting uselessly into the thin margin of shadows thrown onto the water by the woods that crowded against the limestone cliffs.

Finally they tried one last spot. After tying up close to the bank, they pulled the boat under a thick shelter of oaks. From across the lake the boat was almost hidden, but no one noticed. The bass boat had been piddling along for three-quarters of an hour now, and all of the attention on the water was attracted to the skiers who blazed up and down in their lanes in the lake's center. Summer afternoons on this part of the lake were given over to water sports that were louder and faster than fishing.

From the clifftop homes above, the bass boat hadn't been visible at all for the last half hour.

The boat hugged its shady bower for nearly twenty-five minutes. The ski boats continued to plow liquid furrows in the lake, only to have them dissipate in swells that headed slowly for the shores in a lugubrious flight from the boats that had created them.

Finally the anglers had had enough. Slowly the boat emerged from overhanging vegetation under the high cliffs and moved out into the lake. After crossing to the other side, it turned southward and picked up speed as it headed downriver toward the main part of the city. Soon the boat was clipping along, wasting no time. It was too far from shore and moving too fast for anyone to see clearly under the deep shade of its canvas canopy. But anyone who had had the opportunity, or cared enough to follow closely the boat's progress up, and now down, the river, would have made the curious observation that there seemed to be only one angler in the bass boat now.

When the telephone rang, Rita picked it up in Titus's office, where she was still making calls about Carla.

"May I please speak to Mr. Cain?" a man asked.

Rita froze. He had a Spanish accent. All of the planning, all of the tactical maneuverings, were taking place over secure transmissions. What was this? Was it unrelated? She threw a look at Janet, who was standing at the window.

"May I tell him who's calling?"

"He's expecting me."

Another alarm bell.

"Just a second," she said, "I'll have to connect you to his phone." She punched the hold button and spoke to Janet. "This is someone asking for Titus. Mexican accent. Won't leave his name."

"Just put him through," she said, and then she turned aside and spoke softly into her mike.

Herrin was tapping away on the laptop found in the orchard, with Titus and Cline looking over his shoulders. Cline, who was wearing headphones and a mike on a long cord, was the communications hub for everyone. He heard all transmissions among the bodyguards and all the phone calls.

"Uhhh . . . ," Herrin said.

The three of them were looking at a picture of Rita just about as naked as anyone could be and still be wearing clothes. She was beautiful.

"Son of a bitch," Titus said. "How many of those are there?"

"Uhh . . . one other," Herrin said, closing the image.

"Let's see it," Titus said, and Herrin hit the keys.

Unbelievable.

"Delete it," Titus said, "and keep going." Jesus Christ. He was furious, and uneasy with the creepy feeling that came over him as an image popped into his head of some guy crouching behind the stone wall taking nearly nude pictures of Rita.

Herrin's fingers snapped over the keys in double time, as if to get the hell away from those images as fast as possible. Then he hit the ones he was looking for. Five shots. He went through them quickly, slowing on the last two. He threw them both on the screen at the same time. The three of them stared at the photos.

"I just don't see how you could identify him from those," Titus said.

"I guess that depends on what kind of software they're going to use," Herrin said.

"Yeah, I guess so," Titus agreed. "But, right off the bat, I don't see how this is any great revelation for them."

The phone rang on the coffee table in front of the sofa. Surprised, Titus saw that it was coming from his office. He went over and picked it up. He glanced at Cline, who seemed to be listening to some other communication.

"Titus," Rita said, "this is some guy with a Spanish accent for you. Wouldn't give his name."

"Did he say what he wanted?"

"He said you were expecting the call."

Titus turned to Cline, who was already nodding at him and heading for the digital trace-and-record setup sitting on folding tables against one wall.

"Titus, I'm coming over," Rita said. "I want to hear this."

Before he could object she disconnected, and he glanced at Cline.

"She can use those headphones over there," Cline said, pointing at the other end of the table. "We're good to go."

Titus punched the button on the phone.

"This is Titus."

"My name is Jorge Macias. I believe you know about me already."

Titus, stunned, said nothing.

"I think you do," Macias said. "I want you to know that I am taking a deadly risk by making this call to you. I have to meet with you, Mr. Cain. We have to talk."

Another pause. Titus didn't know what to say. The cottage door flung open and Rita and Janet came in. Herrin caught them, cautioned them to be quiet, and guided Rita to the head-phones across the room.

"I don't know who you are," Titus said. "What's this about?"

"Listen to me," Macias said. "There is no time to play games here. Your situation is critical. Things . . . out of my control, are happening. Things that were not anticipated. We are now in a situation that is getting very close to being all or nothing—for both of us. And if we don't talk, we are both going to regret that we didn't."

"And I'm supposed to believe this?"

"Believe it. All I have to do when I hang up here is push one button on my cell phone and everything on this end of this situation disappears." Pause. "But, Mr. Cain, I think you know by now that that will not be the end of it for you. And, believe me, you have no idea how much worse it can get."

Silence.

"Does that mean anything to you?" Macias asked.

Long pause. Titus saw no use in pretending any further.

"Yeah," he said, "it means something to me. Tell me, though, what's happened . . . what's changed that makes you want to talk to me?"

"I have to tell you that in private. Only you and I can make the decisions we have to make. We have to understand each other very clearly."

Titus glanced at Rita, whose eyes were wide open as she shook her head no.

"You understand, don't you," Titus said, "that if some-thing happens to me—"

"Mr. Cain, you're missing the point. Nothing's going to happen to you. In fact, now that I've made this call I can't af-ford for anything to happen to you. You're wasting time. When can you meet?"

Titus's antennae were vibrating. You didn't have to be an expert in intelligence tradecraft to see that this could be a major shift in the momentum of this ordeal. Was it possible that Macias was thinking of compromising Luquín? Titus's gut told him this could be a crucial turning point.

Or it could be a trap.

"I'll have to get back to you."

"In twenty minutes I will call you again," Macias said, and the line went dead.

Rita whipped off the headphones. "You can't be considering this," she said, and the mixture of anger and fear in her face was painful to see.

"Damn right I am," Titus said, and Rita shot a look at Janet as if seeking help. Janet met her gaze stoically, saying nothing.

Titus looked at Herrin and Cline. "Get García on the line and play that conversation to him. Then I'll talk to him."

While they were doing that, Titus turned back to Rita.

"I'm not going to do anything stupid," he said. "If this really is a new development, not a part of Luquín's plans, if this really is an unexpected opportunity for us to end this thing quickly, then I've got to do it."

"But why you? You've got two professionals right out there"—she gestured outside—"who can handle this kind of thing."

"Didn't you hear what he said? It's got to be me. In private."

"Sure, he's going to say that."

"Rita, what if this is legit—"

"Oh, Titus!" Tears of frustration were glistening in her eyes. "What? Were you going to say 'legitimate'? That word has no *meaning* with these people."

"García's getting ready to call you," Cline said.

Titus nodded at Cline and then looked at Rita. "Let's just take it one step at a time," he said. "Okay?"

The expression on her face passed from incredulity to a fearful resignation as they stared at each other. Then she nodded.

"Yeah," she said, "okay." She was sucking it up. Rita knew how to do that. When the time came that they needed her to do that, she would do it.

Chapter 43

This time it was clear that Burden was riding in a boat. He had to speak into the cell phone with a raised voice, and the surrounding thrum was drowning out any other ambient noise.

"No, this isn't a trap," Burden said. "That isn't the way these two men work."

"How can you be so sure?"

"A trap is risky; it's messy. A trap in Bogotá, Rio, fine. Anything goes wrong there, they shoot their way out and disappear. But it's a different story here. Here what they want is quiet. Silence. And, as you can see with our own situation, that places a hell of a constraint on them."

"Then what's the deal here?"

"Macias is breaking his own rules. Luquín trusts Macias as much as he's capable of trusting anybody. He's comfortable that at the first sign of something suspicious Macias will give the signal, and they'll all vanish. And that's exactly what should have happened. But it looks like the only guy in the world who's capable of mortally betraying Tano Luquín is thinking about doing just that."

"Then this is it, isn't it," Titus said, aware of the amazement in his own voice even as he said it. "This is our big break."

"With that one phone call," García said, "Jorge Macias crossed the Rubicon. That's the great risk he referred to. He's going to burn Luquín. Maybe."

"Maybe? What's the matter? You think he recognized you, then?"

"I don't know, but he didn't really have to. He saw the armed bodyguards. He saw an unknown somebody walking off into the woods talking on a cell phone. That was enough right there to cause him to abort this thing."

"But that's not the way it's coming down, is it," Titus said. This was deal-making. This was something Titus could understand. He knew an ass-saving maneuver when he saw one. "He's trying to work something out, find a way of cutting his losses without losing the whole thing. Shit! We've got to move fast on this. Don't give him time to reconsider. He's got to be strung out, knowing he's risking everything. That's a good negotiating position for us."

"Hold on, Titus. I've already set the wheels in motion on this end. We need to make sure we don't start something with Macias that's going to cross up what's already under way. I don't want to let any of these guys get away from us. Any of them." Pause. "Let me check some stuff. Just a second."

Titus held on to the encrypted cell phone as though it were a lifeline. He wanted to do this. He was surprised at how badly he wanted to do it. This was his chance to transform himself from the victim into the pursuer, and he didn't want to lose it.

"Now listen, Titus," Burden said, back on the line. "Go ahead and arrange the meeting, but make it as late as you can. No earlier than ten-thirty. And even after that if you can. The later the better. I need time to get my people in place. I want every single one of his people covered, and that's going to take some fast and careful planning. This is where all that stuff from last night's going to pay off."

"What about the location?"

"He's going to insist on picking that. But stick with your late hour. Negotiate. Have a good reason why it can't be earlier."

"How do you want me to handle his proposal?"

"Just hear him out and do the best you can. Do this, though: Make him happy. Bargain with him, but let him think he's getting away with something, that he's cutting the best deal that he can."

"What if he wants me to agree to something that'll put you at a disadvantage later down the road? How will I know that?"

"Well, you can't ask for more time to think it over. That'll make it even more obvious that you're not the last word here, that someone else is running the negotiations. That could kill this thing. Macias may be willing to stick his neck out, but he's not going to leave it out there long enough for you to cut his throat. He's going to be paying attention to every word, every nuance. He's the one who's going to be looking for the trap."

"Is there anything I absolutely shouldn't do at that meeting so I don't screw up things for you afterward?"

There was a long silence at the other end. Again Titus was left to interpret the reason for that.

"Listen, Titus," Burden said. "There's not going to be any afterward for these guys. This is it. We're going to use this meeting to close them down."

Titus couldn't believe it.

"It doesn't matter what you promise the guy," Burden said. "Whatever you promise him, it's not ever going to happen."

Titus glanced at Rita. Her eyes were riveted on him.

"So, this is it," he said.

"This is it."

Before he got off the phone, Burden wanted to talk to Janet. Titus handed the phone to her, and then he and Rita walked out to the patio behind the cottage. The patio walls were covered with *moneda* vines, and star jasmine crawled up trellises in the corners. A window in the patio's walls, covered with decorative wrought iron, looked out toward the end of the laurel allée and the valley beyond.

Titus told her about the conversation, and when he came to the end, to Burden's remark, she gasped.

"Yeah," he said. "That was a shocker to me, too."

She had been standing in front of the jasmine, which was in full bloom. It was late in the day, and the patio was cooling in deep shade now. To his surprise, she seemed to wilt. She un-folded her arms and buried her face in her hands. The vine's tiny, star-shaped bursts of white blossoms were a dazzling backdrop for her. Nearly perfectly framed behind her head was the grilled window through which he could see in the distance the last of the sun on the tops of the hills across the valley.

"This is too much," she said through her hands. He could see her chest moving, searching for air. He looked at the top of her head, her thick buttery hair parted in the middle and pulled back. "The damned tension," she said, and took her hands down and looked at him with red eyes. "Titus, I'm so afraid."

He went over to her and gently put his arms around her. He felt her simply fold herself into his embrace, a rare moment for Rita as she completely gave in to the vulnerability that she could no longer overcome. It was an emotion that she had con-quered again and again throughout her life, a conquest that had earned her the reputation for being a strong, rock-solid woman. But this time she just couldn't do it.

"It's going to be all right," he said. "I'm afraid, too, no doubt about it. But we both know that I've got to do this. And I want to do it. I've never wanted to do anything in my life more than I want to do this."

Chapter 44

When Macias started back into the house from the shade around the pool where he'd been on the phone, he saw Luquín through the tinted glass walls, looking at him. Luquín was wearing sunglasses because he was looking outside, and he was watching Macias as if he were watching a fish in an aquarium. But Macias feared there was more on Luquín's mind than idle curiosity.

Macias closed the door behind him, walked over to the sofa, and flopped down where he'd left a soft drink in a glass of ice on the coffee table. The nine-foot television screen was flickering with a movie that Roque had been watching, sitting in an armchair like a cruel imbecile with his headphones on. Luquín didn't like the damn television, but he let Roque watch it because it was one of the few things the guy liked to do besides reading the sepia-toned adult comic books that he devoured.

"So, what's going on?" Luquín asked when Macias picked up his soft drink.

"What do you mean?"

"You been on the phone a lot."

"I don't want any screwups," Macias said. "If we can believe what we heard Cain tell his wife, things are going to start heating up. So far it's been fairly smooth. I want it to stay that way."

Luquín took off his sunglasses and put his hands in his pocket. He looked down and walked from one side of the glass wall to the other, thinking. Macias glanced at the movie. He didn't recognize it. He looked at Luquín. He had to admit that Luquín's pensive mood made him uncomfortable.

And it should have. In the last hour Macias had initiated steps that, if followed through, would change the rest of his life no matter what happened. Actually, even if he didn't follow through, that call would change the rest of his life. If the people working with Cain were smart, they would know that by simply contacting them for a meeting, Macias had ended his relationship with Luquín. They could use that phone call—again, if they were smart, they would have recorded it—to blow things apart.

Did Luquín suspect any of this? You had to always fear that Luquín suspected everything. He was uncanny about this sort of treachery within his ranks. And sometimes—Macias had seen it more than a few times—he even wiped out completely loyal men because he suspected them, wrongly.

Macias had one thing in his favor: He was Luquín's *número uno*. So far Luquín had never turned on anyone that high. It was the bane of a tyrant that at some point he had to trust someone. He had to. But not forever.

"I've been thinking—" Luquín suddenly interrupted himself and turned from the windows where he'd been standing, jingling the American nickels and dimes in his pocket. "You started the thing on Cain's wife yet?"

"Yeah," Macias lied, trying to sound on top of it. Luquín took it for granted that if Macias said a certain thing was in the works, then it was in the works, and it would be done. He was getting complacent in his middle age. He relied on others to take care of the details for him.

"I've been thinking," Luquín continued, picking up where he had interrupted himself. "I want that to be one special hit. It's got to be an accident, you know, like the rest of them so he'll know what happened—but even so, you know, a special accident. Something so that, when it happens it brings shame on her, public shame, so that he can't cover it up."

Macias stared at him. This guy was something. "You have an idea?"

"No, not really. Drugs, sex, those things. But the important thing . . . not something he can cover up. That'll be the thing, you know, the twist of the knife."

"That may take a little while to develop."

"That's okay. When it happens, he'll know. Maybe that will even be better. He thinks he's rid of me and then . . . ughhh." He made a gesture of knifing someone in the stomach with an underswinging thrust, holding, then twisting. "But for sure, the thing is, I want it to be a very shameful thing." He turned back to the window, looking out. "That *pendejo* really pissed me off. Shit." He turned again. "And I want pictures. I can send him those pictures for years." He turned back to the window.

Macias said nothing.

Luquín gave it some more thought. He turned around and wandered in Macias's direction.

"Never go away, Jorge," he said, almost to himself. "That's the best torment of all. Hell, I just put it on the damn calendar and forget about it. When the date rolls around I just do it, whatever it is. For them it's worse than just the memory of something terrible. That fades with time. But knowing that I'm going to come back, sometime, some way, and remind them of it with a fresh approach, hell, they can't stop worrying about that. That's real torture. The anxiety consumes them like a fucking disease."

Macias had never heard Luquín talk like this before. What

was this? Did he know something after all? Did he suspect? Was he trolling for a reaction from Macias that would tell him something about his suspicions? If ever Macias had to have himself under control, it was now. The fact was, Luquín could not know what Macias had decided to do, because aside from talking to Cain, the betrayal was entirely within Macias's head. He hadn't uttered a word of it to anyone. There was only the telephone call, that's all. Macias knew that Luquín was capable of playing mind games, and he cautioned himself not to be drawn into them.

"You think about it," Macias said, and he turned up his glass and finished his soda to cover his discomfort. "Whatever you want to do." He looked at his watch. "Later tonight I'm going to meet with my people. That will take a couple of hours. Is there anything you want me to know before I do that? This will probably be the last time I'll see them personally before this is over. I want to make sure they understand what we're expecting."

"And what are we expecting?"

"If Cain pays ahead of schedule, as we hope, I want to release most of these people quickly. Having them here is only a risk. Whatever you decide about Cain's wife can be handled separately."

"Of course, Cain hasn't yet told us what he is going to do."

"No," Macias said, crossing one leg over the other and putting an arm on the back of the sofa, doing his damnedest to seem relaxed. "And what if he changes his mind and doesn't pay up immediately?"

But Luquín didn't answer. Though he was looking at Macias, the slight smile on his face belonged to other thoughts.

"This," Luquín said, "is a lot of money, Jorge. You are going to be a very wealthy man."

"Good," Macias said.

Chapter 45

When Burden returned to the rental house, he was hot and tired, and his jeans were wet to the knees. He had already released the three-man encryption crew that had helped them decipher the messages picked up by the Beechcraft, and all that remained were Romolo Calò's three men and his own surveillance van crew of three.

One man was sitting in the van monitoring the LorGuides and their yellow and green dots representing the human and vehicle moles Titus had managed to put in place. The rest of them were on the humid and airless screened porch, lying about listlessly like Bedouins, trying to get through the late afternoon heat. Pieces of paper, maps, and photos were scattered everywhere as they had been trying to work out the logistics of what they needed to do.

Burden got an RC out of an ice chest, opened it, and walked onto the porch. He sat with his back to the wall, put the can of RC on the floor, and unbuttoned his shirt without saying a word. Everyone looked at him. He took a long drink of the soda.

"Recent developments," he said, and proceeded to tell them what had just happened.

Calò whistled softly under his breath.

"So, essentially," Burden said, "Cain thinks Macias has just sold out his boss. I have to say, I agree. More important, Macias himself has given us the answer to the problem of how to isolate Luquín in the house. Follow me, Calò, and see if my count is the same as yours.

"From our surveillance run last night, it seems that there are six of them staying in the house. Luquín, his bodyguard, Roque, and their driver. They use the black Navigator. Macias, his bodyguard, and their driver travel in the blue Navigator. We needed to get these last three out of the house, which would leave a driver, Roque, and Luquín at the house."

"That leaves the two guards and the driver in the Pathfinder," Calò said. "When Macias leaves, they'll probably come into the neighborhood close by to be ready to move in if Luquín should need them. So, we have three problem spots: Three armed men in Macias's car, that's including Macias. Three armed men in the Pathfinder. And nobody to cover their surveillance van." He looked at Burden. "We're short by one crew."

Burden said, "You're just going to let the surveillance crew go?"

"And keep the van."

"Okay, then, I'll get Gil to put together a team to take care of the surveillance van for us."

Calò nodded. "And then what do you want done with Macias himself?"

Burden squeezed the sides of his RC can in and out, making a little popping sound, the only sound in the room besides the roaring of cicadas in the cedar brakes just outside.

"He disappears, same as the others."

Calò nodded.

"One other thing," Burden said. "One of the Navigators, I don't care which one, needs to be left at Luquín's house after all of this is done."

"Fine," Calò said.

No one asked him what was going to happen at the house, who was going to take care of the driver left there with Roque and Luquín, or what would become of Roque and Luquín themselves. But Burden's silence about it was enough to kick an imaginative mind into high gear. There were a few glances around the room, but Burden, preoccupied deep within himself, either ignored them or was completely unaware. It didn't matter either way. The matter would go no further.

In Burden's small world, men and women with secrets were the accepted norm. It was what made them who they were. But a rare few were profoundly enigmatic, even to their peers. They were granted unusual trust and latitude in their personal mystery because of their nearly legendary reputations. The impending events at the clifftop house on Las Lomitas were the kinds of things that fed those mythologies.

Burden stood stiffly and stepped away from the group of men. Staring out into the hot woods, he pulled out his cell phone to call Gil Norlin. The high temperature was bringing the essence out of the sap of the cedars, filling the dying day with an aromatic fragrance. When he was finished with his conversation, he continued to stand with his back to the group, lost in thought.

Pacing back and forth in front of his men, Calò ignored Burden while he reviewed yet again the details of the coming operation, which was now only hours away. Again they explored the huge number of possibilities that could be applied to a basic scenario that evolved very quickly. The algebra of a specific tactical operation with limited personnel was minutely explored, theories were proposed, attacked, adjusted, and restated. Then attacked again. The unknowable variables were always there, impossible to eliminate. The suddenly unexpected was the only thing they could count on for sure. The rest of it was rehearsed with a fierce concentration.

At a certain moment, when a fine point of a maneuver proposed by Baas was being shredded by the doubts of the others, Calò turned and went over to stand by Burden. There was nothing to look at, just the woods.

"Did you get Gil?"

"He's going to get back to us. He doesn't think it's a problem, but he'll confirm it with you as soon as he can. I gave him all the particulars about the van and its crew, but he's going to want to get it from you, too. You can tell him where you want the thing delivered."

"Good," Calò said. Silence. "This isn't one of the simplest ones."

"We didn't have enough time," Burden said. "I'm sorry it had to be like this." It wasn't an apology; it was a regret. He reached up and touched the rusty screen with the rim of his RC can, rubbing it along the wire with a tiny thrumming sound. He touched it again and then dropped his hand to his side, holding the can against his leg.

"It's one of the human curses," he said, "being afraid of time and what it can do to us. About a hundred years ago I heard an old woman say—she had just become a widow—that Time was a whore without a conscience. She gave herself to the damnedest people and denied herself to the saints. It was a vivid if kind of confusing aphorism, but I think I understand what she was getting at." He thought about it a moment. "But, in the end, it seems that Time treats everyone the same after all: Sooner or later she runs out on all of us."

Chapter 46

Macias called back in exactly twenty minutes as he had promised. The conversation was quick and brittle. They would meet at La Terrazza, an Italian restaurant on Loop 360. Quarter to eleven. Macias didn't give Titus time to negotiate anything later, but luckily it was within Burden's preferred time frame anyway. The line went dead.

For Titus, the next few hours passed in a complex mixture of grim anticipation, frantic preparation, and busywork to keep from thinking. From his office, he finally dealt with one of the things he had dreaded the most. He put in a call to Carla's daughters.

After that, he also called Louise Thrush. Both calls were excruciating. When he hung up the phone, he was wringing wet with perspiration.

He got up and went down the hallway to the kitchen, where Rita and Janet had been making sandwiches.

Rita looked at him expectantly as he walked in, but he said nothing. He passed up the sandwiches sitting in a tray on the island along with glasses of iced tea and got a bottle of Scotch out of the pantry, put ice in a tumbler, and poured a drink.

"How did that go with those calls?" Rita asked, trying to make the question sound nonprovocative. The waiting was like attending a terminally ill friend; there was simply no way to get away from it. It had to be done, and you had to pretend not to be depressed or afraid or you wouldn't be any good to anyone. It was an exercise in the suspension of normal emotions.

He sipped the Scotch. "Actually, it was terrible," he said. "The twins"—he shook his head—"Leslie cried inconsolably. She just couldn't stop. I don't know what I said to her. Tried to be comforting. I don't know. Lynne was quiet and polite, almost as if she weren't affected at all. Something's changed deep inside her. She's not going to let anything, or anyone, comfort her."

He went to the Scotch again.

"And Louise?" Rita asked.

"Bless her heart. She wanted to review the funeral service. The songs, the scriptures. The order of things. She wanted to talk . . . you know, about Charlie. I took a lot of time with her. She needed me to do that." He paused. "And I wanted to . . . for her."

He shook his head again, then turned and walked out the kitchen door to the veranda. At Kal's request, all the landscaping lights had been turned on, but the lights on the veranda were turned off. Titus took a momentary refuge there, the glow from the kitchen windows falling in puddles on the flagstones. He caught a whiff of honeysuckle on the night air.

But the respite was brief. His cell phone rang.

"This is Ryan. Can you come on over to the cottage? We need to start getting you ready."

"Okay." Titus went to the kitchen door and stuck his head in. "Rita, we're getting things ready to go."

Everyone was there except Burden: the three bodyguards;

Herrin and Cline, wearing headphones and watching the screens and listening to transmissions; and Rita and Titus.

"We all need to be on the same page here," Kal said. "Here's what's set up." He was showing the strain. He and Ryan had been working nonstop to coordinate what needed to be done in the cottage with what was happening with Burden's people. Since Macias's phone call, the cottage had felt like the control tower at DFW. Plans were made and changed in a swirl of perpetual motion. Everyone had a job to do, and they had just enough manpower to cover the operation without a single person to spare.

"We've got about an hour," Kal said, "before you need to drive away from here. García will be mobile the whole time, watching the dots on the LorGuides. There are three groups of Macias's people who need to be dealt with. García has a tactical group from out of town covering two of those. Gil Norlin has quickly pulled together a couple of people to handle Macias's surveillance van. All of them will be in communication with us, each other, and García in his van. And they'll all have LorGuides, too, so they can watch each other's progress."

Kal wiped his mouth. The pressure was bringing on the nervous tics. He was pacing around the room, occasionally referring to a clipboard.

Titus made a mental note about the tactical group from out of town.

"What about Luquín?" Rita asked, looking around as if she wondered why someone weren't addressing the most obvious target of concern.

"Yeah, García's got someone covering him, too," Kal said quickly, and moved on. "There's one mole sensor left," he said, stepping over and handing it to Titus. "Use it, don't lose it."

Titus peeled it off its clear sheet and put it on the inside of his right arm, at just about the spot you'd insert an IV.

"We're going to put a ticker on your Rover," Kal continued, "but they'll assume it's there. Still ..." He shrugged. "They want you to get to La Terrazza early, go on inside to the courtyard, and wait. That'll pull Macias in to you and, maybe, separate him from his driver and bodyguard at the Navigator."

"Then what?" Titus asked.

"Have your conversation. Come home."

Titus nodded. "How long do I keep him there?"

"Until we call you. One of us, or García."

"Then I take the cell phone?"

"Yeah."

"The encrypted one?"

"Yeah."

"What about a wire?"

"Useless. He'll check; he'll find it."

Again Titus nodded. This all sounded too slick.

"Listen," he said, looking at both Kal and Ryan, "I know I don't know a damn thing about what's going on here, or should be going on here, but this just doesn't feel quite right. This just seems a little too neat."

"It seems neat," Ryan said quickly and with unexpected candor, "because we're not telling you everything. The details. A lot of shit's going down, but you're not going to be a part of all of it. It's not your job. You don't need to know." He paused. "And you shouldn't know."

"The point is," Kal added, wiping his mouth, "those other guys don't know what's going on at your end, either. And they don't need to know. But everybody's got to do their thing right if this operation's going to succeed. If you don't hold Macias at La Terrazza long enough, you could be jeopardizing what the other guys are doing. They've got to have the time they need. Everybody knows what the others are doing, in general, so we all understand the rationale for our own responsibilities. But beyond that, you're not any different from anybody else in not knowing all the details."

"Okay," Titus said. That made sense. Shit, he guessed it made sense. "Look, at least give me some idea of where the situation is most critical. When is something most likely to go wrong here?"

Kal nodded at him. "The moment you drive out those gates at the bottom of the hill, from that point on something's likely to go wrong. It's that damn simple. Every moment of every operation is the most critical. You can never—ever—kid yourself about that."

Titus stared at him. But just in case he was having any doubts about it, Ryan spoke up again.

"That's no bullshit platitude," he said. "That's the message of salvation."

Titus and Rita stepped outside and stood at the head of the allée. The landscape lights illuminated the beginning of the long double row of laurels until they converged into the sloping darkness.

"That was sobering," Rita said, referring to their brief tutorial inside. "Okay, Titus, I'm going to be following this every step of the way in there with the rest of them. I insisted. We've already talked about it. But the moment you're in the clear, you call me."

"Yeah, I will," he said. He was suddenly humming with adrenaline. He was aware of a kind of giddy anticipation, but at the same time it was mitigated by the things that weren't said. The stuff he had to read between the lines. It seemed absolutely impossible that Burden and this loose collection of people who seemed underprepared and short on time would be able to do what he knew Burden wanted to do. But they were going ahead with it. He wondered if this was the way it always felt for these people. Or if every operation was different and carried with it a different set of emotions. Was it an unending stream of never-repeated episodes? Was that the juice that kept these people in this business?

"Titus?" Rita had taken his arm and pulled herself to him, close. He could smell her, not her perfume, but her, a far more compelling fragrance. He put his arms around her.

"Tomorrow it'll be over," she said. "And we'll have our lives back. I believe that."

"You know, I do, too," he lied. He didn't believe it because he knew they'd never have their lives back. Not the way they had been, anyway. But they might be free of Luquín, and right now he thought that would be worth any amount of lying and killing. That appalled him even as he thought it, but he wasn't going to pretend that he had moral scruples about what was about to happen.

The door to the cottage opened and Kal stood on the threshold.

"Time to go," he said.

Titus embraced Rita and held her very tight. He felt his throat thicken with emotion. He couldn't say a word. But he knew that she understood exactly what this embrace meant. It was a thing they did. And then she said what she always said when he did it.

"And I love you, too, Titus Cain."

And she kissed him, and he walked away with Kal into the shadows.

Chapter 47

The Dodge van sat in the empty parking lot of the small, green glass office building overlooking Bull Creek Road. The van had been there twenty minutes. At ten-thirty at night, the office had been closed a long time. When the gray van arrived, it had pulled around behind an island of trees, preventing it from being seen from the street in front of the building.

In the back of the van were three communications technicians wearing headphones and small mikes. One of the technicians checked in with Macias every half hour as required. Their job was routine at this point, just listening mostly, making sure there were no breakdowns in communication between Macias and the other teams. At the moment they were listening to transmissions between the Pathfinder and Macias's blue Navigator, which was just now pulling away from the house on Las Lomitas. Macias was making sure the Pathfinder was pulling in to cover the house while he was gone. Macias didn't say where he was going. Aside from Tano Luquín, he was the only man on the job who didn't have to explain himself to anyone.

When the black Lexus came into the lot off the street, the

three men in the van froze. One of them slowly got up and moved forward and sat behind the steering wheel. He intently watched the Lexus through the darkened windshield.

The car's lights went off, and for a second nothing happened. Then the driver's door opened, and in the light that came on in the car's interior, the man in the van saw a petite blonde sitting behind the wheel. She wore a light tank top and shorts and was digging through her purse.

"Whoa, will you look at that," the man said, and he leaned over and picked up a pair of binoculars from the passenger's seat while his two companions peered through one of the large windows darkened by one-way glass.

"What's she doin', Del?" one of the guys asked, a set of headphones dangling around his neck.

"Looking for keys, I guess," the driver said.

Del was Anglo, the other two were Mexican Americans. All three were from Juarez.

The woman got out of the car and slung her purse over her shoulder. She punched the remote car lock on her key chain and headed for the front of the building at a brisk walk.

"Woman on a mission," Del mused to himself. "I got a mission for her."

"She forgot something. Working at home," one of the other men said, shrugging.

"Look . . . at . . . that . . . ass," Del said. The nightvision binoculars brought her up close, way close.

The two men in the back glanced at each other.

"Pull your eyeballs back in, Del," one of them said.

The woman went to the double glass doors and put a key into the latch. She had her back to them now, fiddling with the lock.

"Looks like it no workey," Del said.

Frustrated, the woman headed back to the car. Her body

language said she was pissed. As she approached the car, she reached out and punched the remote lock again, and just as she was swinging the door open, she stopped. Slowly she leaned to the side and looked down at her left rear tire.

"Uh-oh," Del narrated, "look at thiiis. Oh, baby, we got a flat *tire.*"

"What?" The two guys in the back of the van leaned over again to look out the window, ignoring for the moment the bank of monitors in front of each of them.

"You got to be kidding," one of them said.

The woman stood and stared at the tire, dumbfounded.

"Watch her whip out the old cell tele," the other one said. But she didn't. Instead she slammed her purse on the ground and kicked the side of the car.

"She pissed!" Del said.

"She left the thing at home," one of the men speculated. "She just ran up here real quick to grab something, and she got the wrong keys and left the cell on the table at home. There you go," he said, "that's how life does you. Man, it was supposed to have been so simple . . . just run up there and get this thing . . ."

"She can't change the damn tire," Del said. "Fifty bucks says she can't do it."

The woman raised her arm again and pointed the remote at the trunk and the lid came open. She went around to the back and looked inside. She just stood there and looked in. Then she turned and looked at the drive that led up from the street.

"No help in sight," Del narrated, still peering through the binoculars, still going over her legs, savoring the size of her sweeties. "Shit," he said, "duty calls."

"What!" both voices cried in startled unison.

"What the hell are you talking about!" said one of the techs.

"No way!" the other one added.

But Del was already putting down the binoculars, grinning.

"She'll freak out, Del. Man, you'll get us killed. Macias will kill us."

"Who's going to tell him?" Del asked, looking back at them. "What if you could get a piece of ass for changing a flat? Is that worth it, or what?"

"What are you talkin' about, man? She's not gonna put out to get her flat fixed, you stupid fuck."

"She's gonna run screaming," the other one said.

But Del was already opening the door.

She wasn't fifty meters away, but she hadn't seen the van. Del knew she could freak out, so when he came around the front of the van he called out, "Hey, lady!" and kept walking.

The woman flinched and spun around. He could see her face—astonishment—rape written all over it.

"I was just over there in the van waiting for friends I'm supposed to go fishing with, supposed to meet here, and saw your situation . . ." He wanted to keep talking, that would calm her. "I'd almost dozed off and you drove up and . . . I don't mean to scare you, but I can change that tire for you if you want. . . ."

The woman lunged for her purse and scrambled and came out with mace or pepper spray or something like that, and she held it up to him, backing away.

He stopped. "Hey, no." They looked at each other. "Look," he said. "A proposition. You hold that spray—here, you stand over here—you hold that stuff on me, and I'll change your tire, and then you get in the car and drive off."

She thought about it, glancing past his shoulder toward the van to see where he'd come from. One beat. Two beats. Three beats. Four . . . And she started moving away from the car, clutching her purse under one arm, holding the aerosol can of whatever it was at him as if she were holding up a cross in front of a vampire.

"Yeah, that's good," he said, gradually changing positions with her. "Don't squirt me, now. Just get on over there. I don't blame you for being scared, but what was I supposed to do, just sit over there and watch you?"

Now that he was closer, he saw that she really was a good-looking woman. And as he came in closer, moving to the back of the car as she orbited around him, holding up the mace, he noticed something else, too. Woman was wearing a tiny head mike, the little pea-size mouthpiece just at the side of her face, partially hidden by her hair. He began to process what that meant.

As the two men in the back of the van stood up from their seats, crouching, peering out the window at the stupid spectacle Del was causing, the back door of the van flew open and a man stood there, pointing an automatic the size of a loaf of bread at them.

"Don't touch a thing," he said. "We're okay here," he said into his mike.

At the Lexus the blonde asked, "What's your name?"

He said, "Del," feeling dumb and busted, but not really understanding yet just how thoroughly he'd screwed up.

She reached into her purse again, pulled out an oversize automatic, and pointed it at him. "Well, Del, let's walk over to the van."

Chapter 48

Calò and Baas arrived at La Terrazza an hour before Titus was supposed to meet Macias. The Italian restaurant was a stone-and-terra-cotta tile re-creation of a Tuscan inn tucked into the oaks and cedars on the western slope of one of the hillsides. It was a popular place in the evenings, and most afternoons people gathered there for drinks after work as well, because its stone-walled courtyards provided cooling shelters against the falling sun.

The parking lot was a cluster of small multicar pockets carved out of the dense cedars and connected by a gravel drive. There were no lights in the parking area, so as soon as you left the ambit of the restaurant's illumination, most of which was provided by lanterns hanging in the courtyards, you were gradually absorbed into the darkness.

At nine-thirty, when Calò and Baas drove into the parking area, the restaurant was in full swing, a typical Friday night. They drove through the parking area looking for either of the Navigators, but neither was there. They found a parking spot that afforded them a view of the entrance to the restaurant as well as the approach from the highway, turned off the motor and lights, and settled in to wait.

"Okay, we're in place," Calò said into his mike, then got a confirmation through his earpiece. He leaned forward and adjusted the LorGuide mapper under the dash. He could see the yellow signal of Macias's blue Navigator headed toward them and Titus's yellow signal on the way as well. But he was behind Macias.

"Okay, the first screwup is shaping up," he said sarcastically. "Looks like Macias is going to get here first."

"Wonderful." Baas had nightvision binoculars pressed to his eyes and was concentrating on the long tunnel of trees that led from the highway.

"Macias has turned off the highway," Calò said.

"And there he is," Baas said. "Blue Navigator."

Calò put his binoculars to his eyes as well.

"Two . . . three heads," Baas said. "Yeah, definitely three."

Silence as they watched the Navigator roll into the parking area, hesitate, and then begin making its way toward the back spaces, where they slowly pulled into a spot and cut the engine.

"They're talking," Calò said, slumped down in the car, his eyes glued to the binoculars as he peeped over the dash.

The Navigator's front passenger door opened and the bodyguard got out.

"Shit! He's hand-holding night goggles," Baas said.

The man began walking along, looking into the cars.

"Okay," Calò said, "we get out, let him see us, nothing to hide. We just go in, go to the bar, and wait until Macias comes in."

They opened the doors and got out, talking normally, ignoring the guy walking along behind the cars. He froze when he heard them coming along to his right on the other side of an island of trees. They passed him by, ignoring him.

They sat in the bar where they could see the front door and waited for Macias.

"They're going to sit in the car with the windows open," Calò said, elbow to elbow with Baas at the bar. "With that gravel, we'd never be able to get close to them. Got to do it another way now."

It didn't take the bodyguard fifteen minutes to check all the cars in the lot, and in twenty minutes Macias came through the front door of the restaurant. But one of the bodyguards was with him.

Calò moaned under his breath.

"No problem," Baas said, and watched the bodyguard as he stopped at the courtyard door and waited until Macias had found a table. The guard quickly surveyed the other patrons in the courtyard and then stepped into the bar and took a small, round bistro table from which he could watch both Macias and the front door. Calò and Baas paid and returned to their car.

Inside the car they took a few moments to check out the Navigator again through their binoculars. The remaining guard sat behind the steering wheel. They fiddled a little with their equipment, and then Calò backed out of their parking space and started around toward the front of the restaurant. The turns in the gravel drive were tight, and negotiating the parking area was a slow go. As they approached the rear of the blue Navigator Calò slowed to a crawl and finally stopped when the rear of the car was just past it. He put it in reverse and backed up to straighten the car into the turn. Forward again, then reverse again. Suddenly he plowed into the rear fender of the Navigator.

For a second nothing happened. He and Baas sat in the car, waiting. Then Calò put the car in gear again, pulled a foot or two forward, reversed it again, and crunched into the Navigator's fender a second time. This time the driver's door came open, and they could see the guy getting out in the red glow of Calò's taillights. Calò got out, too, leaving his door open as he stepped to the back of the car.

"Shit," Calò swore. "What the hell?" He looked at the driver. "Man, you're sticking out two feet here."

The man said something in Spanish as he threw his arms out and gave Calò an incredulous "What the hell's this?" look.

"Yeah, two feet," Calò said, deliberately avoiding Spanish, "you're sticking out two feet here, for Christ's sake." He kicked the Navigator's bumper.

Now Baas got out, too, walking around the front of the car, putting him on the same side of the crunched fender as the bodyguard.

"Oh, man," Baas said, his eyes fixed on the damaged fender.

"What're you going to do?" Calò said to the driver as he looked at his fender. "I got damage here, too, you know. You're sticking out two feet, for Christ's sake."

The bodyguard moved up, looking at Calò's fender.

Then Baas spoke to the guard in Spanish from the other side of the car. Swearing at him. The guard took a step toward him, bringing him within arm's reach of Calò.

Without warning Calò swung his arm around and slammed his fists squarely over the Mexican's heart. The force of the blow drove a needle into the Mexican's chest and simultaneously penetrated a cyanide pellet inside a gas canister hidden in Calò's closed fists. The propellant drove home the drop of cyanide.

The Mexican fell to the gravel between the cars as if he'd been dropped from the sky. Calò jumped into the car and pulled it around to another parking spot to avoid drawing attention, then rushed back to help Baas load the man into the back of the Navigator.

Chapter 49

Just before he turned off the highway, Titus received a phone call from a very calm Herrin, telling him that Macias had beaten him to La Terrazza. No problem, Herrin said. It might have been an advantage for Titus to have been there first, but it wasn't crucial.

Fine, Titus said. He knew they didn't want to rattle him. He figured it would have to be pretty bad before they'd let him hear them actually get excited. Be flexible, he told himself. Just breathe deeply and be flexible.

He drove through the parking lot, wondering where Macias's two bodyguards would be and wondering when Burden's men were going to deal with them and how they would do it. Quietly, he knew that much. How, then, would they deal with Macias? All questions that Titus hadn't been able to get answers to. It wasn't part of his job. His job was keeping Macias at that table until he got a telephone call.

He found an open parking spot and headed for the restaurant, going through the front courtyard, through the bar, and out into the large courtyard in back, where tables were scattered about under the trees. Macias wasn't hard to spot, a very handsome Mexican dressed in a stylish linen shirt and trousers. And alone.

Titus headed straight for him, and as he approached, he was taken aback to see Jorge Macias smile in recognition, stand, and stick out his hand to shake as he said, "Titus, it's great to see you."

Titus had a flash of Charlie Thrush being ripped to pieces by a chain saw. A flash of Carla fighting someone—how, exactly, had that happened?—and then dying slowly of anaphylactic shock. He couldn't do it. He couldn't touch the guy, much less shake hands with him. He sat down immediately, leaving Macias to make the best he could of his hand hanging in the air. Macias sat down, too.

"You've got to play along with this, Mr. Cain," Macias said in a low voice, still smiling. "We cannot attract attention to ourselves. We have to be civil."

"No, I don't have to be civil," Titus said. "What do you want?"

There was a bottle of wine on the table that Macias had ordered and was already drinking, and he poured some in the other glass and pushed it an inch toward Titus.

"Drink it," he said. "It might make this a little easier to do."

Titus did, taking in Macias as he turned up the glass. He was disconcertingly handsome, a neat haircut, manicured nails, a close shave around a perfect mustache. His short-sleeved shirt revealed a trim build with muscular shoulders and arms.

The tables around them were filled with people, but Titus hadn't noticed a single one of them. Macias had chosen a table well situated for a quiet conversation. He took a drink of wine, too, and his smile fell away.

"Permit me, please," he said, and just above the edge of the table he produced a small black device the size of a cell phone and pointed it at Titus. It threw a thin red horizontal bar across Titus's chest. Macias slowly moved it down Titus's body to the top of the table, then moved the device below the table and finished going down Titus's torso to his feet. Macias looked unobtrusively at the dial on the instrument.

He nodded. "Very good," he said, and put the device away. "I have a proposition that is very straightforward and simple: You deposit ten million dollars into a certain account in the Caymans, and I will give you Cayetano Luquín. You can stop him and save forty-four million at the same time. And, of course, you will save lives."

For the second time, Titus was caught off guard. Where was the interrogation he had been cautioned about so much? Where was the wily measuring of words, the calculated reading between the lines? If Titus said yes, would that be the end of it? Would they stand and walk away?

He remembered Burden's instructions: Just keep Macias there as long as you can. Say whatever you have to say. Just keep him there until you hear from Kal.

"Why are you offering me this deal?"

"I make more money this way."

His response was blunt and easy, as if the answer were obvious, like cutting a better deal on a new SUV.

"And I'll be doing you a favor, too, won't I," Titus added, "by getting rid of that son of a bitch."

Macias tilted his head to one side in a shrug. "That would be true, yes."

"Let's say I'm able to do that," Titus proposed. "The money, get rid of Luquín. How do I know one of his people won't come after me and carry out Luquín's threats? How do I know you won't come after me later?"

Macias nodded. "First of all, no one is going to do anything for Tano Luquín after he's dead. He does not inspire that kind of loyalty. There will be many people who will be sorry that the cash flow has been stopped; but no one will be sorry that Tano is dead.

"Second, I can easily imagine how angry you are about what has happened to you. And I can easily imagine how much you have learned from this experience. With your money and with what you've learned, I can imagine, too, that you will create your own guarantee that this sort of thing will never happen to you again. There's no warranty that I could give you that would be more assuring to you than your own determination."

"That's no comfort to me."

"That's only because you don't understand the risks from my side of the enterprise."

"And how will you 'give' me Luquín?" Titus asked.

"We can work out the details," he said. "But first, are you interested in the proposition?"

"It's possible. But I have to know the details first."

"Why the details first?"

"I've never done business with a killer before," Titus said evenly. "I'm going to be very cautious."

Macias's face was immobile. He didn't like Titus's choice of words. A dew of perspiration appeared in the creases on either side of his mouth.

"And how would you get the money to me?" Macias asked in turn.

"I can do it with a phone call. The same way I did the other ten million."

"When?"

"In the morning. You'll get confirmation from your bank within an hour of my call."

Macias nodded again. "When I get the phone confirmation about the money, I'll tell you precisely step by step how to do it."

"Not good enough."

Macias studied him a moment. "I know you have someone working with you. I don't know what's going on there. I have to protect myself."

"Well, we seem to be at an impasse, then."

"What would you propose?" Macias asked. "As a compromise?"

"Look," Titus said. "You've seen me give Luquín ten million already, like I said I would. And I'll put it in your account, too, just like I say I will. But the only thing I've seen from your side of this deal has been lies and death. Now you tell me you're willing to give up Luquín. Well, tell me how he's protected—exactly how. You don't do that it makes me think you're going to screw him—and me—and skip out on both of us. So my feeling right now is, fuck you."

Macias studied Titus again. He was trying to reconcile this hard stance against what he'd heard over the bug. But, of course, the moment he'd contacted Cain with his proposal to sell out Luquín, Cain's situation had shifted radically. What Macias was seeing here was how quickly Cain's competitive mettle came to the forefront when he saw even the slightest opening. Macias might have more to deal with here than he had expected.

Macias drank quickly from his glass, weighing the upside, the downside. He was smelling the $10 million, and more important, he was thinking what life would be like without Cayetano Luquín breathing down his neck and not actually having to do anything about it himself. But Cain was right, of course; he needed something to believe.

"What does it matter to you how he's protected," Macias

asked, "if you are only going to turn the information over to the police?"

"Did I say I was going to turn the information over to the police?"

"What is this, then?" he asked cautiously and with an amused smile. "Your own personal vengeance? But this is such a Latin thing, Mr. Cain."

Titus could feel himself trembling from the high-voltage energy produced by the adrenaline pumping through him.

"Did you really think I was going to watch that man kill my friends and steal my money, and then let him go? He told me that if I didn't do what he said, he'd haunt me the rest of my life by killing my friends, my family. Well, I did what he said, and he killed people anyway." He paused. "Or rather, you did it for him."

The smirk stiffened on Macias's face.

Titus went on. "Did he really think . . . I was going to let that happen without any kind of response? Fifty-four million dollars. If he thinks that kind of money is going to enable him to get certain things done, to buy certain information, to have people killed, what makes him think it won't do the same things for me? Does he think I'm an idiot?"

Titus had no idea that he was going to say all of this, but suddenly as he looked at Macias several obvious ideas converged. The advantage that Macias had over everyone—first, with Luquín over Titus; and now, working only in self-interest, over Luquín as well—was based solely in his willingness to simply disregard the rules by which everyone else in society agreed to play. Even the trust that Luquín had put in Macias, twisted though it was, had its own rules of order. And now Macias was ignoring even those corrupt boundaries.

But what really infuriated Titus was that Macias apparently assumed that Titus would continue to obey the traditional rules of society, that Titus would not resort to Macias's own lawless tactics, even though not doing so would put him at every conceivable disadvantage. The condescension of that presumption suddenly struck Titus like a lightning bolt. What in the hell had Titus been thinking about?

He fixed his eyes on Macias and lowered his voice.

"Has Luquín ever stopped to think how much revenge that amount of money will buy . . . me?"

Macias said nothing. He waited. He was dealing with the unavoidable reality that everything Cain said about Luquín was directed at him as well.

"I'm not going to pay for more lies," Titus concluded. "Unless I can believe what you tell me, I'll just keep my ten million."

Macias was suddenly scrambling to reevaluate his position. This kind of talk from Cain was not what he had anticipated. Why was he suddenly so confident? How much more did Cain know than Macias had thought he knew? If Cain was after revenge, then maybe he was on his own after all. No legitimate law enforcement agency would be involved in that kind of operation. Was it possible that Cain had hired some very capable professionals? Maybe Macias had caught this just in time to prevent a debacle of his own tightly planned scheme.

"Maybe I can tell you a few things," Macias said, buying time to think.

"How's he protected?" Titus asked again. "What will my people be facing if you 'give' him to me? How many guards? Where are they located? Give me some details to believe. But I've got to have a hell of a lot more than a promise from a man like you before I'll fork over another dollar."

Macias's handsome face was stiff with anger and more than a little suspicion.

"You are asking a lot for a man who has Cayetano Luquín

hanging on to his balls with both hands. Maybe I should just let him go ahead and take your fifty-four million . . . and however many more lives he wants in the process."

Titus put his elbows on the table and leaned forward, way forward, almost in Macias's face, to make his point. "Listen to me, you sick son of a bitch. Just sitting here with you makes me want to puke. Don't . . . threaten . . . me."

Even as he spoke, it occurred to Titus that he had juiced himself up so much that maybe he had said too much. Maybe he had gone way too far, way past smart. But from the moment he'd walked into the courtyard and seen Macias, the idea of conversing with this man had been repugnant to him. It was suddenly fantastical to him that he should be sitting down and talking calmly with the man who had orchestrated the deaths of Charlie and Carla.

But now maybe he had really screwed up. He could see from the look on Macias's face that he knew something was definitely wrong here. Why the hell couldn't Titus have contained his temper for another hour? And where the hell was Kal's phone call?

Chapter 50

Cope and Tito checked in with Calò just moments before they drove past the Pathfinder parked down the street from Luquín's house. They passed it only once, slowly, going in the opposite direction, with Cope driving and Tito slumped down out of sight in the seat beside him.

"Windows down," he said. "I think I heard a radio."

Two blocks away they pulled to the curb in front of a darkened house.

"They're parked beside an embankment," he went on, "to the side of the house. The yard sits about four feet higher than the street. The garage opens up right at the rear of the Pathfinder. There's some kind of hedge, about six feet high, at the top of the embankment to give the house privacy from the street. There's a bush jammed up next to the rear of the Pathfinder, planted right at the curb to hide the trash cans."

"What about the approach?"

"We could come at the house from the back of the garage through the street side of the neighbor's yard. From the corner of the garage we'd be protected from their rearview mirrors by the big bush. They can't see the rear right corner of the Pathfinder from inside the vehicle."

Tito was silent.

"I don't like the high-speed drill and gas idea," Cope said. "This has to be bloody quick, and with the windows open we can't guarantee we'll get bloody quick."

"Then it's got to be the CS grenade," Tito said. "We drive by and I'll toss it in, bam. They won't be able to get another breath for about thirty seconds. It's like getting slapped in the face with a board. But then it wears off quick, so we have to get in quick and do our thing."

"What kind of noise does it make?" Cope asked.

"None."

"Flash?"

"None."

Cope thought a moment. "We can't risk them getting a shot off, not even one."

"Their throats and lungs are locked up, man," Tito assured him. "They can't even draw a breath . . . for thirty seconds. After that, they're going to start coming around."

Silence. Cope looked at his watch. "Okay, then I'll just pull up and you toss the bomb. I'll jam on the brakes, and we bail out. The second you know it's okay, jump in and get behind the wheel, and I'll go into the back."

That was it.

Cope pulled away from the curb and slow-rolled to the intersection. He eased out, looking right. Two blocks ahead they could see the Pathfinder up the slight rise in the street, looking like a sitting duck. He turned into the street and started up the hill.

Suddenly the taillights of the Pathfinder came on.

"Shit." Tito leaned forward over the dash, but then the taillights went out again. "Guy's just shifting in his seat."

Cope was watching his rearview mirror for approaching traffic, but they were so far off Bull Creek Road that there was no through traffic, and at this hour the neighborhood was quiet.

He noodled along, not wanting to change pace when they pulled past the Pathfinder. Then they were there.

He looked to his right just as they were even with the Pathfinder driver, and Tito lobbed the CS grenade as if he were tossing back a wadded piece of paper into a trash can. The little canister sailed right past the surprised face of the driver.

Cope slammed on his brakes, stopping just past the front left fender of the Pathfinder so that Tito could fling open his door. Cope scrambled around the back of the car to find the Pathfinder's opened windows swirling with gas.

"Wait," Tito barked. They stood there three beats, and then: "Go!"

As Tito was opening the door, he reached in and shot the driver in the face twice with his suppressed USP, then shoved the dying man from under the steering wheel as he crawled in. At the same instant, Cope plunged into the backseat and shot the gagging guard in the mouth twice, crawled over his body, and shot the passenger-side guard three quick bursts in the left ear as he pushed him down into the floorboard out of sight. Then he was out and back into the idling car.

In less than fifteen seconds it was over. Inside the Pathfinder, three men were in various stages of dying as Tito slowly pulled the SUV away from the curb and eased out into the street. Cope followed him at a distance.

The man had crouched in the pocket of deep shade among the cedars and settled in to endure the stifling heat of the afternoon. The sun beat down on the thick canopy of the woods above him, sucking all the air out of the underbrush. Forty meters away, the lake water lapped against the rocks. Cicadas throbbed in the hot trees, and their drone blended with the occasional drone of ski and pleasure boats plying the long, narrow lake. Peering through a break in the brush, he had found a spot across the lake halfway up the sloping hillside, a terra-cotta tile roof, and he concentrated on it, using it as his gateway out of time.

Everything else that happened for the next four and a half hours happened in his parallax view and in his head. He was fully aware of the changing light, but not in the gradual way that an observant person might be aware of it. For long periods of time his eyes took in nothing—that is, nothing of which he was aware. He was gone, traveling in his mind.

Then, as if playing catch-up, his eyes registered the changing light of the past hour or so all in the space of just a few moments, like a time-lapse film. The clouds skimmed northward across the valley, and the sunlight flickered rapidly as the clouds flitted past, and then underlying it all was the changing light resulting from the angle of the falling sun.

And then again everything held still while he passed through terra-cotta into other worlds.

He got up once to remove his clothes, jamming them into the small canvas duffel bag. He turned aside and urinated into the grass, then squatted on his haunches and returned to the tile roof.

Another hour or so passed and the mosquitoes had gotten so bad that he turned to the duffel bag again and took out two round, plastic containers holding charcoal and olive body paint. Methodically, without any attention to time at all, he began to smear his body with the camouflage paint. He didn't pay much attention to what he was doing, as if it didn't matter much how it was done. But he was thorough, head to toe, inside his ears and nostrils, between the crevice of his buttocks, and even his genitals.

Dusk.

Now he squatted among the weeds, invisible. With the dying light, the swarms of mosquitoes grew exponentially. Frustrated by the repellent in the paint, they formed a cloud around him. He heard them, a high-pitched whining sound enveloping him in its harmonics, exactly like the dusk in Espíritu Santo when he was waiting to kill the man from Andradína and was astonished to hear the sound of time passing. It was an aural sensation precisely the same as the cloud of mosquitoes. It was so odd to discover that.

Time passed. A long time . . . in a darkness blacker than old blood.

When the telephone vibrated in his hand—he had held it throughout, laying it down only to put on the body paint, and even then carefully resting his toes on it so that he would feel the vibrating if it should happen—he answered it by saying only, "Yes."

"Macias has left," Burden said. "I believe that only a guard, Roque, and Luquín remain. That's the best we can figure it."

"Macias won't return?"

"No."

"I have the rest of the night, then?"

"No. You have to leave by two o'clock, at least. You have the directions to the airstrip."

"Yes. But nothing has changed?"

"No."

Silence. He wasn't sure how long it lasted, but he was aware of it, which meant it might have been a long time. But Burden didn't hang up. He was there.

"You want to know something, García?"

323

"Yes. What is it?"

"I didn't think this would ever happen. I thought I would die and this would never have happened."

Silence.

"I won't thank you," the man said. "I will spare you having to have that on your conscience."

Silence.

"But if I could thank you, I would do it. And if I believed in God, I would thank him for it, too, but he wouldn't want my gratitude, either. *Gracias a Dios,* but he would stop it from reaching him. Such gratitude."

Silence.

"Do you hear the insects?"

"Yes," Burden said.

"I am engulfed by mosquitoes," he said. "A cloud of them. They are singing time at me."

Silence.

"I don't ever want to see you again, García. You understand that."

"I understand. Yes."

Silence.

"I look like an insect," the man said.

Again there was silence, and after waiting a moment or two, he turned off the phone.

Chapter 51

After Burden's phone call, the man's heart began to fibrillate. He was used to that and recognized the onset of his familiar disturbance. Something happened to you when you took off all your clothes and covered your body with the colors of earth and vegetation. You began to slough off your human-ness. And that was good.

Wearing only tennis shoes that he'd also smeared with camouflage paint, he began moving up through the lake-level woods to the hillside. The mosquitoes formed a whirring aura around him, and he felt as though he were suspended in the sound of time but not touched by it. He moved through the darkness in a cocoon of timelessness.

The move up the cliff was slow, but not especially difficult. This was simply a steep climb, with a couple of spots where the placement of feet and fingers was important but not critical. He was careful not to dislodge any rocks and send them crashing noisily into the brush.

The pool was set solidly into the stone face of the bluff, but the deck that surrounded it was supported by thick, stolid concrete pilings sunk into the rock face below. When he reached the pilings he stopped to rest a moment before climbing the last twenty feet by crawling over the boulders that had been pushed over the bluff when the pool was built. Then he reached a cinder-block room that housed the pool's plumbing underneath the deck. From there stone steps led up to a tall louvered gate that opened onto the deck and pool area.

He crouched at the gate a long time, holding the little duffel bag with his clothes and a few other things. When he heard no one talking, he carefully unlatched the louvered gate, which opened up into a blind corner of the pool area, and moved inside. He laid the duffel bag in the shadows against the house, unzipped it, and took out the small, dull gray automatic pistol that Burden had given him. It was specifically modified to fire subsonic "cat's sneeze" loads. The rounds had soft lead noses that exploded on impact.

The pale light coming through the glass walls—it looked like television light—threw too much illumination onto the deck and pool. He wouldn't be able to cross to the other side from here. Leaving his duffel bag, he went back out the gate and made his way down the first flight of steps. At the first turn left, he stepped right into the brush that separated the houses along the cliff. To avoid the noisy vegetation as much as possible, he hugged the outside walls of the house.

When he reached the front corner of the house, he snuggled up under a large shrub and waited. He knew Luquín's security. At night, someone always stayed outside in the dark. He waited. The living human being made noises.

He waited. He heard his own blood in his ears. Not too different from the whirr of passing time. He waited.

The guard farted. The man adjusted for the distortion of the architecture and vegetation. The front of the house was a U-shaped courtyard. And luckily, there were hedges. He eased down on his side, his bare back against the house, and advanced under the hedges, groveling inch by inch.

The guard yawned with a groan. The man corrected his audio perception. He was closer than he thought. A few more feet, mulch and twigs digging into his skin. The hedge took a left turn at the patio's edge. The man waited, then slowly eased his head from under the hedge. He saw the guard about two and a half meters away in a lawn chair.

When he shot the guard, there was only the muffled pop of his skull and a soft splash on the stones. The man was quickly on his feet. He took the AK out of the guard's lap and laid it on the stones. He left him lolling in the chair.

He went to the front door and tried the knob. It was unlocked. He opened the door by millimeters and heard the television. Good. He eased his head around the door. A foyer, lucky. Roque would be within twenty feet of Luquín. As he made his way through the foyer, the television threw a pale, flickering light through the opened doorway. There were no other lights on. Lucky again.

He saw through the room's glass walls to the lighted deck outside where he had just been standing a few minutes before. Making sure there were no lights behind him, he eased forward and saw Luquín lounging on the sofa, facing the television. He was nodding off, hardly awake. Another step forward, but no Roque.

Suddenly he heard a toilet flush down the hall and turned just in time to see Roque coming around the corner at the other end of the hallway, fumbling at the zipper of his pants. He was hardly on his guard and probably had been nodding off in front of the television too before he got up to go to the bathroom. The man straightened his arm out horizontally in the dark hallway, and Roque walked right into its muzzle.

The cat sneezed, and Roque's head flew back as if he'd

been hit with a mallet, and his feet shot out from under him. He hit the floor with a sloppy *whump*, half a second after most of his brain hit the hallway wall.

The man wheeled around and was standing in front of the huge entertainment screen facing Luquín while Luquín was still trying to get to his feet. When he finally righted and steadied himself, the man was holding the remote control on the screen. The sound went off.

They stood facing each other in the silence, the coffee table between them.

"*Siéntese,*" the man said. Luquín's expression was slack, and the pale light from the screen was jumping all over his face, heightening his expression of shock. "Sit down," the man repeated in English.

Luquín dumbly complied, collapsing into the exact spot from where he'd struggled so hard to get up a moment before. The man walked to the coffee table. Then he stepped around it, looming over Luquín, his camouflaged genitals dangling an arm's reach away from Luquín's face. The man sat down slowly on top of the coffee table, his knees almost touching Luquín's knees.

"Take off your shirt."

A couple of beats passed before Luquín began unbuttoning his *guayabera*. When he had it off, the man reached out and took it from him. Slowly he began wiping his face with it, smearing away the paint, his eyes latched on to Luquín's eyes as firmly as if they had been little hands holding him. Luquín stared, watching as the color of the man's flesh emerged from underneath the paint. His eyes narrowed a couple of times involuntarily as he tried instinctively to recognize the man underneath the paint.

Suddenly he realized who it was.

Luquín went limp and sank back on the sofa. The odor of

feces filled the room as Luquín's mouth sagged in stupefaction. Some men have a sixth sense about their last moments, something that tells them that this time it will not be a close call. Often such an intuitive certainty is dumbfounding, and that moment of realization sucks everything out of them. That's the way it was for Cayetano Luquín. Now there were only two things left: death, and the fear of death.

The man was surprised by this sudden collapse. He had always anticipated that Luquín would fight insanely, like a rabid coyote. This was unanticipated. But it meant nothing, one way or the other.

"Get on the floor."

Luquín looked at him blankly, without comprehension.

The man stood. "Get on the floor."

Luquín hesitated, then slid sideways off the sofa and onto the floor. He didn't know what position to take on the floor, so he kind of knelt there, almost on his side, eyes rolled at his adversary.

"On your back," the man said. Then, standing over Luquín, he bent and unbuckled Luquín's belt and then the waistband of his trousers. Then he flipped off Luquín's expensive alligator loafers. He grabbed the bottom of his silk trousers and pulled them off. He stood back, looking at him.

"Pull off your underwear."

Luquín rolled around on the floor, squirming out of his feces-soaked underwear.

"Stuff them in your mouth."

Luquín did, without hesitation.

Then the man went back to the coffee table and sat down again. He looked at Luquín, studying him. His body was surprisingly well kept for a man his age. Almost athletic.

"What do you think, Tano," the man asked, "is fear different for different people? Is there only 'fear,' a single thing

that is the same for everyone? Or are there fears?" He thought
a moment. "A child's fear. Do you think it's different from a
man's fear?" He paused as if he were letting Luquín contem-
plate that. And then he said: "How could it not be?

"And how long can a human being be afraid, Tano?" the
man asked in a quiet, conversational tone. He waited for an
answer, as though he actually expected Luquín to respond. "A
few days? Weeks? Months?" Pause. "To me, it seems that after
a time, and that time is probably different for different people,
fear turns into something else. For you, a person so experienced in such things, who knows, that period of time might
be . . . endless."

He pondered this a moment.

"What do you think?" he asked Luquín again. "You're
something of a philosopher on the subject."

Luquín lay on the floor transfixed, his fecal-drenched underwear hanging out of his mouth, his forearms raised, wrists
cocked back in a posture of benumbed disbelief.

"Here's what I think, Tano," the man continued. "I think
that after a lengthy time, if that thing which causes fear continues and does not go away, then fear itself is transformed, almost like a chemical reaction. It turns to horror. And that, I
think, is a more intense experience. Horror is *miedo pro-
fundo.*"

The man noted that Luquín's eyes were beginning to acquire the glassy look of disassociation. A film covered the eyes
in such moments, like a cataract, though not milky in that way,
but rather glittery, reflective, so that the film caught the light
and obscured the eye behind the reflection.

The man studied Luquín in the pale, flickering light of the
television, the perfect aura for what was about to happen. It
was just the right shade of pale. And its jerky light was just the
right modulation for horror.

Luquín was motionless, his forearms still raised, wrists still cocked back.

"Let us explore together these philosophical questions, Cayetano, you and I. You, *el maestro del horrible.* And I the *novicio.* Between us, surely, we can come to some deep and secret understanding of this timeless subject."

Chapter 52

Jorge Macias produced his own cell phone and pushed a button. "Bring the car around," he said, his eyes never leaving Titus.

In an instant Titus felt everything shifting. His own stupidity had triggered something here, and he had the sickening feeling that he had turned a very serious corner.

Speaking carefully, Macias said, "You're going to go with me now. At this moment someone is pointing a gun at you, so please cooperate. No problems. Let's go."

Titus's options were few. If nothing else, Burden had hammered into his head the downside of making a scene. A scene had an aftermath, it had ramifications. They didn't want ramifications. Doing as Macias wanted seemed the prudent course. If it wasn't too damn late to be prudent.

With a sure and casual air, Macias guided Titus through the courtyard and into the waiting area just outside the bar. A Mexican man was waiting there for them.

"Luis isn't answering," the man said. "What's going on?"

"I don't know," Macias said.

Titus's phone rang.

Macias's head snapped around as he took Titus's arm. "Answer it," he said. "And be very careful."

As Titus answered the phone, Macias and his man walked him toward the men's room.

"Yes," Titus said.

"There's been a glitch," Kal said.

"Yeah, I know."

They were inside the men's room now, and Macias's guard put his foot against the door as Macias grabbed the phone from Titus.

"Who is this?" he snapped.

Hesitation. "This's Kal."

"My driver isn't answering his phone, Kal," Macias said.

Hesitation. "Who is this?"

"Jorge Macias."

Hesitation. "I don't know what you're talking about . . . a driver . . . ?"

"Listen to me. Cain is standing right here with me, and I've got a gun pushed into his stomach and he's going to stay with me until we get something worked out here. Now do you know what I'm talking about?"

Hesitation.

"I can think faster than that," Macias said, "and you wouldn't like what I'm thinking. Now. Where is my driver?"

"He's been removed."

"Removed." Macias felt as if he were hyperventilating. "Listen to me, you fuck"—he was rigid with tension—"you tell your people that we're going to leave here. I want my car brought to the front door of this place. When the driver gets out, have him leave the front driver's door open, and then open the back door. Then tell him to get the hell out of the way. And remember this: I do not want to see anybody following me. I assume you have a bug on the car, fine. But I do not want to see any surveillance."

He punched off the phone without waiting for a response and put the phone in his pocket.

"You heard what's going to happen," Macias said. "Stay close to me. Be careful, I'll blow your liver all over this place."

Macias was sweating. He was scared, but he was the kind of man for whom personal danger was a fierce motivator to concentration. It didn't rattle him. He became keenly focused.

"When we get outside," Macias said to his bodyguard, "you get in the front passenger's seat. Cain, you get behind the wheel. I'll be behind you in the backseat."

Titus stared at him. This sounded like a disaster in the making.

"Hey!" Macias barked, jamming a gun in Titus's ribs. "You understand?"

"Yeah, okay, I've got it. I've got it."

They walked out of the rest rooms and down a short corridor to the main entry. People were milling around, leaving, arriving, waiting for friends. The three of them went to the front door. The courtyard was two steps down. Titus could see the arched entry that led from the courtyard to the parking area.

The casual ambience of the people in the foyer seemed ridiculously innocent to Titus, so enormously rich in its banality and thoughtless ease.

Then the Navigator appeared in the arch of the gateway, and he felt Macias's automatic gouge into his kidneys, and they were moving. Most of the tables in the front courtyard were occupied, people waiting for tables inside, talking quietly over drinks.

No one paid any attention to them as they crossed to the stone arch where the wrought-iron gates were thrown back.

The man who got out of the Navigator threw a meaningful glance at Titus as he turned and opened the backseat door, and then he walked away. Titus and Macias got into the Navigator and closed their doors simultaneously.

"Go to the highway and turn left," Macias said, "and be very careful."

Titus eased down the narrow gravel drive from La Terrazza to Loop 360. The loop was a divided highway through the hills, and the restaurant drive came out onto the northbound lanes. Titus crossed these two lanes, continued on the crossover to the southbound lanes, and turned left.

The bodyguard kept his eye on the outside rearview mirror, but Titus could only guess what Macias was doing behind him. He could hear him breathing, and the tension inside the Navigator was so dense that it replaced the oxygen.

"What are you going to do?" Titus asked as he picked up speed.

Macias didn't answer.

Titus drove with his right hand and reached up with his left hand, feeling for the mole in the bend of his arm. It was still there.

Macias was silent behind him, and Titus imagined his mind was going wild with calculation. Titus reviewed his options. Macias could kill him. But why? That would only bring him grief and leave him vulnerable. Macias might kidnap him for the ransom that he wasn't going to get now, but Titus guessed that Burden would never let them get out of the United States with it. Titus couldn't even come up with a scenario for what might happen. But whatever it was, he was reasonably sure that Macias knew it was likely they would try to kill him. That had to dominate his thinking right now and determine the scope of his options.

The Navigator was eating up the miles. Titus shifted in his

seat, thinking of the pistol pointed at him. He thought of the man who had pulled the Navigator up to the gate. What in the hell had his expression been trying to convey? Or had his face simply reflected the intensity of their situation?

The seat belt was digging into his right hip where the buckle side was anchored to the car seat. He hadn't even remembered putting it on and was surprised that he had. He put his right hand down by his right hip to shift the seat belt clasp and felt something in the crack of the seat. He put the back of his hand against the clasp to shift it from rubbing him . . . and felt the grip of a handgun. Shit!

Suddenly he began to recalculate everything.

"Turn off at the next exit," Macias said, "and then turn back under the highway and head toward the city."

Titus turned off on Highway 2222 and did as he was told. The bodyguard said something to Macias, and he replied, *"Bueno."* Titus guessed that Kal and Burden were following Macias's instructions to keep their distance.

"So you are working with professionals?" Macias asked.

"Yes."

"Who?"

"A guy named Steve Lender."

"Do they know everything?"

"Everything I know. Which obviously isn't everything."

Macias said something in Spanish to the bodyguard, who took out a cell phone and dialed a number. He listened.

"Nada," he said.

Macias said something else. The guard dialed again.

"Nada," he said again.

Without being told another time, he dialed again.

"Nada," he repeated.

"¡Chinga——!" Macias swore. "How many people are involved here?" he asked Titus.

"I don't know."

He felt the barrel of Macias's automatic at the base of his neck.

"He said it was best if I didn't know," Titus said. "I just don't know."

Titus was panicked about the safety on the automatic. He had felt it on the left side of his thumb, but he didn't know if it was on or off. How would the guy have left it? Cocked, he thought. Safety off and cocked. This thing was ready to go.

"How long's this guy Lender been involved?"

Titus hesitated. The barrel of Macias's automatic dug into the base of his skull again. He could feel it twisting.

"From the beginning."

"Fuck," Macias said.

In the following silence, Titus tried to guess where Macias's mind was going. Obviously the bodyguard had tried to contact their other people, with no luck. Now he had to know that by some quirk of chance he had escaped the same fate as his other crews by only a few moments and that his whole elaborate scheme had completely disintegrated. He had to be just about as desperate as a man could be.

Chapter 53

Burden's surveillance van stayed on Loop 360, pulling off on residential streets whenever they needed to be out of sight. Besides his driver, there were two technicians, himself, and Gil Norlin inside the van, monitoring the rapidly changing events as each element in their four-phased operation was accomplished. In spite of their disadvantages, everything was going unexpectedly well.

Until the last few moments at La Terrazza.

During all of this, the radio and telephone traffic between Burden and Kal and the others at the guest house was continuous. Rita Cain was watching the LorGuides with them, but she didn't have access to the audio transmissions. Whatever she understood about what was happening she had to piece together from only one side of the conversation. And they were being careful about what they were allowing her to hear.

In Burden's van all eyes were on the LorGuides, watching the Navigator as it sped down the highway with its blips from the moles on Titus and on Macias's bodyguard, who Titus had tagged the night before.

When the Navigator slowed as it approached the Highway

2222 exit, and then turned and headed toward the city, Burden said, "Oh, shit."

Norlin leaned in close to the monitor. "I don't believe this."

Calò, driving the chase car, saw it, too. "What do I do, García?"

"Just keep your distance—and wait."

Burden snatched his phone and started dialing the cell number of the man he had left on the shore below Luquín's safe house. The phone rang and rang and rang.

"There's no way he's going to answer," Burden said. "He's going to think the call is to wave him off for some reason, and he's waited too long for this."

Then he started dialing Titus's cell phone, knowing that Macias had surely taken it away from him. No answer. That wasn't a surprise, either. They could only stare in stunned silence as the two signals closed the distance between them and Luquín's house.

"Why the hell's he going back?" Norlin asked.

"He's left something," Burden said. "It's got to be that. Information, probably, that he can't let get away from him."

"Jesus," Norlin said. "You've got to get somebody over there."

"There's no one left."

"Calò's behind them."

"He's got a LorGuide in his car, and I'm going to need him out there in the dark if they leave. Baas is headed to the airstrip with the body of the other guard in Titus's Rover. Your people are holding their surveillance van, waiting to hear from us, and besides, they're not trained for what they might encounter when they get there. Tito and Cope are headed to the airstrip with the bodies of the guys from the Pathfinder. Cope could pull away, but he's already fifty minutes out, at least."

"What about one of the guys at Cain's house?"

"I'm not taking a single gun away from Cain's wife."

The inside of the van was hot from the heavy load of humming electronics. It was cramped, and everyone was sweating.

"What's going to happen to her if you pull off one of those guards?" Norlin said.

"I wouldn't send just one over there, and if I send two, then that leaves only one with Rita."

"Look, everybody's dead anyway. Who's left to go after her?"

"Where's the guy who took the pictures?" Burden asked. He waited for Norlin's answer, just for emphasis. "The guy didn't figure into our body count for the planning. I'm just not taking any chances with that one."

Norlin said, "You just going to let whatever—"

"That's right," Burden interrupted stoically. "There's nothing we can do about it. We wait it out. Cain'll just have to take his chances."

The van pulled to the side of the highway near the Highway 2222 exit and stopped.

The silence in the guest house changed. Rita had seen Titus's signal leave the restaurant, too, and she had managed to keep quiet. Her personal anxieties aside, she knew perfectly well that she could unwittingly misinterpret anything she might see. She knew that a lot of it wouldn't make sense to her and that her instincts wouldn't serve her well, that they would even be counterintuitive to the circumstances.

But when she saw Titus's signal leave La Terrazza with the signal of one of Luquín's people, a signal that she knew Titus himself was responsible for planting, she began to feel as if her own restraint would cause her to explode.

"I want to talk to García," she said. She didn't yell. Her

voice didn't quiver. There were no histrionics. But everyone in the room turned and looked at her.

"Any problem with that?" she asked calmly. But it was the calmness you reached when you've traveled to the other side of drama. It was the calmness of unshakable determination, and everyone knew it instantly.

"Uh," Herrin said, and looked at Kal.

"Here, you can use these," Kal said, offering a set of headphones that she had not been allowed to use earlier.

"I want a private conversation with him," she said.

Herrin gaped at her again.

"I mean, you're all listening to each other on those, aren't you?" she asked.

"Yeah," Kal said, wishing he didn't have to admit it.

"Well, I want a private conversation with him."

"Look," Kal said, "he's right in the middle—"

"You're not saying no, are you?" Rita asked. She had stood up from the chair where she'd been sitting.

"What I'm saying is," Kal responded, "that I'll ask him if that's something he can do right now."

"You do that."

Kal put his headphones back on, bent his head, and walked away from the group, talking in a low voice. They all waited, concentrating on the screens or just about anything else. All except Janet, who was looking at Rita with the beginnings of a bemused smile on her mouth.

Kal turned and reached into his pocket and took out a cell phone.

"Push talk," he said, handing it to Rita.

Rita took it and walked to the other side of the room. She wanted to go outside to the patio, but she knew that wouldn't be allowed.

"Yeah," Burden said.

"What's happening?"

"Titus and Macias are still talking."

"That doesn't tell me what's happening."

"It looks like Macias is on to us. He's holding Titus until he can get a guarantee that we'll let him go."

"And then what?"

"He's agreed to leave Titus with the Navigator and talking on a cell phone as proof to us he's alive, and while that's happening he drives away and we let him go."

She could tell by his voice that he was being deliberately blunt with her. She wanted to play it straight? He'd play it straight.

"And where are they now?"

"They went to the place where Macias was staying with Luquín."

"Why?"

"We think Macias wants to recover some stuff he doesn't want to get away from him before he makes his escape."

"Macias doesn't know that you were going to kill Luquín, does he."

"Yeah, he does now."

"Is Luquín dead?"

"We don't know."

She couldn't believe what she was hearing. "And what are you doing about this?"

"Not much we can do. We're just waiting so Macias can do his stuff and then leave Titus somewhere with the Navigator like he's supposed to do."

"Supposed to do," she said. It made her heart crawl right up into her throat. "Supposed" had never carried so much import, had never sounded so flimsy and menacing.

"I can't sit here and watch this," she said. "We know exactly where Titus is, don't we?"

"Yes."

"Then I want to be as close as I can get to him."

"You are as close as you can get to him."

"Not as close as you."

Silence.

"You're staying as close as you can, right?" she continued, pressing her point, "without endangering Titus's life, without screwing up the situation?"

Silence.

"Then I want to be where you are."

"Impossible."

There was a moment when neither of them spoke, and Rita swallowed the bile in her throat and smothered the rage in her head. But she resisted the temptation to give in to her gut instincts. She had seen enough of how Burden operated to know the behavior he exhibited himself and probably respected. If she was going to get what she wanted, she had to meet him where he lived.

"Let me tell you what's impossible," she said with the kind of evenness under duress that Burden himself was known for. "I'm not a fool. I know that you can't guarantee Titus's life and safety. This isn't your nightmare. It's ours.

"But . . . if anything happens to him, and I'm not as close to him as reasonably feasible, then . . . it's impossible that I will keep my mouth shut about all of this. If anything happens to that man, and I am not as close to him as you are capable of getting me . . . then it's impossible that I will not drag you and whoever's behind you through the media for *years*. If I'm forced to sit here and watch my husband's death—if that's what it comes to—as if it were a goddamned video game . . . then it's impossible that you will ever again know the anonymity that you're so damned proud of."

She paused.

"And yes," she added, "I remember your threats—rather, your good counsel, your cautionary word. And no, I'm not intimidated."

She stopped. There was silence in the room behind her and silence on the other end of the cell phone. Her anger had scorched her face, and she could feel it burning.

"Give the phone to Kal," Burden said.

She started to go on, to say, Well, what the hell are you going to do, then? But then she realized that she had said all that she had meant to say, and she had meant all that she had said. He had better believe that.

She turned around and held the phone out to Kal across the room. He came over and took it and turned his back to her as she stood right there while he said, Yeah, and, Yeah, and, Okay, and, Got it.

He turned around, pocketing his phone as he looked at her.

"Come on," he said.

Chapter 54

Titus could almost hear Macias thinking. The headlights of the Navigator panned over the cliffs and hillsides as they twisted their way through the hills toward the city. To their left they could see the lights of the houses close and high above them on the dark hillsides. To their right they caught glimpses of the river far below them and the lights of the homes on the broad, upward-sloping valley on the other side, where Titus lived and Rita waited anxiously for him.

Following Macias's directions, they turned off and slipped down into the escarpment that led to a lower level of cliffs above the river. The dark streets twisted back upon themselves and were crowded with houses set close together and nestled into dense woods. Macias directed Titus back and forth on the streets while Macias and the bodyguard kept up a staccato exchange in Spanish. They seemed to be evaluating the feasibility of stopping at one of the houses, which Titus realized they must have driven past several times now. He could see from glimpsing between the houses that these homes were on the cliff high above the river.

Was this where Luquín had been staying?

"Do you know anything about how they were going to deal with Luquín?" Macias asked. "Don't lie to me."

"I have no idea."

"Shit!" Pause. "Pull over."

Titus stopped. They were looking at the house two houses up and on the right.

"Luquín is in there," Macias said. "I've left a computer notebook in there. I might as well be dead now if I have to leave without it." He thought a moment. "They were going to kill him."

"Yes."

"And then what?"

"I have no idea."

"Shit shit shitshitshit," Macias was muttering.

"Look," Titus said, "I do know that . . . well, this guy, Lender, his big deal is, you know, leaving no trace . . . that anything had ever happened. If Luquín is killed, I doubt they would do it in there if they could help it. They're going to want to leave the house clean, without any sign of anything having gone wrong."

Silence.

"What's this guy's name again?"

"Lender."

Macias said nothing, but he was thinking about this. He said something in Spanish to the bodyguard. They talked. More silence. *"Vamos a ver,"* Macias said, and then to Titus, "We're going in."

Titus put the Navigator in gear, and they eased along the street and pulled into the driveway. The driveway to the garage was protected from the street by a high hedge, and when they rounded the corner they saw the black Navigator in the driveway.

Macias swore. "Stop!"

He and the bodyguard talked in Spanish some more, now whispering illogically.

"Go on in and park," Macias said.

Titus pulled up beside the other Navigator and cut the motor.

"Get out," Macias said.

They left the doors ajar, and the bodyguard started toward the front porch with his pistol ready at his side. They passed a knee-high privet hedge with Titus in between the two men.

Suddenly the bodyguard hissed loudly. He looked back at Macias. *"Lo hicieron,"* he whispered, and gestured at a lawn chair where a man was sprawled awkwardly, his head hanging back over the chair. "Rulfo," he said.

Titus began to feel that strange, unreal humming sensation again. He couldn't believe he was doing this. He wondered what Burden and the others were thinking as they watched his mole sensor at Luquín's clifftop house. Were they sending help? Was there going to be a shoot-out after all, despite everyone's elaborate efforts to maintain silence?

The bodyguard put his hand on the doorknob of the front door and twisted it slowly. He pushed carefully. The door eased open, and he followed it in as if he were part of it. Macias nudged Titus forward with his pistol. The bodyguard looked toward the pale flickering light that came from the room just off the main hallway. Television. Lots of light, big screen. The moment Macias cleared the front door, the bodyguard stopped again. He turned around and looked past Titus at Macias behind him and pointed to the hallway floor. Another dead man. Instinctively all three of them waited, listening.

Nothing. Apparently the volume was off on the television.

Wait. From the far side of the family room, water started running. The kitchen. The sound of the water in the sink would create a kind of white noise for the person standing there, so the bodyguard made a quick move to get across the opening into the family room, past the body in the hallway, and to the next opening that came into the back of the family room, nearer the kitchen.

Titus's underarms were slick with perspiration, and suddenly he caught the odor of feces. Feces? He looked at Macias, whose eyes were fixed on his bodyguard as if he were the canary in the coal mine. The bodyguard motioned: One man.

With that information, Macias urged Titus forward into the first opening at the same moment that the bodyguard stepped into the other one. At that instant, both Titus and Macias looked toward the bodyguard for another cue, but the man was stone still, looking around frantically. When he'd turned back after motioning to Macias, he'd lost his man.

Fear defined him in that moment, and Titus knew that he knew that he was going to die. The only sound was the dull *smack!* of the slug hitting his forehead and blowing out the back of his skull, a sound weirdly soft and out of proportion to the sight of his head being flung back violently with a neck-popping velocity that knocked him off his feet. And because his head seemed to recoil at an angle, it was difficult to tell which direction the shot had come from.

Titus went cold. The inexplicable physics of what he'd just seen added to the weirdness of the fact that he was even there.

Then a figure like a demon stood up from behind the sofa, naked, his body smeared with muddy brown and fecal green (a stunning confusion with reality), his hair spiky wild. Titus didn't really understand what he was looking at, and he didn't understand the compression of time, but before either he or Macias could react, the man was holding a small gun to Macias's forehead as he took his automatic away from him and tossed it aside on the floor.

"Who are you?" he asked Titus. Hispanic accent. His eyes were calm but tortured, red rimmed. The whites were very white.

Titus couldn't speak. He smelled the body paint now. And something else, too. There was blood all over the demon, and the odor of it was thick and sweet. Titus could hardly believe his senses. This man-thing wasn't big, but the intensity of its presence was scintillating.

"Who are you?" he asked Macias. He reached around with his left arm and cradled the back of Macias's head with his hand so that his right hand could press the barrel of his strange-looking pistol to Macias's forehead with what must have been a painful force.

"Jorge Macias."

"We're supposed to be alone here," the demon said. "Why are you here?"

"I came to get a computer," Macias said with an honesty that seemed childishly absurd.

"Is that all you want?"

"Yes."

"Where is it?"

Macias carefully raised a hand and pointed to the dining room table a few feet from Titus.

"Get it," the demon said to Titus. "Yes. Yes. Go get it."

Titus went to the table and closed the notebook. It was plugged in. As he was unplugging it, he looked down and saw photographs scattered on the table. They were of various sizes, some in black and white, some in color, some yellowed and limp with age. The images were horrific; a little girl of ten or eleven in various acts of sexual intercourse with men, sometimes several men. Bruises were clearly visible on her little body, which hadn't yet begun to take on the contours of puberty.

Titus struggled with a memory, a recognition. A child . . . what did he know about a child? Jesus Christ! He remembered . . . Burden had told him a harrowing story about Luquín . . . and a little girl . . . and her father. Artemio. Ospina.

He looked around at the man, who was still holding Macias's head wedged between his gun barrel and his hand, and he was looking at Titus. What the hell was going on here?

Something else caught Titus's eye. A cell phone on the table was ringing. The sound was turned off, but a red light stuttered . . . stuttered . . . stuttered.

"Is this your phone?"

The man said nothing.

"It's ringing," Titus said.

"Yes, I know."

Titus's phone rang in Macias's pocket.

"Let me get that," Titus said. "That's my phone. This guy's kidnapped me. . . ."

"No," Macias said, his eyes walled as he rolled them at the man holding him. Then he spoke to him in Spanish, and the man cut his eyes again at Titus.

"I don't know what he's saying," Titus said, suddenly terrified at Macias's ploy, "but he and Luquín had been extorting money from me, and they've killed my friends. . . . Wait . . . wait. I know, you work for García Burden, don't you?"

At the mention of Burden's name, he saw recognition in the demon's eyes. And there was no mistaking the recognition in Macias's eyes, either. Though Titus was actually out of his field of vision, Macias's eyes were rolled in his direction, wide with stunned discovery, as if those two words dazzled with revelation in the shadowy room, like the visionary writing on Belshazzar's wall.

"I hired García to get me out of this thing with Luquín and Macias. Maybe he hired you—"

This wasn't working fast enough, wasn't advancing his argument fast enough.

"These pictures," he said quickly, "I know about those pictures. Just a few days ago, in San Miguel, García told me. She's the daughter of a guy García knows. García was explaining to me what kind of a man Luquín was, wanted me to know what I was up against."

Everything froze. No sound. No one spoke. This information had done something to the demon that nearly sucked the air out of the room.

And then Titus heard a single, faint snick.

The little pistol had misfired.

Macias and the man both realized what had happened a millisecond before Titus did, and in a flash Macias's right fist drove one, two, three times into the man's upper thigh near his naked groin as Macias charged in a powerful burst of energy, carrying the man backward, both of them falling over the coffee table and onto the floor. Macias dropped the small switchblade as he scrambled for his gun and came up with the gun before the man could recover and just as Titus hurled the laptop across the sofa, catching Macias flat in the chest, knocking him into a backward stagger. He fell back against the giant television screen but kept his balance and came up with the automatic leveled at Titus, who had barreled across the room to within a few feet of him.

Again everything stopped. Everybody was breathing hard, wired, adrenaline pumping.

"Okay," Macias said. "Pick up the laptop." He only had to move the automatic inches to cover both men. "Try to throw it again, and I'll kill you. I've got nothing to lose now." To the naked man: "Is Luquín dead?"

"Almost." He was holding his thigh, blood all over the sofa.

Macias motioned to Titus to move toward the front door. "We're leaving," Macias said to the man. "You finish what you came here to do. Don't leave that son of a bitch alive."

Clutching his wounds, the man watched them as they made their way through the entry hall to the front door. Before Titus opened the door, with Macias's automatic again jammed into his kidneys, he glanced back. The pale light from the television flickered on the bloody sofa. The man was gone.

Chapter 55

Suddenly, after an agonizingly long silence, Titus's signal moved out of the house.

"Unbelievable." Norlin was on the edge of his chair, his neck craning toward the screen.

"The bodyguard's signal's not moving," a technician said.

"You think they killed him?" asked the other one.

Burden gazed at the screens, ignoring their questions.

"You think Cain is alone?" Norlin asked.

Burden punched the send call on his cell and waited. No answer. He shook his head. "No, he's not alone."

The blip made its way through the neighborhood and then turned left at Highway 2222 and headed west.

"Coming our way," said a technician.

"We've got a choice," Burden said to no one in particular, thinking out loud. "Macias has an escape plan. Always. Just for him. Whatever it is, he's headed for it now. He assumes the car's tagged, so he'll be dumping it. He's going to think he has to keep Cain as insurance. If it goes on like this, it could end in a confrontation. We don't know what happened back at Luquín's, maybe a shoot-out. Don't know if Artemio's dead.

Don't know if Luquín's dead. Police may be on the way. And that means discovery. If there's a shoot-out trying to get Cain back, that means discovery. If Cain is killed, even without a shoot-out, that means discovery. If Macias kidnaps him, that means discovery and possibly Cain's death, too."

"You want to let him go, then?"

"If we can guarantee Cain's life, yes," Burden said. "If we can guarantee silence for this operation, yes. We have to. Even though it means that someone's going to have to deal with the son of a bitch again sometime down the road."

"Calò's in behind them again," a technician said.

"One more thing," Burden said. "Now the gun in the seat is in play again. If it hasn't already been found and dealt with."

"Man, that is such a risk," Norlin said. "That is such a risk. He'll get killed if he tries to use that thing. Hell, we don't know if he can use it. Why the hell did Calò do that?"

"I don't know that it was the wrong thing to do. It might save his life."

"Shit, it's going to get him killed."

"I don't know, I might've done the same thing. There was opportunity, and not a lot of time to think. It was a choice."

Burden's phone rang, and he snapped it up and answered.

"García Burden," Macias said. It was just a statement.

"Hello, Jorge."

"This explains a lot," Macias said. "I couldn't figure out why so much careful planning was falling apart so fast."

"Is he still alive?"

"Who?"

"Cain."

"Yes."

"Let me speak to him."

Macias held the phone beside Titus's head. "Tell him you're alive."

"I'm okay," Titus said.

"You hear that?" Macias asked.

"We need to talk about where we stand, Jorge."

"Go ahead. I can't wait to hear this."

"Is Luquín dead?"

"He probably is by now."

"What's the situation there?"

"Call your fucking crazy man and ask him."

"I've been trying to."

"Well, he looked like he was very busy."

Silence.

"You've been wiped out," Burden said. "That's where you stand."

"Keep going."

"We want to make a deal. We'll stop right here, and you can walk away. But Cain walks away, too. Very simple. On the other hand," Burden added, "if he dies, you die. Guaranteed."

"Maybe I'll just take him with me," Macias said.

"That's not an option."

Macias already knew that Burden would say that. But maybe they disagreed about what Macias's options were. He wasn't going to tell Burden, but Macias thought that there was some room to be flexible here. Burden would not be bargaining if Macias didn't have a good shot at doing what he wanted to do here.

"How do you propose to do this?" Having to ask the question galled him. It was like asking permission, admitting that Burden had the upper hand. For the moment, at least. But his humiliation was nothing compared to the raw rush of fear that gripped him. He had come so close to being killed, and now he had this one last opportunity to save his ass. He couldn't make any mistakes.

"The car's bugged," Burden said, "and so is Cain. So we know where he is at every moment. He swallowed it, Jorge, so don't worry about taking all of his clothes off and shit like that. I know you have an escape plan. I know you're planning on dumping the car, so go ahead and do that. But leave Cain with it. Alive. If you do that, you live. Anything else, you don't.'"

"Yes, I know. You've already made that point." Macias's mind was racing. Shit. Shit. The one thing that sounded too neat here was Cain swallowing a bug. Why would Burden tell him that? It seemed to Macias that if it was true, it was the sort of thing you'd want to keep secret. Why else would he swallow it? So why would Burden say that? Because once Macias dumped the car and Burden's people lost visual contact with Macias, then Burden wouldn't have any idea where Cain was. Burden was trying to make Macias believe that he had no choice except to leave Cain with the Navigator. But Macias wasn't buying it. Not that part of the deal, anyway.

Other than that, how the hell was he going to make sure they would let him go if he did what Burden wanted?

"This is a delicate moment, García. Do something to make me believe you will do what you say."

"I need to talk to Cain to make it work."

Macias froze.

"Just hand him the phone," Burden said, sensing Macias's instant suspicion. "I need to calm him down, Jorge. You don't understand, yet, what you're dealing with there."

Macias tried to sort it out, his mind stumbling over itself. He was losing the thread here, getting confused, trying to anticipate all the traps, and afraid he wasn't seeing even the obvious ones.

"Hand him the phone, Jorge. He'll hand it right back to you."

This was a fucking mistake, Macias thought, but he had to make a decision fast. The car was flying down the highway. Soon they were going to have to turn off.

"If you don't do this," Burden said, "it's not going to work. It's all over."

Macias had every reason in the world not to believe this.

"He wants to talk to you," Macias said, handing the phone over the seat to Titus.

Sweating, his nerves fraying, Titus reached out, touching Macias's hand as he fumbled for the phone being handed over his shoulder, repulsed at the feel of the other man's flesh.

"Yes."

"Titus," Burden said, "in just a second you're going to hand the phone back to Macias, so I'm going to talk fast. Do you know about the gun?"

"Yes."

"Okay, while I'm talking right now take the mole off your arm and put it on the gun without letting him see. Then let him have the gun when he asks for it. I told him you'd swallowed a bug, and that we know where you are at all times. He needs to believe that. I'm going to try to get him to leave you with the Navigator in exchange for letting him go. Quickly, what did he go back to Luquín's for?"

"Laptop."

Macias snatched the phone from Titus with a slap to the side of the head that was so hard, it caused him to swerve off the highway and plow along a hundred yards of the median before he regained control and got back on the pavement.

"You're a goddamned idiot!" Macias screamed into the phone. He was rattled and furious.

"Listen, Jorge," Burden said slowly. "We want to be very

careful here, okay? Remember, he lives, you live. Anybody dies, everybody dies." He was stretching it out, giving Titus time to switch the mole. "When my men brought you the car at La Terrazza, they jammed an automatic down in between the seats by Cain's right side. He's already found it. It's ready to fire, safety off. I told him to let you have it when you reached over the seat to get it."

"I'll blow his head off, García," Macias yelled, "I've got it to his head right now. I'll fucking shoot him!"

"Damn it, it's no trick, Jorge."

Macias kept the phone to his ear and spoke to Titus.

"What did he tell you?"

During Macias's exchange with Burden, Titus had carefully peeled the mole from his right arm with his left hand and was now pressing it into the scored handle of the pistol. He was still shaken from the blow against the side of his head, but he managed to move his hand slowly away from the gun to the bottom of the steering wheel as he answered.

"He said not to use the gun that's in the seat here. He said to let you have it."

Macias calculated the time they'd spent on the phone. Burden really couldn't have said much more than that. He screwed the muzzle of the automatic into the base of Titus's skull and slowly reached over the seat. He found the handle of the gun, jammed between the seats, and slowly brought it out. There was a suppressor on it.

"Now what?" Macias said into the phone.

"Okay, you see how this is going?" Burden asked.

"Yeah, I see."

"We just want to bring this to an end, Jorge. If we get Cain back safely and in one piece, then you get a free pass. You're lucky this time. Very, very lucky."

Macias knew that Burden was speaking the truth, about

this one thing, anyway. He had this little opportunity *solo por suerte*. Every moment counted now. He'd kept glancing out the rear window. He hadn't seen headlights at a consistent distance, which meant that they probably were locked on to them with a tag, like they said. They didn't need somebody up close. If that was the case, then, that distance between him and whoever was back there—he wasn't stupid, he knew there was somebody back there—that distance was his opening. His only opening. And his next move had to be done in that space, and in absolute privacy.

"What about it, Jorge? Have we got a deal?" Burden asked him.

"Yeah, we've got a deal."

"Okay, now it's your turn to make us believe you," Burden concluded. "When you drop him with the Navigator, you've got to put him on the phone so we know he's alive when you leave. We'll keep talking to him until we get to him. When we've got him, you're in the open."

"¡Hecho!" Macias said, and punched off the phone.

He hesitated a second, calculating, going through the mental paces of what lay before him to make sure he didn't miss a step that would throw off his timing. Then he punched in a code on his cell phone and immediately pushed the time elapse feature on his watch, setting it for forty-five minutes.

Free pass. Yeah. Did Burden think he was so scared that he'd lost his mind? No fucking way was he going to give up Titus Cain until he was safely out of this mess . . . and maybe not even then. He'd have to see how it went. But in the meantime, maybe the lie would buy him a little time.

Chapter 56

"Jesus," Norlin said.

Burden could feel him looking at him. They were close in the van, their eyes jittering over the screens.

"That," Norlin said, "was a ballsy call."

"You mean heartless, don't you," Burden said without looking at Norlin. "You could've said heartless."

"No, I mean ballsy. If you're wrong . . . then it was heartless. You've almost got everything you wanted, García. More than you expected you'd get. You could've let it go."

"And I probably would have—if he hadn't gone back for that laptop. But if he risked his life for it, then I want it."

"Even if it cost Cain *his* life?"

"Cain is one life. God knows how many lives that laptop could save."

"What if it can't? What if it can't even save one?"

"You're acting like Cain's already dead. Look, if Macias believes that Cain's swallowed a bug, then he'll leave Cain with the car because he's got to isolate himself. If he does that, I want Calò to be able to get to him."

"That's a damned big if."

Burden said nothing, ignoring Norlin, his eyes fixed on the monitors.

"And if Macias doesn't buy that story?" Norlin persisted.

Burden turned to him. "Think about it, Gil. We wiped out this entire operation. Hell, I can hardly believe that myself. That's got to scare the hell out of him. I've got to guess that at this point Jorge Macias is entirely focused on saving his ass."

"But what if he doesn't buy the lie about the swallowed bug?"

"Then he'll take Cain with him. And even if he does that, he'll have to be thinking, in the back of his mind, that maybe he's guessed wrong. That maybe I'm watching this monitor, and I can see Cain's bug leaving with Macias and not staying with the Navigator like we'd agreed. He'll remember that I said that if he did anything other than what we agreed on, then he's a dead man. The second he deviates from our agreement— if he does—he's going to be sweating blood. People who sweat blood make mistakes." He looked at the monitor. "Calò's still on him."

"Yeah, way back," the technician said. "More than a mile."

The van was on the move again, too, just about a mile behind Calò.

Burden kept his eyes on the LorGuides. Up until now everything had worked far better than he'd had any reason to expect it would, but now he had no men to spare, and what happened next was largely out of his hands. All he could do was listen to it happening.

"There's another way to look at his thinking," Burden said. "He knows damn well that his security is tied to Cain. He may hang on to him like a drowning man hangs on to a piece of driftwood. There's that possibility. If that's the way it goes, and if he tosses that gun for any reason at all, or loses it, or forgets it in the panic, Calò will go straight to it, and we're screwed."

"Cain's screwed," Norlin corrected him.

"They've turned off onto South Loop One," a technician said.

"Pull up the maps in the southwest part of the city," Burden said.

"If Macias continues on his course"—Norlin leaned across and pointed to the map on the largest of four screens—"he'll go into Oak Hill. He's headed for an intersection where he'll have to make a choice between two highways. One, a state highway, goes toward the lakes and on to Llano; the other one, a U.S. highway, better condition, can take you to Fredericksburg or south to San Antonio. All of them go through ranch country."

Burden stared at the map. Macias was headed into his escape plan. For it to work, he was going to have to drop off the LorGuides somehow. He had to disappear.

Titus's hands were shaking on the steering wheel from the rush of adrenaline that just didn't stop coming. They drove south on Loop 360, where the city had effused into the rolling hills with up-market developments that overflowed into the wooded valleys and crawled along the crowns of the ridges, their lights spreading like a sparkling mildew into the rolling landscape. They stayed with the Loop as it turned back east on the southern side of the city, and when it intersected Loop 1, Macias told him to turn right and head south.

Macias wasn't talking, and Titus found it particularly unnerving that he didn't ease off with the automatic, which he kept screwed into the base of Titus's skull. He could actually feel the roundness of the barrel, and it felt like a coffin to him.

When Loop 1 intersected Highways 290 and 71, Macias

directed him to exit on the access road. From there they headed off into the more traditional housing developments, street after street of ranch houses interspersed with shopping centers and apartment complexes.

"Pull in here," Macias said, and Titus wheeled into a new shopping center carved out of acres and acres of new ranch houses. There was a twenty-four-hour supermarket, a twenty-four-hour home repairs complex, a twenty-four-hour pharmacy franchise, a twenty-four-hour restaurant franchise, and several smaller businesses, their common sprawling parking area brightly lighted by towering halogen street lamps.

"Park here," Macias instructed, directing Titus to one of the largest clusters of cars in the area. He got out and opened Titus's door.

"Come on," he said, but as Titus turned to get out, Macias reached in and put the barrel of his pistol to Titus's Adam's apple. He said nothing, but he pressed so hard that Titus could feel the cartilage of his trachea rolling under the steel. Then Macias jabbed the gun sharply for emphasis, bringing tears to Titus's eyes.

"Get the keys and hand them to me," Macias said.

Titus did, and then Macias stepped back and let him get out.

Standing next to the Navigator, he watched Macias pull out his shirttail to cover the automatic with the suppressor and the mole, which he crammed into the front waistband of his pants. Titus cringed, hoping he didn't rake the mole off in the process.

Macias put his arm around Titus and draped his left hand over the top of his shoulder. "I know you want to keep your kidneys," he said. "Let's go."

But Titus froze. "Hold it. This isn't what we agreed on. They'll kill you if I don't stay with the Navigator."

"They'll have to find us first."

"Look," Titus said, "I've . . . I'll be honest with you. I'm hot. I've swallowed a bug. They know where I am every second. When they see my signal leaving the car, you're screwed."

"Then why in the hell are you telling me this?"

"Because I'm not an idiot. I don't want to get killed in a shoot-out, and I'm telling you, if I leave this Navigator, they're going to come after you."

They were standing face-to-face, and Macias smelled of stale cologne and perspiration. Both men were dealing with fear and with the mystery of the odds of chance. Titus could smell Macias's breath, too, and he thought it smelled of desperation.

Chapter 57

Rita looked out of the backseat windows of Kal's Jeep Cherokee as it pulled off the Loop 1 South expressway and into the
parking lot of the La Quinta Inn. Kal was driving, Ryan was
sitting in the front passenger seat beside him, and Janet was sitting next to Rita behind them.

They pulled up beside a van just as its rear door opened,
and García Burden stepped out into the parking lot. They all
got out of the Cherokee and stood at the opened door of the
van to talk. Rita could see inside the van, its cramped, dark interior glittering with banks of computer screens covered in col-
ored lights. A clutter of transmission noises wafted out to her.

Burden spoke directly to her. "Two things: I don't have any
more people, and before this is over I may need your three
bodyguards here. So this is good for me. The other thing,
you're right. If he's going to die, you shouldn't have to watch
it like that. If this involved a lot of people, as it did earlier in
the evening, I wouldn't have allowed this. But it's down to just
Titus and Macias.

"Titus's signal has stopped moving," he went on, "and it's

369

coming from somewhere in all those shopping center lights over there."

He pointed across the expressway. The back of his saggy shirt was black with perspiration. He seemed wrung out. "Calò's over there, trying to get as close as he can. If we're lucky, that's where Macias is planning to leave Titus with the telephone."

Ryan turned and stepped inside the van and immediately came back out with one of the technicians, who was carrying a LorGuide that they'd disconnected. They went to the Cherokee and started installing it between the driver and the passenger in the front seat.

"Hey," Norlin said from inside the van. "It looks like the signal's leaving the Navigator."

Burden was instantly back inside the van, and the others crowded around the opened rear door.

"This's a big supermarket," Norlin said, pointing to the schematic graphics on one of the screens. "It looks like the signal's going in."

Burden got Calò on the telephone.

"Yeah, I see that," Calò said. "I'm easing into the lot. I'll try to get to the Navigator."

Nobody had to say it: This wasn't good. The signal was on the gun. Titus was supposed to be on the phone talking to them when Macias left the van. He wasn't.

Rita remembered her conversation with Burden earlier. She'd been stubborn, wanting to be closer to it all, and now here she was. She'd be damned if she'd fold and get whiny. She wasn't going to do it. Titus wasn't dead. She would know it if he was. She'd feel it, like the vibrations of a tuning fork, some subtle fibrillation within her stomach. She believed that as surely as she believed the sun would come up again in the morning. She stared into the dark van and waited.

* * *

Titus started walking, and they headed for the supermar-ket.

Inside the huge and brightly lighted store, Macias slowed down and they walked as casually as possible past the cereals and the soft drinks and the refrigerated goods, past the fresh produce and the meat market, and headed through the double swinging doors into the back of the store. Some of the work-ers threw them curious glances, but they weren't being paid enough to be too curious, and Titus and Macias went right on through to the back of the warehouse and out the back metal door into the alley without anyone saying a word to them.

Outside again, Macias glanced around to see that they were still alone. Now he had his gun out in the open and jammed into Titus's kidneys again and shoved him forward, fast walking down the alley, past the Dumpsters with their ran-cid odors hanging in the still summer air. On the other side of them, a tall fence of wooden slats ran the length of the long alley behind the stores, hiding it from the housing develop-ment.

To Titus the alley seemed more isolated than the Antarctic, but Macias kept checking the rears of the stores, and when he passed into the shadows between the security lights over the back doors of a pet store and camera shop, he guided Titus with pressure from his pistol barrel, and they veered to the fence.

They slowed to a walk, then a slow walk, then they stopped and went back a few steps. Macias scanned the backs of the stores again, seeming to check his bearings, and then they went up to the fence, lifted the bottoms of three adjacent slats, and crouched into the backyard of a small ranch house. The yard, lighted by the street lamps in the adjacent alley, was overgrown with weeds; the house was dark.

Macias unlocked the back door of the house and pushed Titus in first. The alley lights were the only thing that lighted the darkened kitchen through its small windows, and then Titus saw a seam of light at the bottom of a closed door.

"Over there," Macias said, and he pushed Titus forward. When they got to the door, Macias told him to open it, and they stepped into the garage. A black Honda Accord was waiting there, backed into the garage, and there was a man sitting on the trunk, his feet on the rear bumper.

"Whoa," the guy said, suddenly alert and getting off the car cautiously, eyeing Titus with alarm. "Oh, shit, what's going on here, Jorge?"

He was in his late twenties, maybe, Hispanic, though he didn't speak with an accent. He wore jeans and a short-sleeved nylon shirt, open, over a white T-shirt.

"No questions," Macias said.

Titus was judging the younger man's reaction. He looked as though he wanted to bolt, his eyes darting back and forth between Titus and Macias.

"Look," the young man said, "when you called me and told me to be here, you said you'd pay me off. I . . . don't want anything to do with this."

"You don't have anything to do with it, Elías," Macias said. "You've got one more chore and you're through."

"One more? I thought I was coming here to get my last payment for the photographs. And you said you'd reimburse me for them taking my laptop."

Titus looked at the young man. This was the guy who had taken the pictures of Rita? Macias must've been reading his mind, because he again jabbed the automatic into his kidney, telling him to keep his mouth shut. Titus's lower back was getting sore from his repeated jabbing.

Macias pulled the Navigator keys out of his pocket and tossed them to the young man.

"In the shopping center over there, there's a Lincoln Navigator parked in front of the supermarket. Dark blue. I want you to go over there and get it and drive it to San Marcos. Watch for the first Texaco station on your right as you come into town. Exit off there and go to the station. You'll find another Navigator just like the one you're driving. Your money's in the glove box. Drive off. You're through."

Elías Loza stared at him. "Why am I doing that all of a sudden? That wasn't in the deal." He glanced at Titus. "It looks to me like shit's coming apart here. There was no driving a car in the deal. If this . . . if shit's coming apart here—"

"Nothing's coming apart," Macias said. "We're just staying flexible. You gotta be flexible, too."

"I don't want flexible. I want the rest of my money."

"Well, your money's flexible . . . it's not here. It's in the other car . . . in San Marcos."

Loza stared at Macias. Titus could see him thinking: Either the money's in the other car or . . . this son of a bitch could shoot me right here.

"That's it, then?"

"Yeah, that's it."

Disgusted, but more scared than anything, Loza bent down and got his camera bag. When he straightened up he looked at Titus and then back at Macias.

"I don't know what's going down here," Loza said, "but, me doing this, it doesn't feel right. And I don't have a gun, nothing. . . ."

Macias swore. Titus guessed he'd love to just shoot the guy and get the hell out of here, but he wanted the tag that he thought was on the Navigator to be headed out of the city. Suddenly he lifted his shirt and pulled the automatic from the waist of his trousers. He tossed it to a surprised Loza, who caught it against his stomach with his free hand.

"Get the hell out of here," Macias said.

Loza looked at the gun, then at Macias, and cut a glance at Titus. For a brief, sweet moment, Titus thought Loza was going to shoot Macias. But it was a fool's moment, and Loza turned and walked out of the garage.

Chapter 58

Romo Calò found the Navigator in a cluster of other cars in front of the supermarket. Rather than trying to work at a distance, he decided to barge in close and go for broke. He parked three cars away from the Navigator so that he was on the opposite side of it from the grocery cart storage rack.

Walking away from his car, he fiddled with his keys as he passed the Navigator on the way to the cart storage. He saw nothing. He pulled out a cart, pretended he forgot something in the car, and walked past the back of the Navigator again. Still he saw nothing. At his car, he opened the door and pretended to get something and then once again walked toward the Navigator on the way to the cart he'd left at the storage rack.

Still seeing nothing that made him suspicious, he got even with the back of the Navigator, left the cart, and slipped in between the cars and looked in. Nothing. Quickly he went to the cart again and headed toward the front of the supermarket as he pulled out his cell phone.

"The car's empty," Calò said to the van. *"Nada."*

"Keep your eyes on it," Burden said. "We'll get back to you."

As Calò closed the phone, he glanced back just in time to see a man walking toward the Navigator through the aisles of cars. He was looking around, pausing, looking, and coming on. Finally his attention focused on the Navigator, and he headed straight for it. Quickly, Calò reversed his direction, pushing his cart. The guy glanced around and saw Calò, but disregarded him.

Calò watched the guy as he began checking out the Navigator as if he were unfamiliar with it. The guy looked up and looked around. What was this? Was he going to steal it? Then the guy walked up to the door and pointed his remote key lock at it; the Navigator squeaked, and the guy opened the door.

He still had one leg outside on the pavement when Calò moved around the rear bumper of the Navigator and blocked the door just as the guy tried to swing it closed. Instantly Calò's automatic was in his face.

"Don't breathe," Calò said. "Are you alone?"

The guy nodded yes.

"Who are you?"

"Elías Loza."

Calò moved the barrel of his automatic to Loza's mouth, touching his lips. Now he saw that Loza had been carrying a bag, and it was sitting in the seat with him.

"What's in the bag?"

"Camera."

"Armed?"

The guy nodded yes.

"Where?"

Loza looked down. "Right here."

Calò moved the barrel between Loza's eyes and reached in and found the automatic in the front waistband of his pants.

He was surprised to see it was the same gun he'd jammed down between the car seats for Titus. He hit the clip release, but it was empty.

"Where the fuck'd you get this?"

Loza didn't even have to guess if the name would have any meaning. "Jorge Macias."

"Where is he?"

"Look, I don't have anything—"

"Where!?"

"Over there . . . other side of the shopping center . . . one of those houses . . ."

"What are you doing here?"

Loza told him.

"What's the address over there?"

Calò was already pulling out his phone as Loza gave him the address.

"Another man with him?" Calò asked.

"Yeah."

"Anybody else?"

"No."

"Where're they headed?"

"I don't know."

Calò hit Loza in the mouth with his gun so fast, the barrel was already back between his eyes by the time Loza could react.

"No no no . . . ," he pleaded, blood pouring from a busted lip and a tooth knocked out of his gums. "Oh, oh, shit, ohhh . . . really, no no no . . . I don't know where the hell they're going. I don't . . . I don't know anything about this. . . ."

With his eyes focused on Loza's eyes, the barrel of his automatic still pressed between Loza's eyebrows, Calò spoke fast to Burden and told him everything.

"And the bad news," Calò said. "I'm holding the damn gun with the mole on it."

"Check the gun," Burden said. "Is the mole still there?"

"What's your signal say?"

"Says it's about five hundred meters west of you."

"Really?" Calò shoved Loza over and told him to curl up on the floor. Loza did as he was told, moaning, moaning, and Calò held the gun up to the interior light. It took him almost a minute of searching to decide it wasn't there.

Burden got into the Cherokee with Rita and the others, and they headed across the expressway, where Janet and Ryan took charge of Loza, driving away with him in the Navigator to check out Macias's safe house and make sure Titus hadn't been left there.

Calò returned to his car, and Rita continued in the Cherokee with Burden and Kal. In the backseat alone, she listened as the three men discussed the best way to handle the encounter with Macias. But before they could even get out of the massive parking lot, the signal left the address to which they were headed six blocks away.

"Calò," Burden said, watching the LorGuide, "get in behind him again. I don't know what's happened to the damn mole, whether it was moved from the gun deliberately or accidentally, but we have to play it safe and assume Macias doesn't know we're still with him. First thing, though, try to get close enough to the signal to get a sighting of the Honda. We've got to find out if it's carrying the signal, or if Macias has managed to somehow put it on a decoy vehicle."

After that, the transmissions fell dead, and everyone was glued to the LorGuides.

*   *   *

Again Macias got into the back and Titus drove, following directions that took them through the neighborhoods to Loop 1 South, where they headed for Oak Hill. Titus took stock of his situation. It wasn't good. Now that the mole had taken off for San Marcos, and Burden's people had no visuals on Titus, he was on his own. He knew that Burden had had a small crew to begin with, and if everything was going according to plan, there was no one else to spare for this little unexpected development. Another blindside for Burden.

Macias had made it plain that Titus's life was only as good as Macias's own personal security. Titus understood that, but what happened when Macias decided he was safe? And how safe would he have to be before he made his decision about what to do with Titus? No matter how many times he went over it, Titus couldn't see how there would be any profit in it for Macias to kill him when he no longer needed him.

On the other hand, Titus didn't know what other factors waited in the background that might completely change that simple deduction. God knows he had seen reversals in spades during the last few days. Despite the fact that he told himself his odds were better as a hostage if he remained optimistic, he found it impossible. Right now the darkness outside was a pretty good metaphor for the way he was feeling about his situation.

"Watch the speed limit," Macias said behind Titus's head. "No cops."

Titus checked Macias in the rearview mirror. He was still monitoring the traffic behind them. He was nervous, maybe feeling a little better now that he thought he had some breathing room. But Macias was a realist. He knew that the margin of his advantage was hair thin.

Titus wanted to try to get some feel for his state of mind.

379

He wanted to hear him say something, maybe give Titus a little insight into his intentions.

"There's not any money in San Marcos, is there," Titus said. "I'll bet there's not even another Navigator there."

"That's his problem," Macias said. "He'll deal with it. You've got a different set of problems you need to think about."

They were moving through the incorporated village of Oak Hill on the southwest edge of Austin. In a few minutes Macias had a decision to make. Either way, the traffic was about to get scarce, and it was going to get easier to spot a tail.

"How are you going to make sure Luquín's dead?" Titus asked.

"After seeing the spook show that was going on back there at that house, I don't think I have to worry about Tano being alive tomorrow morning. It looks like everybody wants Luquín dead. It's his time. When dogs smell blood, they all turn on the bloodiest dog first."

Now they were at the intersection.

"Keep going straight here," Macias said, and they stayed on Highway 290. That would eventually take them to Fredericksburg or San Antonio. Titus guessed San Antonio.

"What I want to know is," Macias said, "how the hell did you find García Burden?"

Titus told him the truth, without using names.

"And you went to see him the very next day?"

"Right."

"How?"

Titus told him the truth again.

Macias shook his head. "And that was just three days ago?"

"Right."

Silence. He heard Macias hiss under his breath.

"Only García Burden could fuck up nearly two months' planning in just three days," he said. "*Completely* fuck it up."

Well, not completely, Titus thought. Macias was still holding a gun to his head.

They left the city and the suburbs behind. The lights in the flanking hills gradually diminished with the churning numbers on the odometer. Mostly now it was only darkness on either side of the highway.

"How far are we going?" Titus asked.

"Don't worry about it," Macias said.

Titus could imagine Macias kicking him out of the car at some vacant strip center or on some dark street in San Antonio. Then he could walk to a pay phone, and it would all be over. Titus couldn't wait for that, for the whole insane thing to be over. He focused on the center stripe in the highway and tried to keep his mind off of . . . everything.

But he couldn't keep it off the guy in the backseat. He thought of what Rita had said, that as horrible as it was, she couldn't keep from imagining Charlie tangled in the chain saw, Carla suffocating, gasping for breath. She couldn't help but wonder how all of that had happened, how it had actually happened. Neither could Titus. It was infuriating to him that the man who had orchestrated all of that was sitting behind him and that Titus himself was complicit in his escape. God, and neither Carla nor Charlie had even been buried yet.

"Slow down," Macias said.

Chapter 59

When it was clear that Macias was taking 290 west, Burden got on the radio with Calò.

"Calò," he said, "do you still have your night goggles?"

"Yeah."

"Okay, at this hour of the night the highway's going to be damn near empty. Put on the goggles, turn out your headlights, and catch up with the signal and see if it's the Honda. He's going to be driving the speed limit, so with luck you can catch up with him."

"What about cops?"

"If you get busted, ditch the goggles and just take the ticket. You've got good ID, right?"

"Yeah. I'll be okay."

During the next twenty minutes, Kal watched his speedometer while Calò kept up a running commentary of his progress screaming down the dark highway without head-lights, the world in front of him apple green and black.

For Rita it was nearly half an hour of unbelievable tension, her eyes glued to the LorGuide, her ears straining to pull more information out of Calò than the typically terse tactical communications provided. Her stomach began to hurt, and she saw nothing of any help in the dash-lighted faces of Kal and Burden as they watched the LorGuide, too, and listened with passionless expressions.

"Got 'em!" Calò broadcast suddenly. "Brake lights. They're slowing . . . way down. . . ."

"Where? What's there?"

"Nothing. Dark ranch country. Nothing. I'm braking hard. I've got to stop. . . ."

Titus was startled back to the moment. Slow down? Was Macias just going to shove him out on the roadside?

"Slow down," Macias repeated.

Titus was confused. They were out in the middle of nowhere, nothing out there in the darkness.

"Okay, see the red reflectors on the fence up there? There's a cattle guard there. Pull over and go through it. Now, quickly."

There were no cars on the highway in either direction, Titus noticed, and that was the way Macias wanted it. And that was what he got.

Titus pulled off on the shoulder and then turned into the cattle guard. His headlights picked up the caliche ruts of a ranch road. The center of the ruts was grown up with range grass that was already burned up in the July heat.

"Cut the lights and stop," Macias said.

Titus did as he was told.

"Roll down the windows," Macias said.

The car was filled with the sound of night insects and the smell of range grass. As their eyes adjusted to the darkness, the caliche ruts began to glow in the light of the half-moon like dull phosphorus.

"You can see enough to drive," Macias said. "Go on."

Titus put the car in gear and slowly moved along the over-grown road. The tall grass between the ruts dragged against the undercarriage of the car as the road rose up a slight rise and then leveled off after a gradual decline. They could see the rolling hills spread out in front of them in the darkness, the pale, moon gray of the grasses, the charcoal splotches of the woods, and above it all the night sky scattered with icy blue stars.

"Stop here and cut the engine," Macias said.

Titus didn't like this.

They got out of the car, Macias carrying his laptop and his gun, and started walking. The hills were covered with rocks and clump grass and scattered cedar trees that rose out of the half-moon darkness like black bears.

As they walked, Titus's heart began to race. He couldn't imagine any kind of resolution here except a bad one. They went down into a draw, stumbling over rocks, barging into cactus, the moon providing just enough light to make them think they could see where they were going but leaving out the details. Then they came up on the other side of the draw to a ridgetop.

"Sit down," Macias said, putting the muzzle of his auto-matic to the top of Titus's shoulder to make the point. Then he pulled out a cell phone and punched a button.

"*Estamos aquí*," he said. "*¡Ándale! ¡Ándale!*"

Both of them were heaving and sweating, their shoes full of broken twigs and rocks, their socks riddled with the spines of needle grass.

Titus's mind was lurching. Then he heard a deep, fulsome sound unlike any he'd ever heard, a rapid, accelerated cough-ing with undertones of a deep *whoosh*ing. Looking toward the sound in the far-off star scatter, he saw two stars growing out of the darkness. But their light was bluer than the others, and they were approaching rapidly, driven by an eerie, monstrous chuffing. As the two blue lights grew larger, the other stars around them disappeared, blocked out by the black silhouette of a helicopter descending toward them. The wind of its rotors finally reached them with a blast, and the chopper sank slowly in near silence and hovered in front of them.

"Let's go," Macias said, still gripping the laptop and urging Titus to his feet with the barrel of the gun.

As Titus came up from his knees, he brought a rock with him in his right hand, a rough stone the size of a grapefruit. The darkness gave him the only advantage he needed.

He swung with all his might, but the rock slipped out of his hand and the blow was only a glancing one, catching Macias against his left ear, staggering him and sending the laptop flying into the darkness. But he didn't go down. Titus charged him the way Macias had charged Artemio, throwing a shoulder into Macias's stomach with all the strength he could manage. The force of it took both of them off the ground, and they landed five feet away on Macias's back, an impact that knocked the air out of Macias, but not his senses. Immediately he began hammering Titus with the butt of the gun, slamming it again and again into Titus's face as Titus tried to ward off the unstoppable energy of the younger man. Then somehow Titus found another rock and smashed it into Macias's forehead just as he began firing.

Titus rolled away from the gunfire as Macias struggled to regain his senses, dazed, frantic to save himself. His arm came up with the automatic, but he was too stunned to control it. More shots went off *bam! bam! bam!* into the sky, into the ground, zinging past Titus's face.

Titus fell on him again before Macias could get to his feet and went crazy, beating him with both fists, never even giving Macias a chance to clear his head. The gun went off again, the barrel against Titus's neck when it fired, blasting a seared path upward under the side of his jaw. Now Titus went for the gun, breaking fingers, wrestling the gun away from Macias's hand, and then shooting him—somewhere in the stomach. Then he shot again, blowing off part of Macias's face—Titus actually saw it in the light of the flash. Then again—somewhere, anywhere. And again and again and again until the thing wouldn't fire anymore.

At the flashes of gunfire in the darkness, the helicopter hesitated thirty feet above them. A brilliant sapphire floodlight came out of its belly, lighting Titus in a laser blue glare as he stood over Macias's body.

Macias's phone began ringing in his pocket, but Titus's legs gave way, and he crumpled on the hardscrabble ground, slumping beside Macias's body, still holding the gun, heaving, unable to get enough air into his lungs, buffeted by the storm from the rotors of the helicopter.

Suddenly the floodlight went out, and very slowly the star lights came on again and the creature began to slip sideways, the wind and mystery of it drifting away over the tops of the trees. It stayed low. The muted pounding of its engine began to fade immediately, but the diminishing blue lights took longer, and Titus, exhausted, continued watching them recede until they were tiny bright dots and he couldn't even distinguish them from the stars.

Chapter 60

The isolated airstrip was on a private ranch nearly fifty miles northwest of Austin. It was an expensive landing site in the dead center of a long narrow valley a mile and a half off Highway 71. There was a small hangar (empty) with a workshop attached. Two fuel tanks sat fifty meters away. Another fifty meters from the tanks sat an old Cessna Grand Caravan, painted a flat charcoal gray, lights out, doors open for loading, waiting. The pilot and helper were sitting in the dark to one side of the aircraft, smoking.

Baas was the first to arrive, the headlights of Titus's Range Rover flickering through the dense cedar brakes as he came down the side of the wooded hills into the valley. He pulled up to the Cessna as if he'd done it a million times and got out. Quickly the pilot and helper ran over to the Rover to help Baas with the body of Macias's guard. They wrestled him out of the Rover and carried him to the cargo door of the Caravan. The interior of the plane had been stripped for cargo transportation, and the body, already discoloring from the cyanide, was laid on the bare aluminum floor.

By the time the body had been loaded into the plane, Tito

was arriving in the Pathfinder, followed by Cope in the car. The job of unloading the three bodies from the Pathfinder was more gruesome because of the profusion of blood.

After the three dead men were piled into the bare cargo hold with the body of the other guard, Tito drove the Pathfinder to the edge of the tarmac by the hangar. They opened all the doors and began sprinkling laundry detergent around the bloody interior. Cope had bought the detergent at a convenience store in Paleface, where the highway crossed the Pedernales River. Then they stretched the water hose from the corner of the hangar and began hosing down the Pathfinder, the suds boiling out of the interior in foaming pink billows.

When that was done, Cope and Tito took off their clothes, washed them with the detergent, too, and laid them over the limbs of the cedar trees to dry in the July night. They all sat down to more cigarettes while they waited for one more arrival.

An hour passed, and then another, with no communication with Calò or Burden. Then Tito's phone rang.

"Tito," Calò said, "I'm on the highway approaching the turnoff."

"What? What's happened?"

"Nothing wrong. Just some unexpected developments. You'll see in a few minutes. Is Luquín there?"

"No. We haven't heard anything."

They waited eagerly, watching the brush for the headlights of Calò's car. Everyone was standing, waiting for him, as he drove the length of the airstrip and pulled up next to the plane.

Calò got out of the car, sweating profusely, and opened the trunk without saying a word. Cope, Baas, and Tito came up and looked in.

"Bloody hell," Cope said.

They just stood there.

Baas looked up. "What happened?"

While they unloaded Macias's body, Calò told them what had happened, of his arrival just as the strange helicopter was sliding away into the darkness and how he had thought he was too late and that Macias had abducted Titus. Then he'd heard someone coughing, and he'd stumbled through the darkness to find Titus. When Burden and Kal arrived with Rita, Calò left with Macias's body, racing for the airstrip to beat the departure deadline.

"The bloody mole, then," Cope asked. "What the hell happened there? Macias took it off? Where'd he put it?"

"We were still getting signals from it when everyone got there," Calò said. "Cain was stunned. He thought the thing had gone with Loza when he left with the gun. We found it tangled in the hair on Macias's stomach. Guess Cain hadn't put it on the gun good enough, and it came off when Macias stuffed it into his pants, or when he pulled it out and gave it to Loza."

Calò checked his watch and then threw a worried look toward the far end of the airstrip. "Come on," he said, "let's clean out the trunk."

By the time they'd finished, it was twenty minutes before three o'clock, the "go no matter what" deadline for the Cessna Caravan's departure. The time came and went.

"Give it ten more minutes," Calò said.

"If he was anywhere near, you'd think he'd call," Tito said.

"Here we go," Cope said, and they all turned and saw the headlights of a vehicle pulling around the knob of the hill and heading toward the airstrip. Together they all watched as Cayeteno Luquín's black Navigator approached along one side of the tarmac. It was in no hurry.

The Navigator pulled up to the Caravan and stopped beside the six men who stood ready to help the driver with the bodies. No one knew who this man was, and they would never know. The driver's door opened and the man who stepped out was wearing dress trousers and that was all. Barefoot and shirtless, he was completely covered in camouflage paint—though his face had been wiped partially clean—which seemed to be mixed in even with his wildly matted hair. The whites of his eyes flashed spookily at them in contrast with his blotchy, marbled flesh.

He said nothing to any of them as he came around to the back of the Navigator and opened the door. But instead of the bodies that they had expected, the Navigator held a pile of black, heavy-ply, double-bagged garbage bags.

There was a moment of hesitation and surprise, but no one said anything. They began unloading the bags, two men to a bag, their lumpy contents shifting and falling around inside, making them difficult to handle.

When all eight bags had been loaded inside the plane, Baas said to Tito, "Don't forget, they can't stay in the bags. They've got to come out of the bags first."

Tito nodded. "Yeah, I know. I've already thought about it."

Cope whistled under his breath.

During the last of the loading, the pilot had been in the cockpit going through his checklist, and now he started the engines without anyone saying anything to him. The man who had brought the bags squatted in the door of the cargo hold. Apparently he was ready to go, too.

Tito looked toward the door reluctantly. "Shit. Okay," he said to the others.

"That's okay, I'll make the flight since I'm here," Calò said. "Tito, call García and tell him we've got to have two more drivers out here. When they get here, drive everything to the San Antonio chop shop, just as we planned. Stay until they're broken down. Then you pick up the surveillance van from Norlin's people. You're clear on that meeting place, right?"

Tito nodded. "Right," he said.

Calò glanced at the plane, and the pilot gave him a thumbs-up. He nodded. "And Tito, tell García that Luquín made it after all."

"*Bueno,*" Tito said. He looked at the cargo hold. "I owe you one, *Jefe.*"

Calò looked toward the cargo door, too. "Shit," he said.

When the Cessna Caravan cleared the runway at the end of the valley and climbed into the early morning darkness, the pilot cranked the Pratt & Whitney turbo prop to its maximum airspeed at the lowest possible altitude. Then, running in reverse the radar-laced air corridor favored by drug smugglers, he headed straight for the closest crossing on the Mexican border, midway between Del Rio and Eagle Pass.

It was still dark when they crossed into the Mexican state of Coahuila and entered the great, arid desert of northern Mexico. Turning slightly more westward, they held their course and climbed higher, passing over the Sierra Madre Oriental. As the darkness began to thin in the east, they approached a carefully charted spot just over the Coahuila-Chihuahua border.

At a precise point of navigation, roughly in the most remote expanse of the north Mexican desert that covered well over a thousand square miles of desperate isolation, the Caravan cut its speed to minimum and seemed to hover in the fleeing darkness.

The lower cargo door opened, and bodies, and parts of bodies, began to fall through the predawn light. With the bare floor of the cargo plane slick with blood, it was a grisly chore, one that Calò and the other man had all to themselves. The pilot's helper stayed in the co-pilot's seat and didn't look back.

When the last piece of anatomy had been jettisoned, Calò

reached for the lower hatch of the cargo door to pull it up. Suddenly the man grabbed his wrist to stop him. For a frozen moment Calò looked him in the eyes. Then the man let go of Calò's wrist, leaned forward, and made a lazy somersault into the cold dawn air.

Chapter 61

With two funerals back to back, there was no time to sit and brood about what had happened. In keeping with Burden's nothing-ever-happened design for the whole affair, Titus and Rita had to act as if nothing had. It would've been impossible to do if they weren't already in shock at having lost two close friends in as many days.

They had somehow gotten through the night, talking, talking, holding each other, catching snags of unconsciousness. It could hardly be called sleep. The next morning, nothing was right. They got up together and Titus made coffee. But he didn't know how to act. He had brutally killed a man less than twelve hours before. Despite what you saw in movies and read in novels, that was a hard thing to live with, no matter what the guy was like. Titus sure as hell didn't feel like making wisecracks and getting back to life as usual. In fact, if he knew nothing else, he knew enough to know that life as usual wasn't going to be there anymore.

The coffee tasted right, but there was no appetite to deal with. As much as anything, it was the nearly unbearable constraint pressed upon them to pretend that nothing had happened that created so much stress for them. If there could have been some kind of ritual aftermath of their harrowing four days, the police, the consolation of friends, the presence of attorneys or doctors . . . or something, they might have been able to handle it more easily. Or at least they might have begun to heal a little.

But there was no transition. Somewhere during the hours of ten o'clock and midnight nine people had died, one of them by Titus's own hand, and then immediately after that everyone and every body (literally) disappeared. Burden remained behind on the rocky hilltop while Kal drove Titus and Rita home. That was the last they saw of García Burden. No good-byes. No one seemed to want to do it, and there was a kind of atmosphere of "we'll tie up loose ends later" that everyone seemed to prefer. The bodyguards stayed the night, but by noon the next day, the three of them, along with Herrin and Cline, were gone. It was bizarre.

Charlie's funeral was on a bright, sunny Sunday. They buried him on his ranch, a breeze blowing through the valley as they gathered under a huddle of live oaks on the hill across the stream from the house. After speaking, Titus sat down and didn't hear another word anyone said. At one point he was shaken out of his preoccupation by the scream of a red-tailed hawk circling high overhead.

Family and friends gathered at the house afterward, and Titus sat for a long time in the shade of the porch and visited with Louise. After a while, at the appropriate time—neither too early nor too late—he and Rita drove away.

Carla's funeral on the following Monday was wrenching. There was a huge crowd at the late afternoon service in the church where she was a longtime member, the sanctuary filled with CaiText employees. Again, Titus spoke, but he and Rita were sitting with the girls, and when he sat down there was no time for him to indulge in his own reveries while Carla's daughters needed his attention.

Titus and Rita opened their home for the reception afterward. The last people didn't leave until dusk.

In the days that followed, Titus was immediately forced to deal with the total loss of his life savings. His attorneys and financial advisers were still trying to make sense of his Cavatino investments. There would be some sticky moments getting all that sorted out, but it wasn't an insurmountable problem.

But CaiText was still a strong company with bright prospects, so it wasn't like starting over from scratch. Still, it was a sobering loss, and he threw himself into CaiText's business in a way that he hadn't done in the last several years.

At home, he and Rita continued to talk endlessly about what had happened. It was strange and frustrating to have had this life-transforming experience in absolute isolation from the rest of the world. It was disconcerting suddenly to have powerful secrets that they would never be able to share with anyone. For a long time it obsessed them both. They hardly thought or spoke about anything else when they were alone. The whole experience was schizophrenic.

Over time, however, they gradually worked the nightmare into the fabric of their lives. They had to, or those four days would have become the only thing that had meaning for them in life. It would have defined them. Luquín and Macias would have stolen more than friends and money from them.

But Titus was restless. One night he went through the complicated process of contacting Gil Norlin again. He told him he wanted to try to arrange a meeting with García Burden. Why? Because he just wanted to talk to him. He wanted the guy to sit still for a few hours and talk to him. Norlin said he would see what he could do. But Titus never heard from either of them.

Chapter 62
Epilogue

It was a cold, drizzly evening with a heavy mist fuzzing the city's lights when Titus got out of the taxi in front of Galileo. He paid the driver and went inside, where one of the booths along the wall was waiting for him as he had requested.

He was in D.C. for business and would be returning to Austin the next day. After a week in the capital with back-to-back appointments, he had deliberately left the evening open. He just wanted a slow meal alone and time to read the newspaper.

He got a bottle of good wine and ordered dinner. When it came, he ate slowly and continued to noodle through the newspaper. He was three-quarters through the meal when he was aware of someone approaching his table. He looked up and was stunned to see García Burden standing there.

"Titus," Burden said, smiling and holding out his hand, "do you mind if I join you for a few minutes?"

He was dressed handsomely, even elegantly, Titus thought, and seemed as comfortable in his expensive, double-breasted suit as he had been in his jeans and baggy linen shirt. He sat down, and the waiter brought another glass. They waited while he poured wine for Burden and took away Titus's plate.

"This is no accident," Titus said.

Burden smiled. "I'm here on business, too, but Gil Norlin called me when he learned we were in the city at the same time. So I tracked you down."

Titus could only imagine. And how in the hell did it happen that Norlin knew that Titus was in Washington?

"I understand you'd wanted to talk to me," Burden said. "Sorry it couldn't happen sooner."

Titus nodded, studying him. The clothes might have changed, but he had the same sorrowful cast of the eyes that Titus remembered and the same air about him that suggested he had seen or done things that separated him from most other men.

"I was feeling . . . pretty desperate back then, when I called Norlin," Titus said. "Time has helped that a little bit. Rita and I have worked through some things, come to terms with some things, since then."

Burden nodded.

Titus sipped his wine. They stared at each other.

"One thing, though. The man who . . . at Luquín's that night. That was Artemio Ospina, wasn't it? The girl's father."

Burden nodded again.

"Why'd you lie to me about him being dead? I don't see the point of it."

"Didn't lie to you. I said the guy had destroyed himself. That's what was so awful about it. He would've been better off dead. He became a professional killer, but that was just a sideline. His real reason for living was to track down the five guys who showed up at his house that night. He hunted them down one by one over the years. Luquín was the fifth one. After that, Artemio just ended it."

"He quit killing?"

Burden told him how Artemio had died.

"Jesus!" Titus was astonished, surprised that he could still be surprised by anything connected with those astounding four days in July. He studied Burden. The high-strung intensity that had been so much a part of him during that short ordeal was tempered now to an interesting subtlety. He was thoughtful, relaxed. He was in no hurry to end the conversation.

Burden glanced around the room, a flick of his eyes, an involuntary reflex that signaled a change in the conversation. He leaned forward a little more, his forearms on the table, his long fingers touching the stem of his wineglass, moving it slightly toward the candle on the table. He tilted it, letting the light pass through the ruby liquid.

"That laptop Macias was so desperate to get?" Burden said.

Titus nodded.

"It contained the entire operational details of their scheme against you. Names. Names. Names. It expanded our criminal intelligence database about Mexico and its relationship to international crime by thirty percent. That's massive. It was a gold mine for us.

"Gil told me later that he'd told you and Rita about Mourad Berkat. Well, Tano Luquín was a key figure behind the Berkat episode. He was the one who had the Hamas connection, oddly enough. He dropped off our radar screens after that. When you came down to San Miguel and identified his picture in my files, I couldn't believe it.

"Macias is a different story. He knew about Luquín's connections to radical factions in the Middle East, and he'd started building secret files on Luquín's contacts. A man like Macias is addicted to information. Collects it like a junk dealer collects junk. You never know when you might be able to make a buck off some bit of information. Macias knew that eventually information about Luquín's Middle Eastern contacts would be valuable. He also knew that Luquín's dealings with these people could eventually be Luquín's downfall. So Macias began hedging his bets big time, hoarding every grain of information he could dig out of the cracks about Luquín and the terrorists. That laptop was full of dots, and Macias was already well on his way to connecting them."

He stopped and looked at Titus, slowly righting his glass so that the ruby smear on the tablecloth moved like a red ghost back into the glass.

"Tano Luquín was running a very dangerous game, Titus. After you left San Miguel, I followed a hunch and had a team sweep a house Luquín owned in Rio de Janeiro. They found, among other things, a telephone number that rang in a house in the Polanco district in Mexico City. When I had another team go to the house in Polanco, they found it empty. Hastily empty. The man who had been leasing the place for the past two months was named Adnan Abdul-Haq. More phone numbers. One of these numbers rang at a house in Beirut, a house that belongs to Hezbollah.

"Further checking revealed that Luquín had been in Beirut twice in the past six months. Also, remember the accounts through which Cavatino was going to scatter your ten million?"

"One was in Beirut."

Burden nodded. "Yeah, it's a popular money-laundering destination. But in this case none of the money went there. Not initially, though eventually that's where it all ended up."

"Jesus. So what was going on?"

Burden stared at Titus and then sat back. "We may never know."

"If you could've questioned—" Titus stopped. That was Burden's point, wasn't it?

Burden smiled a little and shrugged.

"And Abdul-Haq?" he said. "We don't have a clue who that guy is. His name hasn't turned up in any intelligence database that we have access to. The man will most likely remain a mystery to us. At what cost? We may never know that, either. Or we may find out the hard way: too late."

Burden finished the wine in his glass and looked around. His eyes seemed to flicker at something of interest over Titus's shoulder, and then it was gone. The man didn't allow himself much room to live life as it came to him. He was always watchful of his own behavior, afraid, it seemed, of an involuntary betrayal of something within him.

"I can understand the . . . necessity for the list," Titus said, lowering his voice, leaning in toward Burden, "but I don't understand why, with so much to learn from Luquín, he wouldn't be more valuable to you alive than dead. Or any of the names on the list, for that matter."

"Intelligence is . . . unstable," Burden said. "It has a half-life that's measured in instants. It has value only if the subject of the intelligence doesn't know we have it. The moment he knows, or his connections know, that you have it, its value dissipates like smoke. It becomes worthless."

"Because everything changes," Titus said.

"That's right. If we picked up Luquín, everyone who ever had anything to do with him would burn their bridges. Anything that used to be connected to him—contacts, procedures, routes, systems, processes, safe houses . . . everything—would be compromised and immediately changed. Everyone would start conducting their business differently, and we'd have to start from scratch trying to find out who, when, where, how, why.

"But if he dies," Burden went on, "odds are that the information we have is still good. His death doesn't taint the security of their connections, everyone keeps using the same methods and procedures, though maybe with a little extra care, since they can't be sure who it was who got to him."

"But removing him causes a void," Titus went on, beginning to see the logic, filling in the information to his own question. "It breaks up whatever operations he was driving, maybe kills them for good, and takes a major player out of the mix."

Burden nodded. "It's one way of doing things. Right now, for us, it works. We're still playing catch-up as we revamp our intelligence programs. We need some breathing room. Checking names off that list buys us time."

The waiter came and asked if they wanted another bottle of wine. Titus looked at Burden, who shook his head. The waiter retreated.

"How are you doing with it, then?" Burden asked after a few moments of silence. "In terms of the sum of your life."

Titus found it a curious question and was surprised that Burden would even want to know.

"To tell you the truth," he said, "there's no getting over it. No getting away from it, either."

Burden nodded as if he knew what Titus was talking about, but he said nothing.

"It's having to keep quiet about it," Titus added, "pretending it never happened. Somehow that makes it harder to live with. Almost unbearable sometimes."

"Keeping silent and pretending it never happened are two different things," Burden said. "You can't pretend it didn't happen. That'll drive you crazy. This thing is part of who you are now, and there's nothing you can do about it.

"Listen, what happened to you came out of nowhere, unbidden and unwanted, like disease or heartbreak . . . like all misfortune. Nobody on this earth would've traded places with you."

He regarded Titus across the dim light of the table.

"As for the silence, I'm not going to lie to you. It's going to change your life. Doesn't mean it's got to change it for the worse, it's just going to be different. You'll learn how to live with it."

"Then that's the end of it?" Titus asked. He just wanted the damn thing to have an ending, a place where it stopped. He wanted to hear Burden say, finally, officially: It's over.

Burden studied him before answering. "Why was Luquín putting money *into* a Hezbollah account?" he asked. "If he was doing some service for them, helping them establish a base in Mexico within striking distance of the U.S.—which is something we're definitely watching for—then why wasn't it the other way around? Why weren't they paying him? Or were they doing a service for him? And what in the hell could that have been? And, whatever it might have been, did it end with Luquín's death? Or was he only one of many elements in a larger scheme, just as you were?"

There was a dribble of wine left in Burden's glass, and he drained it into his mouth. Carefully he put the glass on the tablecloth, smoothing a wrinkle with its wafer-thin base. He looked at Titus.

"For you and Rita, yes, it's over. You need to let it go, make peace with it."

"What about you?" Titus asked.

Burden seemed to consider something and then rejected it.

"History never knew about it," he said, "and silence keeps its own counsel."